DAVID GIBBINS has worked in underwater archaeology all his professional life. After taking a PhD from Cambridge University he taught archaeology in Britain and abroad, and is a world authority on ancient shipwrecks and sunken cities. He has led numerous expeditions to investigate underwater sites in the Mediterranean and around the world. He currently divides his time between fieldwork, England and Canada.

THE LAST GOSPEL

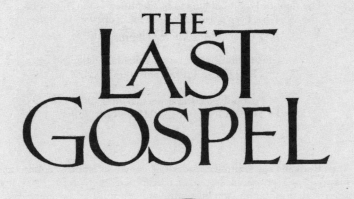

DAVID GIBBINS

headline

First published in Great Britain in 2008
by HEADLINE PUBLISHING GROUP

First published in paperback in 2008
by HEADLINE PUBLISHING GROUP

1

Cataloguing in Publication Data is available from the British Library

978 0 7553 3516 9 (A-format)
978 0 7553 4734 6 (B-format)

Typeset in Aldine 401BT by Avon DataSet Ltd,
Bidford-on-Avon, Warwickshire

Printed and bound in the UK by
CPI Mackays, Chatham ME5 8TD

HEADLINE PUBLISHING GROUP
An Hachette Livre UK Company
338 Euston Road
London NW1 3BH

www.headline.co.uk
www.hachettelivre.co.uk

Acknowledgements

With huge thanks to my agent, Luigi Bonomi of LBA, and to my publishers Harriet Evans at Headline and Caitlin Alexander at Bantam Dell. To Tessa Balshaw-Jones, Gaia Banks, Alexandra Barlow, Alison Bonomi, Chen Huijin Cheryl, Raewyn Davies, Darragh Deering, Sam Edenborough, Mary Esdaile, Emily Furniss, George Gamble, Siân Gibson, Pam Feinstein, Janet Harron, Jenny Karat, Celine Kelly, Nicki Kennedy, Colleen Lawrie, Stacey Levitt, Kim McArthur, Tony McGrath, Taryn Manias, Peter Newsom, Amanda Preston, Jenny Robson, Barry Rudd, John Rush, Emma Rusher, Jane Selley, Molly Stirling, Katherine West and Leah Woodburn. To my brother Alan for his work on my website, to my mother Ann for reading and advice, and to Angie and Molly for much inspiration. To the many friends who worked with me during expeditions from the Universities of Bristol and Cambridge to excavate shipwrecks off Sicily, and to the bodies that sponsored those projects and other exploration that lies behind this novel, including the British Schools of Archaeology in Rome and Jerusalem, the Palestine Exploration Fund and the Winston Churchill Memorial Trust. To Anna Pond, my Latin teacher at school in Canada, who first introduced me to the world of Pompeii and Herculaneum and the letters of the Younger Pliny. And lastly, to my father Norman for passing on to me his passion for the writings of Robert Graves and the life of Claudius, and the tales of Pliny the Elder, and for time together exploring the antiquities of Rome. *Equidem beatos puto, quibus deorum munere datum est aut facere scribenda aut scribere legenda, beatissimos vero quibus utrumque.*

Disclaimer

This is a work of fiction. Names, characters, institutions, places and incidents are creations of the author's imagination and are not to be construed as real. Any resemblance to actual or other fictional events, locales, organizations or persons, living or dead, is entirely coincidental. The factual backdrop is discussed in the author's note at the end.

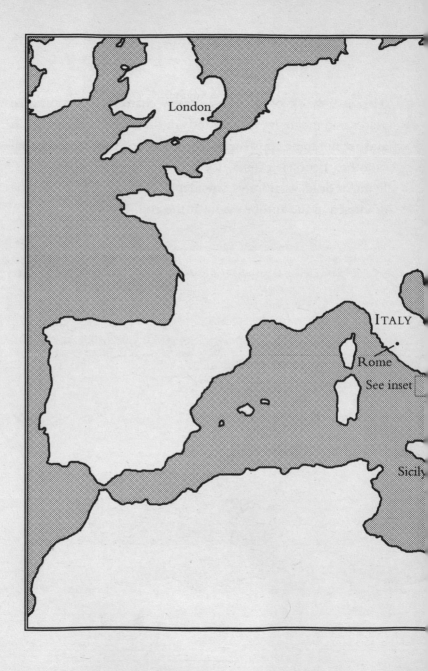

CAMPANIA

Naples

Cumae

Mt Vesuvius

Herculaneum

Misenum

Ponipeii

Stabiae

BAY OF NAPLES

Roman
Shipwreck

MEDITERRANEAN
SEA

Sea of Galilee

Jerusalem

. . . he perished in a catastrophe which destroyed the loveliest regions of the earth, a fate shared by whole cities and their people, and one so memorable that it is likely to make his name live for ever; and he himself wrote a number of books of lasting value: but you write for all time and can still do much to perpetuate his memory. The fortunate man, in my opinion, is he to whom the gods have granted the power either to do something which is worth recording or to write what is worth reading, and most fortunate of all is the man who can do both . . .

Pliny the Younger
Letter to the historian Tacitus. *c.* AD 106

Prologue

24 August AD *79*

The old man limped to the brink of the chasm, the firm grasp of his freedman all that prevented him from pitching forward. Tonight was a full moon, a red moon, and the swirl of vapours that filled the crater seemed to glow, as if the fires of Vulcan were burning through the thin cusp of ground that divided the world of the living from the world of the dead. The old man peered over the edge, felt the warm blast on his face and tasted the tang of sulphur on his lips. Always he was tempted, but always he held back. He remembered the words of Virgil, the poet whose tomb they had passed on the way to this place. *Facilis descensus Averno.* It is easy to descend to the underworld. Not so easy to get out again.

He turned away, and drew his hood up to conceal his face. Behind them he glimpsed the dark cone of Vesuvius over the bay, the towns of Herculaneum and Pompeii glimmering like sentinels on either side. The great bulk of Vesuvius was reassuring on nights like these, when the earth shuddered and the reek of sulphur was almost overwhelming, when the ground was littered with the bodies of birds which had flown too close to the fumes. And always there were the harbingers of doom, madmen and charlatans who lurked in the shadows ready to prey on the gullible, on those who came to this lookout to gape and gawk, but who never went further. One was here now, a wild-haired Greek who leapt up from an altar beside them, hands cupped forward in supplication, flailing and foaming, babbling about a great plague, that Rome would burn, that the sky would rain blood, that the land below Vesuvius would be consumed by the fires within. The freedman pushed the beggar roughly aside, and the old man muttered in annoyance. This was not a place where anyone needed a soothsayer to interpret the will of the gods.

Moments later they slipped through a fissure in the rock known only to the crippled and the damned, where the old man had first been brought as a boy more than eighty years before. He still remembered his terror, standing here weeping and trembling, his head jerking uncontrollably with the palsy. There was to be no cure, but those who took him in gave him solace, gave him the strength to defy others who wanted him never to be seen in Rome again. Even now he had not shaken off the fear, and he whispered his own name, steeling himself. *Tiberius Claudius Drusus Nero Germanicus. Remember who you are. Remember why you are here.*

Slowly they descended, the old man dragging his bad leg behind him, his hands leaning heavily on his freedman in front. On most nights the heavens were visible through the rent at the top of the fissure, but tonight the rock-cut steps were wreathed in a swirl of vapour that seemed to suck them down. Dark corners were lit by burning torches, and in other places orange light flickered through from outside. They reached a ledge above the floor of the crater, and the old man strained to see what he could not make out from above. Swirling gases seemed to float on a layer of emptiness over the rocky floor, an invisible poison that extinguished flames and suffocated all who fell into it. Somewhere beyond lay the entrance to Hades itself, a burning gash that split the rock, surrounded by the charred skeletons of those who had left their bodies behind on the way to Elysium. For a second he saw slits of red like glowing eyes in the rock, and then he watched a molten mass seep out and solidify, leaving shapes like gigantic limbs and torsos imprisoned in a writhing mass on the crater floor. The old man shuddered, and thought again of Virgil. It was as if those who had chosen to leave the mortal life in this place were straining for renewal, as giants and titans and gods, yet were doomed to eternity as inchoate, Protean forms, forms that nature had begun but would never finish, forms like himself.

The scene vanished in the vapours like a dream, and they pressed on, the old man staggering and panting behind the freedman. His vision tunnelled and blurred, as it did often these days, and he paused to rub his eyes and squint ahead. They reached a causeway, a raised path shrouded in yellow smoke rising from vents in the ground and hemmed in on either side by pools of boiling mud, heaving and juddering. He had been told that these were the tormented souls in purgatory pushing upwards, desperate to escape, that the hissing gas was their exhalations, like the ill humours rising from a charnel pit. The old man had seen that before, when his legionary commanders had brought him to the pits where they had flung the dead Britons, bodies that still shifted under the soil weeks after the slaughter. He grimaced, remembering his nausea, and they pressed on, past the steaming fumaroles into the gloom ahead.

Out of nowhere hands reached towards him, and he could sense ghostly forms lining either side of the causeway, some hauling themselves up on withered limbs from the edge of the crater. His freedman walked ahead with arms outstretched, his palms facing outwards and touching theirs, creating a space behind for the old man to follow. He heard low chanting, a soloist and then many voices responding, a rustling noise like fallen autumn leaves lifted on a gust of wind. They were singing the same words, over and over again. *Domine Iumius*. Lord, we shall come. There was a time when Claudius would have walked among them, been one of them. But now they made the sign with their hands as they reached towards him, fingers crossed, and they whispered his name, then the name of the one they knew he had touched. His friend Pliny had seen it too, had gone in disguise among his sailors at the naval base at the head of the bay, had seen knots of men and women listening in dark alleyways and the back rooms of taverns, had heard talk of a new priesthood, of those they called *apostoles*. The great poet Virgil had foretold it, Virgil who had trodden this very path a hundred years before, who had sought his wisdom too in the message of the leaves. *A boy's birth. A golden race arising. A world at peace, freed from never-ceasing fear. Yet a world where temptation lurked, where men would once again arise to place themselves between the people and the word of God, where terror and strife might rule again.*

The old man kept his gaze steadfastly down, and limped on. For twenty-five years now he had lived in his villa beneath the mountain, a humble historian with a lifetime's work to complete. Twenty-five years since he, ruler of the greatest empire the world had ever known, had supposedly died by poison in his palace in Rome, spirited away one night never to return. An emperor who lived on not as a god, but as a man. An emperor with a secret, with a treasure so precious it had kept him alive all these years, watching, waiting. Few others knew of it. His friend Pliny. His trusted freedman Narcissus, here today. Yet now these others treated him with a strange reverence, hung on his every word as if he were a soothsayer, as if he were the oracle herself. The old man muttered to himself. Tonight he would fulfil a promise he had made beside a lake long ago, to one who had entrusted him with his word, his written word. It was the old man's final chance to shape history, to achieve more than he ever could as emperor, to leave a legacy that he knew could outlast even Rome itself.

Suddenly he was alone. Ahead of him the causeway disappeared into a cavernous darkness, a place where the rising heat of the pit met a chill exhalation from within, to form a shimmering mirage. He reached for the dice he always kept in his pocket, turning them round and round, trying to calm his tremor. It was said that the cave had a hundred entrances, each one with a voice. Beside him was a low basin, and he dipped his hand in the lustral waters, splashing his face. In front of him was a low stone table, wisps of brown smoke rising from a smouldering mass spread over the surface. Eagerly he lurched over, grasping the smoothed edges of the table, his eyes tightly shut, sucking the smoke deep into his lungs, coughing and retching, holding it there. Pliny called it the *opium bactrium*, the extract of poppy brought from the far-off kingdom of Bactria in the east, from the bleak mountain valleys conquered by Alexander the Great. But here they called it the gift of Morpheus, god of dreams. He sucked in again, feeling the heady rush that reached into his limbs, bringing feeling back where it had almost gone, dulling the pain. He needed it more now, needed it every night. He leaned back, and felt as if he were floating, face upwards and arms outstretched. For a fleeting moment he was back again in the other place where he had sought healing, long ago beside the lake in Galilee, laughing and drinking with his friends Herod and Cypros and his beloved Calpurnia, with the Nazarene and his woman, where he had been touched by one who had known his destiny, who had foreseen this very day itself.

He opened his eyes. Something was coming from the cave, a writhing, undulating form that seemed to press against the mirage like a phoenix rising. It broke through, and he saw a huge serpent, standing upright as tall as he was, its flat head lowered and its tongue flicking in and out, swaying from side to side. Pliny had told him these were hallucinations brought on by the morpheum, but as the snake drooped down and slithered round his legs the old man felt the silky sheen of its skin, and smelled its musty, acrid odour. Then it slid away, slithering into a crack at the side of the cave, and there was another smell, overpowering the sulphur and the morpheum and the snake, a smell like a chill wind wafting through a rotting tomb, a smell of ancient decay. Something flickered, a shape barely visible in the darkness. She was here.

'*Clau-Clau-Claudius.*'

There was a low moan, then a sound like a mocking laugh, and then a sigh that echoed through all the different passageways in the rock, before it died away. Claudius peered into the darkness, waiting, his head spinning. It was said that she had lived for seven hundred ages of men, that Apollo had granted her as many years as the grains of sand she could hold in her hands, but that the god had refused her eternal youth after she had spurned his advances. All Apollo had allowed was the voice of a young woman, so that as she shrank and decayed the voice of her youth remained to torment her, to remind her of the immortality she had forsaken. And now she was the last of them, the last of the oracles of the earth goddess Gaia, last of the thirteen. She who had held sway in her lair since before Rome was founded, bewitching all who came before her, whose riddles had brought emperors to their knees.

'S-Sibyl.' Claudius broke the silence, his voice tremulous, harsh with the sulphur. 'I have d-done as you instructed. I did what you ordered me to do for the Vestals, in Rome. And now I have been to the thirteenth, to Andraste. I have been to her tomb. I have taken it to her. The prophecy is fulfilled.'

He dropped a bag of coins he had been carrying, and they clunked out, dull gold and silver, the last batch he had saved for this night, coins bearing his portrait. A shaft of light fell in front of the table, revealing the worn stone surface of the passageway beneath the swirls of vapour. On the floor were leaves, oak leaves arranged like words, the inked Greek letter on each leaf just visible. Claudius lurched forward, falling on his hands and knees and peering at the leaves, desperate to read the message. Suddenly there was a gust and they were gone. He cried out, then slowly bowed his head, his words rent with despair. 'You took my ancestor Aeneas to see his dead father Anchises. He came here after Troy, seeking the underworld on his way to found Rome. All I asked was to see my father Drusus. My dear brother Germanicus. My son Britannicus. To glimpse them in Elysium, before Charon takes me where he will.'

There was another moan, thinner this time, then a shriek

that seemed to come from everywhere at once, as if all hundred mouths of the cave were turning inwards on him.

'Day of wrath and terror looming!
Heaven and earth to ash consuming,
Clau-Clau-Claudius' words and Sibyl's truth foredooming!'

Claudius staggered to his feet, his body shaking and jerking, convulsed with fear. He peered again at the pool of light. Where the leaves had been was now a pile of sand, the grains trickling down the sides. He watched as a final sprinkle fell from somewhere high above, a shimmer that dropped like a translucent curtain. Then everything was still. He looked around, and realized that the snake had gone, had sloughed off its skin and left it empty in front of him, had slithered down into the poison above the crater floor. He remembered the words of Virgil again, the coming of the Golden Age. *And the serpents too shall die.*

Claudius felt his head clear, and saw the mirage in front of the cave drop away. He was suddenly desperate to leave, to cast aside the yearning that had bound him to this place and to the Sibyl for so long, to return to his villa beneath Vesuvius to finish the work that he and Pliny had planned for that evening, to fulfil the promise he had made by that lake so long ago. He turned to go, then felt something on the back of his neck, a touch of cold that made his hairs stand on end. He thought he heard his name again, softly whispered, but this time they were the words of an old woman, impossibly old, and were followed by a rustling like a death rattle coming closer. He dared not turn around. He began pressing forward, limping and slipping over the rock, looking around frantically for Narcissus. Over the lip of the crater he could see the dark form of the mountain, its summit wreathed in flickering lightning like a burning crown of thorns. The clouds were rushing overhead, tumbling and darkening, glowing orange and red as if they were on fire. He felt a terrible fear, then a sudden lucidity, as if all his memories and dreams had been sucked out of him by the vortex ahead. It was as if history itself had sped up, history which he had kept at bay since vanishing from Rome half a lifetime ago, history which had waited for him like a coiled spring that could no longer be held back.

He staggered on. Behind him he felt a baleful presence pushing him forward, onward through the sulphurous haze towards the floor of the crater. He grasped the dice again, pulled them out of his pocket then dropped them, heard them rattle on the rocks then stop. He looked despairingly, but saw nothing. On either side spectral forms emerged from the pit, no longer in supplication but joining him like a silent army, shrouded in hot flecks of ash which had begun to fall from the sky like snow. He felt his mouth go dry, a desperate thirst. On the top of Vesuvius he saw a burning ring of fire, racing down the slopes towards the towns, fields of flames in its wake. Then the scene was obliterated by blackness, a swirling funnel that descended into the crater and blotted out all but the narrowing void ahead. He heard screams, a muffled roar, saw bodies ignite like torches in the darkness, one after the other. He was getting closer. Now he knew, with dread certainty.

The Sibyl had kept her promise. He would follow in the footsteps of Aeneas.

But this time there would be no return.

1

Present day

Jack Howard eased himself down on the floor of the inflatable boat, his back resting on one pontoon and his legs leaning against the outboard engine. It was hot, almost too hot to move, and the sweat had begun to trickle down his face. The sun had burned through the morning haze and was bearing down relentlessly, reflecting blindingly off the cliff face in front of him, the limestone scarred and worn like the tombs and temples on the rocky headland beyond. Jack felt as if he were in a painting by Seurat, as if the air had fragmented into a myriad pixels that immobilized all thought and action, that caught him in the moment. He pushed his hands through his thick hair, feeling the heat on his scalp, and stretched out his long arms to either side. He shut his eyes and took a deep breath, took in the utter stillness, the smell of wetsuits, the outboard engine, the taste of salt. It was everything he loved, distilled to its essence. It felt good.

He opened his eyes and peered over the side, checking the orange buoy he had released a few minutes before. The sea was glassy smooth, with only a slight swell rippling the edge where it lapped against the rock face. He reached out and put his hand on the surface, letting it float for a moment until the swell enveloped it. The water below was limpid, as clear as a swimming pool, and he could see far down the anchor line into the depths, to the shimmer of exhaust bubbles rising from the divers below. It was hard to believe this had once been a place of unimaginable fury, of nature at her cruellest, of untold human tragedy. *The most famous shipwreck in history*. Jack hardly dared think of it. For twenty years he had wanted to come back to this place, a yearning which had nagged at him and become a gnawing obsession, ever since his first doubt, since he had first begun to reassemble the pieces. His intuition rarely failed him, tried and tested over years of exploration and discovery around the world. It was an intuition based on hard science, on an accumulation of facts that had begun to point unswervingly in one direction.

He had been sitting here, off Capo Murro di Porco in Sicily in the heart of the Mediterranean, when he had first dreamed up the International Maritime University. Twenty years ago he had been on a shoestring budget, leading a group of students driven by their passion for diving and archaeology, with equipment cobbled together and jerry-built on the spot. Now he had a multi-million budget, a sprawling seafront campus on his former family estate in south-west England, the place where Howards had lived for generations before Jack's father turned the house and grounds over to the fledgling institution. There were museums around the world, state-of-the-art research vessels, an extraordinary team at IMU who took the logistics out of his hands. But in some ways little had changed. No end of money could buy the clues that led to the greatest discoveries, the extraordinary treasures that made it all worthwhile. Twenty years ago they had been following a tantalizing account left by Captain Cousteau's divers, intrepid explorers at the dawn of shipwreck archaeology, and here he was again, floating above the same site with the same battered old diary in his hands. The key ingredients were still the same, the hunches, the gut feeling, the thrill of discovery, that moment when all the elements suddenly came together, the adrenaline rush like no other.

Jack shifted, pushing his diving suit further down around his waist, and checked his watch. He was itching to get wet. He glanced overboard. There was a slight commotion as Pete and Andy, the divers who had been sent down to anchor the shotline, pulled the buoy underwater. Jack could see it now, refracted five metres below, deep enough to avoid the props of passing boats but shallow enough for a free diver to retrieve a weighted line that hung from it as a mooring point. He had already dared to look ahead, had begun to eye the site like a field commander planning an assault. Their research vessel *Seaquest II* could anchor in a sheltered bay around the cape to the west. On the headland itself the rocky seashore dropped in a series of stepped shelves, good for a shore camp. He rehearsed all the ingredients of a successful underwater excavation, knowing that each site produced its fresh crop of challenges. Any finds they made would have to go to the archaeological museum in Syracuse, but he was sure the Sicilian authorities would make a good show of it. IMU would establish a permanent liaison with their own museum at Carthage in nearby Tunisia, perhaps even an air shuttle as a package trip for tourists. They could hardly go wrong.

Jack peered down, checked his watch again, then noted the time in the logbook. The two divers were at the decompression stop. Twenty minutes to go. He cupped his left hand in the sea and splashed the water over his head, feeling it trickle through his thick hair and down his neck. He leaned back, stretched his long legs down the boat, made himself relax and take in the perfect tranquillity of the scene for a moment longer. Only six weeks earlier he had stood by the edge of an underwater cavern in the Yucatán, drained but exhilarated at the end of another extraordinary trail of discovery. There had been losses, grievous losses, and Jack had spent much of the voyage home ruminating on those who had paid the ultimate price. His boyhood friend Peter Howe, missing in the Black Sea. And Father O'Connor, an ally for all too brief a time, whose appalling death had brought home the reality of what they were ranged against. Always it was the bigger stake that provided the solace, the innumerable lives that could have been lost had they not relentlessly pursued their goal. Jack had become used to the greatest archaeological prizes coming at a cost, gifts from the past that unleashed forces in the present few could imagine existed. But here, he felt sure of it, here it was different. Here it was archaeology pure and simple, a revelation that could only thrill and beguile any who came to know of it.

He peered into the glassy stillness of the sea, saw the rocky cliff face underwater disappear into the shimmering blue. His mind was racing, his heart pounding with excitement. Could this be it? Could this be the most famous shipwreck of all antiquity? *The shipwreck of St Paul?*

'You there?'

Jack raised his foot and gently prodded the other form in the boat. It wobbled, then grunted. Costas Kazantzakis was about a foot shorter than Jack but built like an ox, a legacy of generations of Greek sailors and sponge-fishermen. Like Jack he was stripped to the waist, and his barrel chest was glistening with sweat. He seemed to have become moulded to the boat, his legs extended on the pontoon in front of Jack and his head nestled in a mess of towels at the bow. His mouth was slightly open and he was wearing a pair of wraparound fluorescent sunglasses, a hilarious fashion accessory on such an unkempt figure. One hand was dangling in the water, holding the hoses that led down to the regulators at the decompression stop, and the other was draped over the valve of the oxygen cylinder that lay down the centre of the boat.

Jack grinned affectionately at his friend, who meant far more to him than his official role as IMU's chief engineer. Costas was always there to lend a hand, even when he was dead to the world. Jack kicked him again. 'We've got fifteen minutes. I can see them at the safety stop.'

Costas grunted again, and Jack passed over a water bottle. 'Drink as much as you can. We don't want to get the bends.'

'Good on you, mate.' Costas had learned a few comically misplaced catchphrases in his years based at the IMU headquarters in England, but the delivery was still resolutely American, a result of years spent at school and university in the States. He reached over and took the water, then proceeded to down half the bottle noisily.

'Cool shades, by the way,' Jack said.

'Jeremy gave them to me,' Costas gasped. 'A parting present when we got back from the Yucatán. I was truly moved.'

'You're not serious.'

'I'm not sure if he was. Anyway, they work.' Costas passed back the bottle, then slumped down again. 'Been touching base with your past?'

'Only the good bits.'

'Any decent engineers? I mean, on your team back then?'

'We're talking Cambridge University, remember. The brightest and the weirdest. One guy took a portable black-board with him everywhere he went, and would patiently explain the Wankel rotary engine to any passing Sicilian. A real eccentric. But that was before you came along.'

'With a dose of good old American know-how. At least at

MIT they taught us about the real world.' Costas leaned over, grabbed the bottle again and took another swig of water. 'Anyway, this shipwreck of yours. The one you excavated here twenty years ago. Any good finds?'

'It was a typical Roman merchantman,' Jack replied. 'About two hundred cylindrical pottery amphoras, filled with olive oil and fish sauce on the edge of the African desert, in Tunisia due south of us. Plus there was a fascinating selection of ceramics from the ship's galley. We were able to date it all to about AD 200. And we did make one incredible find.'

There was a silence, broken by a stentorian snore. Jack kicked again, and Costas reached out to stop himself from rolling overboard. He pushed his shades up his forehead and peered blearily at Jack. 'Uh huh?'

'I know you need your beauty sleep. But it's almost time.'

Costas grunted again, then raised himself painfully on one elbow and rubbed his hand across his stubble. 'I don't think beauty's an option.' He heaved himself upright, then took off the sunglasses and rubbed his eyes. Jack peered with concern at his friend. 'You look wasted. You need to take some time off. You've been working flat out since we returned from the Yucatán, and that was well over a month ago.'

'You should stop buying me toys.'

'What I bought you,' Jack gently admonished him, 'was an agreement from the board of directors for an increase in engineering personnel. Hire some more staff. Delegate.'

'You should talk,' Costas grumbled. 'Name me one

archaeological project run by IMU over the last decade where you haven't jumped on board.'

'I'm serious.'

'Yeah, yeah.' Costas stretched and gave a tired grin. 'Okay, a week by my uncle's pool in Greece wouldn't go amiss. Anyway, sorry. Was I dreaming? You mentioned an incredible find.'

'Buried in a gully directly beneath us now, where Pete and Andy should have anchored the shotline. The remains of an ancient wooden crate, containing sealed tin boxes. Inside the boxes we found more than a hundred small wooden phials, filled with unguents and powders including cinnamon and cumin. That was amazing enough, but then we found a large slab of dark resinous material, about two kilograms in weight. At first we thought it was ship's stores, spare resin for waterproofing timbers. But the lab analysis came up with an astonishing result.'

'Go on.'

'What the ancients called *lacrymae papaveris*, tears of the poppy, *Papaver somniferum*. The sticky, milky stuff that comes from the calyx of the black poppy. What we call opium.'

'No kidding.'

'The Roman writer Pliny the Elder writes about it, in his *Natural History*.'

'The guy who died in the eruption of Vesuvius?'

'Right. When Pliny wasn't writing, he was in charge of the Roman fleet at Misenum, the big naval base on the Bay of Naples. He knew all about the products of the east from his sailors, and from Egyptian and Syrian merchants who put in there. They knew that the best opium came from the distant land of Bactria, high in the mountains beyond the eastern fringe of the empire, beyond Persia. That's present-day Afghanistan.'

'You're kidding me.' Costas was fully alert now, and looked incredulous. 'Opium. From Afghanistan. Did I hear you right? We're talking the first century AD here, not the twenty-first century, right?'

'You've got it.'

'An ancient drug-runner?'

Jack laughed. 'Opium wasn't illegal back then. Some ancient authorities condemned it for making users go blind, but they hadn't refined it into heroin yet. It was probably mixed with alcohol to make a drink, similar to laudanum, the fashion drug of Europeans in the eighteenth and nineteenth centuries. The seed was also pounded into tablets. Pliny tells us it could induce sleep and cure headaches, so they knew all about the pain-killing properties of morphine. It was also used for euthanasia. Pliny gives us what may be the first ever account of a deliberate Class A drugs overdose, a guy called Publius Licinius Caecina who was unbearably ill and died of opium poisoning.'

'So what you found was really a medicine chest,' Costas said.

'That's what we thought at the time. But a very odd find in the chest was a small bronze statue of Apollo.'

'Apollo?'

Jack nodded. 'I know. When you find medical equipment it's more commonly with a statue of Asclepius, the Greek god of healing. A few years later I visited the cave of the Sibyl at Cumae, on the edge of the active volcanic zone a few miles north of Misenum, within sight of Vesuvius. Apollo was the god of oracles. Sulphur and herbs were used to ward off evil spirits and maybe opium was added to it. I began to wonder whether all those mystical rites were chemically assisted.'

'It could have been smoked,' Costas murmured. 'Burned like incense. The fumes would have been quicker than a draught.'

'People went to those places seeking cures, to the Sibyl and other prophets,' Jack said. 'Organized religion at the time didn't provide much personal comfort, often excluding the common people and fixated on cults and rituals that were pretty remote from daily concerns. The Sibyl and her kind provided some kind of emotional reassurance, psychological relief. And the Sibyls must have known it, and played on it. All we hear about from ancient accounts is the message of the oracle, obscure verses written on leaves or issued as prophetic pronouncements, all sound and fury and signifying God knows what. But maybe there was more to it than that. Maybe some people really did find a cure of sorts, a palliative.'

'And a highly addictive one. It could have kept the Sibyl in business. Cash offerings from grateful clients would have kept the supply rolling.'

'So I began to think our little ship wasn't carrying an apothecary or doctor, but a middleman travelling with his precious supply of opium for one of the oracles in Italy, maybe even procured for the Sibyl at Cumae herself.'

'A Roman drug-dealer.' Costas rubbed his stubble. 'The godfather of all godfathers. The Naples Mafia would love it.'

'Maybe if they found out, it would teach them a little respect for archaeology,' Jack said. 'Organized crime is a huge problem for our friends in the Naples archaeological superintendency.'

'Doesn't one of your old girlfriends work there?' Costas grinned.

'Elizabeth hasn't been in contact with me for years. Last I heard she was still an inspector, pretty low down on the food chain. I never really worked out what happened. She finished her doctorate in England before I did and then had to go back, part of her contract with the Italian government. She swore to me that she'd never return to Naples, but then it happened and she completely shut down communication with me. I suppose I moved on too. That was almost fifteen years ago.'

'Ours is not to reason why, Jack.' Costas shifted. 'Back to the opium. Procured from where?'

'That's what worried me.' Jack rolled out a laminated small-scale Admiralty chart of the Mediterranean over the equipment on the floor of the boat, pinning its corners under loose diving weights. He jabbed his finger at the centre of the chart. 'Here we are. The island of Sicily. Bang in the middle of the Mediterranean, the apex of ancient trade. Right?'

'Go on.'

'Our little Roman merchantman, wrecked against this cliff

with its cargo of north African olive oil and fish sauce. It does the trip to Rome three, maybe four times a year, during the summer sailing season. Up and down, up and down. Almost always within sight of land, Tunisia, Malta, Sicily, Italy.'

'Not a long-distance sailor.'

'Right.' Jack stabbed his finger at the far corner of the chart. 'And here's Egypt, the port of Alexandria. Fifteen hundred miles away to the east of us, across open sea. Everything points to the drug chest coming from there. The wood's Egyptian acacia. Some of the phials had Coptic letters on them. And the opium was almost certainly shipped to the Mediterranean via the Red Sea ports of Egypt, a trade in exotic eastern spices and drugs that reached its height in the first century AD.'

'The time of St Paul,' Costas murmured. 'Why we're here.'

'Right.' Jack traced his finger along the coastline of north Africa from Egypt. 'Now it's possible, just possible, that the opium was shipped along the African coast from Alexandria to Carthage, and then went north to Sicily in our little merchantman.'

Costas shook his head. 'I remember the navigational advice in the *Mediterranean Pilot* from my stint in the US Navy. Prevailing onshore winds. That desert coastline between Egypt and Tunisia has always been a death trap for sailors, avoided at all costs.'

'Precisely. Ships leaving Alexandria for Rome sailed north to Turkey or Crete and then west across the Ionian Sea to Italy. The most likely scenario for our opium cargo is one of those ships, blown south-west from the Ionian Sea towards Sicily.'

Costas looked perplexed, then his eyes suddenly lit up. 'I've got you! We're looking at two overlapping shipwrecks!'

'It wouldn't be the first time. I've dived on ships' graveyards with dozens of wrecks jumbled together, smashed against the same reef or headland. And once that idea clicked, I began to see other clues. Take a look at this.' Jack reached down into a crate beside him and picked up a heavy item swaddled in a towel. He handed it across to Costas, who sat up on the pontoon and took the item on to his lap, then began carefully lifting the folds of towelling away.

'Let me guess.' He stopped and gave Jack a hopeful look. 'A golden disc covered with ancient symbols, leading us to another fabulous lost city?'

Jack grinned. 'Not quite, but just as precious in its own way.'

Costas raised the last fold and held the object up. It was about ten inches high, shaped like a truncated cone, and weighed heavily in his hands. The surface was mottled white with patches of dull metallic sheen, and at the top was a short extension with a hole through it like a retaining loop. He eyed Jack. 'A sounding lead?'

'You've got it. A lead weight tied to the end of a line for sounding depths. Check out the base.'

Costas carefully held the lead upside down. In the base was a depression about an inch deep, as if the lead had been partly hollowed out like a bell, and below that was a further depression in a distinctive shape. Costas raised his eyes again. 'A cross?'

'Don't get too excited. That was filled with pitch or resin, and was used to pick up a sample of sea-bed sediment. If you were heading for a big river estuary, the first appearance of sand would act as a navigational aid.'

'This came from the wreck below us?'

Jack reached across and took back the sounding lead, holding it with some reverence. 'My first ever major find from an ancient shipwreck. It came from one end of the site, nestled in the same gully where we later found the drug chest. At the time I was over the moon, thought this was a pretty amazing find, but I assumed sounding leads were probably standard equipment on an ancient merchantman.'

'And now?'

'Now I know it was truly exceptional. Hundreds of Roman wrecks have been discovered since then, but only a few sounding leads have ever been found. The truth is they would have been expensive items, and only really of much use for ships regularly approaching a large estuary, with a shallow sea bed for miles offshore where alluvial sand could be picked up well before land was sighted.'

'You mean like the Nile?'

Jack nodded enthusiastically. 'What we're looking at here is the equipment of a large Alexandrian grain ship, not a humble amphora carrier.' He carefully placed the lead back in the crate, then pulled out an old black-bound book from a plastic bag. 'Now listen to this.' He opened the book to a marked page, scanned up and down for a moment and then began to read: '"But when the fourteenth night was come, as we were driven to and fro in the sea of Adria, about midnight the sailors surmised that they were drawing near to some country; and they sounded, and found twenty fathoms; and after a little space, they sounded again, and found fifteen fathoms. And fearing lest haply we should be cast ashore on rocky ground, they let go four anchors from the stern, and prayed for the day."'

Costas whistled. 'The Gospels!'

'The Acts of St Paul, Chapter 27.' Jack's eyes were ablaze. 'And guess what? Directly offshore from where we are now, the bottom slopes off to deep water, but diagonally to the south there's a sandy plateau extending about three hundred metres out, about forty metres deep.'

'That's a hundred and twenty feet, twenty fathoms,' Costas murmured.

'On our last day of diving twenty years ago we did a recce over it, just to see if we'd missed anything,' Jack said. 'The very last thing I saw was two lead anchor shanks, unmistakably early Roman types used to weigh down wooden anchors. By the time of our north African amphora wreck, anchors were made of iron, so we knew these must have been lost by an earlier ship that had tried to hold off this coast.'

'Go on.'

'It gets better.'

'I thought it would.'

Jack read again: ' "And casting off the anchors, they left them in the sea, at the same time loosing the bands of the rudders; and hoisting up the foresail to the wind, they made for the beach. But lighting on a place where two seas met, they ran the vessel aground; and the foreship struck and remained unmoveable, but the stern began to break up by the violence of the waves." '

'Good God,' Costas said. 'The drug chest, the sounding lead. Stored in the forward compartment. What about the stern?'

'Wait for it.' Jack grinned, and pulled out a folder from the bag. 'Fast-forward two millennia. August 1953, to be exact. Captain Cousteau and *Calypso*.'

'I was wondering when they were going to come in to it.'

'It was the clue that brought us here in the first place,' Jack said. 'They dived all along this coast. Here's what the chief diver wrote about this headland. "I saw broken amphoras, concreted into a fold in the cliff, then an iron anchor, concreted to the bottom and apparently in corroded state, with amphora sherds on top." That's exactly what we found here, the Roman amphora wreck. But there's more. On their second dive, they saw "des amphores grecques, en bas profound".'

'Greek amphoras, in deep water,' Costas murmured. 'Any idea where?'

'Straight out from the cleft in the rock behind us,' Jack said. 'We reckoned they hit seventy, maybe eighty metres depth.'

'Sounds like Cousteau's boys,' Costas said. 'Let me guess. Compressed air, twin hose regulators, no pressure gauge, no buoyancy system.'

'Back when diving was diving,' Jack said wistfully. 'Before mixed gas took all the fun out of it.'

'The danger's still there, just the threshold's deeper.'

'Twenty years ago I volunteered to do a bounce dive to find those amphoras, but the team doctor vetoed it. We only had compressed air and were strictly following the US Navy tables, with a depth limit of fifty metres. We had no helicopter, no support ship, and the nearest recompression chamber was a couple of hours away in the US naval base up the coast.'

Costas gestured pointedly at the two mixed-gas rebreathers on the floor of the boat, and then at the white speck of a ship visible on the horizon, steaming towards them. 'State-of-the-art deep-diving equipment, and full recompression facilities on board *Seaquest II*. Modern technology. I rest my case.' He waved at the battered old diary Jack was holding. 'Anyway, Greek amphoras. Isn't that before our period?'

'That's what we assumed at the time. But something was niggling me, something I couldn't be sure of until I saw those amphoras with my own eyes.' Jack picked up a clipboard from the crate and passed it over to Costas. 'That's the amphora typology devised by Heinrich Dressel, a German scholar who studied finds from Rome and Pompeii in the nineteenth century. Check out the drawings on the upper left, numbers two to four.'

'The amphoras with the high pointed handles?'

'You've got it. Now, in Cousteau's day, divers identified any amphora with those handles as Greek, because that was the shape of wine amphoras known to have been made in classical

Greece. But since then we've learned that amphoras of that shape were also made in the areas of the west Mediterranean colonized by the Greeks, then later under the Romans when they conquered those areas. We're talking southern Italy, Sicily, north-east Spain, all major wine-producing regions first developed by the Greeks.' He passed over a large black and white photograph showing high-handled amphoras leaning against a wall, and Costas peered at it thoughtfully.

'A wine storeroom? A tavern? Pompeii?

Jack nodded enthusiastically. 'Not Pompeii, but Herculaneum, the other town buried by the eruption of Vesuvius. A roadside bar, preserved exactly as it was on 24 August AD 79.'

Costas was quiet for a moment, then squinted at Jack. 'Remind me. What was the date of St Paul's shipwreck?'

'Best guess is spring AD 58, maybe a year or two later.'

'Put me in the picture.'

'A few years after the death of the emperor Claudius, in the reign of Nero. About ten years before the Romans conquer Judaea and steal the Jewish menorah.'

'Ah. I'm with you.' Costas gave Jack a tired smile, then narrowed his eyes again. 'Nero. Gross debauchery, throwing Christians to the lions, all that?'

Jack nodded. 'That's one take on the history of the period. But it was also the most prosperous time in ancient history, the height of the Roman Empire. Wine from the rich vineyards of Campania around Vesuvius was being exported in those Greek-style amphoras all round the known world. They've even been found in the furthest Roman outposts in southern India, traded for spices and medicines like the opium in that chest. And they're found in Britain. They're exactly what you'd expect to find on a large Alexandrian grain ship of this period. According to the New Testament account in the Acts of the Apostles, there were more than two hundred and seventy people on board that ship with St Paul, and diluted wine would have been their staple drink.'

'Last question,' Costas said. 'The big one. From what I remember, St Paul's shipwreck was supposed to have been in Malta. How come Sicily?'

'That's why it never clicked twenty years ago. Then I did a bit of lateral thinking. Geographically, I mean.'

'You mean you had a way-out hunch.'

Jack grinned. 'It's like this. All we have to go on is the Gospels, the Acts of the Apostles. There's no other account of St Paul's shipwreck, no way of verifying the story. Right?'

'It's all about faith.'

'In a way, that's the nub of it. The Gospels, the New Testament, were a collection of documents chosen by the early Church to represent the ministry of Jesus, or perhaps their view of the ministry of Jesus. Some of the Gospels were written soon after Jesus' life, by eyewitnesses and contemporaries, others were written later. None of them were written as historical documents as we would understand the term, let alone geographical ones. To those who put the texts together, it was probably a matter of little consequence which island Paul was actually wrecked on.'

'I had all this drummed into me by my Greek Orthodox

family. Acts was written by a survivor of the wrecking, by Paul's companion Luke.'

Jack nodded. 'That was what everyone was taught. Acts tells us that Paul was accompanied by two men, Luke from Asia Minor and a Macedonian from Thessaloniki.'

'Aristarchos.'

'I'm preaching to the converted,' Jack grinned. 'You should be telling this.'

'I can only give you the bare bones,' Costas said. 'After Paul was arrested in Judaea, they joined him on the voyage north from Caesarea to Myra in southern Turkey, where they transferred to an Alexandrian ship destined for Rome.'

'That's what we're told,' Jack said. 'But we need to stand back from the detail. It goes back to what I said about reading the Gospels as history. That wasn't their primary purpose. Some scholars now think Acts was composed several decades later by someone else, maybe based on an eyewitness account. And then there are questions over textual transmission. The Gospels went through the same process as all the other classical texts, all those except the fragments we've actually found in ancient sites. Sieved, purified, translated, embellished with interpretations and annotations which became part of the text, censored by religious authorities, altered by the whim or negligence of the individual copyist.'

'You're saying take the details with a pinch of salt.'

'Be circumspect.'

'A favourite word of yours these days.'

Jack grinned. 'The earliest surviving fragment we have of

Acts dates to about AD 200, almost 150 years after Paul, and it only contains the first part of the story. The earliest version with the wreck dates several hundred years later. It gets translated from Greek to Latin to medieval languages, to seventeenth-century English, goes through numerous scribes and copyists. It makes me very cautious, circumspect, about a detail like the word Melita, whether it even means Malta. Some ancient versions even render it as Mytilene, an island in the Aegean more familiar to Greek copyists of the Gospels.'

'Treasure-hunting 101,' Costas said solemnly. 'Always authenticate your map.'

'St Paul's shipwreck is just about the first time in history that we can hunt a known wreck, but like so many wreck accounts it's fraught with pitfalls. You have to stand back from it, open your mind to all the possibilities and let them fall into place, not force them towards a foregone conclusion. I think that's what I've been doing over the years since I last dived here, since the idea first began to dawn on me.'

'That's why you're an archaeologist, and I'm an engineer,' Costas said. 'I don't know how you do it.'

'And that's why I leave robotics and submersibles to you.' Jack grinned at Costas, then looked towards the eastern horizon. 'There's nothing else in Acts to corroborate Malta as the location, and all that happens on the island is that Paul heals some local man. Sicily makes a lot more sense. It's in the right neck of the woods, a far more likely landfall for a grain ship blown off course in the Ionian Sea by a north-east wind. Acts even mentions Syracuse, just round the headland from us, where Paul and his companions spent several days on their eventual trip to Rome after the wrecking. According to Acts, they hitched a lift on another grain ship which had overwintered in Malta, but I believe that was far more likely to be a ship in the Great Harbour at Syracuse itself.'

'So two thousand years of Biblical scholarship is wrong, and Jack Howard has a hunch and is right?'

'Careful reasoning based on an accumulation of evidence, pointing . . .'

'Pointing unswervingly to one conclusion,' Costas finished. 'Yeah, yeah. A hunch.' He grinned at Jack, then spoke with mock resignation. 'Okay. You've sold me. And now that I look at it, that cleft in the cliff face beside us, your marker for the wreck site. Have you noticed how it also looks like the Greek letter chi? Like a cross?' Costas grinned. 'While we're on the subject of leaps of faith, don't tell me you're above a little sign from on high.'

Jack squinted at the rock, then grinned. 'Okay. I'll go with that. Twenty years on, you see things with different eyes.' He leaned back on his elbows, and shook his head. 'I can't believe it's taken me so long to put all these pieces together.'

'You've had a few other projects on your mind.'

'Yes, but this could be the biggest of them all.' Jack sat up and leaned towards Costas, his face ablaze with excitement. 'Anything, anything at all, that identifies this shipwreck with St Paul would make it a treasure trove like we've never seen before. Nobody has ever found anything so intimately linked with the lives of the evangelists, with the reality behind the

Gospels. We're looking at a time when a few people truly believed in a kingdom of heaven on earth, a dream that pagan religion didn't offer the common people. A time before churches, before priests, before guilt and confession and inquisitions and holy wars. Strip away all that and you go back to the essence of what Jesus had to say, what drew so many to him.'

'I never knew you were so passionate about it.'

'It's the idea that individuals can take charge of their own destiny and seek beauty and joy on earth. That seems to be about as uplifting as you can get. If we can find something that will draw people back to that, take them back to the essence of the idea and make them reflect on it, then we'll have done humanity a service.'

'Holy cow, Jack. I thought we were just treasure-hunters.'

Jack grinned. 'Archaeology isn't just about filling up museums.'

'I know. It's about the hard facts.'

'A shipwreck could be a time capsule of the period like Pompeii and Herculaneum, only with a direct connection to the most potent figures in western history. It would capture the imagination of the world.'

Costas shifted and stretched. 'We still have to find it yet. And speaking of excitement, we've got company.' He jerked his head towards the cascade of bubbles now erupting on the surface, and they watched as the two divers came into view a few metres below them. They surfaced simultaneously and both gave the okay signal. Jack noted down the time in the log and then glanced at Costas. 'This place was a fulcrum of history,' he continued. 'Whatever we find, we'd be adding to a story that's already pretty fantastic. In 415 BC the Athenians landed at this spot to attack Syracuse, a key event in the war with Sparta which almost destroyed Greek civilization. Fast-forward to another world war, July 1943, Operation Husky. My grandfather was here, chief officer of the armed merchant ship *Empire Elaine*, just inshore from the monitor HMS *Erebus* as she bombarded the enemy positions above us with fifteen-inch shells.'

'This place must be in your blood,' Costas said. 'Seems like a Howard was present at just about every famous naval engagement in British history.'

'If many English families knew their background, they'd be able to say the same.'

'Anything left to see?'

'The Special Raiding Squadron, an offshoot of the SAS, parachuted on to the cliff above us and forced the Italian coastal defence battery to surrender, throwing their arms into the sea. When we first dived here the site was strewn with ammunition.'

Costas rubbed his hands. 'That's what I like. Real archaeology. Beats bits of old pot any day.'

'Let's keep our eyes on the prize. You can play bomb disposal later.'

Costas grinned, and held up the feed hose from his rebreather. 'Lock and load.' He clicked it home, then watched Jack do the same.

'Done.' Jack angled his neck down to check his equipment, then eyed Costas. 'You up for it?' he said. 'I mean, going deep?'

Costas raised his eyes, then gave an exaggerated sigh. 'Let me see. Our last dive was in an underground passageway beneath the jungles of the Yucatán, being swept towards some kind of Mayan hell. And before that it was inside a rolling iceberg. Oh, and before that, an erupting volcano.'

'You saying you've had enough, or can manage one more?'

Costas gave his version of the thousand-yard stare, then gave a haggard grin and began pulling up his diving suit. 'You just say the words.'

'Time to kit up.'

2

Maurice Hiebermeyer leaned back against the wall of the passageway, panted heavily a few times and eyed the ragged hole ahead of him. He would not be defeated. If the Bourbon King Charles of Naples could do it, an ample girth if there ever was one, then so could he. Once again he heaved himself up on his hands and knees, aimed his headlamp at the hole and threw himself bodily forward, his hard hat clattering against the ceiling and the jagged protrusions tearing at his overalls. Once again he ground to a halt, stuck like a cork in a bottle. It was no good. He looked through the filthy sheen on his glasses at the dust cloud he had created in the tunnel beyond. He could hardly believe it. The Villa of the Papyri at Herculaneum, the greatest unexcavated treasure in Italy. Buried by the eruption of Vesuvius in AD 79, rediscovered by the Bourbon kings of Naples in the eighteenth century, hardly excavated since. And then an earthquake, a rushed international response, and here he was, first archaeologist ever to reach this far into the villa, stopped dead by his own girth. He felt like weeping. They would have to get in a pneumatic drill, widen the hole. It would mean more delays, more frustration. Already they were two weeks behind schedule, days spent pacing and sweating in the superintendency lobby while the bureaucracy inched towards releasing their permit. Precious time he could ill afford to lose, with his new excavation in full swing in the eastern desert beside the Red Sea.

Then he saw it.

He gasped, and whispered in his native German. *'Mein Gott. No, it can't be.'* He reached out, and felt the smooth surface. A snout. 'Yes, it is.' He let his hand drop, and stared in amazement.

The guardian god of the dead.

A few feet ahead the grey mottled wall of the eighteenth-century tunnel had fallen away to form a shallow cavity, no more than a foot in depth. In the centre was a head, peering out, black and shrouded with dust but unmistakable, the ears pointing high up and the snout jutting out defiantly. *He who walked through the shadows and lurked in dark places, guardian of the veil of death.* Hiebermeyer stared at the sightless eyes, surrounded by the thick black line of kohl, then shut his own eyes tight and silently mouthed the name. Here, at the threshold of the unknown, at a place of unimaginable terror and death, where those who last lived truly saw the fires of hell. *Anubis*. He opened his eyes again, and saw three vertical lines of hieroglyphs running down the chest of the statue, the text instantly recognizable. *A man remains over after death, and his deeds are placed beside him in heaps. Existence yonder is for eternity, and for him who reaches it without wrongdoing, he shall exist yonder like a god.* Hiebermeyer stared past the statue into the empty blackness of the tunnel beyond. For a brief, bizarre moment he pitied all of them, the ancients who placed such store in the world beyond, whose crumbled dreams of the afterlife had become his own kingdom of the dead. Not for the first time he felt he was on a mission, that his true calling as an archaeologist was to bring those in limbo some semblance of the immortality they had so craved.

'Maurice.' A muffled voice came through from behind.

'Maria.'

'Relax for a moment.'

There was a massive jolt and he sprang forward, tumbling awkwardly down the cascade of rock fragments that filled the tunnel entrance. He began to cough violently and quickly replaced the dust mask where it had been wrenched off. He grimaced, pulled his legs through, then crouched upright in the narrow tunnel.

'Sorry.' Maria's face appeared through the hole, capped with a yellow hard hat and wearing protective glasses and a dust mask, her long dark hair tied back. Her voice was strong and mellifluous, English with a hint of a Spanish accent. 'Always best to catch people unawares, I find. If you tense up it's hopeless.'

'You've done that often?'

'I've been through a few holes in my time.' She slipped effortlessly through and crouched beside him, their two bodies exactly filling the width of the tunnel with scarcely enough headroom to stand upright. 'I hope you're still intact. A few bruises seemed better than another sentence to the superintendency office, begging for a pneumatic drill.'

'My thoughts precisely.' Hiebermeyer rubbed his left leg gingerly. 'The permit only allows us to follow this old tunnel, not to dig new ones. Even widening that hole created by the earthquake would be a criminal transgression. It's madness.' He peered back through the dust. 'Not that the super-intendency people will notice what we do right now.'

'They'll be catching up to us soon.'

Hiebermeyer grunted, then raised his safety glasses and eyed Maria thoughtfully as he cleaned the lenses. 'Anyway, I rather enjoyed our time together in the office. A crash course on medieval manuscripts from a world expert. Fascinating. And I was about to read you my doctoral thesis on the Roman quarries opened up by the emperor Claudius in Egypt.'

Maria groaned. 'You're supposed to be in your element here, Maurice. Underground, I mean. Remember, I was on board *Seaquest II* when Jack took the call, after the earthquake here. Get an Egyptologist, he said. Someone used to catacombs, burrowing in the ground, the Valley of the Kings and all that.'

'Ah, the Valley of the Kings,' Hiebermeyer sighed. He watched as Maria backed up until her head was inches from the snout of the jackal. 'But you're right. I am in my element now. It's fabulous. We have a new friend.'

'Huh?'

'Turn around. Slowly.'

Maria did as instructed, then yelped and threw herself back. '*Dios mia*. Oh my God.'

'Don't worry. It's just a statue.'

Maria was splayed against the tunnel entrance, but far enough back to take in everything that had been revealed. 'It's a dog,' she whispered. 'A wolf. On a human torso.'

'Relax. It won't bite.'

'Sorry. My nerves are a little frayed.' Maria took a deep breath, then leaned forward and peered closely. 'It's not possible,' she murmured. 'Hieroglyphs? Is this thing Egyptian?'

'Anubis,' Hiebermeyer said matter-of-factly. 'A life-sized statue of the Egyptian god of the dead, in black steatite. The hieroglyphs are a copy of the *Instructions for Merikare*, a text of the third millennium BC, but that cartouche at the bottom is a royal inscription of the Twenty-Sixth Dynasty, of the Sixth century BC. I wouldn't be surprised if this came from the royal capital at Saïs, on the Nile delta.'

'That rings a bell,' Maria said. 'Wasn't that where the Athenian Solon visited the high priest? Where he recorded the legend of Atlantis?'

'You've spent some time with Jack.'

'I'm an adjunct professor of the International Maritime University now, remember? Just like you. It's like we're all back at college again. He told me the whole story on board *Seaquest II* on our voyage back from the Yucatán. I was completely hooked. It really helped to refocus me.'

Hiebermeyer peered back at her through the dust. 'I know this may seem an odd time to say it, but I do know what you went through. In the Yucatán, I mean, the kidnapping and torture, your friend O'Connor in Scotland. Jack told me on the phone before you joined me in Naples. I haven't mentioned it before because the time was never right. Like now. Just so you know.'

'I know.' Maria straightened up and dusted off her sleeves. 'Jack said he'd told you. Thank you, Maurice. Much appreciated. End of topic.'

Hiebermeyer paused as if about to say something, then nodded. 'So. Atlantis.'

'Jack and Costas have plans to go back to the Black Sea to the site and find a Greek wreck they saw nearby, a trireme I think.'

Hiebermeyer grunted. 'I wish Jack would give me some time instead. I've got something much better for him. It's supposed to be our job, feeding him any new leads. I've been trying to tell him about this one for months now.' He sighed in exasperation, then looked at the statue. 'But back to what we've got here. The Greek historian Herodotus also visited Saïs and described a lake outside the Temple of Neith, a sanctuary surrounded by statues like this, pharaohs and gods brought from older sites all over Egypt. By the Roman period Saïs was silted up and abandoned, but it would have been accessible to Roman ships and stripped of all its precious stone and statuary.'

'You're saying this was looted?'

'I prefer the word transferred. The Romans who built this villa had access to great works of art from all over the Mediterranean and beyond, from many different cultures stretching far back in history. They were just like private collectors or museum curators today. Some of the best Greek bronze statues ever found came from this very villa, discovered only yards away from us when well-diggers broke through in the eighteenth century. Some Romans equated Anubis with Cerberus, guardian of the river Styx in the underworld, but to many he was a figure of derision, the barking one, a dog. This statue would have been an antiquity, a curio, probably seen as an amusing work of art and nothing more.'

'I don't know,' Maria said quietly. 'He seems to be staring at us, half in and half out of history, exactly like a guardian.' She peered at Hiebermeyer. 'Do you ever get superstitious, Maurice? I mean, King Tut's tomb, the curse of the mummy, all that?'

'No.' Hiebermeyer spoke curtly. 'I'm just a dirt archaeologist.'

'Come on, Maurice. You must at least be thrilled by this. Remember when we were undergraduates, and you talked all the time about Egypt? And I mean all the time. Admit it.'

Hiebermeyer looked at the jackal head, and allowed himself

a rare smile. 'I am thrilled. Of course I am. It's wonderful. I can't wait to see the rest of the inscription.' He pressed the palm of his hand against the polished steatite, then looked down the tunnel. 'But I really think this is the end of the road. This statue must have been revealed in the seismic aftershock last night, and we must be the first to see it. But others have been this far in the tunnel before us, before it was sealed up to get it ready for our arrival. The local site security people will have been in here as soon as that first earthquake opened it up. If they found anything it's probably on the black market already. I doubt whether we'll find anything else.'

'I can't believe you're so cynical.' Maria seemed genuinely affronted. 'They'd never have allowed it. Have you forgotten where we are? The Villa of the Papyri at Herculaneum. Site of the only known library of papyrus scrolls to survive from antiquity, yet everyone knows that more of it must remain here to be found, sealed up behind these walls. You don't just let anyone walk in here and pilfer it.'

'Also one of the greatest disappointments in archaeology,' Hiebermeyer said. 'Almost all the excavated scrolls are by Philodemus, a third-rate philosopher of no lasting significance. No great works of literature, hardly anything in Latin.' He replaced his glasses. 'Ever wonder why the villa was never fully excavated?'

'Lots of reasons. Structural issues. Undermining the modern buildings above. Resources needed for maintaining the existing excavation, the main part of Herculaneum already revealed. Bureaucracy. Lack of funds. Corruption. You name it.'

'Try again.'

'Well, there are huge problems working out the best way of conserving and reading the carbonized papyri. You remember our visit to the Officina dei Papyri in Naples? They're still working on the stuff found in the eighteenth century. And they need to determine the best way of excavating new material, of recovering any more scrolls that may exist. This place demands the best. It's a sacred site.'

'Precisely.' Hiebermeyer clicked his fingers. 'The last thing you said. A sacred site. And like other sacred sites, like the caves of the Dead Sea Scrolls in Israel, people yearn to find out what lies inside, yet they also fear it. And believe me, there's one very powerful body in Italy that would rather not have any more written records from the first century AD.'

At that moment the dust in the air seemed to blur and there was a palpable tremor, followed by a sound like falling masonry somewhere ahead. Maria braced her hands on the floor of the tunnel and looked at Hiebermeyer in alarm. He quickly whipped out a palm-sized device with a prong and jammed it on to the wall of the tunnel, watching the readout intently as the tremor subsided. 'An aftershock, a bit bigger than the one last night but probably nothing to worry about,' he said. 'We were told to expect these. Remember, the walls around us are solidified pyroclastic mud, unlike the ash and pumice fallout on Pompeii. Most of it's harder than concrete. We should be safe.'

'I can hear the others, coming up the tunnel behind us,' Maria said quietly.

'Ah yes. The mysterious lady from the superintendency. You know she's an old friend of Jack's? I mean, close friend. It was after you'd left, when he was finishing his doctorate and I was already in Egypt. For some reason they don't talk. I can see the torch light now. Best behaviour.'

'No, I didn't know,' Maria said quietly, then looked up at the snout. 'Anyway, Anubis should stall them.'

'Anubis will probably halt the whole project,' Hiebermeyer said. 'It'll be hailed as a great discovery, vindication of their decision to explore the tunnel. It'll be enough for them to withdraw our permit and seal this up. The only reason we're here is that someone leaked the discovery of the tunnel to the press after the earthquake, and the archaeological authorities had no choice but to put up a show.'

'You're being cynical again.'

'Trust me. I've been in this game a long time. There are much bigger forces at play here. There are those who are fearful of the ancient past, who would do all they can to close it off. They fear anything that might shake the established order, the institutions they serve. Old ideas, ancient truths sometimes obscured by those very institutions which sprang up to protect them.'

'Ideas that might be found in a long-lost library,' Maria murmured.

'We're talking the first century AD here,' Maurice whispered. 'The first decades anno domini in the year of our Lord. Think about it.'

'I have.'

'It's your call whether or not we continue down the tunnel to see what else we can find before they shut us down. I've got an excavation in Egypt waiting for me. You need a rest.'

'Try me.'

'I take it we're in agreement.'

'Let's take the chance now while we've got it,' Maria said. 'You've found your treasure, now I need mine.'

Hiebermeyer stowed the oscillator in his front overall pocket, sneezed noisily then peered at Maria. 'I can see what Jack saw in you. He always said you might make something of yourself, if you got out of the Institute of Medieval Studies at Oxford and took a job with him.'

Maria gave him a withering look, then crawled forward until she was just beyond the statue. The dust was settling, and ahead of them they could just make out a white patch where another fragment of the tunnel wall had been dislodged by the tremor. As the beams of their headlamps concentrated on the fracture, they could see something dark at the centre. Hiebermeyer pulled himself forward and turned to Maria, his face ablaze with excitement. 'Okay, we've passed Anubis, and we're still in one piece.'

'Superstitious, Maurice?'

'Let's go for it.'

3

23 August AD *79*

Claudius gulped at the wine, holding the cup with trembling hands, then shut his eyes and grasped the pillar until the worst of the fit was over. Tonight he would go to the Phlegraean Fields, stand before the Sibyl's cave for the last time. But there was work to do before then. He lurched sideways on to the marble bench, lunging wildly at his toga to stop it from slipping off, then tripped and fell heavily on his elbows. His face twisted in pain and frustration, willing on tears that no longer came, retching on empty. In truth he was going through the motions. He barely felt anything any more.

He raised himself and peered rheumily at the moonlight

DAVID GIBBINS

that was now shimmering across the great expanse of the bay, past the statues of Greek and Egyptian gods that lined the portico of the villa. The nearest to him, the dog-headed one, seemed to frame the mountain, its ears and snout glowing in the moonlight. From his vantage point on the belvedere of the villa he could see the rooftops of the town he knew intimately but had never visited, Herculaneum. He could hear the clinking and low sounds of evening activity, the rising and falling of conversation, peals of laughter and soft music, the lapping of waves on the seashore.

He had all he had needed. Wine from the slopes of Vesuvius, rich red wine that flowed like syrup, always his favourite. And girls, brought for him from the back alleys below, girls who still gave him fleeting pleasure, years after he had stopped pondering what it did for them.

And he had the poppy.

He sniffed and wrinkled his nose, and then looked up. The soothsayers had been right. There was something about the sky tonight.

He looked across the bay to the west, past the old Greek colony of Neapolis towards the naval base at Misenum, on the far promontory beside the open sea. The shadow of the mountain darkened the bay, and all he could make out were a few merchantmen anchored close inshore. He was used to looking out for the phosphorescence left in the wake of the fast galleys, but tonight he could see nothing. Where was Pliny? Had Pliny got his message? It was hardly as if he was away on naval manoeuvres. Claudius knew exactly what the commander of the Roman fleet at Misenum did. The fleet had not put out for action since Claudius' grandfather Mark Antony had been defeated at Actium, over a century before. *Pax Romana*. Claudius nodded to himself. He, Tiberius Claudius Drusus Nero Germanicus, *Imperator*, had helped to keep that peace. He looked back towards the half-empty pitcher on the table. Pliny had better get here soon. What he had to say tonight demanded a clear head. It was getting late.

He reached out to pour himself another cup, letting the wine overflow and trickle down the table to join the wide red stain that had permeated the marble floor over the years. He could see back into his little room and the line of wax images ranged along the wall, caught in the moonlight. Ancestral images, the only things he had saved from his past. His father Drusus, cherished in memory. His beloved brother Germanicus. With his waxen skin, Claudius felt he was already one with them. He was old, old enough to have lived through the Age of Augustus, the Golden Age tarnished for ever by the debauchery of Tiberius and Caligula and then Claudius' successor, Nero. Sometimes, in his bleaker moments, usually after the wine, he felt that time had made a monster of him just as it had ruined Rome, not by some hideous malformity but through a slow and inexorable wasting, as if the gods who had inflicted the ailment on him, the palsy, were making him endure the full extremity of torment in this life before they pitched him into the fires below.

He shook himself out of his trance, coughed painfully and

looked over the balcony of the villa again, over the rooftops of Herculaneum. When he had faked his own poisoning and escaped Rome, when his work there was done and he craved his former life as a writer and a scholar, his old friend Calpurnius Piso had blocked off an annex to his villa and made a home for him here, his hideaway now for almost a quarter of a century, overlooking the sea and the mountain. He missed nothing in Rome that was not already gone, and had all that a scholar could need. He knew he should be more grateful, but there were irritations. Calpurnius' grandfather had been a patron of the Greek philosopher Philodemus, whose library of unreadable nonsense was always in the way. And then poor Calpurnius Piso had been forced to commit suicide, here, in front of Claudius' very eyes, after his failed plot against Nero, leaving the villa to a grudging nephew who did not even know who Claudius was, who thought he was just another one of the Greek charlatans who seemed to beg their way into every aristocratic household around here. It was exactly the anonymity that Claudius sought, but it was also the ultimate humiliation.

But he had the memories, one above all others. The fisherman by the inland sea, that afternoon all those years ago. The promise Claudius had made him. Everything the fisherman had predicted had come to pass. Now forces beyond Claudius' control were closing in on him. Claudius would not let him down.

'*Ave, Princeps.*'

Claudius straightened with a start. 'Pliny? My dear friend. I told you to stop calling me that. We have known each other well since you were a young cavalry officer with my legions in Germany. You have been my closest companion since I summoned you to visit me here when you took up your appointment with the Fleet. I stopped being *Princeps* when you were still a young man. It is I who should be honouring you, a veteran and an admiral. But we are both citizens of Rome, no more, no less, for what that is worth these days.'

Pliny came quickly in and helped Claudius back to his seat, taking his cup and filling it. He passed it over and poured himself one, holding it up formally. 'The gods give you salutations on your ninetieth year.'

'That was three weeks ago.' Claudius waved his hand dismissively, then looked at the other man with affection. Pliny was tall, unusually so for a Roman, but then he did come from Verona in the north, the land of the Celts. Rather than a toga he wore the emblazoned red tunic and strap-on boots of a naval officer, and he had a sinewy toughness about him. He was everything that Claudius most admired, a decorated war veteran, a natural leader of men, a prodigious scholar who was author of countless volumes, and now the new encyclopedia. Claudius clenched his fist to stop his stutter. 'Have you b-brought me the book?'

'The first twenty volumes. My present for your birthday, *Princeps*, even if a little belated. I could not imagine a more auspicious occasion or a more exacting reader for my work.' Pliny pointed proudly to a leather basket beside the door, carefully placed away from the wine, brimming over with scrolls. 'A few details on the flora and fauna of Britannia I want to check with you, and of course the space you asked me to keep in the section of Judaea. Otherwise complete. The first natural history of the world not written by a Greek.'

Claudius gestured at the half-empty shelves in the room, then at the scrolls lying in bundles on the floor. 'At least now I've got space to store them. Narcissus has been helping me to box up these other scrolls. I've never been able to bring myself to throw any book away, and I never had the heart to tell old Calpurnius, but these ones by Philodemus aren't worth the paper they're written on.'

'Where do you want them? My books, I mean. I can shelve them for you.'

'Leave them where they are by the door. Narcissus is making space in my library tomorrow. Yours will have pride of place. All of that Greek nonsense will be removed.'

'Narcissus still does all your writing for you?'

'He castrated himself, poor fellow, so he could serve me, you know. It was when he was a boy, a young slave. I was going to free him anyway.'

'I've never quite trusted Narcissus,' Pliny said cautiously.

'You can always trust a eunuch.'

'It's always been your Achilles' heel, if I may say so. Wives and freedmen.'

'Achilles is one thing I'm definitely not. I may be a god, but I'm no Achilles.' Claudius stifled a giggle, then looked serious. 'Yes, Narcissus is a bit of a mystery. I sometimes think his fall from being Prefect of the Guard in Rome to being little more than the slave of an old hermit must be hard for him to bear, being part of my own disappearing act. But Nero would have executed him if he hadn't faked his death too. Narcissus has always been a shrewd fellow, with his business interests in Britannia. And his religion, the quirky stuff he picked up when he was a slave. He's a very pious chap. And he's always been very loyal to me.' Claudius suddenly smiled, lurched up, and caught Pliny by the arm. 'Thank you for your books, my friend,' he said quietly. 'Reading has always been my greatest joy. And there will be much to help me with my own history of Britannia.' He pointed to an open scroll pinned on the table, one edge splattered with wine. 'We'd better get to work while I've still got a modicum of common sense left in me. It has been a long day.'

'I can see.'

The two men hunched together over the table, the curious hue of the moonlight giving the marble a reddish tint. It was unseasonably hot for late August, and the breeze wafting over the balcony was warm and dry like the sirocco that swept up from Africa. Claudius sometimes wondered whether Pliny the great encyclopedist was not just flattering him by calling on his expertise on Britannia, a hollow victory if there ever was one. Claudius had been there, of course, had ridden out of the freezing waves on a war elephant, pale and shaking, not in fear of the enemy but terrified that he might have a seizure and fall off, bringing dishonour to his family name. Yet Britannia was his one imperial achievement, his one triumph, and he had devoted himself to writing a history of the province from the earliest times. He had read everything there was to read on the subject, from the journal of the ancient explorer Pytheas, who had first rounded the island, to the blood-curdling accounts of headhunting that his legionaries had extracted from the druids before they were executed. And he had found her, princess of a noble family, the girl the Sibyl had told him to seek out, she who would rise and fall alongside the warrior-queen.

'Tell me,' Claudius suddenly said. 'You saw my father in a dream?'

'It was why I wrote my *History of the German Wars*,' Pliny replied, repeating the story he had told Claudius many times before. 'It was while I was stationed on the Rhine, in command of a cavalry regiment. I awoke one night and a ghost was standing over me, a Roman general. It was Drusus, I swear it. Your revered father. He was committing me to secure his memory.'

'He d-died before I even knew him.' Claudius glanced at the bust of his father in the room, then clasped his hands together in anguish. 'P-poisoned, like my dear brother Germanicus. If only I had been able to live up to his legacy, to lead the legions like Germanicus, to earn the loyalty of the men.'

'But you did,' Pliny said, looking anxiously at Claudius. 'Remember Britannia.'

'I do.' Claudius slumped, then smiled wanly. 'That's the trouble.' He began fingering a coin on the table, a burnished sestertius with his portrait on it, turning it over and over again, a nervous habit Pliny had seen him indulge many times before, but he let it slip out of his fingers and roll towards the scrolls by the door. Claudius sighed irritably and made as if to get up, but then slumped down again and stared morosely at his hands. 'They've built a temple to me there, you know. And they're building an amphitheatre now, did you know that? In Londinium. I saw it on my secret trip there this summer, when I went to her tomb.'

'Don't tell me about that again, *Princeps*, please,' Pliny said. 'It gives me nightmares. What about Rome? Your achievements in Rome? You constructed many wonderful things, Claudius. The people are grateful.'

'Not that anyone would see them,' Claudius said. 'They're all underground, underwater. Did I tell you about my secret tunnel under the Palatine Hill? Right under my house. Apollo ordered me to make it. I worked out the riddle in the leaves, in the Sibyl's cave. Let me see if I can remember it.'

'And Judaea,' Pliny said quickly. 'You granted universal toleration for the Jews, across the empire. You gave Herod Agrippa the kingdom of Judaea.'

'And then he died,' Claudius murmured. 'My dear friend Herod Agrippa. Even he was corrupted by Rome, by my vile nephew Caligula.'

'You had no choice,' Pliny continued. 'With nobody to replace Herod Agrippa, you had to make Judaea a Roman province.'

'And let it be ruled by venal and rapacious officials. After all that Cicero warned a century ago about provincial administration. The lessons of history,' Claudius added bitterly. 'Look how I learned them.'

'The Jewish Revolt was inevitable.'

'Ironic, isn't it? Fifteen years after Rome grants universal toleration for the Jews, she does all she can to eradicate them from the face of the earth.'

'The gods willed it.'

'No they did not.' Claudius took a long shuddering drink. 'Remember the temple you told me about during your last visit? The one Vespasian had erected in Rome? To the deified Claudius. I'm a god too now, remember? I'm a god, but this god did not will the destruction of the Jews. You have it on divine authority.'

Pliny quickly rolled up the scroll and slid it into a leather satchel beside the table, away from the splatter of wine, then hesitantly pulled out another. 'You were going to tell me something about Judaea. Another day?'

'No. Now.'

Pliny sat poised with a metal stylus over the scroll, eager and determined. Claudius peered at the writing already on the scroll, at the gap in the middle. 'Tell me, then,' Pliny said. 'This new Jewish sect. What do you think of them?'

'That's why I asked you here.' Claudius breathed in deeply. 'The followers of the anointed one. The Messiah, the *Christos*. I know about them from my visits to the Phlegraean Fields. They are just the kind of people the Nazarene wanted to follow him. The crippled, the diseased, outcasts. People who so desperately crave happiness that their yearning becomes infectious, leading others to find their own release from the burdens of life, their own salvation.'

'How do you know all this?'

'Because I am one of them.'

'You are one of them?' Pliny sounded incredulous. 'You are a Jew?'

'No!' Claudius scoffed, his head jerking sideways. 'A cripple. An outcast. Someone who went to him for a cure.'

'You went to this man? But I thought you never travelled to the east.'

'It was all Herod's doing. My dear friend Herod Agrippa. He tried to help, to take me away from Rome. He had heard of a miracle-worker in Judaea, a Nazarene, a man they said was descended from King David of the Jews. It was my only trip ever to the east. The heat made my shuddering worse.'

'So the trip was wasted.'

'Except for a few hours on a lake.' Claudius suddenly had a far-off look in his eyes. 'The town of Nazareth lies on a great inland body of water, the Sea of Gennesareth they call it. It's not salt water at all, you know, but really a vast lake, and lies several *stades* below the level of the sea.'

'Fascinating.' Pliny was writing quickly. 'Tell me more.'

'He was a carpenter, a boatwright. Herod and I and our women went out with him on his boat, fishing, drinking wine. I was with my lovely Calpurnia, away from the clutches of my wife. We were all about the same age, young men and women, and even I found an exuberance I thought I could never have. I spilled wine in the lake and he joked about turning water into wine, catching the fish that way.'

'But no miracle.'

'After the fishing we sat on the shore until the sun went down. Herod grew impatient, and went off to the town seeking his pleasure. The Nazarene and I were left alone together.'

'What did he say?'

'He said I must bear my affliction, that it would protect me and propel me to a greatness I could scarcely imagine. I had no idea what he was on about: me, Claudius the cripple, the embarrassing nephew of the emperor Tiberius, barely tolerated in Rome, hidden away and denied public office while all the other young men were finding glory with the legions.'

'He saw a scholar and a future emperor,' Pliny murmured. 'He knew your destiny, *Princeps*. He was a shrewd man.'

'I don't believe in destiny. And there you go again. *Princeps*.'

Pliny quickly steered him back. 'What of the man's own future? The Nazarene?'

'He spoke of it. He said that one day he would disappear into the wilderness, then all the world would come to know of him. I warned him not to be brought down by the sticky web of those who would exploit and deceive him. That was my advice for him. Nazareth was a pretty out-of-the-way place, and I don't know if he realized then what men are capable of. I doubt whether he'd ever even seen a crucifixion.'

'And Herod Agrippa?'

'Herod was still with us when the Nazarene had said he wanted no intermediaries, no interpreters. Herod used a Greek word for them, *apostoles*. Herod was a straightforward man, blunt, a dear fellow. He had no interest in the visions of the Nazarene, but he could see I had been affected, and he was fond of me. He determined that if he came to power he would tolerate the Nazarene.'

'But this man was executed, I believe?' Pliny said.

'Crucified, in Jerusalem. In the final years of the reign of my uncle Tiberius. The Nazarene had told me he would offer himself as a sacrifice. Whether he truly foresaw his own execution, his crucifixion, is another matter. The man I met had no death wish. He was full of the joys of life. But we talked about the ancient legends of human sacrifice among the Semites, the Jews. He knew his history, how to reach his people. I think the sacrifice he meant was symbolic.'

'Fascinating,' Pliny murmured absently. 'The Sea of Gennesareth, you say? Not the Dead Sea? That sea is remarkably briny, I believe.' He was writing in the final narrow space he had left on his scroll, dipping his quill in an ink pot he had placed beside him. 'This will make a splendid addition to my chapter on Judaea. Thank you, Claudius.'

'Wait. There's more. I haven't even given it to you yet.' Claudius got up and hobbled unsteadily over to the bookcase where Philodemus' library had been, sweeping aside the few remaining scrolls on the middle shelf and reaching into a dark recess behind. He lurched back to the table, sat down heavily and passed a small wooden scroll tube over to Pliny.

'There it is,' Claudius panted. 'That's what I wanted you to have.'

'Acacia, I shouldn't wonder.' Pliny sniffed the wood. 'What the Jews call *sittim*, from the stunted tree that grows along the shores of the east.' He uncorked the tube and reached gingerly inside, extracting a small scroll about a foot square. It was yellow with age, though not as old as Philodemus' papyrus scrolls, and some of the ink had crystallized and smudged on the surface. Pliny held the sheet close and sniffed the ink. 'Probably not sulphate,' he murmured. 'Though it's hard to tell, there's so much sulphur in the air today.'

'You smell it too?' Claudius said. 'I thought it was just me, bringing it back from my visits to the Phlegraean Fields.'

'Bitumen.' Pliny sniffed the ink again. 'Bitumen, no doubt about it.'

'That makes sense,' Claudius said. 'Oily tar rises to the surface all round the Sea of Gennesareth. I saw it.'

'Indeed?' Pliny scribbled a note in the margin of the text. 'Fascinating. You know I have been experimenting with ink? My Alexandrian agent sent me some excellent gall nuts, cut from a species of tree in Arabia. Did you know they are made by tiny insects, which exude the gall? Quite remarkable. I crushed them and mixed them with water and resin, then added the iron and sulphur salts I found on the shore at Misenum. It makes a marvellous ink, jet black and no smudging. I'm writing with it now. Just look at it. Far better than this inferior stuff, oil soot and animal skin glue, I shouldn't wonder. I wish people wouldn't use it. Whatever this writing is, I fear it won't last as long as old Philodemus' rantings.'

'It was all I could find.' Claudius took a gulp of wine and wiped his mouth with the back of his hand. 'I'd used up all my own ink on the voyage out.'

'You wrote this?'

'I supplied the paper, and that concoction that passes as ink.'

Pliny unrolled the papyrus and flattened it on a cloth he had laid over the sticky mess on the table. The papyrus was covered with fine writing, neither Greek nor Latin, lines of singular flowing artistry, composed with more care than would normally be the case for one accustomed to writing often. 'The Nazarene?'

Claudius twitched. 'At the end of our meeting, on the lake shore that night. He wanted me to take this away and keep it safely until the time was right. You read Aramaic?'

'Of course. You have expertly taught me the Phoenician language, and I believe they are similar.'

Pliny scanned the writing. At the bottom was a name. He read the few lines directly above it, looked up, then read them again. For a moment there was silence, and utter stillness in the room. Claudius watched him intently, his lower lip trembling. A waft of warm air from outside the balcony brought with it a sharp reek of sulphur, and from somewhere inland came a distant sound like waves along the seashore. Claudius kept his eyes on Pliny, who put down the scroll and raised his hands together, pensively.

'Well?' Claudius said.

Pliny looked at him, and spoke carefully. 'I am a military man, and an encyclopedist. I record facts, things I have seen with my own eyes or had recounted to me on good authority. I can see that this document has the authority of the man who wrote it, and who signed his name on it.'

'Put it away,' Claudius said, reaching out and grasping Pliny's wrist. 'Keep it safely, the safest place you can find. But transcribe those final lines into your *Natural History*. Now is the time.'

'You have made copies?'

Claudius looked at Pliny, then at the scroll, and suddenly his hand began shaking. 'Look at me. The palsy. I can't even write my own name. And for this I don't trust a copyist, not even Narcissus.' He got up, picked up the scroll and went over to a dark recess beside the bookcase filled with papyrus sheets and old wax tablets, then knelt down awkwardly with his back to Pliny. He fumbled around for a few moments, got up again and turned round, a cylindrical stone container in his hands. 'These jars came from Saïs in Egypt, you know,' he said. 'Calpurnius Piso stole them from the Temple of Neith when he looted the place. Apparently they were filled with ancient Egyptian hieroglyphic scrolls, but he burned them all. The old fool.' He put the jar down, then picked up a bronze-handled dish filled with a black substance and held it over a candle, his hands unusually steady. The air filled with a rich aromatic smell, briefly disguising the sulphur. He put the dish down again, picked up a wooden spatula and smeared the resin around the lid of the container, let it cool for a moment, and then handed the cylinder to Pliny. 'There you go. It is sealed, as I was instructed in the leaves, according to divine augury.'

'This document,' Pliny persisted. 'Why so urgent?'

'It is because what he predicted has come to pass.' Claudius shuddered again, ostentatiously clutching his hand as if to stop it from shaking. He fixed Pliny with an intense stare. 'The Nazarene knew the power of the written word. But he said he would never write again. He said that one day his word would come to be seen as a kind of holy utterance. He said that his followers would preach his word like a divine mantra, but that time would distort it and some would seek to use their version of it for their own ends, to further themselves in the world of men. He was surrounded by illiterates in Nazareth. He wanted a man of letters to have his written word.'

'The written words of a prophet,' Pliny murmured. 'That's the last thing a priesthood usually wants. It does them out of a job.'

'It's why the r-ridiculous Sibyl speaks in r-riddles,' Claudius said, flustered. 'Only the soothsayers can interpret it. What nonsense.'

'But why me?' Pliny insisted.

'Because I can't publish it. I'm supposed to have died a quarter of a century ago, remember? But now that your *Natural History* is nearly finished, it's perfect. You have the authority. People will read you far and wide. Your work is one of the greatest ever written, and will far outlast Rome.

Immortal fame will await those whose deeds are recorded by you.'

'You flatter me, *Princeps*.' Pliny bowed, visibly pleased. 'But I still don't fully understand.'

'The Nazarene said that his word would first need others to preach it. But there would come a time when the people would be ready to receive his word directly, when there would be enough converts for the word to be spread from one to the other, when they could dispense with teachers. He said that time would come within my lifetime. He said I would know when.'

'A *concilium*,' Pliny murmured. 'They are forming a *concilium*, a priesthood. That's what he was warning about.'

'In the Phlegraean Fields. They use that very word. *Concilium*. How do you know?'

'Because I hear it among my sailors at Misenum.'

'I told you about those in the Phlegraean Fields, the followers of *Christos*,' Claudius continued. 'More and more are going into the fold, the *concilium*. They are talking about a *kyriakum*, a house of the Lord. There is already dissent, there are already factions. Some say Jesus said this, some that. They are speaking in riddles. It is becoming sophistry, like Philodemus. And there are men who call themselves fathers, *patres*.'

'Priests,' Pliny murmured. 'Men who would rather nobody knew what we now know.'

'While I was still emperor in Rome, one came here, a Jewish *apostolos* from Tarsus named Paul. I was in disguise, making one of my visits to the Sibyl, and I heard him speak. He found followers in the Phlegraean Fields, many who are still there today. Yet none of these people knew the Nazarene, not even Paul, none of them touched him as I did. To them the man I knew was already some kind of god.' Claudius paused, then looked intently at Pliny. 'This scroll must be preserved. It will be your ultimate authority, for what you write in the *Natural History*.'

'I will keep it safe.'

'It's worse.' Claudius suddenly looked down in despair. 'The poppy makes me talk, makes my mind wander, makes me say things I can never remember afterwards. They know who I am. Every time I go now they seem to appear out of the mist, reaching out for me.'

'You should be more careful, *Princeps*,' Pliny murmured.

'They'll come here. All my life's work, all my manuscripts. They'll destroy everything. That's why I've got to give it to you. I don't trust myself.'

Pliny thought for a moment, then took the scroll of the *Natural History* he had been writing on and placed it on the bookshelf. 'I will return for this tomorrow. It will be safe here for one night, and I will add more to it about Judaea, anything more you can tell me. I will return. There is someone else I must visit here tomorrow evening. Maybe even tonight. I have been starved of her for too long. You will join me?'

'I sometimes avail myself. But these days I think more and more of my dear Calpurnia. Such pleasures are in the past for me, Pliny.'

'Tonight I will take my fast galley straight to Rome, I'll be back here by the morning. After I see you again, I will make the same additions into my master version, then send it to the scribes in Rome for copying,' he muttered, half to himself. 'The *Natural History* will be complete at last. The final edition. Unless you can tell me anything more about Britannia, that is.' He thought for a moment, drumming his fingers on the table, then tapped the cylinder Claudius had given him. 'And I think I know just the place for this.' He tucked it in a pouch under his toga, then took down the *Natural History* scroll on Judaea from the shelf, placed it on the table, picked up the stylus and wrote a few lines, paused for a moment, smudged the lines out with his finger, then made a note in the margin. Claudius watched, and grunted his approval. Pliny let the two ends of the scroll roll loosely together and replaced it quickly on the shelf, suddenly remembering the time and his visit to the woman that night. At that moment there was a shuffling sound at the entranceway, something that might have been a knock, and a stooped old man appeared, dressed in a simple tunic and carrying two woollen cloaks.

'Ah, Narcissus,' Claudius said. 'I am ready.'

'You go to the Sibyl?' Pliny asked.

'One last time. I promise.'

'Then one last thing, *Princeps*.'

'Yes?'

'I do this for you as a friend, and as a fellow historian. It is my job to present the facts as I know them, and to hold nothing back.'

'But?'

'You? Why is this so important to you? This Nazarene?'

'I too am loyal to my friends. You know that. And he was one of them.'

'My sailors speak of a Kingdom of Heaven on earth, that people with goodness and compassion can find it. Do you believe in this thing?'

Claudius started to speak, hesitated, then looked Pliny full in the face, his eyes moist and suddenly etched with his years. He reached out and touched his friend's arm, then gave a small smile. 'My dear Pliny. You forget yourself. I'm a god, remember? Gods have no need of heaven.'

Pliny smiled back, and bowed. *'Princeps.'*

4

Present day

Jack and Costas hung weightless in the water eight metres below the Zodiac boat off south-east Sicily, their equipment reflecting the sunlight that shone as far down as the cliff base thirty metres below. Jack was floating a few metres away from the shotline, maintaining perfect buoyancy with his breathing and watching the extraordinary scene overhead. The Lynx helicopter from *Seaquest II* had arrived a few minutes before, and its deflected propwash created a perfect halo around the silhouette of the boat. Through the tunnel of calm in the middle, Jack could see the wavering forms of the two replacement divers who had been winched down to provide safety backup should anything go wrong. He could feel the vibration, the drumming of the propwash on the water, but the roaring of the engines was muffled by his helmet and communication headset. He had been listening to Costas giving instructions to the departing divers, a complex checklist that seemed to run through the entire IMU equipment store.

'Okay, Jack,' Costas said. 'Andy says we're good to go. I just wanted to get the logistics people moving on *Seaquest II* in case it's showtime.'

His voice sounded oddly metallic through the intercom, a result of the modulator designed to counter the effects on the voice of helium in the gas mix. Jack tilted upright and finned back towards the shotline. The twin corrugated hoses of his regulator made him feel like a diver of Cousteau's day, but the similarity ended there. As he approached Costas he cast a critical eye over the yellow console on his friend's back, its contoured shell containing the closed-circuit rebreather with the cylinders of oxygen and trimix they needed for the dive. The corrugated hoses led to a helmet and full-face mask, allowing them to breathe and talk without the encumbrance of a mouthpiece.

'Remember my briefing,' Costas said. 'Lights off, unless we find something.'

Jack nodded. With their eyes accustomed to the gloom, he knew they would have a greater range of vision for spotting a wreck mound than with the limited cone of light from a headlamp. 'Dive profile?' he asked.

'Maximum depth eighty metres, maximum bottom time twenty-five minutes. We can go deeper, but I don't want to risk it until *Seaquest II*'s on station and the recompression chamber's fired up. And remember your bailout.' He pointed to the octopus regulator that could be fed into the helmet if the rebreather malfunctioned, bypassing the counterlung and tapping gas directly from the manifold on the cylinders.

'Roger that. You're the divemaster.'

'I wish you'd remember that the next time you see treasure glinting at the bottom of the abyss. Or inside an iceberg.' Costas pressed a control on his dive computer and then peered at Jack through his visor. 'Just one thing before we go.'

'What is it?'

'You said anything that touches on the life of Jesus is like gold dust. People must have been searching for the shipwreck of St Paul since diving began, even before Cousteau. It's one of the biggest prizes in archaeology. Why us?'

'That's what you said about Atlantis. A few lucky breaks and a little lateral thinking. That's all I've ever needed.'

'And a little help from your friends.'

'And a little help from my friends.' Jack grasped the dump valve on his buoyancy jacket. 'Good to go?'

'Good to go.'

Seconds later, Costas was hurtling down into the depths, approaching the dive in his customary way as if he were going over Niagara Falls in a barrel. Jack followed more gracefully, his arms and legs outstretched like a skydiver, exhilarated by the weightlessness and the panorama that was opening out below them, listening to the sound of his own breathing. It was exactly as he remembered it, every gully and ridge of the cliff base etched on his mind from twenty years before, from hours spent measuring and recording, poring over the wreck plan and working out where to excavate next. Costas was right about the technology. Underwater archaeology had advanced leaps and bounds in the past two decades, as if physics had progressed from Marie Curie to particle accelerators in a mere generation. Back then, measurements had been taken painstakingly by hand; now it was laser rangefinders and digital photogrammetry, using remote-operated vehicles rather than divers. What had taken months could now be achieved in a matter of days. Even the discomforts of diving were greatly reduced, the E-suits insulating them from the temperature drop at the thermocline. Yet with new diving technology greater depths beckoned, depths that brought new boundaries, new thresholds of danger. The cost was still there, the risks even greater. Jack was drawn on, always pushing the limits of exploration, but before committing others to follow in his wake he needed to be certain that the prize was worth it.

Directly below, he saw where Pete and Andy had anchored the shotline in the gully where he had found the sounding lead, and from there he saw a wavering line encrusted with algae extending down the slope into the depths. He stared at it, suddenly feeling in a time warp. It was the line he had paid out on his final dive all those years ago, still lying exactly where he had left it, as if the site had been waiting for him, unfinished. Costas had seen it too, and somehow brought himself to a halt before augering into the sea bed. He waited for Jack to reach him, then together they finned slowly side by side over the line until they reached the last plateau, fifty metres deep, the furthest point where amphoras had tumbled from the Roman shipwreck. As they swam over the plateau, a bar-like shape appeared below them in the silt, about two metres long with a rectangular aperture just visible in the centre.

'My old friend.' Jack tweaked the control on the side of his helmet to get his voice to sound normal. 'It's the lead Roman anchor shank I saw on my final dive, and there should be another identical one about fifty metres ahead, on the edge of the plateau. It's exactly what you'd expect to see from a ship using two anchors to hold offshore, one paid out behind the other. We can use them to take a compass bearing.'

'Roger that.'

They swam on over the line and soon saw the second shank just as Jack remembered it, wedged in a cleft above a dropoff. From there he could see the line tapering off, its end hanging over a ridge, the deepest he had dared to go on his final dive twenty years before. It was like the end of divers' safety lines he had followed inside caves, haunting relics of extraordinary human endeavour that beckoned others to surpass them. Without pausing they passed beyond, and dropped down to the base of the rocky cliff where the sea bed became a featureless desert of sand. On the edge Jack saw a belt of corroded machine-gun cartridges, draped over a clip of larger cannon rounds from an anti-aircraft gun. He remembered seeing them before, relics of the Second World War. Costas slowed down, and reached for the dump valve on his buoyancy compensator.

'Don't even think about it,' Jack said.

'Just looking,' Costas said hopefully, then finned away. Beyond them the sand seemed to extend to infinity, a blue-grey desert with no visible horizon. About fifty metres on they swam over a small outcrop of rock, then saw an undulation where the sand rose in a low dune. As they approached it looked more and more unnatural, like some sea creature lurking beneath the sediment, the undulation extending ten metres or more in either direction from a central hump with another ridge running at ninety degrees through it. Costas gave an audible intake of breath. 'My God, Jack. It's an aircraft!'

'I was wondering if we'd see one of these,' Jack murmured. 'It's an assault glider, a British Horsa. Look, you can see where the high wings have collapsed over the fuselage. That night in 1943 when the SAS dropped in on the Italians, the British also sent in an airlanding brigade. It was the only major glitch in the whole Sicily invasion, and it was a pretty horrific one. The gliders were released too far offshore against a headwind, and dozens of them never made it. Hundreds of guys drowned. There are going to be bodies in there.'

'That's one place I definitely don't want to go,' Costas said quietly.

'Topside you'd sometimes believe old wars never happened,' Jack said. 'Everything's cleaned up and sanitized, but underwater it's all here, just below the surface. It's haunting.'

'Depth seventy-five metres.' Costas was concentrating hard on his computer, as they finned over the last of the shadowy form in the sand. 'Not looking too good on the time front, Jack. Ten minutes max, unless we really want to stretch the envelope.'

'Roger that.'

'I take it we're not looking for a giant cross sticking out of the sea bed.'

Jack grinned through his visor. 'I wish it were that easy. At this date we don't even know whether the cross was a Christian sign. If it's the shipwreck of St Paul, we're talking twenty, maybe twenty-five years after the crucifixion. Most of the familiar Christian symbols, the cross, the fish, the anchor, the dove, the Greek letters chi-rho, only start appearing in the following century, and even then were only used secretly. The archaeology of early Christianity is incredibly elusive. And remember, Paul was supposed to be a prisoner, under Roman guard. He's hardly going to have relics with him.'

Jack looked at his depth gauge. Seventy-seven metres. He could feel the compensator continuously bleeding air into his suit as he descended, counteracting the water pressure. He felt elated, preternaturally aware, at a depth where he would have been one step from death twenty years before. He remembered too well the numbing effect of nitrogen narcosis, the thick, syrupy taste of compressed air below fifty metres, into the danger zone. Breathing mixed gas was like drinking wine without alcohol, all expectation but no buzz. He realized that he missed the narcosis, that his mind was overcompensating. It was euphoria of a different kind to descend to these depths clear headed. He felt acutely alive, focused, his lucidity sharpened by the threshold of danger just ahead, revelling in the moment as if he were a novice diver again.

'They must have been narked out of their minds,' Costas said.

'Cousteau's boys?'

'I can't believe they got this deep.'

'I can,' Jack replied. 'I dived with the last of that generation, the survivors. Tough French ex-navy types. They took a slug of wine before diving to dilate the blood vessels, and the last breath they took before the regulator was a lungful of Gauloise. Going deep was like a drinking competition. Real men could take it.'

'Take it and die.'

Then out of the gloom Jack saw them. First one, then another. The unmistakable shapes of pottery amphoras, half buried and shrouded in sediment. The trail of amphoras led back to the cliff face, the way he and Costas had come, in the right direction, but the forms were too encrusted to identify. They could be Greek, they could be Roman. Jack needed more. He looked at his depth gauge. Eighty metres. He swam over the last shape, Costas behind him. Suddenly they were at another cliff, only this time there was no sandy shelf below, only inky blackness. They had reached the edge of the unknown, a place as forbidding as outer space, the beginning of a slope that dropped through vast canyons and mountain ranges to the deepest abyss of the Mediterranean, more than five thousand metres below. It was the end of the road. Jack let the momentum carry him a few metres over the edge, his mind blank in the face of the immensity before them.

'Don't do it, Jack.' Costas spoke quietly, his voice now sounding distorted as the helium level increased. 'We can come back with the Advanced Deep Sea Anthropod, check out the next hundred metres or so. Do it safely.'

'We haven't found enough to justify it.' Jack's voice sounded distant, emotionless, too overwhelmed to register his feelings, masking his disappointment. 'Cousteau's divers, the account in that diary, they must have meant that scatter of amphoras on the shelf. There's no way they could have gone deeper, down that slope. We're well into the death zone for compressed air.' He turned slowly, then on a whim switched on his helmet headlamp. There was nothing to lose now. The glare was blinding, and showed how dark it was around them. He played the beam down the rock face, revealing occasional patches of red and orange marine growth which had been invisible in the natural light. Very little lived at this depth. He swept the beam back up from the limit of visibility below, then swept it back down again.

Bingo.

A narrow ledge, concealed from above by the cornice of the

cliff. A mound of forms, twenty, maybe thirty of them, identical to the ones they had just seen. *Amphoras*.

'I've got it,' Jack said excitedly. 'About ten metres below us.'

Costas swam alongside, switched on his headlamp and peered down. 'Looks like a wreck mound to me,' he murmured. 'A sandy gully. Could be good for preservation.'

'It must be the stern,' Jack said fervently. 'The bow strikes the cliff, the stern floats back, dropping amphoras as it goes, then sinks here. It's where the best artefacts should be, ship's stores, personal possessions, stuff to identify it.'

'Can you see the amphora type?'

'No way. I need to get down there.'

'Jack, we can do it, but I'd have to reconfigure the dive profile. It's exactly what I didn't want. It puts us into an extended decompression schedule, before *Seaquest II* arrives and without any backup. Even the safety diver's no use. And we'd only get an extra ten minutes.'

'Every dive's a risk,' Jack murmured. 'But if you can calculate the risk, you can do it safely. That's what you always tell me and you've just calculated it.'

'Remember what you said about all the new diving technology, about missing the edge? Well, you're on it now.'

'I trust your equipment, you trust my intuition. This could be the best wreck we've ever discovered.'

'We could wait. Surely we've found enough now to come back.'

'We could.'

'I'll cover your back, you cover mine.'

'That's always the deal.'

'Let's do it.'

They dropped over the cliff together, Costas reprogramming his wrist computer as Jack panned his light over the mound of amphoras below. Just before they reached the ledge he let out a whoop of excitement. 'Graeco-Italic,' he exclaimed. 'Dressel 2 to 4. Look, you can see the high handles, the angular shoulder. First century AD, Italian type, from Campania around Mount Vesuvius. That's it. We've found what we need. We've got a mid first century AD wreck.'

'We've got another nine minutes,' Costas said. 'I've programmed it in, and we may as well use the time.' They both dropped down and knelt on the sea bed beside the amphoras, and began sweeping the site with their headlamps, the light revealing the red colour of the amphoras and reflecting off a sheen of silt suspended in the water. Jack saw other shapes protruding from the sediment under the amphoras, bar shapes about a metre long. He sank down further and wafted away sediment with his hand, then unsheathed his knife and scraped cautiously. 'Just as I thought,' he murmured excitedly. 'Lead ingots.'

'This one has lettering on it.'

Jack sheathed his knife and swam over to Costas, then fanned the sediment away for a clearer view. *TI.CL.NARC. BR.LVT.EX.ARG.* For a moment there was silence. 'Well I'll be damned,' he murmured. 'Tiberius Claudius Narcissus.'

'You know this guy?'

'A slave of the emperor Claudius. When he was freed he

adopted the emperor's first two names, Tiberius Claudius. He was Claudius' secretary and became one of his chief ministers, but was murdered by Claudius' wife Agrippina after she had her husband poisoned.'

'How does this help us?'

'Freed slaves were the nouveau riche of the time. They weren't restricted by aristocratic snobbery about investing in trade and industry. It was just like the nineteenth century. We already know that Narcissus had his fingers in a number of pies in Rome, some of them pretty muddy. This ingot shows what a crafty character he was.'

'*BR* means Britain?'

'Yes. *LVT* was Lutudarum, in Derbyshire, one of the main lead-mining centres in Britain. *EX ARG* means *ex argentariis*, from the lead-silver works. I guessed it when I scraped that other ingot.'

'High-quality lead,' Costas said. 'Produced from galena, lead sulphide, a by-product of silver production. Fewer impurities, less stuff to oxidize, brighter. Am I right?'

'Correct. We know that British lead was exported to the Mediterranean, from the analysis of lead pipes at Pompeii. It's just what you'd expect a wealthy shipowner to have on board his vessel, to repair lead sheathing on the hull. Our sounding lead was pretty pure, not blackened with corrosion, and my guess is it was cast from this metal somewhere along the way.'

'Fascinating, but I still don't see where this gets us.'

'Britain was invaded by the Romans in AD 43, the lead mines were in operation by AD 50. Wily old Narcissus gets straight in on the act and snaps up a lucrative contract, just like a modern mining speculator. These ingots must date to the early fifties. That gets us closer, a whole lot closer, to the magic date for St Paul's shipwreck.'

'Got you.'

There was a crackling on the intercom, and then a staccato beep indicating a relay message from *Seaquest II*: 'You take it,' Jack said. 'I need to concentrate.' He toned down the external receiver on his helmet and rose a few metres above the wreck site, while Costas sank down beside an amphora as he listened to the message. Jack swept his headlamp over the tumbled rows of amphoras, knowing he and Costas only had a few minutes left. They had found more than he had expected, much more, and with a huge sense of elation he realized that the excavation would now go ahead. Suddenly everything here was sacrosanct, no longer a frontier of discovery but a forensic scene, an interlocking matrix of evidence where every feature, every relationship could contain precious clues. He began to drop down again to pull Costas off the site, just as the three-minute warning flashed inside his helmet.

'Uh-oh,' Costas said. 'It's your old buddy Maurice Hiebermeyer. Just when you thought he was up to his neck in mummies in Egypt, he pops out of a hole in the ground in Italy.'

'Maurice?' Jack said. 'Not now.'

'He says it's urgent. He won't go away.'

'He's been working with Maria at the Roman ruins of Herculaneum,' Jack said. 'There was an earthquake, and it's a kind of rescue excavation. They've been having problems with the authorities who control their part of the site, so maybe there's been some kind of lull. He's been badgering me for months about a papyrus, something to do with Alexander the Great. Last time he collared me was when we were raising that cannon from the great siege of Constantinople. He really chooses his moments. Tell the radio officer I'll talk to him while we decompress.'

There was an insistent beeping sound, and Costas looked at his computer. 'We're on amber, Jack. Two minutes, max.'

'Roger that. I'm good to go.'

'Jack.'

'What is it?'

'This amphora in front of me. It's got some kind of inscription on it.'

Jack was directly above Costas now, and could clearly see the letters painted on the shoulder of the amphora. *EGTERRE*. 'It's a Latin infinitive, means "to go". Fairly standard export marking.'

'No. Not that. Below it. Scratched markings.' Costas wafted his hand gently at the side of the amphora as Jack sank down beside him. 'It looks like a big asterisk, a star maybe.'

'Pretty common too,' Jack murmured. 'Bored sailors, passengers whiling away their time doodling on the pottery, playing games. If it was a long-haul voyage, we'll find plenty of that. But I'll get the remote-operated vehicle guys to photo this on their first run over the site.'

'Aristarchos,' Costas said slowly. 'Greek letters. I can read it.'

'Probably a sailor,' Jack said distractedly, his tone now urgent as he looked at his computer. 'Plenty of Greek sailors then. Probably an ancestor of yours.' He suddenly caught his breath. 'What did you say?'

'Aristarchos. Look for yourself.'

Jack sank down and peered at the pottery. A common name. The letters were confident, bold, not the crude scratches of a sailor. Yet could it be? He hardly dared think it. *Aristarchos of Thessaloniki?*

'There's another,' Costas said, excited. 'The same hand, by the looks of it. Loukas, I think. Jack, I'm remembering the Acts of the Apostles. Paul's two companions.'

Jack's mind reeled. Loukas. *Luke*. He looked back at the symbol scratched above the names, the star shape. 'I was wrong,' he said hoarsely. 'We were all wrong.'

'What do you mean?'

'That symbol. It's not a star. Look, the vertical line has a little loop at the top. It's the Greek letter R, and the X is the Greek letter Ch. It's the chi-rho symbol. So they *did* use it in the first century.' Jack could hardly believe what he was saying. 'The first two letters of the word *Christos*, the Greek for Messiah,' he whispered.

'I think it's about to get better. A whole lot better.' Costas had been wafting sediment off the amphora below the word *Loukas*, and a third scratching appeared. The letters were as clear as day. They both stared speechless.

Paulos.

Paul of Tarsus, St Paul the Evangelist, the man who had scratched his name and those of his companions on this pot almost two thousand years before, below the symbol of the one they already revered as the Anointed, the Son of God.

Jack and Costas pushed off and rose together, towards the opaque shimmer of light where the sun shone on the surface almost one hundred metres above. Jack seemed to be in a trance, looking at Costas but not seeing him, his mind's eye on the foredeck of a great grain ship plying the Mediterranean two thousand years before, in the age of the Caesars, taking its passengers inexorably into the annals of history.

'I take it,' Costas said bemusedly, 'we're in business?'

5

Jack lifted his helmet briefly to ease the ache in his neck, his senses suddenly overwhelmed by the roar of the Rolls-Royce turbine just behind him, then pulled the helmet back into place and pressed in the ear protectors until the noise was dampened and the microphone repositioned. He was physically exhausted but too excited to rest, elated by their discovery of the shipwreck the day before, itching to get back, but now full of anticipation for a new prize that lay ahead. Hiebermeyer had been able to say little, but it had been enough for Jack to know that this was real. He checked his watch again. They had been flying due north in the Lynx helicopter for just over an hour from the position where they had left *Seaquest II* before dawn, in the Strait of Messina off

Sicily, and Jack had set the autopilot to keep them low over the waves. Monitoring the altimeter was critical, and it was keeping him awake. It had been less than twelve hours since they had surfaced from their dive, and their bloodstreams were still saturated with excess nitrogen which could expand dangerously if they gained any more altitude.

He checked again, then switched off the autopilot and engaged the hand controls and pedals of the helicopter, bringing the Lynx round thirty degrees to the north-east so that it was angled towards the coastline. He reactivated the autopilot, then settled back and looked again at the image he had been contemplating on the computer screen between the seats. It was an image he had grown up with, a centrepiece of the Howard Gallery, the art collection Jack's grandfather had accumulated and which was now housed in a building on the IMU campus in Cornwall. It was a miniature watercolour by Goethe, painted during an eruption of Mount Vesuvius in 1787. In the background was a flat grey sky, and in the foreground a luminous yellow sea. In the centre was the dark mass of the volcano, the shoreline beneath it fronted by flat-roofed buildings similar to the ancient Roman towns below Vesuvius then being unearthed for the first time. The image seemed whimsical, almost abstract, yet the streaks of red and yellow above the volcano betrayed the violent reality of the event that Goethe had witnessed. Jack gazed out of the cockpit windscreen towards the bay ahead of them. It was as if he were seeing a version of the watercolour, pastel shades drifting across the horizon in the sunrise, the details melded and obscured by the layer of smog in the atmosphere just below their altitude.

In the co-pilot's seat Costas had been dozing fitfully, but he shifted forward when Jack adjusted the course. He woke with a start as his sunglasses slipped off his helmet and wedged on his nose.

'Enjoying off-gassing?' Jack said through the intercom.

'Just keep us below fifteen hundred feet,' Costas replied blearily. 'I want to keep those nitrogen bubbles nice and small.'

'Don't worry. We'll be on the ground soon enough.'

Costas stretched, then sighed. 'Fresh air, wide-open spaces. That's what I like.'

'Then you should choose your friends more carefully.' Jack grinned, then nosed the helicopter down a few hundred feet. They broke through the layer of haze, and the mirage became a reality. Below them the dramatic shoreline of the islands and the mainland coast was sharply delineated, expanses of sun-scorched rock surrounded by azure sea. To the east was the great expanse of the city, and beyond that a smudge on the horizon where the bay ended, the haze just concealing a looming presence below a burst of orange where the sun was rising above the mountains beyond.

'The Bay of Naples,' Jack said. 'Crucible of civilization.'

'Civilization.' Costas yawned extravagantly, then paused. 'Let me see. That would be corruption on a seismic scale, drug crime, the Mafia?'

'Forget all that and look at the past,' Jack said. 'We're here for the archaeology, not to get embroiled in the present.'

Costas snorted. 'That'd be a first.'

Jack looked out at the extraordinary scene in front of them, and was infused by the sense of history he had experienced at other cities in the Mediterranean: Istanbul, Jerusalem, where the superimposed layers of civilization were still visible, different cultures which had left their distinctive mark yet were bound together by the possibilities that settlement and resources at the place had to offer. The Bay of Naples was one of the great staging posts for the spread of ideas into Europe, where the Greeks had first settled in the ninth and eighth centuries BC when they came west, trading with the Etruscans for iron at a time when Rome was just a few huts above a swamp. Cumae, where the alphabet was first brought west, Neapolis, Pompeii, all these places became centres of the new Greece, Magna Graecia, fuelled by trade and by the hinterland of Campania with its rich agriculture. Jack stared at the slopes of Vesuvius, then had a sudden flashback to their underwater discovery the day before. He turned to Costas. 'Remember those wine amphoras on the shipwreck? They were from here.'

'Rich volcanic soil, perfect for vineyards.'

'And a lot of Greek influence,' Jack said. 'Even after the Romans took over in the fourth and third centuries BC, making this place a kind of Costa del Sol for the wealthy, Greek culture stayed strong. People think of Pompeii and Herculaneum as the quintessential Roman towns, but actually they existed for centuries before the Romans arrived. They were still highly cosmopolitan in AD 79, with people speaking Greek and local dialects as well as Latin. And the Bay of Naples continued to be the first port of call for all things from the east, not just Greece but also the Near East and Egypt and beyond, exotic trade goods, new art styles, foreign emissaries, new ideas in philosophy and religion.'

'Now fill me in on the volcano,' Costas said.

Jack tapped the computer keyboard and the Goethe watercolour was replaced by a black-and-white photograph showing a distant view of a volcano erupting, a great plume of rolling black cloud hanging like a malign genie over the city. 'March 1944, during the Second World War,' Jack said. 'Fast-forward nine months from the Allied landings in Sicily, where we've just been diving. A few months after the liberation of Naples, while the Allies were still slogging towards Rome. The most recent major eruption of Vesuvius.'

Costas whistled. 'Looks like the gods of war unleashed hell.'

'That's what people thought at the time, but fortunately it was just an immense venting of gas and ash and then the fissure closed up. Since then there's been nothing as dramatic, though there was a bad earthquake in 1980 that killed several thousand people and left hundreds of thousands homeless. There's a lot of concern about the recent seismic disturbances.'

'Three weeks ago.'

'That's why we're here.'

'And in ancient times?' Costas said. 'I mean, the eruption of AD 79?'

Jack tapped again, and another painting appeared. 'This is

the only known Roman image of Vesuvius, found on a wall painting in Pompeii. It's fanciful, with the god of wine laden with grapes to the left, but you can see the mountain's rich with vegetation and vineyards growing up the slopes. Vesuvius had been completely dormant since the Bronze Age, and the Romans only knew of it as an incredibly bountiful place, with rich soils that produced some of the best wines anywhere. The eruption in AD 79 was a massive shock, psychological as well as physical. Pompeii, Herculaneum, Stabiae, the villas around the volcano, were all gone for ever, though eventually life reasserted itself in Campania. The psychological effects were probably more damaging, reverberating down the centuries. It's hard to make a modern analogy, but imagine if the San Andreas fault split open destroying Hollywood and devastating Los Angeles. Many would see it as the coming apocalypse.'

'So they really had no clue about what was going to happen?'

'The clues were there, where we're headed now, but they had no reason to link them with the mountain.'

Jack pulled the helicopter in a wide arc to the north, and Costas peered down at a barren landscape. 'What's that place?'

'That's what I wanted you to see. We're over the north-west shore of the Bay of Naples, about twenty-five kilometres west of Vesuvius. This was the one area of extensive volcanic activity in the Roman period, though even Pliny never made the connection with Vesuvius. The Phlegraean Fields, the fields of fire. Listen to this. It's from the *Aeneid* by Virgil,

Rome's national poet. I've got the text on screen. "There was a deep rugged cave, stupendous and yawning wide, protected by a lake of black water and the glooming forest. Over this lake no birds could wing a straight course without harm, so poisonous the breath which streamed up from those black jaws and rose to the vault of sky." Now look outside. That's Lake Avernus, which means birdless. Over there you can see the most active crater today, Sulfaterra. That's what Virgil was on about. And by the coast you can just make out the overgrown acropolis of ancient Cumae, one of the first places the Greeks settled.'

'Where the Sibyl hung out.'

'Literally. According to some accounts, she was suspended in a cage in the back of her cave, never fully visible and always wreathed in smoke.'

'High in more ways than one.'

Jack grinned. 'In the Roman period, the Phlegraean Fields was a big tourist attraction, much more so than it is now. The entrance to the underworld, a place that reeked of fire and brimstone. People came here to see the tomb of Virgil, buried beside the road from Naples. And the Sibyl was still here too, at least before the eruption. Augustus consulted her, and other emperors too. Claudius went to the Sibyl,' he added.

'So the Greek colonists brought the first Sibyl with them?'

'Yes and no.'

Costas groaned. 'Facts, Jack. Facts.'

'Supposedly there were thirteen Sibyls across the Greek world, though the earliest references suggest they derived from the idea of a single all-seeing prophetess. The site of Cumae is one of the few places where archaeology adds to the picture. In the 1930s, an extraordinary underground grotto came to light, exactly as the Romans described the cave of the Sibyl. It's a trapezoidal corridor almost fifty metres long, lit by side galleries and ending in a rectangular chamber, all hewn out of the rock. In Virgil's *Aeneid*, this was where the Trojan hero Aeneas consulted the Sibyl, to ask whether his colony in Italy would one day become the Roman Empire. And this was where she took him down into the underworld, to see his father Anchises.'

Costas pointed to the steaming crater below them. 'You mean the fields of fire, the Phlegraean Fields?'

'There were probably open volcanic vents here in antiquity. It must have been a vision of Dante's inferno if there ever was one,' Jack said. 'People are always drawn to these places, creation and destruction together in one terrifying cauldron. It was the perfect location for the Sibyl, who must have seemed like an apparition from the underworld itself. Supplicants were probably led through the fumaroles and boiling mud, so would have been shaking with fear even before they stood in front of her cave.'

'If my memory serves me, Aeneas was a Trojan prince escaping from the Trojan War, at the end of the Bronze Age,' Costas said thoughtfully. 'That means Virgil thought the Sibyl was here already, way before the Greeks or the Romans arrived.'

'All of the mythology we know today associated with the

Cumaean Sibyl was Greek, especially her relationship with the god Apollo. But this may have been what the Greeks brought with them, and layered on to a goddess or prophetess who already existed in prehistoric Italy. The Greeks and the Romans often fused their gods with similar native gods, even as far away as Britain.'

'So there may have been a much older female deity here.'

'Our friend Katya has a theory about that. Her team at the Palaeographic Institute in Moscow are almost ready to publish the Atlantis symbols. You remember the Neolithic mother goddess of Atlantis?'

'Could hardly forget her. I've still got the bruises.'

'Well, we already knew that corpulent female figurines were being worshipped across Europe at the end of the Ice Age, at least to the time of the first farmers. For years archaeologists have speculated about a prehistoric cult of the mother goddess, a cult that crossed boundaries between tribes and peoples. Well, Katya thinks the survival of that cult owes everything to a powerful priesthood, the men and women who led the first farmers west, whose descendants preserved the cult through the Bronze Age and to the classical period. She even thinks the druids of north-west Europe were connected.'

'I remember,' Costas murmured. 'From Atlantis. The wizards with conical hats. Lords of the Rings.'

'The idea of Tolkien's Gandalf, like Merlin in the King Arthur stories, may ultimately derive from the same tradition,' Jack said. 'Men with supposedly supernatural powers who could pass from one kingdom to the next, who knew no borders. Healers, mediators, prophets.'

Costas peered down again at the Phlegraean Fields. 'Seems that every culture needs them,' he murmured.

'And the mother goddess also survived in different guises. The Roman goddess Ceres, the Greek Demeter. Magna Mater, the Great Mother.'

'Every new culture adds its own layer of paint, but it's the same old statue underneath.'

'And the same allure, the same mystery. I've just been giving you the facts as we know them. Part of me can't help thinking that there was something about the Sibyls that defies rational explanation, something so powerful that it allowed them to maintain the mystique over centuries, so alluring that it even drew in the Romans, the most rational and practical of peoples. Something the Sibyls themselves believed in.'

'Don't go all supernatural on me, Jack.'

'I'm not suggesting it. But if the Sibyls believed in themselves, and if others with the power to shape the world, emperors, believed in them, then it becomes something we have to take seriously.'

Costas grunted, then peered down through his visor at the indented shoreline that was now directly beneath them. 'What's that place now?'

'Pozzuoli. Roman Puteoli.'

'So that was where St Paul was heading? After Sicily, after surviving the wreck?'

'According to the Acts of the Apostles, he and his

companions sailed up from Syracuse on a ship of Alexandria, then stopped at Puteoli. That's the ancient Roman grain port you can see now. It complements the naval port beside it at Misenum.' Jack tapped the screen. 'The words are: "We found brethren there, and were intreated to tarry with them seven days.'

'Brethren? Fellow Christians? What about persecution?'

Jack jerked his head to the north. 'The Phlegraean Fields. Perfect hideaway. Probably always a place for outcasts, beggars, misfits.'

'And then Paul goes to Rome. Where Nero had him beheaded.'

'The New Testament doesn't actually say so, but that's the tradition.'

'Might have been better for him if he'd gone down in that shipwreck after all.'

'If that had happened, then western history might have been utterly different.' Jack banked the helicopter to starboard, then nosed it towards the smudge on the eastern shore of the bay. 'We might have ended up worshipping Isis, Mithras, or even the great mother goddess.'

'Huh?'

Jack adjusted the throttle, glanced at the air traffic screen and flicked on the autopilot. 'That shipwreck really was one of the pivotal events of history, not because of what was lost but because of who survived. Remember, Jesus' ministry in his lifetime was confined to Judaea, mainly his home province of Galilee. The idea that his word should spread to

Jewish communities abroad, and then to non-Jews, only seems to have taken hold after his death. Paul was one of the first generation of missionaries, of proselytizers. Without him, many of those who proved receptive to Christianity might have been seduced by one of the other cults on offer. At the time we're talking about, the spread of the Roman Empire and the *Pax Romana* meant that the Mediterranean world was awash with new cults, new religious ideas, some brought back by soldiers from newly conquered lands, others brought by sailors to ports such as Misenum and Puteoli. The Egyptian goddess Isis, the Persian god Mithras, the ancient mother goddess, any one of these could have provided the kernel of a monotheistic religion, giving the common people something they craved in the face of all the gods and rituals of Greece and Rome. If one of those religions had truly taken hold, it might have been enough to repel Christianity.'

'Phew,' Costas said. 'And I thought with the crucifixion it was all a done deal.'

'That was really just the beginning,' Jack said. 'And the amazing thing is, there's no indication that Paul ever met Jesus in life. Paul was a Jew from Asia Minor who had a vision of Christ on the road to Damascus, but only after the crucifixion. And yet he may have been responsible more than any other for the foundation of the Church as we know it. The spread of the concept of Jesus as the son of God, as the Messiah, the meaning of the Greek word *Christos*, all seem to owe a huge amount to his teaching. The word Christian probably first appears about the time of his travels, and the emphasis on the cross. It's as if, a generation after Jesus' death, after people's personal experience of him, the focus had shifted from Jesus the man to the risen Jesus, almost as if he'd come to be seen as a god, been put on a pedestal.'

'That's what people would have understood,' Costas said. 'No one worships a man.'

'Exactly,' Jack said. 'It was a world where emperors were deified after their death, where the imperial cult was a huge unifying factor in the Roman Empire. And like all good missionaries, Paul was a shrewd operator who knew what he had to do to get the word across, the compromises and incorporation of age-old ways of thinking and seeing the world he would have thought necessary to get the light to shine through.'

'So you're saying this is the place where it all took hold, the Bay of Naples?'

'The Acts of the Apostles suggest that there were followers of Jesus already here when Paul arrived in the late fifties AD, only twenty-odd years after the crucifixion. But Paul may have been responsible for making them truly Christian, for turning their thoughts from the message of Jesus, the imminent kingdom of heaven, to Christ himself, the Messiah. This is the place where Paul may have created the first western Church, the first organized worship, maybe somewhere hidden out there among the craters and the sulphur of the Phlegraean Fields. Taught them what they should believe, how they should live. Given them the Gospel.'

'I wonder how much of it was the original one.'

'What do you mean?'

'Well, Paul didn't know Jesus in life, had never met him. And Jesus never wrote anything down, right? It makes you wonder.'

'Paul claimed to have had a vision, to have seen the risen Christ.'

'I grew up with all this stuff, remember? Greek Orthodox. I loved the beauty of it, the rituals. But I'm just a nuts-and-bolts man, Jack. If we can follow a trail of hard facts, then I'm good with it. This early Christianity stuff is like looking through one of those kids' kaleidoscope tubes, endlessly shifting lenses and prisms. I want facts, hard data, stuff written by those who were there at the time, texts that have never been tampered with. As far as I can tell, the only hard facts we have are those names scratched on that amphora we found yesterday at the bottom of the Mediterranean.'

'I hear you.' Jack grinned, and flipped off the autopilot. 'Speculation out, facts in.'

'I wonder what the old Sibyl would have thought of it all.'

'What do you mean?'

'Christianity. Followers of a new religion, gathering here under her very nose.'

'Okay. Final bit of speculation,' Jack said. 'Hard facts first. By the late Roman period, Cumae had become a focus for Christian worship. The temples were converted to churches, the cave of the Sibyl was reused for burials. The place is riddled with Christian tombs, almost like a catacomb.'

'And the speculation? I'll allow you.'

'There's a long-standing Christian tradition that the Sibyl foretold the coming of Christ. In Virgil's *Eclogues*, poems written about a hundred years before Vesuvius erupted, we're told of being at the end of the last age predicted by Cumae's Sibyl, and of a boy's birth preceding a golden age. Later Christians read this as a Messianic prophecy. And then there's the *Dies Irae*, the Day of Wrath, a medieval hymn used in the Catholic requiem mass until 1970. I've just been looking at it again, while you were asleep. The first lines are *"Dies irae! Dies illa Solvet saeclum in favilla teste David cum Sibylla!* Day of wrath and terror looming! Heaven and earth to ash consuming, David's word and Sibyl's truth foredooming!"* It's usually thought to be medieval, thirteenth century, but there may be an ancient source behind it, one that's now lost to us.'

'The Sibyl would certainly have had her ear to the ground, in that cave,' Costas said.

'Go on.'

'Well, that verse all sounds pretty apocalyptic,' Costas said. 'I mean, heaven and earth to ash consuming. That sounds like a volcanic eruption to me.'

'Pure speculation.' Jack smiled at Costas, then put his hands on the helicopter controls. He stared out of the window, thinking hard. It was possible, just possible, that the Sibyl knew something big was about to happen. There had been a catastrophic earthquake a few years before, in AD 62, bad enough to topple much of Pompeii. Maybe creating the

Sibylline prophecies involved keeping a close eye on the Phlegraean Fields, divination and augury based on all the changing moods of the underworld. It suddenly seemed plausible. That mystique, that power, based on knowledge that few others had, on hard science. Jack turned back to Costas. 'The Sibyl may have known her days were numbered. Already she was becoming a curio, a tourist attraction. Only a few supplicants were now coming seeking utterances, with few of the gifts and payments that had sustained the oracle in the past. And she had a pretty good idea where Vesuvius was heading.'

'And what better way to go than with a bang,' Costas added.

'Precisely. Maybe the Sibyl fed this idea to the Christians who lived here, hung out in the Phlegraean Fields. There's no clear indication that Jesus' teaching had the kingdom of heaven preceded by an apocalypse, even though this idea has gripped Christians over the centuries. Maybe it has its origins here, in the Christians who may have perished in the inferno of AD 79. I hate to think what was running through their minds in those final moments. When Paul had brought the Gospel to them twenty years before, I doubt whether they envisaged the end being a pyroclastic flow followed by incineration.'

'Speculation built on speculation, Jack.'

'You're right.' Jack grinned, and brought the Lynx out of its circling pattern and on to a course due east, along the coast towards the rising sun. 'Time to find some hard facts. We're coming inbound.'

'Roger that.' Costas flipped down his designer sunglasses and stared to the east. 'And speaking of fire and brimstone, I'm seeing a volcano dead ahead.'

6

Jack leaned forward on the railing over the archaeological precinct, taking in the extraordinary scene in front of him as the morning sunlight began to pick out the alleyways and dark spaces of the Roman town below. He felt tired, as tired as he ever had been, with the sense of heaviness that always came after a deep dive. He knew that his system was still working overtime to flush out the excess nitrogen from the dive the day before, yet the feeling also came from a profound sense of contentment. In the space of twelve hours he had moved from one of the most remarkable underwater discoveries of his career to one of the most famous archaeological sites in the world, a place that had left an indelible impression on him when he had first visited as a schoolboy.

Herculaneum. It had been a scorching afternoon, and he had found the *frigidarium* of the bathhouse, a cool, dark place where he had sat in a corner for over an hour, listening to the drip of condensation from the damp walls and conjuring up the people who had last used it almost two thousand years before. Herculaneum seemed shabbier now, neglected in places, but had changed little over the years, and it still took his breath away. He could hardly believe that they were about to be the first archaeologists in over two hundred years to excavate the place, inside the tunnel Maria and Maurice had discovered the day before.

'Text message for you, Jack.' Costas passed up the cell phone without looking. He was squatting with his back against the railing, focusing entirely on a complex systems diagram on his laptop. 'It's from Maria.'

Jack read the message, and grunted. 'Another half-hour, maybe less. Good news is, the transaction's been done.' He and Costas had already been waiting over an hour since landing the helicopter, time well spent showing Costas round the archaeological site, but neither of them was used to being at the beck and call of officialdom and the delay was becoming an irritation.

Costas took back the phone, and squinted up at Jack. 'I still can't believe we're doing this. Paying baksheesh. It's like something from *The French Connection*.'

'That's Naples for you,' Jack said. 'Bandit country.'

'So the idea is our money goes towards the upkeep of the site, conservation work.' Costas turned round and gestured at a dusty roof above a crumbling ancient wall. 'Like all the other foreign money that's been pumped in here in the past.'

'I was frank with the IMU board of directors,' Jack said. 'There's no way round it. If you want to work in this place, you cough up.'

'Basically, we're paying a bribe.'

'Not exactly how I put it to the board, but that's about the size of it,' Jack replied, looking at his watch. 'Now we just have to wait while they confirm the electronic transfer. You may as well stick with your work for a while longer. I'm going back to the first century AD.' Jack turned again towards the site, took a deep breath and slowly exhaled. As a child travelling around the world, he had developed an unusual imagination, an ability to use a few images to transport himself back into the distant past, almost a trance-like state. But here he hardly needed it, as the past was in front of him with extraordinary clarity, complete in almost every detail.

Herculaneum was that rarest of archaeological sites, without the compressions and distortions of time, with little of the complex layering of history seen in most ancient ruins. Here, the city of AD 79 was so well preserved it was almost habitable, the flat-roofed structures nearly identical to the modern suburb above the edges of the excavated area. Jack's eye moved up beyond the rooftops to the blackened cone of Vesuvius, rearing up in the background. The image seemed to epitomize the underlying continuity of the human condition, and the indomitable power of nature. He looked down at the warehouses on the ancient seafront, where masses of distorted skeletons had been found huddled together in their death agony. Then he looked up at the villas where those same people had been eating and talking and going about their daily lives a few minutes before, everything left as they had abandoned it in those final moments of horror. There was clarity here, Jack reflected, extraordinary clarity, but also opacity. Teasing older history out of this site, before those final moments, was like watching an animation deconstructed, in which the first scenes were sharp and clear, then the next vague, increasingly out of focus, until images that had been dominated by people became a shadowland, with only the artefacts standing out and the people reduced to flitting forms barely discernible in the background.

That was the challenge for archaeologists at this place, Jack reflected, to give depth, to tell stories stretching back hours, days, years. And yet that final apocalyptic scene was a continuous draw, playing on the human fascination with death, with the macabre, the final moments of normality, what that would be like. Earlier, walking into the Roman houses with Costas, he had felt a curious unease, as if he were violating the intimate places of people who had never really left, places where he could still sense the mundane acts of the living, the private smells and sounds of the household. What had happened here had happened so quickly, quicker even than at Pompeii, that the place was still in a state of shock, frozen in that moment just before hell unleashed. Herculaneum still seemed to be reeling, as if the earthquakes of recent weeks were a nervous tremor that had begun on the night of the inferno almost two thousand years before.

'That's a hell of a view.' Costas was standing beside him, and Jack snapped out of his reverie. 'The past, the present, and the big bang. Says it all.'

Jack gave a tired smile. 'I'm glad you see it too.'

'So this is all solidified mud,' Costas said.

'Mud, ash, pumice, lava, everything picked up as it snowballed down the volcano.'

'Pyroclastic flow?'

'You remember Pliny the Elder, who wrote about opium?' Jack said.

'You bet. The workaholic admiral. Somehow found time to write an encyclopedia.'

'Well, his teenage nephew, also called Pliny, was here that day too, staying at his uncle's villa near the naval base at Misenum. The younger Pliny survived the eruption, his uncle didn't. Years later he wrote a letter about it to the historian Tacitus, who wanted to know how the elder Pliny died. From a natural-history viewpoint it's one of the most important documents to survive from antiquity, maybe even more so than his uncle's encyclopedia. It's not only a unique eyewitness account of the eruption of Vesuvius, it's also one of the best scientific observations ever made of a volcanic eruption until modern times.'

'Sounds like a chip off the old block. His uncle would have been proud of him.' Costas watched Jack pull a small red book from his bag, its cover worn and battered. 'You seem to have an endless supply of those. I had no idea so much literature survived from this period.'

'It's what didn't survive that keeps me awake at night,' Jack said, jerking his head towards the ruins in front of them. 'That's what's so tantalizing about this place. But before we go there, listen to this. It's crucial to understanding why Herculaneum and Pompeii look the way they do.' He held the book up so that the site and the volcano were in the background, and then began to read marked passages. ' "Its general appearance can best be expressed as being like an umbrella pine, for it rose to a great height on a sort of trunk and then split off into branches, I imagine because it was thrust upwards by the first blast and then left unsupported as the pressure subsided, or else it was borne down by its own weight so that it spread out and gradually dispersed." ' He traced his finger down the page. 'Then he describes ashes falling, "followed by bits of pumice and blackened stones, charred and cracked by the flames". Later he says that the darkness was blacker and denser than any ordinary night, and on Vesuvius "broad sheets of fire and leaping flames blazed at several points".'

'Sound like a classic ash and pumice fallout,' Costas said. 'But that first bit, about the plume collapsing on itself, that's a pyroclastic flow.'

'That's exactly the difference between the two sites. Pompeii was buried by fallout from the sky, mixed with poisonous gases. Afterwards, some of the rooftops still stuck out, which is why they're not so well preserved today.

Herculaneum was buried by landslides, tons of boiling mud and volcanic material, surging over the site each time the plume collapsed until the buildings were completely buried, up to ten metres above the rooftops.'

'That's a hell of an image, Jack. And that's what those early Christians would have seen, the ones you think were in the Phlegraean Fields, I mean. Rings of fire at the leading edge of each pyroclastic flow, coming down the mountain at terrifying speed.'

'The younger Pliny was watching all that from the villa at Misenum, only a mile or so south of Cumae, the Sibyl's cave. More or less the same vantage point.'

'Post-traumatic stress syndrome,' Costas said.

'Come again?'

'Post-traumatic stress syndrome,' Costas repeated. 'The obsession with hellfire, damnation. I've been thinking about it. If this is the main place where Christianity spread from in the west, then they're bound to have been affected by the experience, right? When we were flying in you mentioned the psychological fallout of the eruption. Once you've seen hell, you don't forget it in a hurry. They were already halfway there in the Phlegraean Fields, living among the fumaroles and the entrance to the pagan underworld. Add a volcanic eruption, and you've got a pretty apocalyptic outlook. Am I right?'

'For a nuts-and-bolts man, that's a pretty fantastic idea. Ever thought of rewriting the history of Christian theology?'

'Nope.' For a moment they were quiet, both looking into the windows of the excavated Roman warehouse in front of them, dark and forbidding like the portholes of a sunken ship. 'No survivors here,' Costas murmured. 'No one who stayed.'

'It's hard to know which would have been worse,' Jack said thoughtfully. 'Suffocated in superheated gas at Pompeii, or incinerated alive at Herculaneum.'

'Come live by the sunny Bay of Naples,' Costas murmured. 'Today, all that happens is you get mugged or run over.'

'Don't speak too soon,' Jack said. 'Remember that picture of the 1944 eruption? The seismologists have been talking doom and gloom for decades now, and the earthquakes are pretty ominous.'

Costas shaded his eyes and squinted at the summit of the volcano, where the sunlight was beginning to radiate off the barren upper slopes. 'Pliny was here? The elder one, I mean. In Herculaneum?'

'According to his nephew, he took one look at the eruption and hared off in a warship towards the volcano, this side of the bay, under the mountain. It was supposedly a heroic mission to rescue a woman.'

'The undoing of many a great man,' Costas sighed.

'It was hopeless. By the time he got here the shore was blocked with debris, floating pumice like sea ice. But instead of returning, he got his galley to row south to Stabiae, another town beyond Pompeii directly under the ash fallout. He stayed too long and was overcome by the fumes.'

'Sounds like a Shakespearean love tragedy. Maybe he was really overcome by grief.'

'I don't think so,' Jack said. 'Not Pliny. Once he saw his

girlfriend was doomed, he would have been on to something else. What he really wanted was to get close to the eruption. I can see him, notebook in hand, sniffing and identifying the sulphur, collecting pumice samples along the shoreline. At least he'd finished his *Natural History*.'

'What with all that multi-tasking, he was probably heading for a burnout anyway.'

Jack rolled his eyes, then caught sight of two figures making their way down the entry ramp into the site, a woman and a man. 'Good,' he said. 'It looks like we're moving at last.' He pushed off from the railing, and ruffled his hair. Maria was wearing desert boots, khaki combat trousers and a grey T-shirt, and her long black hair was tied back. She had a well-honed, lean physique, and the look suited her. Maurice Hiebermeyer was several paces behind her, a cell phone clamped to his ear, and cut a somewhat less svelte figure. He was slightly shorter than Maria, considerably overweight, and was wearing a curious assortment of safari gear over a pair of scuffed leather dress shoes. He was red faced and flustered, constantly pushing his little round glasses up his nose as he spoke into the phone. His shorts reached well below his knees and seemed perilously close to half-mast, almost miraculously free-floating.

'Don't say anything,' Jack muttered to Costas. 'Anything at all.' He fought to keep a straight face, and glanced at Costas. 'Anyway, *you* can smirk. When was the last time you looked in a mirror? You look like you've just walked out of six months in a submarine.'

Hiebermeyer halted before reaching them, gesturing at the phone and turning his back on them, while Maria walked up and embraced them both. Jack closed his eyes as she pressed against him. He had missed seeing her, hearing her sonorous voice, her accent. It had been an intensive time together during the search for the menorah, and Jack had gone through the usual moments of emptiness when the expedition was over. Above all he wanted to see that she was well, that he had made the right move in suggesting that she join Hiebermeyer in Naples. Maria shot him a look from her dark eyes. 'It's been six weeks since I was on *Seaquest*, but it seems a lot longer.'

'It's the company you miss,' Costas said, looking at her with concern.

'I've really tried to put it all behind me,' she said quietly, turning away from them and gazing out over the site. 'I had a text message from Jeremy this morning, and that was the first time I'd really flashed back to our time in the Yucatán, those terrible scenes. It's been good for me to have this new project to focus on, better than going back straight away to my medieval manuscript research at the Institute. And Jeremy's taken care of everything in Oxford. It's just the break he wanted, a chance to serve as acting director while still just a graduate student, and he's brilliant at it.'

'I really want him at IMU full time, you know,' Jack said. 'It's only been a couple of months since he joined us on the trail of the Vikings, but already he seems like a permanent fixture. I always know when someone's right, and the moment he walked through the IMU engineering lab and began talking to Costas about submersibles I knew that was it.'

'How is my favourite new dive buddy?' Costas said. 'Has he told you I passed him with flying colours on his checkout dive? A real natural.'

'Buried up to his neck in the lost library at Hereford Cathedral. He's got some fantastic new stuff, Jack. Another early map, some reference to Phoenicians, I think. He's itching to show you. And he's had an idea for some new diving contraption, Costas. I don't understand a word of it.'

'Really?' Costas said in hushed excitement. 'If it's Jeremy, it's got to be good.' He reached into his hip pouch for his cell phone, but Jack stopped his arm.

'Not now. Bad timing.'

Costas relented, ruefully. 'Just keeping on the ball.'

'No multi-tasking, remember? Let's stick with where we are for now.'

'Yes, boss.'

'I'm grateful you suggested me, Jack,' Maria continued. 'It's a real privilege to be here. And an eye-opener in more ways than one. But it should have been you here from the outset.'

'Then you'd never have had the pleasure of spending time with our old friend Maurice,' Jack said with a smile. 'I know you haven't seen him much since Cambridge.'

Maria sidled up to them. 'He's a dear man,' she whispered, looking questioningly at Jack. 'Isn't he?'

'He is a dear man,' Jack replied quietly, giving her a

knowing look. 'Remember, he and I were at school together, even before we all met up at Cambridge. I had my first real adventures with him, when we were kids. You know, he's treated like a god in Egypt, with some justification. Easily the finest field archaeologist I know. And despite appearances, he's not one of those Egyptologists who thinks all other archaeology is beneath them. He's tremendously knowledgeable, inquisitive across all periods and places. He wouldn't be seen dead in a wetsuit, but he's a perfect adjunct professor for IMU.'

'So what's with the shorts?' she whispered.

'Ah.' Jack looked at Hiebermeyer's backside, and struggled with his expression. 'Genuine German Afrika Corps, *circa* 1940. Seemed appropriate, when he first went to Egypt and needed kit. I gave them to him as a graduation present. He gave me my British Eighth Army khaki bag. I always have it with me too.' Jack patted the battered bag hanging against his side. 'My fault. Sorry.'

'Some suspenders would help,' Maria whispered. 'You know, lederhosen.'

'What Jack's saying,' Costas said with a twinkle in his eye, 'is that Maurice grows on you.'

'He's developed quite a lot since you knew him at Cambridge,' Jack said.

'Just as long as he doesn't expect me to treat him like a god,' Maria whispered, then she stood back and spoke normally. 'Anyway, now I see what it's like to be in Jack Howard's shoes. I just hope I haven't taken the steam out of your sails.'

'We haven't exactly been sunbathing on the foredeck,' Costas said. 'Wait until you hear what we found yesterday.'

Hiebermeyer looked increasingly exasperated, raising his eyes and bunching his fist in the air, then suddenly he listened intently on the phone and flashed a look of relief. He nodded towards Maria, then snapped the phone shut and walked over, shaking hands quickly with Jack and Costas. 'I thought I'd be wasting your time.' His voice was slightly hoarse with stress, his German accent more pronounced. 'I couldn't believe it. All I did was step out yesterday to call you. They weren't going to let us back in.'

'Can you finger anyone?' Jack said. 'I might be able to exert some pressure in the archaeological superintendency.'

'It's not the archaeologists who are the problem, it's the site guards and whoever is topping up their wages. Whoever it is also pulls the strings at the top of the archaeological superintendency. They're always apprehensive, clamped down, even some old colleagues I know personally, and sometimes there's real fear in their eyes. I've never seen anything like it. I feel as if we're walking on very thin ground.'

'Everyone ready?' Maria said, slinging her pack and clipping on her waist strap, then turning back up the ramp. 'Maurice and I have learned the hard way that when you get the go-ahead in this place, you go-ahead pronto. It's about two hundred yards due west from here, but we have to go out of the site and down some back alleys. We'll be met at the entrance.' She eyed Costas' camera bag. 'And watch your valuables, right? Remember where we are.'

7

Twenty minutes later, Jack and the others stood outside a low door at the end of a dark alley in the modern town of Ercolano. They were above the buried remains of the Villa of the Papyri, one of the greatest archaeological sites ever discovered, much of it still entombed under the streets around them. Jack's excitement had increased as they came closer, though the narrowing walls of the alleyway seemed to accentuate the unease he had felt since talking to Hiebermeyer and Maria. It had become hot in the midday sun, and they gathered in the shade against the wall. The scene was astonishingly similar to an excavated street in ancient Herculaeum a few hundred metres away, and for a split second Jack felt completely displaced, uncertain whether he was in the past or the present. He was brought back to reality by the tinny echo of a Vespa scooter as it hurtled down a nearby alley, and by the distinctly modern smells that rose up around them. The sides of the alley were strewn with rubbish, and an alcove beside the doorway was scattered with used hypodermic syringes.

'Watch your feet,' Maria said. 'It's a favourite local shooting-up place.'

'Opium,' Costas said. '*Plus ça change.*'

Maria looked at him questioningly. 'Later,' Jack said. 'We've got some fabulous news. An incredible discovery. But let's do what we've got to do here first.'

The door opened, and an armed security guard appeared. Hiebermeyer spoke a few halting words of Italian and the man looked dubiously at Jack and Costas. He shook his head, grudgingly took the permit papers Hiebermeyer offered him and pushed him back out into the alley, shutting the door again in his face.

'This happens every time,' Hiebermeyer said, his teeth clenched. 'There's always a new guard, and they always need to see the paperwork. Then they insist on keeping the papers, and I have to get new ones issued by the super-intendency in Naples. It took two weeks before they'd let Maria in.'

'I don't know how you can stand it,' Costas said.

'Patience 101,' Jack said. 'Mandatory introductory archaeology course.'

'I can't imagine how you passed that one, Jack.'

'I bribed Maurice to sit the exam for me.'

The door reopened, and the guard jerked his head. Hiebermeyer ducked through and the others filed after him into a small grey courtyard. The guard waved his sub-machine gun towards another entrance. Costas caught his gaze for slightly too long, and the man's look froze.

'Don't,' Jack said under his breath. Before they realized what was happening, the guard was beside them and had casually sideswiped Costas, knocking him into the wall. Jack took Costas by the arm and quickly led him behind Maria and Hiebermeyer towards the other entrance. The guard remained rooted to the ground, watching them, then they heard him sidle away. They passed through the entrance into another small alleyway.

'Nobody does that to me,' Costas seethed, brushing the graze on his arm and trying to push Jack away.

'Keep cool,' Jack said quietly, keeping a vice-like hold on Costas and steering him forward. 'It's not worth it. A little man in a uniform.'

'With thirty rounds of nine millimetre,' Maria murmured.

'I thought you were supposed to be the star attraction around here,' Costas grumbled to Hiebermeyer as Jack released his hold. 'Distinguished foreign archaeologist, flown in from Egypt to help excavate one of the most important sites ever found.'

'That's the public face of it,' Hiebermeyer said, keeping his voice down. 'Come through that entranceway, and it's a different story. They won't even let a film crew in here. This place has been shut down for two hundred years, and somebody somewhere wants it to stay that way.'

'None of the villa's open to the public?'

'After intense international lobbying, a small section was opened with great ceremony a few years ago. We passed the entrance on the way. For the first time, people can visit some of the eighteenth-century excavations. They made a big show of it, even got Prince Charles over from London to cut the ribbon. You've no idea how many scholars and philanthropists have been trying to kick-start work on this place. But from our point of view this progress has been a mixed blessing. It's allowed the authorities to paint a picture of huge achievement, diverting attention away from the most pressing need, which is to resume the excavations.'

'So without the earthquake last month that opened up this new tunnel, we wouldn't be here,' Costas said.

'Not a chance.'

'Thank God for natural catastrophe.'

'You could say that about this place.'

'It's bizarre,' Maria said quietly as they reached the end of the alley. 'It's as if they hate us being here, and have done everything in their power to impede us. It took a geologic age for Maurice to get an extractor fan in to clear out the toxic gas from the tunnel. But in the press releases, Maurice is the big star. He's all over the papers here. Then, once we're inside, it's as if they actually want us to find something, but only enough to allow them to shut the whole place down again for good.'

'That's just about the stage we've reached now,'

Hiebermeyer said. 'I'm convinced this is the last time we'll be let in. You'll see why in a few minutes. Okay. Here goes. Best behaviour.' He led them round a corner into a deep trench, open to the sky, like the foundation pit for a large house. The walls were grey volcanic mud, identical to the main site of Herculaneum, and they could see fragmentary courses of ancient masonry and the odd Roman column sticking out. Half a dozen workmen and a woman with a clipboard were clustered round some tools and planking on the far side of the pit, and two more armed security guards were loitering and smoking in another corner. The guards grasped the barrels of their sub-machine guns and peered suspiciously at his companions. Hiebermeyer took a deep breath, nodded courteously and proceeded to lead the entering group briskly across the floor of the pit. 'The guards are here to prevent the site being pillaged at night.'

'That's a joke,' Costas said. 'Those apes look like they were recruited from the local drugs gang.'

'Keep your voice down,' Maria said urgently. 'There's some authority behind all this that even keeps the guards in control, and I don't think it's the Mafia.' She took the lead, navigating her way around piles of ancient masonry towards a wooden structure against the other side of the pit, which evidently concealed some kind of entranceway. The workmen all glanced up briefly as they passed, but the woman studiously ignored them. She was dark featured, Neapolitan, with wavy black hair going prematurely grey, wearing jeans and a loose-fitting white shirt. A superintendency ID hung around her neck and she wore an orange hard hat. She slipped on a pair of sunglasses as they passed.

'She's our guardian angel from the superintendency,' Hiebermeyer murmured.

'No meet and greet?' Costas said.

'No chance. They're under strict orders not to fraternize with the enemy.'

'Dr Elizabeth d'Agostino,' Jack murmured, fiddling with his cell phone. 'An old friend of mine.' He slipped the phone inside his bag.

'That's her,' Hiebermeyer murmured. 'She knows her stuff, but someone's definitely put a gag order on her.'

'Aren't you going to say hello, Jack?' Maria said.

'I don't want to muddy the waters,' Jack murmured. 'We have a history.' He glanced again at the woman, his expression troubled, and then looked back at Maria. 'As you said, when you get the go-ahead here, you go ahead. I'll try to have a word with her later.'

Costas looked at Hiebermeyer. 'Do the superintendency people join you in the tunnel?'

'Officially, no. They're afraid of a collapse. That's the official reason why they've refused to authorize a full excavation. Any further tunnelling will increase the risk of collapse, threatening the modern town above. Far better to seal up the tunnel again for another two hundred years.'

'And unofficially?'

'Yesterday, as soon as we found what they wanted, Dr d'Agostino and those workmen were in there like a shot. I imagine they've been trying to get the statue out while we've been gone. But she wasn't with us when we went further into the tunnel, and you'll soon see why they won't have tried on their own.' Hiebermeyer pulled at the lock on the door of the wooden structure, then signalled with his hand to one of the guards. 'We have to wait for the guard to unlock it for us,' he grumbled. 'Another little ritual.' The guard saw him, but pointedly continued talking to the other guard, doing nothing. The workmen started up an electric drill, putting them out of earshot. 'The guards know perfectly well what I want. All in their own time.'

'Welcome to the Villa of the Papyri,' Costas said ruefully.

'I didn't think it was going to be this bad,' Jack murmured.

'There are some excellent archaeologists here, and I have good friends in the superintendency,' Hiebermeyer said. 'They do what they can. But they have to battle the system. Some end up thriving on it, getting sucked in. Only here even those people seem subdued, oppressed, as if they've been locked down by some bigger force. Others fall by the wayside, get eliminated.'

'You mean offed?' Costas said in a hushed voice. 'They really do that here?'

'Usually not quite that dramatic, but sometimes. A car crash, a boating accident. Usually it's more mundane. Threats, bribery, intimidation, tampering with personal financial records. People can easily be brought down in this place, if they're honest.'

'If they're honest,' Costas repeated, shaking his head.

'But there are some good ones who do reach the top and hang in there,' Hiebermeyer said. 'The current chief superintendent is one of them, our lady's boss. We wouldn't be here if he hadn't given the go-ahead, against all kind of pressure from somewhere. Needless to say, he has permanent bodyguards, but then that's not uncommon for officials in Naples.'

'I still don't understand what the Mafia could want with this place,' Costas said.

'I don't even know for sure that the Mafia are involved. Nobody seems to know. You just have to assume it. It's not only the trade in stolen antiquities, and you can rest assured that goes on here. There's also a huge amount of money tied up in archaeological tourism.'

'Speaking of archaeology, what's the story here?' Costas said.

'It all began in 1750,' Hiebermeyer said, suddenly animated. 'A Swiss army engineer named Karl Weber took over the excavations at Herculaneum. A few weeks later a well-digger discovered a marble floor, probably right about where we are now. Eventually they tunnelled all over this place, and Weber realized they had a huge villa, bigger than anything else they'd seen. It was smash and grab, statues, mosaics, anything. Then they started finding carbonized scrolls. They didn't realize what they were, and some of the diggers even took them away and used them as firelighters, believe it or not. Then they realized they were papyrus. Eventually most of the legible ones were interpreted as part of the Greek library of an obscure philosopher called Philodemus.'

'He was probably patronized by the rich owner of this house,' Jack said. 'A kind of philosopher mascot. Whether or not there was a Latin library too has always been the big question.'

'And the tunnel, the one we're going into, the one revealed by the earthquake?' Costas asked.

'It's one of the early tunnels, dug by Weber's men, heading towards the area of the villa where the library was found. It was sealed up while Weber was still in charge.'

'Any idea why?'

'That's what we're here to find out.'

'Do we know who owned this place?' Costas said.

'That's the beauty of this period, leading up to the eruption,' Jack replied. 'We know a lot of the names of aristocrats from the Roman historians, from Tacitus, Suetonius, Pliny, half a dozen others.

'Cue your first treat,' Hiebermeyer interrupted, beaming. 'What alerted the superintendency to the earthquake's effect on this site was that part of the solidified mud wall in this trench collapsed, over there. We may as well look at it now while our guard finishes his cigarette.'

They made their way past the group of workmen, who were now clearing away chunks of rocky conglomerate, and came to a gap where a section had fallen away from the trench wall. Elizabeth d'Agostino was standing only a few metres away with a clipboard, talking rapidly to a man with the same ID around his neck, evidently another inspector. Jack tried to catch her eye, but failed. 'It'll be months before they clear all this,' Hiebermeyer muttered to Jack as they picked their way through the rubble. 'Every possible reason for delay will be found. Someone, someone really big, wants this place shut down, and I think they're going to have their way.'

'Not if we can help it,' Jack murmured.

'There are three big forces at play around here,' Hiebermeyer continued quietly, mopping the sweat off his brow. 'The first is the volcano. The second is the Mafia, organized crime.'

'And the third is the Church,' Jack said.

'Correct.'

'Pretty volatile mix,' Costas said loudly, then coughed as he saw the inspector glance at them.

'Makes doing archaeology in Egypt seem like a piece of cake,' Hiebermeyer murmured. 'Sometimes I think they're wishing for another eruption, to seal this place up for ever. It seems that the huge loss of life that would result, the destruction of these sites and all the archaeology and the loss of tourist money would be nothing compared to the danger of what might be found here. What that might be, I don't know, but someone's frightened of something. I suspect someone powerful in the Church is worried about a great revelation, an ancient document that might undermine their authority. Look how much obstruction there was when the Dead Sea Scrolls were revealed in Israel. Another pyroclastic flow from Vesuvius would eliminate the threat here for all time.'

'Let's hope you've found enough to keep the door open before that happens.'

'You're going to be amazed,' Hiebermeyer whispered, looking at Jack intently. 'What we've found. Trust me.' They reached a table covered with safety gear, and he turned and spoke loudly. 'Hard hats on. Health and safety regulations.'

'They have those in Naples?' Costas said pointedly. The inspector looked around again, and Jack shot Costas a warning look. They both donned orange hard hats, followed by the others. Everyone followed Maria and stooped in file under the overhang into a cavity about five metres deep, decreasing in height to the point where Maria at the far end was forced to squat down. Costas crawled in beside Jack and pressed his hand on the irregular grey surface above them.

'See what I mean?' Jack said. 'Hard as rock.'

'Must have been a nightmare to excavate.'

'Here we are.' Hiebermeyer pointed. Emerging from the solidified mud in front of them was a smoothed slab of masonry, veins of blue and green visible on the polished white surface.

'Cipollino,' Jack murmured, stroking the surface appreciatively. 'Euboean marble, from Greece. Very nice. No expense spared in this villa.'

Hiebermeyer flicked on the headlamp on his hard hat, and immediately they could see that the slab was covered with an inscription. It was in three lines, bold capital letters carved deep into the marble:

ΗΒΟΥΛΗΚΑΙΟΔΗΜΟΣΛΕΥΚΙΟΝΚΑΛΠΟΡΝΙΟΝ
ΛΕΥΚΙΟΥ ΥΙΟΝ ΠΕΙΣΩΝΑ
ΤΟΝΑΥΤΟΚΡΑΤΟΡΑΚΑΙΠΑΤΡΩΝΑΤΗΣΠΟΛΕΩΣ

'It's Greek!' Costas exclaimed.

'These kinds of inscriptions were highly formulaic,' Hiebermeyer said. 'You find them in Egypt too, from the time before the Romans when the Greeks ruled. It reads "The council and the people honour Leukios Kalpornios Peison, the son of Leukios, the ruler and patron of the city." '

'Ruler and patron,' Costas whistled. 'The local Mafia boss?'

Jack grinned. 'I remember this. There's an identical inscription in Greece. Calpurnius Piso was Roman governor on the island of Samothrace, in the Aegean. He must have brought this back as a memento.'

'Along with a shipload of statues and other art,' Maria murmured. 'Maurice showed me the stuff they found here in the eighteenth century, in the Naples museum. It's incredible.'

'This particular Calpurnius Piso was probably the father or grandfather of the one we know most about, who lived in the time of the emperors Claudius and Nero,' Hiebermeyer said. 'That later Calpurnius Piso seems to have been especially loyal to Claudius, but hatched a plot against Nero that failed. Piso retired to his house, maybe this very one, where he opened his veins and bled to death. That was in AD 65, eleven years after Claudius' death and fourteen years before Vesuvius blew. We don't know who the owner of the villa was at the time of the eruption, but it was probably another family member or this inscription wouldn't still be here. Maybe a nephew, a cousin, someone who escaped Nero's purge of the family following the assassination attempt.'

'So this clinches it,' Jack said, eyeing Hiebermeyer. 'This really was the home of Calpurnius Piso. Another small step for archaeology. Congratulations, Maurice.'

They moved out into the open courtyard again. Hiebermeyer took off his hard hat and jerked his head towards the looming presence behind the rooftops. 'Don't congratulate me, Jack. It was the volcano that did it, not us. This inscription was revealed by the earthquake. It's what alerted the authorities to what else might have been revealed, old excavation workings that might have opened up. Then they saw the tunnel entrance.'

'It seems to be more Greek than Roman around here,' Costas said, wiping the dust from his hands. 'I had no idea.'

'There are layers of it,' Jack said. 'First the Greeks who colonized the Bay of Naples, then the Romans who rediscovered Greece when they conquered it. The Roman generals in Greece looted all the great works, from places like Delphi and Olympia, and a lot of Greek art starts to appear in Rome, often stuck on Roman monuments. Then wealthy private collectors like Calpurnius Piso bring back their own haul, some of it masterpieces but mostly lesser works, what was left. Then, by the time we're talking about, the early imperial period, Greek artisans are making stuff specifically for the Roman market, just as Chinese potters or Indian furniture-makers produced stuff for western taste in the nineteenth century. That's what you mostly see in Pompeii and Herculaneum, *objets d'art* in the Greek manner, more style than substance.'

'I look at a sculpture,' Costas said determinedly. 'I like it or I don't like it, and I don't care about the label.'

'Fair enough.' Jack grinned. 'The truest kind of connoisseur. But you really have to understand the context here, and that's the beauty of these sites. You can see how the Romans used their art, how they appreciated it. To them, it didn't matter if they had a Greek Old Master or a fine reproduction, because when it came to the crunch they were all just decoration. What really mattered to the Romans were the portraits of their ancestors, images that embodied the virtues they so admired, that emphasized family continuity. Those portraits were kept hidden away, often in a private room, and were traditionally in wax and wood so haven't survived. The Romans get a lot of bad press because art historians of the Victorian period, who glorified classical Greece, mostly only saw collections of ancient sculptures ripped out of context and lined up in galleries and museums. It seemed to show indiscriminate judgement, bad taste, vulgarity. Come here, and you can see that nothing was further from the truth. If anything, it was the Greeks at this period who lacked the edge.'

'Which brings us very neatly to the reason you're here,' Hiebermeyer beamed, pressing his hard hat back on.

They watched as the guard finally roused himself, ambling

over to the wooden doorway and making a big display of unlocking it. 'The greatest lost library of antiquity,' Hiebermeyer said quietly. 'And one of the greatest black holes in archaeology. Until now.'

8

Jack crouched behind Hiebermeyer at the entrance to the tunnel into the ancient villa. It was already cooler, a relief from the baking sun outside. Immediately in front of them was a metre-wide extractor fan with an electric motor, and behind it a flexible corrugated tube that ran out of the temporary wooden structure in front of the entrance to a coil and an outlet high on a wall above the site.

'After coming out of the tunnel yesterday, I played up the danger element just to ensure they wouldn't try going in,' Hiebermeyer said. 'But there really is a toxic gas buildup in there, methane, carbon monoxide. Mostly it's from organic material that's beginning to rot, with the introduction of more oxygen after the tunnel was opened up.'

'Not bodies?' Costas said hopefully.

'In this place, they're either skeletonized, or incinerated,' Hiebermeyer replied. 'Usually,' he added.

'How long do we have to wait?' Maria asked.

'We'll give it a few more minutes, then take the fan in and reactivate it when we reach the grille.'

Jack paused. 'I think this is the first time we've dug together since Carthage.' He turned to Costas. 'The three of us were students together, and we cut our teeth with a UNESCO team at Carthage. I dived in the ancient harbour, Maurice disappeared into a hole in the ground and Maria recorded inscriptions.'

'I feel the odd one out here,' Costas said.

'I think you can join our club.' Jack nudged Hiebermeyer, who tried to look at Costas stonily through his pebble glasses, the hint of a smile on his face, his cheeks streaked with grime. Jack suppressed a grin. 'Maurice found the remains of a great bronze furnace, just as described by the Romans, the first definitive evidence for Carthaginian child sacrifice. It was a fantastic find.'

'Fantastic?' Costas said weakly. 'Child sacrifice. I thought we'd left all that behind on our last little adventure, with the Toltecs in Mexico.'

'The past is a pretty unsavoury place sometimes,' Jack said wryly. 'You just have to take what you get, go with the flow.'

'Go with the flow,' Costas repeated. 'Yeah, right.' He looked into the dark recess behind the gated entrance in front of them, then back at Jack. 'So what delights does this place hold for us?'

'Ever been to the Getty Villa?'

'The Getty Villa. Malibu, California. Yeah,' Costas said vaguely. 'I remember a school trip. Classical design, lots of statues. Big central pool, great for skimming coins.'

Hiebermeyer raised his eyes, and Jack grinned again. 'Well, this place was the basis for the design of the Getty Villa.'

Costas looked doubtfully at the black hole in front of them. 'No kidding.'

'Okay, we're moving,' Hiebermeyer said, eyeing the hole that he and Mana had managed to enlarge slightly the evening before. He lifted up the extractor fan and heaved it forward, pulling the exhaust hose behind him. Jack and the others followed, and within a few metres they were completely enclosed by the tunnel. It was about as wide as a person could stretch, and just high enough for Jack to stand upright. The surface was like an old mine shaft, covered with the marks of chisels and pickaxes, and it smelled musty. Jack felt as if he were walking back into the eighteenth century, seeing the site through the eyes of the first tunnellers who had hacked their way into the rock-hard mud, through the eyes of the engineer Karl Weber as he tried to make sense of the labyrinth his men had dug in their search for loot. He followed Hiebermeyer round a corner, and it became darker. 'No electric lighting yet,' Hiebermeyer said ruefully. 'But keep your headlamps off for a moment. Okay, you can switch them on now.'

Jack activated his beam and shone it forward. He stifled a

gasp, and tripped forward slightly. The head of Anubis was staring out from the side of the tunnel just ahead of him, the black ears upright and the snout defiant just as Hiebermeyer and Maria had first seen it the day before.

'Behold your second treat.' Hiebermeyer twisted back round after having placed the extractor fan just in front of him. 'This is the key find I meant, the clincher for the superintendency. It's exactly what they want. A spectacular find. You can see they've already widened the recess around the statue, ready for taking it out later today. It'll be all over the front pages tomorrow morning. Cue closing up this tunnel. Permanently.'

'Amazing.' Jack was still awestruck by the image, and put his hand carefully on the snout. 'They found one of these in King Tut's tomb,' he said to Costas.

'At least that one was where it belonged, in Egypt,' Hiebermeyer grumbled.

'Greeter of the souls of the underworld, and protector of them on their journey,' Maria said from behind. 'Or so Maurice tells me.'

'I don't like the sound of that,' Costas muttered. 'I thought you said there were no bodies in here.'

Jack tilted his helmet up, and looked past the snout of Anubis to the darkness beyond. He felt as if the eighteenth century had now given way to a much older past, erupting through the walls like the head of Anubis. He also sensed the danger. A few metres beyond the statue was a temporary metal grille across the tunnel bearing the word *PERICOLO* and a large death's-head symbol. Hiebermeyer unlocked the hatch through the grille and pushed the extractor fan inside. He clicked it on, and a red light began flashing, accompanied by a low electronic whirr.

'That's a good start,' he said. 'Believe it or not, the extension lead actually works. We've got electricity.' He checked a digital readout on the back of the fan. 'In about ten minutes this should have cleared the tunnel ahead as far as we got yesterday, to the point where it ends at another wall. When the light goes green we'll take the fan forward until the sensor flashes red again.' He glanced at Jack, and spoke quietly. 'I could have had this running before you arrived, but I didn't want to tempt anyone to sneak in. Your superintendency friend seems perfectly happy with Anubis. In fact she's obsessed with it.'

'That would figure,' Jack said quietly. 'Elizabeth was passionate about Egypt when I knew her. She was paid to study Roman archaeology, but she really wanted to follow in your footsteps, Maurice. I told her all about you. She swore she'd go there once she'd fulfilled her government contract. But something drew her back here. Family connections. Obligations. She only ever hinted at it, hated the whole thing. That's what really baffles me. Why she's still here.'

'You seem to have known her well,' Maria murmured.

'Friends for a while. But not any more, it seems.'

Hiebermeyer pushed up his glasses. 'The bottom line is, as far as they're concerned, the investigation has got its result, and what we're doing now is purely a sideshow, a recce, before the whole thing is deemed unsafe and sealed up again. At the moment, I'm happy to go along with that.'

'How safe is it, exactly?' Costas said.

'Well, the tunnel isn't shored up, and there's the risk of another earth tremor. The place is full of toxic gas. Vesuvius might erupt again. We could be crushed, asphyxiated, incinerated.'

'Archaeology,' Costas sighed. 'To think, I turned down a position at CalTech for all this. Beach house, surfing, martinis on tap.'

'We could also be gunned down by the Mafia,' Maria added.

'Great. That's just the icing on the cake.' Costas sighed, then looked back at Anubis. 'Anyway, I thought by the Roman period this Egyptian stuff was all passé,' he said. 'I mean, what you were saying about this guy Calpurnius Piso. The fashion accessories. Everything had to be Greek.'

'The Warhol collector doesn't necessarily throw away his family collection of Old Masters,' Maria said.

'Actually, ancient Egypt was the very latest rage,' Jack said. 'Egypt was the last of the big old places to be annexed by Rome, after the defeat of Cleopatra in 31 BC. Most of the obelisks you see in Rome today, the one in St Peter's Square, were shipped over by the first emperors. It was just like the pillage of Greece all over again. Everyone wanted a piece of the action.'

'Barbarians,' Hiebermeyer muttered. At that moment the extractor fan flashed green and the fan cut out. He motioned for them to move forward, and crouched through the grille. Jack and Costas picked up the corrugated tube and followed him, with Maria close behind. Ahead of them the passageway was unlit except for the wavering beams of their headlamps. Jack had wondered when he would feel the claustrophobia, and it was now, the point in a tunnel when he suddenly felt removed from the world outside, when progress ahead seemed beyond his own volition, when the tunnel itself seemed to be drawing him in. It was as if the toxic air they were pressing against had bled around them and filled the tunnel behind, sealing them in a capsule that could implode at any moment, sucking them into the vortex of the past. They pressed on, pulling the tube noisily behind them. The tunnel was longer than he had expected, reaching deep into the recesses of the villa site, well beyond the tunnels he had seen on Weber's plan. About thirty metres on they came to the end, to the dark crack in the wall where Maria and Hiebermeyer had stopped the day before. Jack could clearly see the pick marks from the eighteenth century, and he looked at them closely. Some of the marks were on stone, not solidified mud. The tunnel clearly ended at some kind of structure, a stone entranceway. Hiebermeyer heaved the fan inside the crack and activated it again. 'It still shows green, but I'm going to give it five minutes anyway. Better safe than sorry.' He looked at Jack. 'This is as far as we got just before I came out and called you. After I looked inside.'

'I can hardly wait.' Jack turned and peered back down the corridor, where they could see a wavering electric light and hear voices, then the sound of a power tool being tested. 'Will any of them join us?'

'I doubt it,' Hiebermeyer said. 'They're widening the passageway to get Anubis out. Even our lady guardian won't come through that grille.'

'Maybe they think the place is cursed,' Costas murmured. 'Maybe Anubis does it for them.'

'If there was a curse, the authorities would let us know about it,' Hiebermeyer said. 'They've put every other obstacle in front of excavating this place. We're part of their game. A token gesture, so they can say they've done everything they can do, but that the place is just too dangerous.'

As if on cue, there was a shudder and the air shimmered with dust. It was gone as quickly as it had arrived, but there was no doubting the cause. Hiebermeyer took out his seismic oscillator and pressed it against the side wall, then grunted. There was silence for a moment, then a quiet coughing from Maria, and they all clipped on their dust masks.

'Maybe they're right,' Costas said. 'Is there anything more to see, Maurice? I mean, anything really? I'm good to go.'

'Too late to turn back now,' Hiebermeyer said, peering at Jack. 'I hate to admit it, but I'm beginning to understand those eighteenth-century tunnellers. I know where they were coming from. You don't want to linger too long down here. I don't think we're here for a painstaking excavation. Not exactly smash and grab, but something like an archaeological raid.'

'I'm hearing you,' Jack said.

'While we wait, what's this about opium, anyway?'

'You'll never believe what we found in the shipwreck.'

At that moment there was a grunt and a curse. 'I think we've got something here.' Costas had been edging ahead of the others, and now framed the ragged hole at the end of the tunnel. 'I think it might be another statue.' The others quickly came up behind him, their beams converging on the place where the seismic shock had just caused a section of wall to cave in beside the crack. Inside the cavity was a human form, life sized, lying on its front, one arm outstretched and the other folded under its chest, the legs extending back towards the entrance. It seemed to be naked, but the surface was obscured by a darkened carbonized layer that made the material underneath difficult to ascertain.

'My God,' Maria whispered.

'This must have just been revealed,' Hiebermeyer said quietly. 'That tremor just now. It wasn't visible yesterday.'

Jack knelt down and examined the head, then tried to peer through a small hole just below one ear. He could see that the form was hollow, like a bronze statue, but there was no metal visible, not even a corrosion layer. He thought for a moment, then looked again. 'Well I'll be damned,' he murmured.

'What is it?' Costas said.

'You remember I told you about the bodies at Pompeii, shapes preserved as hollow casts in the solidified ash?'

Costas looked aghast. 'You're not telling me this is one.' He edged back.

'Only it's not preserved in ash,' Hiebermeyer said. He had come up beside Jack and taken out his worn old trowel, using it to pick up a small sample of blackened material from beside the body. 'It's bizarre. It's preserved in some kind of carbonized material, something fibrous.'

'My God,' Jack said. 'You're right. I can see the crossed fibres. Clothing, maybe.' He peered at Hiebermeyer, who looked back at him suggestively. Jack thought again, and felt his jaw drop. 'Not clothing,' he whispered. '*Papyrus.*'

'Wait till you see what's in there,' Hiebermeyer whispered back, aiming his trowel at the crack in the wall ahead of them.

'These were scrolls?' Maria whispered. 'This man was covered in papyrus scrolls?'

'They were spilling out of the place that lies ahead of us,' Hiebermeyer replied. 'It's as if this man fell into a bed of scrolls, and they were all blown over him when the blast came. When they found Philodemus' library in the eighteenth century, a lot of the scrolls were strewn around, as if someone were trying to escape with them.'

'Or was searching through them, frantically looking for something precious to salvage before fleeing,' Maria said.

'Let's hope these books were just more of Philodemus' Greek scrolls,' Jack muttered, 'and not the lost Latin library.'

Costas put out his hand and gingerly touched the shoulder of the body. Instantly the entire form shimmered and disappeared in a puff of carbon. His finger was left suspended in mid-air, and for a moment there was silence.

'Whoops,' he said.

Hiebermeyer groaned.

'Not to worry,' Jack sighed. 'An Agamemnon moment.'

'Huh?'

'When Heinrich Schliemann excavated the Bronze Age site of Mycenae, he lifted a golden death mask from a royal grave and claimed to have gazed on the face of King Agamemnon. Maybe he really did see something, some fleeting impression under the mask. You remember Atlantis, the spectral form of the bull on the altar? Sometimes you really do see ghosts.'

'I think it's time for photographs from now on, Jack,' Maria said, pulling out a compact digital camera.

'Absolutely,' Jack said. 'Take everything, several times, different settings. It could end up being the only record we have.'

'Look what's underneath,' Hiebermeyer said, suddenly excited. 'Far more interesting, forensically speaking.' He hunched down close over the place where the head had been and took out a photographer's lens cleaner, gently blowing at the dust. Another form was emerging underneath, grey and blackened. 'It's the skull,' he whispered, his voice tight with emotion. 'It's partially carbonized too, but looks as if it'll hold up. And I can see the vertebrae, the ribs.' He put his finger into a dark sticky mass under the skull, then sniffed it, first cautiously, then deeply. He suddenly gagged, then swallowed hard. 'Amazing,' he said hoarsely, wiping his finger against the wall. 'Never even come across that in a mummy, and I've stuck my fingers in a few.'

'What is it?' Costas said. 'Some kind of resin, pitch?'

'Not exactly.' Hiebermeyer's glasses had slipped down his nose, and he pushed them up with the same finger, leaving a dark streak between his eyes. He looked at Costas, beaming with excitement. 'When the inferno hit this place, the scrolls must have instantly carbonized, but there must have been something in them, a resinous preservative material, that caused the carbonized mass to form the cast around the body. That sealed off the flesh from oxygen, so it couldn't incinerate. Instead, it cooked.'

'Cooked alive,' Maria said.

'He means, this guy melted,' Jack added, peering at Costas.

'Oh no.' Costas swayed back against the opposite wall of the tunnel. 'And you put your finger into it.'

Hiebermeyer held up his finger again, and peered at it with some reverence. 'It's fantastic. Probably some brain in that. Should be perfect for DNA analysis.'

Maria had edged back to where the man's feet had been, looking closely, and then sidled up to Hiebermeyer and peered into the ribcage. 'Look! He's wearing a gold ring!' she exclaimed. Hiebermeyer followed her gaze, tracing the finger bones which were contorted under the ribcage as if the man had been clutching at his chest in his death throes. He took out a mini Maglite, and put his face right up to the bones. 'It's a signet ring, for impressing into wax sealings on documents. It's partly melted into the bone, but I can see the design. It's an eagle impression.'

'An imperial signet ring,' Jack said. 'This guy must have been in the service of the emperor.'

'I'm not sure if this was a guy, exactly,' Hiebermeyer murmured, kneeling up with his hands on his hips. 'There's something odd about this skeleton. Distinctly odd. Rounding

148

of the face, areas of bone structure you'd expect to be more developed in a male, unusual widening of the pelvic area. It's not a woman, exactly, but it's not far off. Very odd.'

'Didn't they have eunuchs?' Costas said.

'An interesting thought,' Jack murmured. He stared at the skeleton, thinking hard. In the early fourth century AD, the emperor Constantine the Great surrounded himself with eunuchs, and so did the later Byzantine emperors. Eunuchs were thought to be a safer bet as secretaries and state officials, less likely to be hard driven and ambitious. Earlier emperors had them, too. He looked up. 'Some scholars think that Claudius' freedman Narcissus was a eunuch.' He paused for a moment, then spoke again, almost to himself. 'But it couldn't be. Narcissus was murdered when Claudius was poisoned, in AD 54. That's a quarter of a century before Vesuvius erupted. There would have been other eunuchs around. This whole area attracted oddities, freaks who came here for the amusement of the wealthy, as well as cripples and other unfortunates who sought cures in the sulphur vents of the Phlegraean Fields. That's the other side of life here in the Roman period, not exactly the tourist image.'

'Whoever and whatever this was, he may have ended up as an imperial freedman, but he certainly started off life as a slave.' Hiebermeyer had shifted to the feet end of the skeleton, and then came back up beside the extractor fan just inside the entranceway ahead of them. 'His ankles have the characteristic contusions caused by shackles, healed over years before. I think he was an old man when he died, very old for this period, maybe in his eighties or even his nineties. But he'd had a pretty rough time of it a long time before, as a boy.'

'From shackles to castration to this,' Costas said, his eyes studiously averted from the slick of black goo under the skeleton. 'Let's hope the years in between weren't so bad.'

'The end was probably pretty quick,' Hiebermeyer said, scraping some of the black material on to his trowel and then into a small specimen phial. 'The terrible shock of that blast of heat, then one lungful and you'd be gone. There would only have been a few seconds of awareness.'

'He must have known something bad was going down,' Costas said, forcing himself to look again. 'I thought the volcano had been erupting for hours.'

'Yes, but the pyroclastic flow that wiped Herculaneum off the map came from nowhere, rushed down that mountain in rings of fire faster than anything any Roman had ever seen. Before that, the eruption would have seemed a terrifying catastrophe, but not necessarily a death sentence. After that it truly was the apocalypse. Nobody would have escaped Herculaneum alive.'

Jack began to sense the smell of the place, not just the familiar smell of dust and old tombs but the smell of recent death, the rusty smell of blood, the scent of animal fear. For a moment the tunnel lost its solidity and became the whirling vortex of death that had encased this man, a terrifying, claustrophobic place which moments before had been a shrine to beauty, a sumptuous expression of freedom and confidence. The whole place still seemed traumatized, still trembling in the aftershock almost two thousand years on. Jack closed his eyes briefly, then moved up behind Hiebermeyer towards the dark entranceway ahead of them. He glanced back, to where he could still see the snout of Anubis peering sightless out of the side wall, to the glimmer of light just visible beyond. The noise of the drill could be heard where the tunnel entrance was being widened, but there was still nobody to be seen. He turned back to the dark crack in the wall ahead.

'You ready for this?' Hiebermeyer said, flicking off the fan. There was now no noise ahead of them, only the silence of a tomb, and even the distant noise of the drill had stopped. Jack looked at the grimy face a few inches away from his, the face of a man which in the blink of an eye could have been a boy. 'Do you remember when we were at school, when we filled that cellar room with home-made artefacts and then sealed it up, pretending it was King Tut's tomb? I was Howard Carter, you were Lord Carnarvon.'

'No.' Hiebermeyer shook his head decisively. 'Other way round. You were Carnarvon, I was Carter.'

Jack grinned, then looked ahead at the dark crack in the wall, his face suffused with excitement. 'Okay. Let's do it.'

9

Jack peered through into the hidden chamber at the end of the tunnel, trying to make sense of the fragments of clarity revealed by his headlamp in the darkness. The tunnel had felt like an old mine working, which was exactly what it was, the result of Weber's digging more than two hundred years before, itself part of the extraordinary archaeology of this place. But now there were glimpses that reminded Jack of exactly where they were, deep inside the buried remains of an ancient Roman villa. At first all he could see were shadows, dusty grey forms, darkness. Then he saw a table, possibly a stone table, and some kind of shelf structure on the far wall. Something was not right. Then he realized to his astonishment what it was. There was no ash, no solidified mud.

'It's perfectly preserved,' he whispered.

Hiebermeyer heaved the extractor fan forward a few feet into the chamber, and it showed red again. He cautioned them to stay back. 'This room is a miracle,' he replied in hushed tones. 'I realized it when I first peered in here yesterday, before we backed out and called you. There are other rooms at Herculaneum that escaped the mud, the pyroclastic flow. Nobody really understands it, but the extraordinary thing about this room is that it escaped the furnace effect as well. It could have been something to do with the elevation, perched on the top floor of the villa above the rooftop level of the town, looking down on it. The hot blast certainly ripped through everywhere else right up to the room, over that body at the entrance. But it missed this chamber itself. We always knew something like this was possible at Herculaneum.'

'Maurice, I can see scrolls,' Jack said, his voice tight with excitement. 'Wound-up scrolls. No doubt about it. In jars, under those shelves.'

'That's what I saw yesterday,' Hiebermeyer replied, almost whispering. 'That's why I called you here. Now you see what I mean. This really could be it.'

'Can you imagine what they might contain?' Jack's voice was hoarse.

The fan suddenly went dead, and Hiebermeyer cursed in German. 'Not now. Please God, not now. He bent over the machine, and seemed to be praying. 'I apologize profusely for everything I have ever said or thought about Naples. Just another five minutes. Please.'

'This happened before,' Maria murmured. 'Dodgy electrical grid in Ercolano. The guards couldn't be bothered to fire up the backup generator, and we had to come out in a hurry. But right now the superintendency are planning to use electrical drills to widen the cavity in the volcanic rock around the Anubis statue, so there's a bit more incentive for the guards to get on with it. We just have to back off and wait.'

Jack looked over at the shadowy recess with the scrolls, hardly able to restrain himself. He closed his eyes, and breathed in deeply. He turned and followed the others, crawling back through the entrance to their start point. Costas reached into the shadows by the wall and picked something up. 'Check this out,' he said excitedly. He held it up, shaking off the dust. It was a metal disc about an inch across, dark green and mottled. 'It looks like a medallion.'

'Not a medallion,' Hiebermeyer murmured, peering closely. 'A bronze sestertius, the biggest base metal denomination of the first century AD. A bit like a quarter.'

'Also the largest type of Roman coin, the best for portraits.' Jack crouched closer to Costas. 'Anything visible?'

'Nero!' Costas exclaimed. 'I can read it. The emperor Nero!' He passed the coin to Jack, who looked at it intently, angling it to and fro in his headlamp. 'Right about the name, wrong about the emperor,' Jack murmured. 'I'm looked at the reverse, the back side. It reads *NERO CLAUDIUS DRUSUS GERMANICUS*. That's the full name of Drusus, brother of the emperor Tiberius. Nero was a family name. Drusus was one of the ablest Roman generals, a decent man and a hero of the people. A real beacon at the beginning of the empire, a time of great promise but also great uncertainty, a bit like 1960s America. Charismatic characters like that seem to be typical of those periods. His death by poisoning and then the murder of his son Germanicus were like the Kennedy assassinations, cast a pall over the whole early imperial dynasty.'

'That was well before the time period we're dealing with here,' Hiebermeyer murmured. 'Drusus was murdered in 10 BC, during the reign of Augustus, almost ninety years before Vesuvius erupted.'

Jack nodded, and peered closely at the coin. The image showed a triumphal arch in Rome, surmounted by an equestrian statue of Drusus galloping between trophies. 'But this isn't a coin of Drusus. It's a coin celebrating him. He was never emperor.' Jack flipped it over. This was a coin of one who survived all the madness of his uncle Tiberius and his nephew Caligula. It dated more than fifty years after Drusus' death. 'This is a coin of Drusus' other son, younger brother of Germanicus. The inscription reads *TI CLAUDIUS CAESAR AUG PM TR P*. That's Tiberius Claudius Caesar Augustus, Pontifex Maximus, Tribunicia Potestas. The emperor Claudius.'

'Poor Claudius,' Maria murmured. 'Claudius the cripple.'

'That's the caricature,' Jack said. 'But it's a bit like Shakespeare's take on the English king Richard III, the hunchback. There was a good deal more to Claudius than that.'

'He was emperor from AD 41 to 54,' Hiebermeyer said, looking again at the extractor fan and seeing the backup sensor still showing red while it cooled. 'Died in Rome a quarter of a century before Vesuvius erupted, probably poisoned by his wife Agrippina.'

'He had bad luck with his wives,' Jack said. 'His one real love seems to have been the prostitute Calpurnia, but she'd also been murdered by then.' Jack paused, entranced by the coin image again. 'This has always been my favourite issue of Claudius, one of my favourite Roman coins of all. It's a rare coin, a very compelling portrait. Look at that face, the expression. He's no cripple here, it's a handsome face, but there's no glorification, no idealization. You can see the features of the Julio-Claudian dynasty, the forehead, the ears, features that hark back to his great-uncle Augustus, to Julius Caesar before that. Claudius would have known the portraits of his ancestors intimately, and would have been proud to look at this portrait of himself, to see the dignity in it. To see beyond his deformities, to know that he shared his revered ancestors' features. There's intelligence in that face too, a yearning, but also sadness and pain. A young man's face clouded by disappointment, eyes older than his years.'

'His illness was probably a palsy,' Hiebermeyer murmured. 'Cerebral palsy, with some element of spasticity. No cure, hardly any palliative treatment back then except copious quantities of wine.'

'What about opium?' Costas suddenly cut in. 'Morphine?'

Hiebermeyer turned and gave Costas a look verging on pity.

'We're talking about the first century AD. Let's keep modern Naples out of this.'

'I'm not kidding. Have you heard about our shipwreck find?'

'Later.' Jack glanced at Costas, and at that moment the extractor fan buzzed to life.

'Speaking of modern Naples,' Hiebermeyer muttered. 'Looks like someone bribed the grid operator to give us some electricity. Or the guards outside finally got off their backsides. Whatever it was, we're good to go. As you would say.' The words sounded slightly absurd in his clipped German accent, and Jack stifled a smile. Hiebermeyer pushed up his glasses and gave Costas another look, this time more quizzical than pitying.

'Hey. He's one of us after all.' Costas returned the look deadpan, then glanced at Jack, then back at Hiebermeyer, grinning. 'Roger that.'

Jack pressed his back against the jagged side of the tunnel to let Maria through. 'I think it's time for our resident manuscripts expert to take the lead.'

'I'm good with that.' Hiebermeyer peered inquisitively at Costas, who gave an enthusiastic thumbs-up, then he pushed up his glasses again and spoke seriously. 'From now on in, we touch only what we have to. The papyrus scrolls in there may be unusually well preserved but they may also be extremely fragile. Even in the driest tombs in Egypt, papyrus with no resin preservative can crumble to dust at a touch.' He kept his gaze fixed on Costas. 'Remember the body at the entrance. The body that disappeared in a puff of smoke. After all the effort we've been through to get the authorities to allow us in here, I don't want to be the latest in a long line of investigators to destroy more than they recover from this place. Okay. The fan shows green. Let's move.'

Jack crouched down and made his way behind Maria over a pile of rubble that had evidently fallen when the earthquake damaged the wall, clogging up the lower part of the crack leading into the chamber. A few moments later they cautiously stood up inside. Jack felt sure that he was now beyond the eighteenth-century tunnelling, that they were the first to stand here since the time of the Roman Empire. It was an extraordinary feeling, and took him straight back to that time as a schoolboy when he had sat alone in the ancient bath building in the main site of Herculaneum, only a stone's throw from where he was now, willing himself to pass back into antiquity and become one of the living, breathing inhabitants of the place almost two thousand years before, in the fateful hours leading up to the eruption. He shut his eyes tight, opened them again, unclipped his dust mask, and took a cautious breath. The air had a slightly sickly tang to it, but there was little dust. For the first time he looked at the room properly, sweeping his headlamp around all four walls, then methodically working his way back through everything he had seen.

'Can we have the fan off now, Maurice?' he murmured. 'I'm worried our voices might travel, be heard by the guards and superintendency people outside, at the outlet of the extractor exhaust.'

'Done.' Hiebermeyer flicked the switch, and suddenly it was eerily quiet. Then they heard the sound of clinking and distant voices down the tunnel, and the whining of electric drills. 'Good. That noise should cover us.'

Hiebermeyer came through behind Jack and Maria, followed by Costas. 'This room seems pretty austere,' Costas said, standing up behind Jack and looking around. 'I mean, not much here.'

'That's the Roman way,' Jack said. 'They often liked to have their floors and walls covered in colour and decoration, but usually had very few furnishings by our standards.'

'No mosaics or wall paintings here,' Maria murmured. 'This room's all stone, white marble by the look of it.'

Jack peered around again, absorbing everything he could, trying to get a sense of it all. To the right, on the south side, the wall was pierced by two entrances, both blocked up with solid volcanic material. He guessed they led to a balcony, overlooking the town of Herculaneum below. It would have been a spectacular view, with Vesuvius rearing up to the left and the broad sweep of the Bay of Naples to the right, the coastline visible as far out as Misenum and Cumae. Jack shifted, and his headlamp beam illuminated a long marble table, perhaps three metres long and a metre wide, with two stone chairs backing against the balcony. On the table were two pottery pitchers, three pottery cups, and what looked like ink pots. Just visible against one leg of the table was a small wine amphora. Jack looked at the tabletop again. *Ink pots.* His heart raced with excitement. He saw dusty shapes that could have been paper, papyrus. He narrowed his eyes. He was sure of it. He forced himself to remain rooted, to remain calm and detached for a few moments longer, and swept his beam to the left. He saw the shelves they had seen from the entrance, that Hiebermeyer had told him he had seen through the crack in the wall the day before. Bookshelves, piled high with scrolls. It was incredible. More scrolls were strewn on the floor, just as Weber had found elsewhere in the villa in the eighteenth century. Jack pivoted further left, to the place where they had come in. Beside the entrance were scrolls in some kind of wicker basket, different from the scrolls on the floor, wound round wooden sticks with distinctive smoothed finials poking out of the ends of each one, labels protruding. There was no doubt about it. Not just blank rolls of papyrus. *Finished books*.

He aimed his beam back to the left wall of the room, between the basket and the shelves, at something he had seen earlier but not properly registered. Now he realized what it was, and drew in his breath in excitement. It was two shadowy heads, portrait busts perched on a small shelf looking towards the table. He took a few careful steps towards them. He needed to find out who had been here, who had been the last person to sit at that desk, almost two thousand years ago. He stood in front of the busts, and saw that they were life-sized. For a moment they had a ghostly quality, as if the occupants of the villa that fateful day had walked out of the wall and were staring straight at him, with lifeless eyes. Jack forced himself to look dispassionately. Typical early imperial portrait busts, extraordinarily lifelike, as if they had been taken from wax death masks. Handsome, well-proportioned heads, slightly protuberant ears, clearly members of the imperial family. Jack peered down at the small pedestals below each bust.

NERO CLAVDIVS DRVSVS
NERO CLAVDIVS DRVSVS GERMANICVS

'Drusus and Germanicus,' he whispered.

'The two guys you mentioned just now? The guy on the coin?' Costas said. 'Father and brother of Claudius?'

'Seems an incredible coincidence,' Maria said.

Jack's mind was racing. He still had the coin in his hand, and he held it up so the portrait was framed by the two busts. The similarity was truly remarkable. *Could it be?* 'There's something about this coin,' he murmured. 'Something staring us in the face.'

'But that one coin doesn't necessarily mean much, surely,' Maria said. 'This villa was like an art gallery, a museum. The great villa owners of Italy in the Renaissance collected medallions, old coins. Why not Roman villa owners too?'

'Possibly.' Jack looked around the chamber pensively. 'But I think we're in the room of an old person, stripped to its essentials. This isn't just Roman minimalism, it's real austerity. Books, a writing table, a few revered portraits, wine. No wall paintings, no mosaics, nothing of the hedonism we associate with the Bay of Naples. The room of someone prepared for the next step, for the afterlife, already swept clean of the past. The twilight of a life.'

'Seems pretty odd for a lavish villa,' Costas said. 'I mean, this room's like a monk's cell.'

Hiebermeyer had squatted down, and was peering closely at one of the scrolls on the floor. 'This papyrus is fantastically well preserved,' he murmured, carefully prising at it with his fingers. 'It's even pliable. I can read the Greek.'

'Ah. Greek,' Jack said, his voice neutral.

'What's wrong with that?' Costas said.

'Nothing,' Jack said. 'Nothing at all. We just want Latin.'

'Bad news, Jack,' Hiebermeyer said, peering closely at the script, then pushing up his glasses and looking at him. 'I may have brought you here on a wild goose chase.'

'Philodemus.'

'I'm afraid so.'

'I thought Greek philosophers were highly esteemed,' Costas said.

'Not all of them,' Jack said. 'A lot of Romans, educated men like Claudius, like Pliny the Elder, thought many of these Greek philosophers around the Bay of Naples were quacks and charlatans, hangers-on in the villas of the wealthy. But there was a lot of this stuff around, and in a typical library here you were probably more likely to pick up a book by someone like Philodemus than one of the great names we revere today. Remember, the classical texts that have survived, that were saved and transcribed in the medieval period, represent the pinnacle of ancient achievement, and only a small part of that.

It spoils us into thinking that all ancient thinkers were remarkable minds. Look at the academic world today. For every great scholar, there are dozens of mediocrities, more than a few charlatans. But they're still all called professors. It was just bad luck for us that old Calpurnius Piso patronized one of the flaky ones.'

'I hope to God we haven't just stumbled into Philodemus' study,' Hiebermeyer muttered. 'I hate to lead you on, Jack. Hardly worth calling you from your shipwreck.'

'I wouldn't miss being here for anything,' Jack said fervently, 'Philodemus or not. And we weren't going anywhere with the wreck until all the equipment for a major excavation's in place, a week at least.'

'It'd be such a pity, though,' Maria said, slumping slightly. 'Some second-rate philosopher. It's hard to believe someone was trying to save it all, when the eruption happened,' she said, waving at the strewn scrolls all over the floor.

'Maybe they weren't,' Costas said. 'Maybe the clearance was already underway, and they were trying to get rid of it.'

'Or searching for something. You said it before.' Jack glanced back at the macabre form of the skeleton at the entrance, its hand seeming to grasp towards the scrolls inside the room. 'But there's something about this place. It doesn't seem like the study of a Greek philosopher. Not at the end, anyway, not in AD 79. It's just too Roman. It's a very private room, a hidden sanctuary almost, a place where someone could live in their own world and forget about impressing others. And I just can't imagine a Greek choosing to have two imperial Roman portrait busts as the only decoration in his study, the only things to look at from his desk.'

Hiebermeyer flipped on the extractor fan again, and it flashed red. 'Let's give it a few more minutes,' he said. 'I think we're still okay to talk, with the noise. I don't think they can hear us down there with that drill going.'

They backed up to the entrance again, clustering round it, and Jack held up the coin. He looked at the statues again, then back at the coin. He realized that the coin had been fingered a lot, in the same place on both sides. 'Maybe this was the memento of an old soldier, an old man who lived here in AD 79,' he murmured. 'Perhaps one who had served under Claudius in the invasion of Britain, or even under Germanicus, sixty years before the eruption. An old man who revered his general, and that general's brother and father.' He paused, troubled. 'But it's still odd.'

'Why?' Costas said. 'It's a great find, but as Maria says, it's just one coin.'

'Well, it would still have been risking it,' Jack said. 'In the Roman period, you didn't hang on to old coins, unless you were hoarding them. You just didn't want to be seen with issues of a past emperor. Coins were hugely important propaganda tools. It was how a new emperor conveyed his image, asserted his power. And the coin reverse had commemorative images which celebrated the achievements of the emperor and his family.'

'The Jewish triumph of Vespasian,' Costas said. *'Judaea Capta*. The menorah.'

Jack grinned. 'A great example. How could we forget. That issue was less than two years after the eruption of Vesuvius. Another famous example is the Britannia issues of Claudius, celebrating his conquest of Britain in AD 43.'

'But this coin commemorates Claudius' father.' Costas took the coin from Jack, and looked at it closely with his headlamp. 'It seems a selfless thing for an emperor to do, a little touching. I think I like this guy.'

'It's not quite what it seems,' Jack said. 'This coin probably dates to the first year of Claudius' reign, before he had anything to brag about. Harking back to a glorious ancestor was a way of giving your claim to the throne some authority, reminding people of the virtues of your ancestors. In AD 41, when Claudius was proclaimed emperor, Rome had just suffered four years of insanity under Caligula, Claudius' nephew. What people desperately wanted was a return to the hallowed old days. Personal honour, integrity, family continuity, living up to your ancestors, that was all very much the Roman way. At least in theory.'

'In Italy,' Costas murmured. 'The family. Sounds familiar.'

'Claudius was Rome's most reluctant emperor,' Jack continued. 'Dragged from behind a curtain by the Praetorian Guard when he was already in middle age, looking forward to his remaining years as a scholar and historian. But he revered the memory of his father, and all his life he wished he'd been fit enough to join the army like his brother Germanicus, whom he adored. Being emperor gave him the chance. And the acclamation of every new emperor, even Caligula and

Claudius' successor Nero, was always accompanied by pious assertions of a return to the ways of the past, the end of debauchery and corruption and a reminder of the virtues of their ancestors.'

'Did Claudius live up to it?' Costas asked.

'He might have done, if he hadn't been ruled by his wives,' Hiebermeyer muttered.

'Britain was a great triumph,' Jack said. 'Claudius was doomed never to cover himself in personal glory, riding out from the waves of the English Channel rather absurdly on a war elephant, arriving in time to see the corpses of the British vanquished but not to lead his legions in battle. But he was a good strategist, a visionary of sorts who had spent his life studying empire and conquest and could see beyond the individual campaign, the triumph. The world would be a very different place today if Claudius hadn't conquered Britain. And remember, for the men in the legions nothing could be worse than Caligula a few years earlier forcing them to line up on the French side of the English Channel and attack the sea god Neptune. With Claudius they didn't mind having a cripple for an emperor, as long as he was sane. And Claudius chose very able field commanders, generals like Vespasian, middle-ranking officers like Pliny the Elder, and they were loyal to him. And the legionaries revered the memory of Claudius' father and his brother.' Jack paused, and looked up again at the portrait bust. 'Just like the occupant of this room.'

'Their loyalty didn't prevent Claudius from being poisoned,' Hiebermeyer said.

'No,' Jack murmured. 'But for a first-century emperor, that was also the Roman way.'

'Speaking of poison, what's all this about opium?' Hiebermeyer said. At that moment the light flashed green, and he reached over and deactivated the fan. 'Sorry. It'll have to wait.'

Jack crouched back into the ancient chamber and went straight over to the table, around to the far side between the chairs. He looked at what lay on the surface. *He had been right.* They were shrouded with grey matter, dust and fallen plaster, but there was no mistaking it. Sheets of papyrus, blank sheets. A pinned-out scroll, ready for writing. Ink pots, a metal stylus poised ready to dip into the ink, left where it had been abandoned for ever, the day when this place became hell on earth. Jack stared down, then glanced up again at the two portrait busts. *Drusus and Germanicus.* There were Romans alive in AD 79 who would still hark back to those glory days. The untimely deaths of two heroes meant that their memory lived on, for generations. Jack remembered something he had thought before. A Roman would have known the portraits of his ancestors intimately. And this was a private room. A room where a man kept his most precious heirlooms, the portraits of his ancestors.

Jack was beginning to think the impossible.

The portrait of his father. Of his brother.

The pieces were suddenly falling together. Jack felt a heady rush of excitement. Something else sprang into his mind, from talking to Costas about Pliny the Elder the day before.

He reached into his bag, his heart pounding, took out the little red book and placed it on the table, under his headlamp beam. He clipped on his dust mask, carefully picked up an ancient sheet of papyrus, shook it slightly, and shone his Maglite through it. He laughed quietly to himself. 'Well I'll be damned.'

'What is it?' Costas said.

Jack held the paper up to the light so the others could see. 'Look, there's a second layer of papyrus underneath, coarser than the upper layer. It means the surface is of the best quality, but underneath it the paper is strengthened, less transparent. And unless I'm mistaken, the sheet measures exactly one Roman foot across.'

'So?'

Jack put down the sheet and picked up the book, his copy of the *Natural History*. 'Listen to what Pliny has to say about paper. Book 13, Chapter 79, on papyrus:

' "The Emperor Claudius imposed modifications on the best quality because the thinness of the paper in Augustus' time was not able to withstand the pressure of pens. In addition it allowed the writing to show through, and this brought fear of blots caused by writing on the back of the paper. Moreover, the excessive transparency of the paper looked unsightly in other ways. So the bottom layer of the paper was made from leaves of the second quality, and the cross-strips from papyrus of the first quality. Claudius also increased the width of the sheet to a foot." '

Hiebermeyer leaned over the table and peered at the sheet

closely with a small eyeglass. 'And unless I'm mistaken, this is the best-quality ink available at the time,' he said excitedly. 'Gall ink, in all probability, made from the desert beetle. I'm a bit of an expert, you know, having studied ink types when we found papyrus documents reused as mummy wrappings in Egypt. Pliny writes about that too.'

'Then I'm about to make an extraordinary suggestion,' Jack said, replacing the sheet carefully on the table and looking intently at the others. 'I think it's possible, just possible, that we're standing in the study of a man who should never have been here, who history tells us died a quarter of century before the eruption of Vesuvius.'

'A man who once ruled an empire,' Maria said softly.

Hiebermeyer was nodding slowly, and whispered the words, almost to himself. 'Tiberius Claudius Caesar Augustus.'

Jack held up the coin, allowing the light to pick out the portrait. 'Not the emperor Claudius, not the god Claudius, but Claudius the scholar. Claudius who may have somehow faked his own poisoning and survived for all those years after his disappearance from Rome, hidden away in this villa. Claudius who must have finally perished just as Pliny the Elder did, in the cataclysm of AD 79.'

There was a stunned silence, and Costas looked keenly at Jack. 'Well,' he said quietly. 'That's another little bit of history you're going to have to rewrite.'

'And not the only bit.' Maria had her back to them, and was hunched over the lower shelf in the corner of the room.

'There's more here, Jack. Much more. Books and books of it.'

Jack came round the table and they all crouched beside her. There was a collective gasp of astonishment. In front of them, below the shelves they had seen from the entrance, were two further shelves packed with several dozen cylindrical boxes, each about eighteen inches high. 'They're lidded, sealed with some kind of mortar,' Hiebermeyer murmured. 'Hollowed-out stone, Egyptian marble by the look of it. They look like reused canopic jars. No expense spared here.'

'This one's open.' Maria took out her Maglite, twisted it on and shone it at the top of the cylinder on the right side of the lower shelf. The hollowed-out interior was about a foot wide, and inside it they could see further narrow cylindrical shapes, with a space where one appeared to have been removed.

'Eureka,' Hiebermeyer said, his voice tight with emotion.

'What is it?' Costas asked.

'Papyrus scrolls,' Hiebermeyer said. 'Tightly wound papyrus scrolls.'

'Jack, they're not carbonized,' Maria whispered. 'It's a miracle.' She reached out, then held back, as if she wanted the spell to remain unbroken, to preserve that moment of realization before their action changed history.

'Any idea what they are?' Costas said.

'There should be *sillyboi*, labels describing each book,' Jack said. 'Scrolls don't have spines, so books were identified with pasted labels, usually hanging out over the shelf. I don't see any here.'

'Wait a second.' Maria peered closely at the top of the sealed cylinder next to the one with the displaced lid. 'There are markings. Engravings in the stone. Words, in Latin. I can read it. *Historiae Carthaginienses Antiquae.*'

'*The History of the Ancient Carthaginians,*' Jack whispered. 'Claudius' lost *History of Carthage*. It's mentioned in other ancient sources, but not a word of it survived. Or so we thought. There may only ever have been one copy, too controversial to publish. The only dispassionate account of Rome's greatest rival. Who else but Claudius himself would have had that, in his own private library? These jars must contain his other works.'

'Wait for it, Jack.' Hiebermeyer had sidled over to the basket of scrolls by the door, and was holding up a flap of papyrus attached to one of the decorative handles. '*Naturalis Historia, G. Plinius Secundus*. My God. Looks like we've got a complete edition of Pliny's *Natural History.*'

'Looks like you've found that Latin library after all,' Costas said.

Jack felt an overwhelming sense of certainty. He looked at the scroll, remembered his sense of the room when he first saw it, those two portraits. There had been another here, another presence, as if the old man so covetous of his private space had allowed in one other, a man whose imprint was still here, around them. 'There's something else that's niggling me about this place,' Jack said. 'About who was here.'

'What is it?'

'Well, we've got what looks like an entire copy of Pliny's

Natural History, hot out of the scriptorium. How does Claudius get hold of that?'

Costas jerked his head towards the skeleton at the door. 'Maybe he sent the eunuch to buy books for him.'

'Let's just think about it,' Jack said. 'Let's say we're right, that Claudius was living here in secret up to the time of the eruption, in AD 79. That's hypothesis, but one of the most famous facts of ancient history is that Pliny the Elder was here, on the Bay of Naples, based at Misenum only a few miles away, admiral of the Roman fleet, and that he died in the eruption.'

'You're saying they may have met each other, here,' Costas said.

Jack flipped open the index pages of his copy of the *Natural History*. 'This is what sparked me off. Pliny the Elder mentions Claudius a number of times throughout the book, always studiously, always lauding his achievements. He owed Claudius his career, when Claudius was emperor and Pliny was a young man, but the passages in the *Natural History* are almost too laudatory, for an emperor who had supposedly been dead for a quarter of a century. Just an example. Listen to this. He talks of Claudius' achievement in having a tunnel dug to drain the Fucine Lake near Rome, taking thirty thousand men and eleven years, an immense operation "beyond the power of words to describe". That final phrase is odd, by itself. For Pliny the Elder, absolutely nothing was beyond the power of words. And another thing. He should have referred to Claudius as *Divus* Claudius, the divine

Claudius, in keeping with his status as a deified emperor, years after his death and supposed apotheosis. But instead, Pliny refers to him as Claudius Caesar. It's almost too familiar, almost as if Claudius is still alive when Pliny is writing this. The clues are all here.'

'It makes sense,' Hiebermeyer murmured.

'From what we know of him, Claudius seems to have been a gregarious man, as was Pliny,' Jack said. 'Claudius may have been forced to live as a recluse, but he had always enjoyed company. He may even have summoned Pliny in secret to this room when he heard that the other man had arrived to take up his naval post at Misenum. And Pliny would constantly have been searching for informants, people who could help with his *Natural History*. He was a practical, straightforward Roman, and Claudius may have been a breath of fresh air for him in this place which would have seemed infested with Greek-loving hedonists, Romans with more money than sense under the spell of weak-minded philosophers like Philodemus.'

'And vice versa,' Maria said. 'Claudius probably felt the same about Pliny.'

'Claudius would have greatly admired Pliny,' Jack said. 'Soldier, scholar, fantastically industrious, a decent man. Pliny claimed he once had a vision of Claudius' father Drusus, telling him to write a history of the German wars. With his bust of his beloved father in front of him here, Claudius would have loved to hear that anecdote from Pliny himself, perhaps over a few pitchers of wine.'

'Claudius would also have been extremely knowledgeable, hugely well read,' Hiebermeyer added, pointing at the shelves. 'It would have been a real meeting of minds. Claudius would have been a great source for Pliny on Britain, though I don't remember much on Britannia in the *Natural History*.'

'Possibly because Pliny died before he could incorporate it,' Jack murmured. 'He had only been based at Naples for a year before the eruption, and he probably hadn't found time. He was too sociable for his own good, constantly doing the rounds of friends, the ladies too. But Claudius would have been a fantastic discovery for him, a tremendous secret. I believe Pliny was here, in this room. I can feel it. I think he came to visit Claudius often, and they had begun to work together. Pliny had given Claudius the latest copy of his *Natural History*, but he was probably poised to make additions, once he realized what a gold mine he'd found.'

'Maybe this is where Pliny was really coming when he sailed towards Vesuvius during the eruption,' Costas said. 'That letter you read me, from his nephew Pliny the Younger. Maybe he only told his nephew he was coming here for a woman. Maybe it was really a secret mission. Maybe he was coming to rescue Claudius, this fabulous library.'

'But he was too late,' Maria murmured.

'I wonder what did happen to old Claudius, if he really was here,' Costas said.

'He was here,' Jack said fervently. 'I can almost smell it. Stale wine, spilt by a shaking hand. A whiff of sulphur, maybe brought back from nocturnal visits to Cumae to see the Sibyl, who we know he consulted when he was emperor. The smell of old gall ink. He was here, all right. I know it in my bones.'

Jack walked back to the desk as he spoke. He suddenly saw that words were visible where there had been none before. He realized that the sheet of papyrus below the blank one he had picked up was covered in writing, perfectly preserved for almost two thousand years. He peered down, and read across the top:

HISTORIA BRITANNORVM CLAVDIVS CAESAR.

'My God,' he whispered. 'So this was what he was writing. This was why he wanted to return to the life of a scholar. *A History of Britain, by Claudius Caesar*. Can you imagine what this contains?'

He scanned the lines of fine, precise writing and then looked back at the title. Underneath it were two words, in the same hand but smaller:

NARCISSVS FECIT

'Of course,' Jack exclaimed, his voice hoarse with excitement. '*Narcissus did this. Narcissus wrote this*.' He looked back towards the doorway, where the outstretched arm of the skeleton was visible in his headlamp beam. 'So it is you after all,' he murmured to himself, then looked at the others, his face suffused with excitement. 'You remember I said that Narcissus was Claudius' freedman? Well, his official title was *praepositus ab epistulis*, letter-writer. This clinches it. We know who that skeleton was after all. He was Claudius' amanuensis, his scribe. I know Pliny always had one, and Claudius must have had one too, especially with his palsy.' Jack looked at the page again, then at some other pages scattered beside it on the table, with no writing but covered in dark red blotches like wine stains. 'It's amazing. I only hope we can find something in Claudius' own hand.'

The sound of the drill at the entrance to the tunnel had stopped, and a woman's voice was shouting, in heavily accented English. 'Dr Hiebermeyer? Dr Hiebermeyer? We are closing the tunnel now. Please come out immediately.'

'*Si, si, si*,' Hiebermeyer bellowed back. Maria immediately came over with her digital camera and began taking pictures, quickly moving through everything on the table, finishing with a close-up sequence of the page of writing before picking up the blank papyrus sheet and placing it on top to protect and conceal the writing.

'We need to decide what to do, Jack,' Hiebermeyer said in a low voice. 'Pronto.'

'As soon as we're out of earshot beyond the villa site, I'm on the phone to my friend at Reuters,' Jack said. 'Maria should now have a disk full of images of everything we've seen here, and those can be e-mailed straight through. But we keep quiet until then. Leak any of this now, to the superintendency people, and we'll never see the contents of this room again. You need to play the danger card, Maurice, big time. We found nothing of much interest, spent our time examining some masonry fragments sticking out of the wall. Far too dangerous for anyone to come beyond that grille again. Tell them their drill destabilized the tunnel even more, and there was a collapse. But by tomorrow morning, when these images are out, splashed across the headlines and TV news everywhere, they'll have no choice but to open up this place. It'll be one of the most sensational finds ever made in archaeology. And by the way, Maurice, and Maria. Many congratulations.'

'Not just yet, Jack.' Hiebermeyer murmured, making his way past the scrolls on the floor towards the extractor fan. 'I've spent too long dealing with these people now to be so optimistic. Let's stall the champagne until this place is more than just a figment of our imagination.'

'Jack, there's an open scroll here.' Costas was standing beside the shelves, peering into the recess behind the marble jars.

'There are scrolls everywhere,' Jack said. 'This place is an Aladdin's cave. We'll just have to leave it.'

'You said you wanted to see Claudius' handwriting. I'm not sure, but this one looks like it might be in two different hands, one of them a little spidery. Looks like someone's jotted notes in the margin.'

'Probably mad old Philodemus,' Hiebermeyer said.

'I doubt it. I think Claudius was having Philodemus cleared out,' Jack said. 'I think he was making room on the shelves for his own stuff.' He walked over to Costas, who moved aside, and peered where he was pointing. The scroll was open, the two ends partly rolled back, with a few inches of writing visible in between. The scroll looked identical to those in the basket by the door, the volumes of Pliny's *Natural History*, with the distinctive rounded finials on the handles. Someone must have been consulting it, then put it down opened at a page. The woman's voice came up the tunnel again, shouting, insistent. 'Dr Hiebermeyer! Jack! Please. Now!' Jack looked up, suddenly distracted at hearing his name spoken by a voice from a past that had never been resolved, as if she were calling to him in a dream. For a second he felt an overwhelming need to leave everything and go back out of the tunnel, to find out what had gone wrong. Maria and Hiebermeyer were already out of the chamber, taking the extractor fan with them. Jack shook his head, looked at Costas and then back at the scroll, forced himself to concentrate for a moment longer, to read the words of the ancient script.

He froze.

He looked again. Two words. *Two words that could change history*. His mind was racing, his heart thumping.

Then, for the first time in his life, Jack did the unthinkable. He lifted the scroll, carefully rolled the two wound ends together, and slid it into his khaki bag. He flipped over the cover of the bag and buckled the straps. Costas watched him in silence.

'You know why I'm doing this,' Jack said quietly.

'I'm good with it,' Costas replied.

Jack turned to follow Hiebermeyer and Maria. 'Right. Time to face the inquisition.'

★

Fifteen minutes later Jack stood with Costas and Maria in the open air outside the archaeological site, waiting for the guard to unlock the door that led back out into the alleyway through the modern town of Ercolano. They had been hit by the heat as they left the tunnel, but the blinding sunlight of their arrival on the site had given way to a lowering grey sky, with dark clouds forming over Vesuvius and blanketing the bay behind them. They had doffed their safety helmets outside the tunnel and made their way past the workmen and the guards in the main trench, leaving Hiebermeyer to make his report to Elizabeth and a male inspector who had been waiting beside the tunnel entrance, impatient to close up the site. The Egyptian statue of Anubis had already been drilled out of the volcanic rock and stood partly crated outside the entrance, a cluster of tungsten lamps to one side ready for the impending media event. A concrete-mixer had already been drawn up next to the tunnel entrance, and workmen were laying wooden formers ready to fill and block up the tunnel for good. Everything seemed to be happening exactly as Hiebermeyer had predicted.

The guard who had jostled Costas on their way into the site was ambling across the small courtyard towards them again, smoking, his sub-machine gun slung over his back. He came directly towards Costas, flicked away his cigarette and made an upwards gesture with both hands. Jack realized that he was planning to frisk him. Jack looked at Costas, then back at the guard, then at Costas again. This was not going to work. They had less to lose now that they had done what they came for, but the last thing Jack wanted was an incident that would lead to full body searches. He put his hand on his precious bag and tried to catch Costas' attention, but Costas' eyes were glued on the guard, expressionless, and Jack could see his hands slowly clenching and unclenching.

At that moment there was a clatter behind them and Hiebermeyer entered the courtyard, followed by Elizabeth and the male inspector. Elizabeth snapped at the guard in Italian and he sneered at her, standing his ground. The man with Elizabeth then said something and the guard backed off a few steps, passing over a bunch of keys. The man went straight to the door and unlocked it, ushering them out. Maria and Costas ducked through. Jack was about to follow, then looked at Elizabeth, catching her eye for the first time. She looked back at him, imploring, and suddenly reached out and grasped his arm, drawing him into the shadows, past the slit-eyed gaze of the guard. For a fleeting moment Jack was back where he had been all those years before, held by those dark eyes that still had the same allure, but in a face more worn and anguished than the passage of time could explain. He barely registered what she whispered to him, a few tense sentences, before she pushed him forcibly away and left quickly the way she had come, back round the corner towards the excavation trench, disappearing out of sight.

Jack was rooted to the spot, and then heard Costas calling him through the doorway. He stumbled past the guard who was now talking intently on a cell phone, his eyes following

Jack, and past the inspector who nodded at him, and then through the entrance into the rubbish-strewn alley. The door clanged shut behind him and he heard the padlock being engaged. He looked up towards the dark cone of Vesuvius looming over the rooftops at the end of the alley, and began following the other three. He clutched his bag, feeling the shape inside, and felt his heart begin to pound. There was no turning back now.

10

The man in the black cassock swept past the *baldacchino* and towards the pier of St Andrew, making the sign of the cross towards the high altar as he passed. He was tall, late middle aged, with fine, aquiline features and scholarly glasses, but with the sinewy toughness of a Jesuit who had spent years in the field. He nodded curtly at the Swiss Guard who stood at the low entranceway into the pier, then glanced back at the *baldacchino*. The great black pillars had been cast by Bernini from bronze taken from the Pantheon, the pagan temple to all the gods, here transformed into baroque splendour and captured beneath the dome of the greatest church in Christendom. To the man this place always made the ancient Roman sense of mastery over nature seem puny, insignificant, just as it made the people appear puny who stood beneath it today. It was a place where all could know the ascendancy of the Holy See, over a congregation far larger than ever could have been imagined by the Roman emperors at the time of Christ.

He sniffed, then wrinkled his nose slightly. The air seemed heavy with the exhalation of thousands of pilgrims and tourists who had passed through that day, as they did every day. They were the power of the Church, yet the man found the base reality of the common people distasteful and always relished passing beyond, into the sanctuaries of the ordained. He reminded himself why he was here, this evening. He recovered his stride and made his way purposefully down the steps into the grotto under the nave, to the level of the Roman hillside where there had once been a hippodrome of Caligula and Nero and a city of the dead, a necropolis, dug into the rock. Now it was the burial ground of popes, and the revered resting place of St Peter. The man made the sign again as he passed that holy spot, then weaved his way through the surviving foundation stones of Constantine the Great's basilica to another door and another flight of steps, leading down into the depths of the ancient necropolis. The door had been opened for him, but as he passed through he took out a key from under his cassock, and with his other hand flicked on a small torch. At the bottom of the stairs the beam danced over rough stone walls lined with niches and shadowy recesses. He bent to pass down a low passageway to the right, descended a flight of rock-cut steps into an empty tomb and felt along the wall, quickly finding what he was looking for. He slid the key into the hole and a concealed door gave way, opening inwards. He ducked through, then turned and locked the door again. He was inside.

He still remembered the thrill when he had first crouched at this spot. It was during the excavation of the necropolis, when all attention was focused on the tomb of St Peter. He and another young initiate had discovered this passageway, an early Christian catacomb sealed off since antiquity. It was better preserved than the rest of the necropolis, with the niches still plastered over and the burials intact. They had gone inside, just the two of them. Then they had made their extraordinary discovery. Only a few had ever been told of it: the pontiff, the head of the college of cardinals, the man who held the position he now held, the other members of the *concilium*. It was one of the greatest secrets of the Holy See, ammunition for the day when the forces of darkness might reach the holy gates, when the Church might need to rally all its reserves to fight for its very existence.

He made his way towards a flickering pool of light at the end of the passageway. Along the way he passed the images they had seen that first day, simple, crude expressions of early faith that still moved him powerfully, more visceral than any of the embellishments in the church above. Christ in a boat, casting a net, a woman seated beside him. Christ on fire, rising with his two crucified companions above the flames, a burning mountain in the background. And names everywhere, on the tomb niches, names made from simple mosaics pressed into the plaster. *Priscilla in Pace. Zakariah in Pace.* Chi-rho symbols, incised images of baskets of bread, a dove holding an olive branch. Images that became more frequent as he drew closer to the source of light, as if people had been yearning to be interred near that spot, crowding in on it. And then he was there. The passageway widened slightly, and he could see that the light ahead came from candles on each corner of a plinth set in the floor, a tomb. It was a simple structure, raised a few inches on plaster, and was covered with large Roman roof tiles. He could see the name scratched on the surface. He made the sign again, and whispered the words that had long been suspected, but that only he and a few others knew to be true. *The Basilica of St Peter and St Paul.*

Two others were already there, cassocked figures seated in low rock-cut niches on either side of the tomb, their faces obscured in shadow. The man made the sign again. '*In nomine patris et filii et spiritus sancti*,' he said. He bowed slightly to each in turn. 'Eminences.'

'Monsignor. Please be seated.' The words were in Italian. 'The *concilium* is complete.'

The catacomb was damp, keeping the dust down, but the wreathing smoke from the candles made his eyes smart, and he blinked hard. 'I came as soon as I received your summons, Eminence.'

'You know why we are here?'

'The *concilium* only meets when the sanctity of the Holy See is threatened.'

'For almost two thousand years it has been so,' the other

said. 'From the time of the coming of St Paul to the brethren, when the *concilium* first met in the Phlegraean Fields. We are soldiers of our Lord, and we do his bidding. *Dies irae, dies illa, solvet saeclum in favilla.*'

'Amen.'

'We accept only the true word of the Messiah, no other.'

'Amen.'

'We have met once already this year. We have thwarted the search for the lost Jewish treasures of the Temple. But now a greater darkness threatens us, a heresy that would seek to destroy the true Church itself. The heresy of those who would deny the sanctity of the ordained, who would seek to poison the ministry of St Paul, who believe that the word of our Lord lies elsewhere, outside the Gospels. For almost two thousand years we have fought it, with all our power and all our guile. Now the heresy has arisen again. That which we had hoped destroyed, lost for ever, has been found. A blasphemy, a lie, ammunition of the Devil.'

'What would the *concilium* have us do?'

The voice when it replied was steely, icy cold, a voice that brooked no debate, that sought no reply.

'*Seek it.*'

The sky was streaked with gold as Jack brought the Lynx helicopter down towards the landing lights on *Seaquest II*'s stern. Maria was in the co-pilot's seat and Costas was stretched out in the rear, snoring heavily. They had waved Hiebermeyer off at the helipad near Herculaneum, just as it began to rain, a heavy, pelting downpour that took Jack's full attention as they lifted off. He had been quiet for the rest of the flight, preoccupied with his own thoughts after his encounter with Elizabeth and then focused on an e-mail exchange on the helicopter's computer. It had taken less than an hour to fly south from the Bay of Naples, skirting the dark mass of the Calabrian mountains and then veering offshore to the ship's position some ten nautical miles north of the Strait of Messina. The evening had become startlingly clear, almost pellucid, the air cleansed and the sea ruffled by the dying breeze from the west, but as the rotor churned up propwash on either side of the ship it was as if they were descending through a vortex of water, the landing lights illuminating the spray like a twister swirling off the stern.

The Lynx thumped to a halt and Jack waited for the rotors to stop before unbuckling himself and opening the door, giving a thumbs-up to the crew chief who was lashing the pontoons to the deck. He took off his helmet, waited as Costas and Maria did the same and then got out and led them straight into a hatchway at the forward end of the helipad. Moments later they were in the ship's main conservation lab, the door shut behind them. Jack chose a workstation with a computer console on one side and a light table on the other, then activated a fluorescent bulb on a retractable metal arm above the table and sat down. He pulled out a two-way radio from his flight overalls and pressed the key for the secure IMU channel. There was a crackle and he spoke into the receiver. 'Maurice, this is Jack. We're on *Seaquest*, safe and sound. I'll update you on any progress. Over.' He waited for an affirmative, then placed the radio beside the monitor and slipped the strap of his old khaki bag over his head, placing the bag on his lap and pulling on a pair of plastic gloves from a dispenser under the table.

'Do you think he can hold the fort?' Costas said.

'Maurice? He's a professional. He knows how to play the authorities. He knows exactly how to shut down an excavation. All he has to do is say that the tunnel's unsafe, in danger of collapse, and they'll board it up. The super-intendency didn't want any new excavation in the villa anyway. And they've got the ancient statue of Anubis to feed the press, more than enough to satisfy the public that the archaeology's being done. We're sticking with my revised plan. Reuters will get told, but not about the library, not yet. As soon as we've seen through wherever this is leading us, I'll make a call which will expose the whole thing. Maria took hundreds of digital pictures, and they're all here. They look like those first views of King Tut's tomb. Absolutely sensational, front-page stuff. The authorities will have no choice but to open up the site properly, for the world to see what we've seen.'

'I'll be back there with Maurice as soon as we've finished here,' Maria said.

'That's crucial, Maria. You can keep his blood pressure down. You obviously make a great team.' He grinned at her, then opened his bag. 'Now let's see what we've got.'

Seconds later the extraordinary find Jack had taken from the villa chamber at Herculaneum lay in front of them on the light table. It looked much as Costas and Jack had first seen it, with each side of the scroll wound round a wooden stick, an *umbilicus*, and lines of ancient writing visible where the scroll was open in between. Jack attached small foam pads with retractor wires to the ends of each umbilicus and carefully drew the scroll wider apart, each wire attached to the edge of the light table and secured with ratchets. Now they could see the entire column of text, similar to the page of a modern book. 'This is how the Greeks and Romans read them, from side to side, unrolling the scroll to reveal each page, like this,' Maria said. 'People often think scrolls were awkward, because they assume they were written as continuous text from one end to the other, unrolled a bit at a time. In fact, they were almost as convenient as a codex, a modern book.'

'We're incredibly lucky we can see any of this at all,' Jack murmured. 'The carbonized scrolls found in the villa in the eighteenth century took years to unravel, millimetre by millimetre. But everything we saw in that room was incredibly well preserved, having missed the firestorm in AD 79. There seems to be some kind of resin or wax in the papyrus which means it's still supple.'

'This looks like two paragraphs in one hand, with a section in the middle in a completely different hand,' Costas said.

Maria nodded. 'The main text is like the printed page, the practised hand of a copyist, a scribe. The other writing is a little sprawling, more like personal handwriting, legible but certainly not a copyist's hand.'

'What are those blotches?'

'At first I thought they might be blood, but then I sniffed them,' Jack said. 'It's what I saw all over that table in the chamber. They're wine stains.'

'Let's hope it was a good vintage on that final night,' Maria murmured.

Costas pointed at a slip of papyrus attached to the top of the scroll, like a label. 'So that's the title?'

'The *sillybos*,' Jack said, nodding. '*Plinius, Naturalis Historia.* This scroll must have been taken out from the batch in the basket by the door, undoubtedly one of the volumes of completed text. I can still hardly believe it. Nothing like this has survived anywhere else from antiquity, a first edition by one of the most famous writers of the classical period.'

'I can see that,' Costas murmured. 'But why are we being so secretive about this?'

'Okay.' Jack pointed to the upper line in the scroll. 'The first clue for me was that word, *Iudaea*. Pliny the Elder mentions Judaea in several places in the *Natural History*. He tells us about the origin and cultivation of the balsam tree, and about a river that dries up every Sabbath. Typical Pliny, a mix of authoritative natural history and fable. But the main discussion of Judaea is in his geographical chapter, where he tells us everything else he thinks worth knowing about the place. That's what we've got here.' Jack opened his modern copy of Pliny's *Natural History* at a bookmarked page, and pressed it down. They could see the Latin on the left-hand side, the English translation on the right. He read out the first line on the page: ' *"Supra Idumaeam et Samariam Iudaea longe lateque funditur. Pars eius Syriae iuncta Galilaea vocatur."* '

He peered back at the scroll, then at the printed text, reading it again under his breath. 'It's identical. Those medieval monks who transcribed this got it right after all.' He read out the translation. '"Beyond Idumaea and Samaria stretches the wide expanse of Judaea. The part of Judaea adjoining Syria is called Galilee."' He then began to work his way down the text, his eyes darting from the translation to the scroll and back again, pausing occasionally where the lack of punctuation in the scroll made it difficult to follow. 'Pliny was fascinated by the Dead Sea,' he murmured. 'Here, he tells us how nothing at all can sink in it, how even the bodies of bulls and camels float along. He loved this kind of stuff. That's the trouble. He was right about the high salinity of the Dead Sea, but there were other wonders he wrote about that were completely fabulous, and he wasn't great at distinguishing fact from fiction. If he had any kind of guiding principle, it was to include everything he heard. He was almost entirely reliant on second-hand sources.'

'At least with Claudius he would have had a reliable inform-ant,' Maria said. 'A pretty sound scholar, by all accounts.'

'Here we go,' Jack said. 'This is just before the gap in the scroll text, before the writing style changes. ' *"Iordanes amnis oritur e fonte Paniade.* The source of the river Jordan is the spring of Panias." Then there's a longer description: "*In lacum se fundit quem plures Genesaram vocant, xvi p. longitudinis, vi latitudinis, amoenis circumsaeptum oppidis, ab oriente Iuliade et*

Hippo, a meridie Tarichea, quo nomine aliqui et lacum appellant, ab occidente Tiberiade aquis calidis salubri. It widens out into a lake usually called the Sea of Gennesareth, 16 miles long and 6 broad, skirted by the agreeable towns of Iulias and Hippo on the east, Tarichae on the south, the name of which place some people also give to the lake, and Tiberias with its salubrious hot springs on the west." '

Jack pointed at a map he had laid on the other side of the light table. 'This time he's not writing about the Dead Sea but the Sea of Galilee, some eighty miles north at the head of the Jordan Valley. Gennesareth was the Roman name for it, the same as the modern Hebrew name Kinnereth. Tiberias is the main town today on the Sea of Galilee, a popular resort. Tarichae he got wrong, it's not south but west, a few miles north of Tiberias. Tarichae was the Roman name for Migdal, home of Mary Magdalene.'

'The place where the Gospels say Jesus began his ministry,' Maria said.

Jack nodded. 'Along the western shore of the Sea of Galilee.' He paused, and sat back. 'Now we come to the gap in the scroll text. This is where it gets really intriguing. There's no gap at all in the modern printed text, based on the medieval transcription, which goes straight on to a discussion of bitumen and the Dead Sea.'

'So our scroll must be a later version, the basis for a new edition that was never published,' Costas murmured. 'Maybe it was one he was working on when he died, with updates and changes.'

'He may have asked his scribe to do him a working copy, leaving gaps where he thought he was likely to make additions,' Maria said. 'And that could be the copy he brought with him to Claudius.'

'Writing the *Natural History* must have been an organic process, and it's hard to believe a magpie mind like Pliny's would ever have been able to leave it alone,' Jack said. 'And remember, more places were being conquered and explored by the Romans every year, so there was always plenty to add. Claudius would have been able to tell him much that was new about Britain, especially as we now know that Britain was foremost in Claudius' mind at the time of the eruption of Vesuvius, with his own history of Britannia in progress. And if Pliny had survived Vesuvius, my guess is we'd have had a whole new chapter on vulcanology.'

'Can you read what's in the gap?' Costas said.

'I can, just,' Jack said. 'It's in a completely different hand to the main text in the scroll – spidery, precise. I've no doubt this is the actual hand of Pliny the Elder.' As he said the words Jack suddenly felt himself transported back to that hidden room in the villa almost two thousand years ago, beneath the lowering volcano, the ink still freshly blotted and the wine stains still reeking of grapes and alcohol, as if the figures on either side of him were not Maria and Costas but Pliny the Elder and Claudius, urging him to join them in exploring the revelations of their world.

'Well, fire away,' Costas said, peering at him quizzically.

Jack snapped back and leaned over the text. 'Okay. Here

goes. This is where those words appear, the ones I saw when we found this scroll in the villa. The reason for all this secrecy.' He glanced at Costas, then paused, scanning the text to pinpoint the beginning and end of the sentences and to put the Latin into coherent English word order. 'Here's the first sentence: "Claudius Caesar visited this place with Herod Agrippa, where they met the fisherman Joshua of Nazareth, he whom the Greeks called Jesus, who my sailors in Misenum now call the Christos."'

Jack felt as if he had delivered a thunderbolt. There was a stunned silence, broken by Costas. 'Claudius Caesar? Claudius the emperor? You mean our Claudius? He met Jesus Christ?'

'With Herod Agrippa,' Maria whispered. 'Herod Agrippa, King of the Jews?'

'So it would appear,' Jack replied hoarsely, trying to keep his voice under control. 'Herod Agrippa, grandson of Herod the Great. And there's more.' He read slowly: '"The Nazarene gave Claudius his written word."'

'His written word,' Costas repeated slowly. 'A pledge, some kind of promise?'

'I've translated it literally,' Jack said. 'It's more than that. I'm sure it means he gave him something written.'

'His word,' Maria murmured. 'His gospel.'

'The gospel of Jesus? The written word of Christ?' Costas suddenly sat back, his jaw dropping in amazement. 'Holy Mother of God. I see what you mean. The secrecy at Herculaneum. The Church. This is exactly what they have most feared.'

'And yet it is something that many have hoped against hope would one day be found,' Maria said, almost whispering. 'The written word of Jesus of Nazareth, in his own hand.'

'Does Pliny say what happened to it?' Costas asked.

Jack finished sorting out the next sentences in his mind, and read out his translation: ' "Gennesareth, that is Kinnereth in the local language, is said to derive from the word for the stringed instrument or lyre, kinnor, or from the kinnara, the sweet and edible fruit produced by a thorn tree that grows in the vicinity. And at Tiberias, there are springs that are remarkably health-restoring. Claudius Caesar says that to drink the waters is to clear and calm the mind, which sounds to me like ingesting the morpheum." '

'Ha!' Costas exclaimed. 'Morpheum. I want Hiebermeyer to see that.'

Jack paused, and muttered under his breath, 'Come on, Pliny. Get on with it.' He read what came next to himself, grunted impatiently and then repeated it out loud. ' "And the Sea of Gennesareth, really a lake, lies far below the level of the Middle Sea, the Mediterranean. And whereas the Sea of Gennesareth is fresh water, my friend Claudius reminds me that the Dead Sea is remarkably briny, and part of it is not water but bitumen." '

'My friend Claudius,' Costas repeated, weighing the words. 'That's a bit of a slip, isn't it? I mean, I thought Claudius' survival was meant to be a secret.'

'That proves it,' Jack said. 'I think this particular scroll was Pliny's own annotated version, one that he eventually intended to take away with him. It got left in Claudius' study, probably deliberately. And I think some of this addition was for Claudius' benefit, too. You have to imagine Claudius sitting beside Pliny as he's writing this, sipping and spilling his wine, keenly reading over the other man's shoulder. Of course, as we know from the published text, Pliny was already perfectly well aware that the Dead Sea was briny and produced bitumen.'

'He was flattering Claudius,' Maria said.

'Classic interrogation technique,' Costas said. 'Never let on what you already know, then people will tell you more.'

'Is there anything else?' Maria said. 'I mean, about Jesus? Pliny seems to have lost himself in a digression.'

'There may be,' Jack said. 'But there's a problem.'

'What?'

'Look at this.' Jack pointed at the bottom of the gap in the scroll text, then at the right-hand margin. 'I've read everything I can make out in the gap. But you can see at the bottom that a few lines have been smudged, wiped out. Then he's written something in the margin beside it, much smaller. He hasn't replenished his ink, maybe even deliberately, so it's barely legible. It's almost as if he wrote at the bottom of the gap something he wanted in the published edition, then thought better of it and erased it, then thought again and put a note in the margin, perhaps a note to himself that he didn't want anyone else to read.'

'But you can read it,' Costas said.

'Not exactly.' Jack swivelled the light table until the scroll was at ninety degrees, then pulled a magnifying glass on a retractable arm over the miniature lines of writing just visible in the margin. He pushed his chair back so Maria and Costas could take a look. 'Tell me what you think.'

They both craned over, and Costas spoke immediately. 'It's not Latin, is it? Is that what you mean? But some of those letters look familiar to me. There's a lambda, a delta. It's ancient Greek?'

'Greek letters, but not Greek language,' Maria murmured. 'It looks like the precursor Greek alphabet, the one they adopted from the near east.' She glanced back at Jack. 'Do you remember Professor Dillen's course at Cambridge on the early history of Greek language? It's a while ago now, but I'm sure I recognize some of those letters. Is this Semitic?'

'You were the star linguist, Maria, not me,' Jack said. 'He'd have been proud of you for remembering. In fact, he already sends his congratulations for the discovery, as we e-mailed from the Lynx when we flew in. When I took this scroll from the shelf in Herculaneum I caught a glimpse of this writing, and I had a sudden hunch. I asked Professor Dillen to provide his latest version of the Hanno Project for us to download. It should be online now.'

'Jack!' Costas said. 'Computers? All by yourself?'

Jack gestured at the keyboard beside them. 'Don't worry. It's all yours.'

'The Hanno Project?' Maria said.

'Two years ago, we excavated an ancient shipwreck off Cornwall, not far from the IMU campus. Costas, you remember Mount's Bay?'

'Huh? Yeah. Cold. But great fish and chips in Newlyn.' Costas had sat down at the computer, and was busily tapping. He turned and glanced at Jack. 'I take it you want a scan?'

Jack nodded, and Costas pushed away the magnifier and positioned a movable scanner arm over the margin of the scroll. Jack turned to Maria. 'It was a Phoenician shipwreck, the first ever found in British waters, dating almost a thousand years before the Romans arrived. We found British tin ingots stamped with Phoenician letters, and a mysterious metal plaque covered in Phoenician writing. Dillen's been working on it ever since. We called the translation project Hanno after a famous Carthaginian explorer. We don't know it was him. Just a name pulled out of a hat.'

'So you think our scroll writing is Phoenician.'

'I know it is.'

'So Pliny read Phoenician?'

'Phoenician was similar to the Aramaic spoken around the Sea of Galilee at the time of Jesus, but that may just be a coincidence. No, I think this has to do with Claudius. You remember those scrolls on the bottom shelf of the room in Herculaneum? Claudius' *History of Carthage*? It was his biggest historical work, one thought completely lost but now miraculously discovered. Well, Claudius would have learned the language in order to read the original sources, the language spoken by the Phoenician traders who founded Carthage. It was virtually a dead language by the time of imperial Rome, and it's just the kind of thing I can imagine Claudius teaching Pliny in their off-time together after finishing their writing, over wine and dice. So when Pliny comes to make this note, he chooses a language that was virtually a code between them. Claudius is watching, and he would have been pleased and flattered by that too.'

'They must have been the only people around who could read this.'

'That's the point.'

'It's ready,' Costas said, hunched over the screen. 'There are four words the concordance has identified as transliterations, that is proper nouns, and it's rendered them first into Latin and then into English. One word is Claudius. The other's Rome. All the other words are in Dillen's Phoenician lexicon. There's one I even know. *Bos*, bull or cow. I remember that from the Bosporus.'

Jack's heart was pounding with excitement. *This could be it.*

'It's appearing on screen now.'

Maria and Jack came up behind Costas. At the top of the scan they could see that the script had been enhanced, with the Greek-style letters more clearly visible. Below it was the translation:

Haec implacivit Claudius Caesar in urbem sub duo sacra bos iacet.

That which Claudius Caesar has entrusted to me lies in Rome beneath the two sacred cows.

Jack stared again. His mind was racing. Only one day after finding the shipwreck of St Paul, they had stumbled on something extraordinary, perhaps the biggest prize of them all. And now he knew he had been right to take the scroll away, to keep it hidden until they had followed the trail to the end.

The word of Jesus. The final word, the word that would eclipse all others. *The last gospel.*

'Well?' Maria said, looking up at him. 'Sacred cows?'

'I think I know where that is.'

'Game on,' Costas said.

11

The next morning Jack and Costas stood beside the Via del Fori Imperiali in the heart of ancient Rome. They had flown the Lynx helicopter from *Seaquest II* to Rome's Fiumicino airport, on the site of the great harbour built by the emperor Claudius, and had taken the train along the course of the river Tiber into the city. Despite the heat, Jack had insisted that they leave the train at Ostiense station and walk through the ancient city walls and over the Aventine Hill, and then down past the Circus Maximus towards the Colosseum and the Roman Forum. As they neared their destination, the assurance and solidity of the modern city gave way to the fractured landscape of antiquity, desolate and empty in places, in others resplendent with structures more awesome than anything built since. It was as if those ruins and the shades of monuments long gone had the power to repel any attempt to better them, an aura which preserved the heart of ancient Rome from being submerged by history. Jack knew that the impression was partly an illusion, as much of the area of the imperial fora had been cleared of medieval buildings in the 1930s under the orders of Mussolini, but even so the Palatine Hill with the remains of the palaces of the emperors remained much as it had been since the end of antiquity, ruinous and overgrown in the many places where archaeologists had still done little more than scrape the surface.

Jack had been talking intently in Italian on his cell phone, and now snapped it shut. A van carrying their gear would rendezvous with them in two hours' time at the foot of the Palatine Hill. He nodded at Costas, and they joined a small throng of tourists lining up behind the ticket desk outside the site of the old forum.

'Doesn't seem right,' Costas grumbled, wiping the sweat from his face and swigging some water. 'I mean, a celebrity archaeologist and his sidekick. They should be paying you.'

Jack pushed his cell phone into his khaki bag and pulled out a Nikon D80 camera, slinging it round his neck. 'I often find it's best to be anonymous at archaeological sites. You're less likely to be watched. Anyway, I'd never convince them with you looking like that.' Jack was dressed in desert boots, chinos and a loose shirt, but Costas wore a garish Hawaiian outfit, complete with a straw hat and his beloved new designer sunglasses.

'They must be used to it,' Costas said. 'Archaeologists' dress sense, I mean. Look at Hiebermeyer.'

Jack grinned, paid for the tickets and steered Costas into the archaeological site, down a ramp and towards the ruin of a small circular building, with fragmentary columns still standing. 'The Temple of Vesta,' he said. 'Shrine, really, as it was never formally consecrated as a temple, for some reason. Where the sacred fire was guarded by the Vestal Virgins. They lived next door, in that big structure nestled into the foot of the Palatine, a bit like a nunnery.'

'A pretty extravagant nunnery,' Costas murmured. 'So all that stuff's really true? About the Vestal Virgins?'

Jack nodded. 'Even the stuff about being buried alive. There's no more sober witness than our friend the younger Pliny, who wrote the famous letters about the eruption of Vesuvius. In another letter he described how the emperor Domitian ordered the chief Vestal Virgin to be buried alive, for violating her vows of chastity. Domitian was a nasty piece of goods at the best of times, and the charge was concocted. But being walled up underground was the traditional punishment for straying Vestals, and she was taken to the appointed place and immured alive.'

'Sounds like a male domination thing, gone badly wrong.'

'Probably right. After the first emperor Augustus became Pontifex Maximus, the supreme priest, the emperor and the chief Vestal were on a collision course. The goddess Vesta was very powerful, guardian of the hearth. The eternal fire, the *ignis inextinctus*, symbolized the eternity of the state, and the future of Rome was therefore in the hands of the Virgins. They called her *Vesta Mater*, Vesta the Mother. She was like the Sibyl.'

'In what way?'

'Well, some of the similarities are pretty remarkable. Vesta was probably an amalgam of an ancient local deity of Italian origin with a Greek import, supposedly brought by Aeneas from Troy. The Sibyl at Cumae has the same kind of history. And the Vestals were chosen as girls from among the aristocracy of Rome, just as I believe the Cumaean Sibyls were. We might find out more here. Come on.'

Jack led Costas up the Sacred Way past the Arch of Titus, where they paused and looked silently up at the sculpture of the Roman soldiers in triumphal procession, carrying the Jewish menorah. They then carried on up the Palatine Hill into the Farnese Gardens, and then to the vast ruins of the imperial palace on the west side of the hill overlooking the Circus Maximus. They were met by a refreshing breeze as they came over the top, but even so the heat was searing and Jack led them to a shaded spot beside a wall.

'So this was Claudius' stomping ground,' Costas said, taking off his sunglasses and wiping the sweat from his face. 'Before he did his Bilbo Baggins disappearing act. It seems a far cry from that monk's cell in Herculaneum.'

'This was where he grew up, then where he spent most of his time as emperor apart from his visit to Britain,' Jack replied. 'But the image we have of this place at that time, the Hollywood image, you can forget a lot of that. Our view of the past is so often conditioned by later accretions, anachronisms. The Colosseum wasn't built yet, was only inaugurated in AD 80, the year after Vesuvius erupted. The imperial palace, the huge sprawl in front of us, was only begun a few years after that by Domitian, the emperor who had the showdown with the Vestals. That was when megalomania really took hold, when the emperors really did begin living like gods. But for Claudius, like his grandfather Augustus, it was crucial to maintain the pretence of the republic, the idea that they were simply caretakers. They lived in a modest house, actually smaller than the Villa of the Papyri at Herculaneum.'

'Where was it?'

'You're leaning against it now.'

'Ah.' Costas put his hand against the worn brick facing. 'So Claudius was here,' he murmured.

'And Pliny the Elder, in AD 79,' Jack said.

'I was wondering when you were coming to that.'

'Right here we're smack in between the House of Augustus and Domitian's palace, and the building in front of us is the Temple of Apollo,' Jack said. 'Hardly anything's left of the temple now, but you have to imagine an awesome structure in white marble. It was embellished with some of the most famous sculptures of classical Greece, taken by the Romans when they conquered the east. Right where we're sitting now was the portico, a colonnaded structure that surrounded the temple. Augustus had an enclave constructed within the portico next to his house, and it contained a library, apparently large enough to hold Senate meetings. The enclave may have had particular administrative functions, including a Rome office for the fleet admirals.'

'Got you,' Costas said. 'Pliny the Elder. Admiral at Misenum.'

Jack nodded. 'Pliny would have known this place well. Augustus also built a new shrine to Vesta at this spot, probably meant to supplant the one in the forum.'

'Right under his bedroom window,' Costas said. 'Talk about control.'

'The Vestal Virgins seem to have resisted the idea of moving their sacred shrine, and continued to patronize the old one. And here's the really fascinating thing, the reason we're here. The shrine to Vesta in the forum contained an *adytum*, an inner sanctum, a hidden place where various sacred items were stored. Its contents were pretty mystical, sacred objects to do with the foundation of Rome. The *fascinum*, the erect phallus that averted evil, the *pignora imperii*, mysterious pledges for the eternal duration of Rome, the *palladium*, a statue of the goddess Pallas Athena supposedly brought by Aeneas from Troy. Only the Vestals and the Pontifex Maximus were ever allowed in, and these items were never shown in public.'

'A secret chamber,' Costas mused. 'So if Augustus was planning this new shrine as a replica of the old, he would have had a chamber built into this one too?'

'My thinking exactly.'

'But if the sacred items remained in the forum shrine, this new one would have been empty.'

'Or not quite empty.'

'Are you saying what I think you're saying?'

Jack opened his bag and pulled out a clipboard with a blown-up photograph of a Roman coin on the front. 'This is the only known depiction of the new shrine, the Palatine Shrine of Vesta. It's from a coin of the emperor Tiberius, of AD 22 or 23. You can see a circular colonnaded building very similar to the old shrine in the forum, clearly emulating it. The circular shape was meant to copy the hut form of the earliest Roman dwelling, the so-called House of Romulus, which was carefully preserved as a sacred antiquity on the other side of the House of Augustus. You can still see the postholes in the rock. What else can you see on that coin?'

Costas took the clipboard. 'Well, the letters S and C above the shrine. *Senatus Consultum*. Even I know that. And the shrine's got a column on either side, a plinth with a statue on it. They're animals, possibly horses.' He paused, then spoke excitedly. 'I've got you. Not horses. *Bulls*.'

'That's what clinches it,' Jack said excitedly. 'We know from the ancient sources that two statues stood in front of the Palatine Shrine of Vesta. Statues of sacrificial animals, sacred to the rites of the Vestals. Both statues were originally Greek, by the famous sculptor Myron of the fifth century BC. Statues of cows.'

'Of course.'

'Remember our clue,' Jack enthused. '*Subduo sacra bos*. Beneath the sacred cows. These two statues were a unique pair. There was nothing else like them in Rome. This can only be what Pliny meant. He hid the scroll here, in the empty chamber under the Palatine Shrine of Vesta.'

'Where exactly?' Costas had taken out a GPS receiver and was looking round, eyeing the featureless ground and dusty walls dubiously.

'My best guess is where we are now, give or take ten metres either way,' Jack said. 'All trace of the shrine is gone, but it seems clear that it would have been on this side of the temple portico, right beside Augustus' house.'

'Ground-penetrating radar?'

'Too much else going on here. The place is honeycombed, building built on building. Even the bedrock's full of cracks and fissures.'

'So what do we do now? Get a shovel?'

'We'll never find it that way. At least not without a lot of money, a lot of bureaucracy, and about a year for the permit to come through. No, we're not going to dig down.'

'So what can we do?'

'We might be able to go up.'

'Huh?'

Jack took back the clipboard, closed his bag and jumped to his feet. He checked his watch. 'I'll explain on the way. Come on.'

Twenty minutes later they stood on a terrace on the north side of the Roman Forum archaeological precinct, with a magnificent view of the heart of ancient Rome stretching out in front of them and the vast bulk of the Colosseum in the background. 'This is the best place to get a sense of the topography,' Jack said. 'At its height this was a huge conglomeration of buildings, temples, law courts, monuments, all crowding in on each other. Strip all that away and you can see how the forum was built in a valley, with the Palatine Hill on the west side. Now look to our right, below the north slope of the Palatine, and see how the valley sweeps round towards the river Tiber. Where we're standing now is the Capitoline Hill, the apex of ancient Rome, the place where the triumphal processions reached their climax. Just to the right of us is the Tarpeian Rock, where criminals were flung to their deaths over a precipice.'

'The miscreant Vestals?'

'Traditionally their place of execution is thought to have been outside the city walls, but Pliny the Younger only mentions an underground chamber. It could have been close by.'

'So tell me about underground Rome,' Costas said. 'Not that I want to go there. Three thousand years of accumulated sludge.'

Jack grinned, opened his bag and pulled out the clipboard again, folding back the sheet with the image of the coin to reveal a copy of an old engraving, the word *ROMA* in large letters at the top. The centre of the map showed topographical features, valleys, hills and watercourses, and around the edge were building plans. 'This is my favourite map of Rome,' he said. 'Drawn by Giovanni Battista Piranesi in the eighteenth century, about the same time that the Villa of the Papyri at

Herculaneum was first being explored. The fragmentary plans of buildings around the edge are drawings of chunks of the famous Marble Plan, a huge mural originally displayed in Vespasian's Temple of Peace. Only about ten per cent of the Marble Plan survives, in fragments like this.' To Jack, Piranesi's map was like a metaphor for knowledge of ancient Rome, like an incomplete jigsaw puzzle with some areas known in great detail, others hardly at all, even building layouts recorded exactly but their actual location lost to history.

'It shows the topography very clearly,' Costas said.

'That's why I love it,' Jack replied. 'Piranesi kept the pieces of the jigsaw to the edges, swept aside the buildings, and focused on the hills and valleys. That's what I wanted you to see.' He angled the map so it had the same orientation as the view in front of them, and traced his finger over the centre. 'In prehistoric times, when Aeneas supposedly arrived here, the forum area was a marshy valley on the edge of a flood plain. As the first settlements spread down the slopes of the hills into the wetland, the stream was canalized and eventually covered over. It became the Cloaca Maxima, the Great Drain, extending beyond where you can see the Colosseum now, then right under the forum, then sweeping round in front of us and flowing into the Tiber. There were tributaries, streams running into it, as well as artificial underground constructions, the channels of aqueducts. It's all still there, a vast underground labyrinth, and only a fraction of it has ever been explored.'

'Where's the nearest access point?'

'We're heading towards it now. Follow me.' Jack led Costas off the terrace and down into Via di San Teodoro, the ruins on the Palatine rearing up to the left and the buildings of the medieval city to the right. They veered right again into a narrow street which opened out into a V-shaped courtyard, with traffic thundering beyond. In the foreground was a massive squat ruin, a four-way arch with thick piers at each corner. 'The Arch of Janus,' Jack said. 'Not the most glorious of Rome's ruins, pretty well denuded of anything interesting. But it stands astride the Cloaca Maxima. The place where the drain disgorges into the river is only about two hundred metres away, beyond the main road.' They went through an opening in the iron railing surrounding the arch and walked under the bleached stone. On the forecourt on the other side a van was drawn up and two clusters of diving equipment were laid out on the cobbles, with two IMU technicians running checks on one of the closed-circuit rebreathers.

'This looks like a setup,' Costas grumbled.

'I thought I'd spring this on you now after giving you a sense of purpose. It's fantastically exciting, the chance to explore completely unknown sites in the heart of ancient Rome.'

'Jack, don't tell me we're going diving in a sewer.'

A man came towards them from where he had been squatting beside the arch. He had a wiry physique and fine Italian features, though he seemed unusually pale for a Roman. 'Massimo!' Jack said. '*Va bene?*'

'*Va bene.*' The voice sounded shaky, and close up the man looked slightly grey. 'You remember Costas?' Jack said. The two men nodded, and shook hands. 'It seems only yesterday that we met at that conference in London.'

'It was my greatest pleasure,' Massimo said in perfect English, only slightly accented. 'We work here under the auspices of the archaeological superintendency, but we're all amateurs. It was a privilege to spend time with professionals.'

'This time, the tables are turned,' Jack said, smiling. 'This will be my first venture into urban underwater archaeology.'

'It's the archaeology of the future, Jack,' Massimo said with passion. 'We come on ancient sites from below, leaving the surface intact. It's perfect in a place like Rome. It beats hanging on the shirttails of developers, waiting for a fleeting chance to find something in a building site before the bulldozers destroy it.'

'You're beginning to talk like a professional, Massimo.'

'It's a pleasure to help. We've been desperate to explore where you're planning to go. We've been waiting for the right diving equipment.'

'What do you call yourselves?' Costas said.

'Urban speleologists.'

'Tunnel rats,' Jack grinned.

'Be careful of that word, Jack,' Massimo said. 'Where you're about to go, it might come back to haunt you.'

'Ah. Point taken.' Jack gave a wry grin. 'You have a map?'

'It's inside the arch. Your people will bring over the equipment. Follow me.' Jack and Costas waved at the two

IMU technicians, and went towards a door in one of the stone piers. 'This leads up to a complex of small chambers and corridors inside the arch, used when it was converted into a medieval fortress,' Massimo said. 'What nobody knew was that the stairway extends below as well, into the Cloaca Maxima. We assumed there must have been an access point somewhere under the arch, and came looking for it a few months ago. The superintendency allowed us to remove the stones.' He pointed to a new-looking manhole cover about a metre and a half round on the floor just inside the door. 'But first, some orientation. The map.' He reached behind the door and pulled out a long cardboard tube, then extracted a rolled-up sheet and held it open against the side of the pier. 'This is a plan of everything we know about what's underground in this part of Rome, from the entrance into the Cloaca Maxima under the Colosseum to the river Tiber just beyond us here.'

'This is what I'm really interested in,' Jack said, using both hands to point to branches leading off the main line of the Cloaca Maxima, then drawing his hands together into the blank space in between.

'Absolutely. That's one of our most exciting finds,' Massimo said. 'We think those branches are either end of an artificial tunnel running right under the Palatine. We think it was built by the emperor Claudius.'

'Claudius?' Jack said, startled.

'He's our hero. A posthumous honorary tunnel rat. His biggest projects were underground, underwater. Digging the tunnel to drain the Fucine Lake. Building the great harbour at

Ostia. His aqueduct into Rome, the *Aqua Claudia*. We think a drainage tunnel under the Palatine would have been right up his street. And he was an historian, would have been fascinated by anything they came across, any vestiges of the earliest Romans, his ancestors. He might even have gone down there himself. One of us.'

'Small world,' Costas murmured.

'What do you mean?'

'Well,' he began, then Jack shot him a warning look. 'Well, Jack was just telling me about Claudius, the harbour, when we were flying into Fiumicino. Fascinating guy.'

'I think we can leave Claudius aside until we actually find something that identifies his involvement,' Jack said sternly. 'Remember, what we're after dates hundreds of years before Claudius' time. What we talked about on the phone, Massimo. The Lupercale cave.'

'The Lupercale,' Massimo repeated reverently, then looked furtively around. 'If you can find a way into that from underground, then we've made history.'

Costas peered enquiringly at Jack, who turned to him stony faced. 'My apologies, Costas. I was waiting till now to fill you in on what we're really after. I didn't want anyone over-hearing, any word leaking out,' he said forcibly, looking at Massimo. 'It's an amazing find. Archaeologists drilling into the ground below the House of Augustus on the Palatine broke through into an underground chamber, a cavity at least fifteen metres deep. They sent in a probe, and saw walls encrusted with mosaics and seashells, like a grotto. It could be the Lupercale, the sacred cave of Rome's ancestors, where the she-wolf nursed Romulus and Remus. A place revered in antiquity but lost to history. It could be one of the most sensational finds ever made in Roman archaeology. We're here to see if we can find an underground entrance. Massimo's even kept the superintendency in the dark. His team are worried about looters getting in, and want to explore the place fully before going public.'

'The Palatine's riddled with caves and fissures,' Massimo enthused. 'God only knows what else lies under there. The Lupercale cave could just be the tip.'

'You're sure this is the best entrance, here under the arch?' Jack asked.

'On the other side of the Palatine, the tunnel runs from the Cloaca Maxima somewhere near the *Atrium Vestae*, the House of the Vestal Virgins,' Massimo replied. 'We haven't got any further than that. This side is definitely your best bet. The branch going from here into the Palatine is on the line of the Velabrum, an ancient stream that was once part of another marshy area, canalized and arched over about 200 BC. We've explored as far as the edge of the Palatine, but then the tunnel drops down and becomes completely submerged. We're not cave divers, not yet. From our farthest point we think it's only about two hundred metres to the site of the Lupercale, and about thirty metres up.'

'What's the geology?' Costas said.

'Tufa, volcanic stone. Easily worked but strong, a good load-bearer. And you sometimes see calcite formations as well, even stalactites and stalagmites, where calcium-rich ground-water has dripped into the Roman conduits.'

'Can we take a peek down that hole?' Jack said, jerking his head towards the open doorway in the arch. 'I want some idea of what we're dealing with.'

Massimo nodded, walked inside and stooped down, then swallowed hard, as if he were about to retch. He glanced back at them. 'You might want to take a few deep breaths. It's a little high down there.' He lifted the manhole cover, and they glimpsed the dark beginnings of a spiral staircase. An indescribable smell wafted up. He closed the lid hurriedly, and dived back outside, clutching his mouth.

'Okay. I see what you mean. We'll kit up here, outside,' Jack said.

Massimo swallowed hard, and his voice was hoarse. 'You'll see a fluorescent orange line running along the edge of the Cloaca Maxima, then into the Velabrum as far as we reached,' he said. 'Beyond that, you're on your own.'

'You're not coming with us?' Jack said.

'I'd love to, but I'd be a liability. I had a bad experience yesterday, just below the Forum of Nerva. A conduit suddenly disgorged a gob of yellow liquid into the Cloaca, and it aerosolized into a mist. No idea what it was, don't want to know. I didn't have my respirator on. Stupid. I've been throwing up every half-hour or so ever since. It's happened to me before, I just need a little time. Occupational hazard.'

'You guys take risks,' Jack murmured. 'So what is down there? Liquid, I mean.'

'You want the full menu?'

'A la carte,' Jack said.

'Well, it's a mixture of runoff from the streets, the things that actually live down there, and leakage.'

'Leakage,' Costas muttered. 'Great.'

'Mud, diesel, urine. Rotting rat carcasses. And the stringy grey stuff, well, it shouldn't be there, but the sewage outlets aren't exactly all they're piped up to be.' Massimo gave them a slightly macabre grin, and coughed. 'But it's an old city. There's always going to be a bit of give and take.'

'Give and take?' Costas said.

'Well, one conduit provides clear, life-giving water, the other takes away putrid effluent. Or, to put it another way, the sewage pipes give to the drains, the drains take it away, the river flows to the sea. Here, it's the natural order of things.'

'Sheer poetry,' Costas muttered. 'No wonder the river Tiber looks green. It's how I'm beginning to feel.'

'We'll be fine in the IMU e-suits.' Jack said. 'Completely sealed in, no skin exposed. Tried and tested in all the most extreme conditions, right, Costas? If this goes well, Massimo, we'll donate you all of our equipment.'

'That would be excellent, Jack. *Perfetto*.' He swayed, and looked as if he were about to throw up. 'You'd better get going. They're forecasting heavy rain this afternoon, and the Cloaca can become a torrent. You don't want to get flushed out into the river.'

'I don't like that word, flush,' Costas muttered.

'The good news is, once you turn the corner from the main

drain into the Velabrum, the water becomes clear,' Massimo said. 'Under the Palatine it comes from natural springs, and because nobody lives there any more there's hardly any pollution. Right under the hill it should be crystal clear.'

Jack took off his old khaki bag, and slung it over Massimo's head. 'Guard this bag with your life, Massimo, and I'll see that our board of directors award Costas a special secondment here as your technical adviser.'

'What?' Costas looked aghast.

'Another honorary tunnel rat.' Massimo gave Costas a feverish grin, and slapped him on the shoulder. 'It's a deal. And now it's my turn to donate some equipment.' He went back into the chamber inside the stone pier and came out with two compact climbers' harnesses, with metal carabiners, a hammer and pitons and a coil of rope. 'It's not exactly what you'd imagine needing under Rome, but trust me, this can be a lifesaver.'

Jack nodded. 'Much appreciated.' He laid the harness down beside the rest of his kit, and waved appreciatively to the two IMU technicians who had gone back to wait by the van. He looked back at the cover over the hole into the Cloaca Maxima, the place where they would soon be going, and took a few deep breaths. Their banter had kept his anxieties at bay, but now he had to face it: this dive was going to force him to confront his worst fear, the one thing that could truly unsettle him. Costas knew it too, and Jack sensed that he was being watched very closely. He pulled the e-suit towards him, and squatted down to take off his boots. He would remain focused. An extraordinary prize could await them. And underwater tunnels always had exits.

Costas peered at him. 'Good to go?'

'Good to go.'

12

The manhole cover above Jack slid into place with a resounding clang, sealing him and Costas off from the rumble of traffic through Rome outside. They had given their final okay signal to Massimo and the two IMU crewmen moments before, and Jack felt reassured that the others would be above the manhole for the duration, awaiting their return. But now that they were entombed in the Cloaca Maxima he found himself weighing up the odds once more. There was no safety backup, no diver poised ready to assist in a rescue. It was another calculated risk, like their dive on St Paul's shipwreck. But Jack knew from hard experience that safety backup was often more psychological than practical, that problems were most often solved on the spot or not at all, that his ability to pull off a dangerous dive often depended on himself and his buddy alone. And any more equipment and personnel would make their operation more visible, and take precious time they could ill afford. He peered at Costas squatting beside him, then angled his headlamp down the spiral staircase into the darkness. This was it. They were on their own again.

'I'll go first,' Costas said over the intercom, peering at Jack through his helmet visor.

'I thought this wasn't exactly your cup of tea.'

'Decision made. Always ready to try a new brew. You okay?'

'Lead on.'

Costas heaved himself up and clunked down the stairs in front of Jack, the halogen beam from his headlamp wavering along the ancient masonry walls. They were wearing the same IMU e-suits they had used on the wreck, all-environment Kevlar-reinforced drysuits that had served them well from the Arctic to the Black Sea, with integrated buoyancy and air-conditioning systems. The yellow helmets with full face masks contained a call-up digital display showing life-support data, including the computerized gas mix fed from the compact closed-circuit rebreathers on their backs. Their only concession to the unusual circumstances were the climbers' harnesses that Massimo had insisted they take along, fitted and tested before they had donned their rebreathers a few minutes before.

'This reminds me of going into that sunken submarine in the Black Sea, hunting for Atlantis,' Costas said as he stomped around the stairs. 'I feel as if I could cut the air with a knife here too.'

Jack swallowed hard. Just before sealing his helmet he had caught a waft of fetid air from below, and he still had the cloying taste in his mouth. The last thing he needed now was to throw up inside his helmet. That was one human reality the IMU engineers had failed to consider. He swallowed again. 'You know, you might want to get the design guys to fit these with a sick bag.'

'I was just thinking the same thing.'

After about thirty steps, the spiral staircase ended at a small platform in front of an arched door, blackened and dripping with slime. Jack came up behind Costas and they both aimed their headlamps through. 'There it is,' Jack said, trying to sound cheery. 'The Great Drain.' Ahead of them a straight flight of steps led down into a wide tunnel, at least eight metres across and five metres high, built of stone and brick dripping with algae. Half filling the tunnel was a surging mass of dark liquid, rushing towards them from the darkness ahead and disappearing out of sight below. Jack turned up his external audio sensor, and his head was filled with the sound of the torrent, almost deafening. He turned it down again and pointed to the fluorescent orange line that began ahead of them where the stairs disappeared underwater. 'That must be Massimo's line,' he said. 'It's pitoned in, and we can haul ourselves along it. There's a ledge about a metre and a half below it that's usually above water, but it looks as if we'll be wading. The entrance to the Velabrum is only about twenty metres ahead of us.'

'That'd be a hell of a waterpark ride if we fell in.'

'It disgorges into the Tiber, but Massimo says there's a big metal grid in the way. Might not be a happy ending.'

Costas walked gingerly on to the first step in the tunnel. Something large and dark scurried off at enormous speed along a narrow ridge in front of him. 'Looks like Massimo left one of his friends down here,' Costas said distastefully.

'At least we shouldn't be seeing any of those where we're going,' Jack said from behind. 'According to Massimo, the conduit leading under the Palatine is pure, doesn't have enough in it to sustain many higher life forms.'

'That's reassuring,' Costas said. They carried on slowly down until they reached the fluorescent line. Costas played his headlamp over the rushing torrent just below them. 'It looks like espresso,' he murmured. 'That foam on top.'

'*Schiuma*, you mean,' Jack said. 'That's exactly what Massimo called it.'

Costas put a foot into the torrent, holding tight with both hands to the rope. His foot created a wide wake, with foam streaming off to either side. He lifted it out, and what seemed to have been brown foam but was actually a stringy mass came out with it. He thrust his foot back in, shaking it violently. 'Jack, that was just about the worst thing that has ever happened to me,' he said, panting. 'Why this? We could be in the crystal-clear waters off Sicily. Lying by a pool, having a long-overdue holiday. But no, we go diving in a sewer.'

'Fascinating.' Jack was squatting on the step behind Costas, peering at a pile of washed-up debris just above the torrent. Costas twisted around, his foot still in the water. 'Have you found it? Can we go now?'

Jack pushed aside some rodent bones, and held up a slimy chunk of pottery. 'Roman amphora sherd. Dressel 2 to 4, unless I'm mistaken. The same type we found on the shipwreck, and in Herculaneum. The wine Claudius would have drunk. This stuff got everywhere.' He put his other hand deep into the sludge, and grunted. 'There's more.'

'Leave it, Jack.'

Jack paused, then pulled out his arm and stood up. 'Okay. Just being an archaeologist.'

'Save it for this secret chamber. If we ever get there.' Costas took the coil of rope from his shoulder. He clipped one end to the piton holding the fluorescent line, and the other end to his harness. 'I think we can sacrifice one rope here, for safety,' he said. 'I refuse to end my days in a torrent of shit. Clip on behind me.' He turned back and stepped down until the liquid was nearly chest-high, flecking his visor with foam. 'I'm on the ledge,' he said. 'Moving ahead now.' Jack followed him, feeling the pressure of the water push hard against his legs and then his waist. They began to progress along, painfully slowly, a few inches at a time. The water felt heavy, cloying, and Jack could see iridescent streams of oily matter on the surface, then shifting blotches of brown and grey, a camouflage colour. He tried to focus on the walls, the ceiling, on stonework which had been built well before the Roman Empire, when the Velabrum was first covered over. He arched his head back, and realized the tunnel had taken a slight curve to the right. The steps they had come down from the spiral staircase were now out of view. He turned forward and slogged on, beginning to pant hard with the exertion. He looked down to check his carabiner on the line and then looked up. Costas had vanished. He blinked hard, and wiped his mask. He was still gone. For a horrified moment he thought Costas must have fallen in, and he braced himself for the whip of the rope as he was swept past. Then he saw a dull glow coming from the wall about five metres in front of him, and a yellow helmet appeared.

'This is the side tunnel,' Costas said. 'I've clipped the other end of the rope to a piton inside.' Jack heaved himself against the current for the final few steps, then Costas reached out and hauled him in. Both men sat for a moment slumped against the side of the tunnel, panting. Jack sucked at the hydrating energy drink stored inside his suit, sluicing it round his mouth to get rid of the unpleasant taste. He looked around. They were in a smaller tunnel, but it was still a good three metres high and three metres across, with an arched barrel-vaulted roof and a flat bottom, a channel filled with water flowing down the centre. The flow was exiting into the Cloaca Maxima, and the water was clear.

'Time for a final reality check,' Costas said, peering at his wrist gauge. 'This must be it. The Velabrum. It's orientated straight into the Palatine Hill, and I can see Massimo's line running ahead along the right side as far as I can make out, to wherever they stopped.'

Jack put his hand on the side of the tunnel. 'This is an impressive piece of engineering,' he said. 'The Cloaca Maxima has masonry and brickwork from lots of periods, from when it was first covered over in the sixth century BC. But this is different, a single-period construction. Regular, rectilinear blocks of stone at the entrance. If I didn't know better, I'd say we were walking into one of the great aqueduct channels made by the emperors.'

Costas looked at Jack through his visor. 'About this Lupercale place, Jack. The cave of Romulus and Remus. I didn't have a clue what you were on about.'

'Sorry to spring that on you. Massimo and I did talk about it at that conference where we met him in London, shortly after the discovery of the cave under the House of Augustus was announced. I told him I'd love to come and take a look, to join his urban speleology group. When I realized yesterday we were coming to Rome, it was the perfect pretext. Once I guessed that Pliny must have hidden the scroll under the Palatine Shrine of Vesta, right next door to the House of Augustus, I also realized it was the site where the Lupercale was found. At the moment we just can't risk bringing anyone else in on this quest. I hate keeping Massimo in the dark, but maybe he'll forgive us once we tell him the role he played.'

Costas grunted, got up and started forward again, the rivulet of clear water from the darkness ahead rising over his ankles.

'I hate to say this, Costas, but you're trailing something.'

Costas turned round, stared, and made a strangulated noise.

A mess of stringy brown tendrils extended back from his left foot towards the Cloaca, and caught in their midst was a writhing form with a long black tail. Costas shook his foot frantically, and the whole mass slithered off out of sight into the drain. 'Never again, Jack,' he muttered. 'I swear to God, you're never doing this to me again.'

'I promise I'll make it up to you. Next dive will be pure heaven.'

'We've got to get out of this version of hell first.' Costas resumed his slog up the tunnel, and Jack followed close behind. He still felt connected to the world outside, only a quick abseil along the rope back to the base of the spiral staircase, but with every step now the underworld seemed to be closing in on him, with darkness ahead and behind and only the immediate walls of the tunnel visible in their headlamps. He forced himself to concentrate, to push aside the claustrophobia, counting his steps, estimating how close they were getting to the foot of the Palatine Hill. After thirty paces he sensed that the angle had changed, that they were going down. The walls appeared buckled, fractured. The fluorescent line ended abruptly at a piton in front of a dark pool, and he could see where the ceiling sloped down into the water about five metres ahead.

'This isn't natural,' Costas murmured. 'I mean, the tunnel wasn't designed this way. It looks like damage from seismic activity, like some of those fracture lines at Herculaneum.'

'They get earthquakes here too,' Jack said.

'A pretty big one, but some years ago, centuries probably. And this might be a dead end for us, though there's still plenty of flow getting through.'

'Time for a swim,' Jack said.

Costas sloshed into the pool, then disappeared in a mass of bubbles. Jack followed close behind, dropping to his knees and flopping forward, hearing the air in his suit expel as his computerized system automatically adjusted to neutral buoyancy. The water was extraordinarily clear, cleansing, like the underground cenote they had dived through in the Yucatán, and even here Jack felt the exhilaration he always felt as he went underwater, the excitement of the unknown. He reached back and slipped his fins down from where they had been tucked up behind his calves, and powered forward after Costas. His depth gauge showed three metres, then six. The earthquake had created a sump in the tunnel, and they were coming back up again. He saw in front of him that Costas had surfaced, and that the floor of the tunnel rose up to less than a metre depth. He swam up as far as he could, pulled his fins up again and rose out of the water beside Costas, who was staring ahead down the tunnel.

'I've got that feeling again,' Costas said.

'What feeling?'

'That feeling of walking into the past. I had it at Herculaneum, even had it diving down on to the shipwreck of St Paul. It's weird, like déjà vu.'

'So you get it, too,' Jack murmured.

'Maybe it's the force.'

'I had it explained to me once,' Jack said. 'It's that you've had exactly the identical emotional response before, in very similar circumstances. Your brain's playing tricks on you. It's a short circuit.'

'No, Jack. I've seen it in you. It's the force.'

'Okay. It's the force. You're right. Maybe you can use some of it to get us through the next sump.' Jack pointed ahead to another dip in the tunnel, to more cracked and fragmented masonry, another pool. He knew they must now be on the very edge of the Palatine Hill, under at least eighty metres of fractured tufa. Costas splashed in again and Jack followed him. This time the tunnel regained its former shape and continued underwater, but about ten metres ahead it constricted. As Jack swam closer he realized that the point of constriction was two ancient columns on either side. Beyond them the tunnel narrowed into a culvert like an aqueduct channel, taller than it was wide, with a barrel-vaulted ceiling. The dimensions would have allowed them to stand upright and walk through it, single file, were it not for the water. He reached out and touched the right-hand column. It was grey granite, with white and black flecks, a stone seen all over the ruins of Rome, in the columns of the Pantheon, in Trajan's basilica next to the old forum. Jack had been with Hiebermeyer to the source, Mons Claudianus in Egypt, the great quarry first opened under the emperor Claudius, another of his distinctive stamps on the architecture of the city.

'Maurice would love this,' he murmured. 'His doctoral

project was Claudius' quarries in Egypt, and that's where this stone came from.'

'Jack, take a look at this.'

Jack rolled over and looked up, and realized that Costas had broken surface about three metres above him, bobbing in a wavering sheen of water that reflected his headlamp in shifting patterns of white. Jack rose up slowly, pressing his buoyancy control to inject air, remembering to exhale as the ambient pressure decreased. His head emerged out of the water, and he gasped in astonishment. Costas' beam was shining at a rock face that rose directly above the columns and the conduit entrance. It extended high above them, at least four metres high and five wide, carved out of the living rock. Above them Jack could see the triangular gable of a pediment, projecting half a metre out of the rock. He looked down into the water again, saw the columns. He realized that the entire structure was a monumental entranceway, carved and decorated as a work of art in its own right. He gazed at it, awestruck. It was like the great rock-cut façades at Petra in Jordan, yet deep under the Palatine, a curious mixture of ostentation and secrecy, the creation of someone who cared about his own achievements but not what other people thought of them.

'Check this out,' Costas said. 'Take a look at the stone face under that gable.'

Jack raised his head again above the surface. An eddy effect from the current below had pushed them closer to the rock face, and he was now within touching distance. He reached out and put his hand on it. What looked like mould and slime was rock-hard, and he realized it was calcite accretion, the seepage from groundwater that Massimo had talked about. He saw tiny rivulets of wet running down the rock, evidently from rainwater far above. Then he saw the regular incisions in the rock. He pushed off, and aimed his headlamp up. *Of course*. It was an imperial monument, and there had to be a monumental inscription. The calcite lay over the inscription like icing, but instead of smudging it seemed to clarify it, crystallize it. There were four registers, the letters only about three inches high, scarcely big enough to be seen from the floor of the chamber. Whoever had made this dedication did it for propriety, for his own private satisfaction and to sanctify the place, not to impress the masses.

TI.CLAVDIVS.DRVSI.F.CAISAR.AVGVSTVS.GERMANICVS
PONTIF.MAXIM.TRIBVNICIA.POTESTATE.XII.COS.V
IMPERATOR.XXVII.PATER.PATRIAE.AQVAS.VESTIAM.
SACRA.SVA.IMPENSA.IN.VRBEM.PERDVCENDAS.CVRAVIT

'This is authentic, no doubt about it,' Jack murmured. 'It has the characteristically archaic spelling of the word Caesar, harking back to the glory days of Julius Caesar, the Roman Republic. The wall's like that too, carved as if it's made of blocks in a rusticated style, the surfaces left rough with almost an exaggerated lack of finish. Absolutely characteristic of Claudius, of buildings where he had a personal involvement. And typical of Claudius to get the epigraphic details right, the archaic reference.'

'You're talking about our Claudius? The emperor? This was his doing?'

Jack translated the inscription: ' "Tiberius Claudius, son of Drusus, Caesar, Augustus, Germanicus, Chief Priest, with Tribunician power for the twelfth time, five times Consul, twenty-seven times Imperator, Father of his Country, saw to the construction at his own expense of the Sacred Vestal Water." '

'That's going to make Massimo very happy,' Costas said. 'It's all we need to tell him. His tunnel rats can have a party down here when they see this. Their hero.'

'The formula's similar to Claudius' inscription on the Aqua Claudia, at the Porta Maggiore where the aqueduct entered Rome,' Jack said. 'But the fascinating thing here, the unique thing, is those three words. *Aquas Vestiam Sacra*. The sacred waters of the Vestals. It means Massimo may well have been right about that too, that this tunnel connects with the House of the Vestals on the other side of the Palatine, with the channel that joins the branch off the Cloaca Maxima he explored under the old forum.'

'The strange thing is, this isn't a drain from the Cloaca,' Costas murmured. 'It's exactly the opposite. The fact that the water's crystal clear on this side suggests it must be on the other side too, flowing down back towards the forum. There must be a pretty big spring smack in the middle of all this, right under the Palatine.'

'Perhaps a sacred spring,' Jack murmured. 'Maybe the Vestals were the guardians.'

Costas eyed his navigation computer again. 'Judging by the direction of this tunnel and the likely angle of the tunnel Massimo explored under the forum, the point of confluence should be almost exactly under where we were sitting by the House of Augustus this morning. Maybe that cave, the Lupercale, was actually an entranceway down to the spring, a secret passage from the palace. Maybe all that myth stuff, Romulus and Remus, could actually have some fact behind it.'

'The Romans never doubted it,' Jack murmured.

'Right,' Costas said. 'The myth could even underline the importance of the spring. The earliest settlement of Rome was on the Palatine Hill, right? Well, control of a spring could have been crucial to their success. Maybe we're about to find the real reason why Rome became great. Water.'

'You never cease to amaze me,' Jack said. 'And it makes sense that the Vestals were involved, an ancient priesthood dating from the foundation of Rome, probably from way before. By sanctifying this place, by keeping it secret and pure, they would also have been safeguarding Rome. No wonder they were feared and revered. Down here under the Palatine they may literally have been the powerhouse of ancient Rome.'

'Time to find out.' Costas pushed off from the rock and vented air from his buoyancy system, dropping under the rock face between the two columns. Jack lingered for a moment, staring at the inscription, his excitement pushing against a feeling of apprehension which had not yet fully grown, but was there. He dropped down and followed Costas, finning into the tunnel, completely submerged again with the tufa vault above him.

'Waterproof concrete,' Costas said. Jack could see the cone of light from his headlamp a few metres ahead, aimed at a section of the conduit wall which had partly cracked and crumbled.

'Another Claudius speciality,' Jack replied, coming up behind him. 'It's how they built the underwater moles of his great harbour at Ostia, and what they used to line aqueducts. In here it was probably used to keep groundwater from leeching down into the conduit, contaminating the springwater. The key ingredient of hydraulic concrete was a dust called *pozzolana*, from ancient Pozzuola. That's Puteoli on the Bay of Naples, beside the Phlegraean Fields.'

'Small world,' Costas murmured as he pressed ahead.

Jack passed the damaged section, and then came under Costas' legs where he had stopped, about fifteen metres beyond the columns that had marked the entrance to the conduit.

'It's all choked up,' Costas said. 'It looks as if there's been a collapse.'

'A dead end?' Jack said.

Costas bent over and delved into the tool pocket on his e-suit. He produced a device about the size of a spoon, activated it and held it out in front of him. Jack watched the flashing red light turn to green. 'The water current meter shows we've still got flow. Wherever the spring is, it's still ahead of us.' Costas pocketed the meter, then looked at the gauge on his wrist. 'And we're still going up at a slight angle, about ten degrees. At this rate we'll break surface about twenty metres ahead, if the tunnel continues at the same angle beyond this rubble.'

Jack edged under Costas, and peered at the jumble of tufa fragments on the floor of the tunnel. He reached down and shifted one, then moved several more. 'Take a look at this,' he said. 'There's a crack underneath us, a fissure in the base of the tunnel. It must have split open when the quake brought down the ceiling. We might be able to get through.'

Costas dropped alongside Jack, and looked into the hole, angling his head so that the beam shone deep inside. 'You may be right,' he said. 'It widens ahead of us, maybe body width, and goes on as far as I can see. The rubble seems to have compacted at the top of the fissure, and not fallen into it. If we can clear the first couple of metres or so, we might reach the point where the fissure's wide enough to fin through.'

'My turn to take the lead,' Jack said. Costas dropped back and peered at him closely, his visor almost touching Jack's, and made the okay sign. The two men knew each other too well, and words were unnecessary. It was always the second sump that did it for Jack, the realization that escape was no longer straightforward, that he would need to go back through several submerged spaces before reaching the final passage to freedom. He had survived a near-death experience as a boy diving a sunken mine shaft, when his air had cut off and his buddy had saved him, and the memory rose up again every time he confronted similar circumstances, every time his mind began to lock into that sense of déjà vu. He had already felt the icy grip of claustrophobia before he saw the inscription, and now he needed all his reserves to fight it, his own secret battle that only Costas knew about. Taking the lead helped him to focus, to concentrate, to see the objective ahead as his own personal quest, to feel responsibility for one who now came behind him.

'We're still at about six metres water depth,' Costas said. 'By my reckoning, we're only about thirty metres from the point directly below the House of Augustus and that temple, where we were sitting on top of the Palatine.'

'Okay. Here goes,' Jack muttered. He angled down and pulled himself through the crack. He finned hard, but got nowhere. He was beginning to hyperventilate. He closed his eyes, then felt a jostle from behind. 'Your coil of rope caught on a rock,' Costas said. Jack felt a hard push, and then was floating free inside the fissure, which had quickly widened to about two metres. He realized that he was dropping, and dropping fast. He looked at his gauge. Fifteen metres depth already. He must have deactivated the automated buoyancy control as he squeezed into the fissure, and he fumbled with the controls on the side of his helmet. There was a hiss of gas into the suit and he slowed down, reaching neutral buoyancy at eighteen metres. For the first time he looked along the length of the fissure ahead of him. The water was still crystal clear, and he could see horizontally at least thirty metres, to a point where the rough volcanic tufa walls on either side seemed to join together again. He looked down. There was nothing, a yawning blackness, an abyss like he had never seen before, deep below the heart of one of the world's most ancient cities.

He heard grunting and cursing through his intercom, and looked up to see Costas part-way into the fissure. He began to swim back up to help him, and then Costas was through, dropping down until they both came level at twelve metres depth. 'This place is phenomenal.' Costas was still panting from his exertion, but was peering down. 'The crack of doom.'

'I can't see the bottom,' Jack said. 'It must be at least fifty metres below us, maybe more.'

'I didn't wager for a decompression dive under Rome,' Costas said. 'We haven't got the gas for that.' They both checked the readout inside their helmets, which showed the gas mixture from their rebreathers adjusting for depth. 'I'd say half an hour, no more, with a twenty-five-metre maximum. Any deeper than that and it's a bounce dive, then we're out of here.'

'We may be lucky,' Jack said. 'Look along the top of the fissure.' He panned his headlamp beam along, and Costas followed it. They could see the glistening reflection of the water surface at their entry point, then nothing but rock for about ten metres, then another wavering patch of white, this one at least three metres long. 'Looks like it breaks surface again,' Jack said. 'Let's go up.'

They began to swim in the direction of Jack's beam. Costas

rolled on his back, peering up and down the fissure, then looking hard at the rock directly above them. 'This fissure's clearly a seismic cleft, tens, maybe hundreds of thousands of years old. It looks as if it's always been filled with water, spring-fed. Then right above it there's that tunnel built by Claudius, buckled by a more recent earthquake. You can see sections of the Roman rock-cut ceiling from the tunnel above us. My guess is, the tunnel was never intended to break into the fissure, but extended above it to that pool we're heading towards. The tunnel must be a kind of outlet, an overflow conduit for when the water here got too high.'

'Look at that,' Jack exclaimed, pointing to the side of the fissure. 'There's a flight of four, five rock-cut steps, leading up to the pool.'

'It looks like a wellhead,' Costas said. 'Maybe this was where they accessed the spring. We're coming up almost directly under the place where those prehistoric huts were found, the House of Romulus on top of the Palatine, about sixty metres above us.'

Jack broke surface first, then cautiously walked up the steps, craning his neck round to ensure there was ample headspace. He looked back to check that Costas was behind him, then reached down and pulled his fins up behind his calves before walking up out of the water on to a flat rock surface. He was inside another tunnel, but it was spectacularly different from the one they had come through. Jack turned around, looking. To the north, about ten metres from him, the tunnel came to an end at what looked like a small chamber, slightly larger than the dimensions of the tunnel. At the other end, about the same distance away, it opened into a rocky cavern, obscured in shadows. The tunnel itself was hewn out of the living rock, about three metres wide and five metres high, with a trapezoidal cross-section like a truncated pyramid. Jack swivelled around and scanned the whole length again, then looked closely at one wall, inspecting the ancient pick-marks. This was old, far older than anything else they had seen. He looked again. It suddenly clicked. 'My God,' he whispered.

'Another tunnel,' Costas said, his dripping form appearing beside Jack.

'Not just another tunnel,' Jack murmured. '*A dromos.*'

'A what?'

'Where have you seen this shape before?'

Costas gazed along the tunnel, the rectilinear profile of the walls framed by his beam. 'Bronze Age,' he suddenly said, sounding triumphant. 'The Greek Bronze Age. Those tombs you showed me at Mycenae, in Greece. A *dromos* was a sacred corridor. The time of the Trojan Wars, Aeneas, all that.'

'And this may finally pin down the origin of Rome, once and for all,' Jack said, his voice hushed. 'We're on the edge of the age of myth again, Costas, just like Atlantis, myth made real. But I'm thinking of somewhere closer to home. This is almost identical to the *dromos* in the cave of the Sibyl at Cumae.'

'The Sibyl,' Costas murmured. 'So she had an apartment in Rome, too.'

'This is all beginning to make sense,' Jack said. 'The

Lupercale, the sacred cave of Rome's origin. I'll bet that's what lies ahead of us, that cavern. And we've just emerged from the spring, vital for the survival of Rome. A sacred place, sanctified and protected. We know the ritual at Cumae involved lustral waters, rites of purification. The Vestals probably did that too. And then there's the dark side.'

'The crack of doom,' Costas said.

'The entrance to the underworld.'

'Just like Cumae, the Phlegraean Fields,' Costas said.

'And on top of it all sits a Sibyl.'

'I wonder if she was here when they arrived, the first Romans, or whether they brought her with them?' Costas mused. 'And I wonder how the Vestal Virgins figure in all this?'

'Maybe there are answers here. We need to get to that cave. Come on.'

'Before you do that, Jack, you might want to take a look at the other end of this tunnel. There's something in the middle of that chamber.'

Jack swivelled round to follow Costas' gaze. With their two beams concentrated together the chamber was more clearly illuminated. They walked along the passageway towards it. The ancient walls were streaked with accretion, calcite deposits that covered the tufa like dirty whitewash. They reached the edge of the chamber. It was a perfect dome, about eight metres in circumference, with small rectangular openings in the ceiling that might once have been air vents, evidently clogged up. On the far side was what looked like the decayed remains of a statue, on a plinth. In front of it was a circular depression in the floor about three metres wide, surrounded by a rock-cut rim and filled with a dark mass, what looked like a black resinous material sealed under calcite accretion. Jack stared at it, and then at the decayed figure behind it. 'Of course,' he whispered.

'What is it?'

'That statue, it looks as if it might once have been female,' he said. 'A seated woman. A cult statue. And this is a hearth, a sacred hearth.' He was suddenly elated. 'That's why the shrines of Vesta in the forum and on the Palatine were never inaugurated, never made into temples. It's because they were outliers, just the public face of the cult. This chamber was the real Temple of Vesta.'

'Jack, the statue. It's got an inscription.'

Jack stepped around the hearth and followed Costas' beam. At the base of the statue was a thin slab of marble veneer, about thirty centimetres across. Jack squatted down and peered at it. 'Odd,' he said. 'It's not a dedicatory inscription, not part of the plinth. It's propped up here loose, or at least was until the calcite glued it in place.' He bent down as far as he could, then got down on the floor. The Latin was clear in his beam, and he read it out:

COELIA CONCORDIA
VESTALIS MAXIMA
ANNO DOMINI CCCXCIV

'Well I'll be damned,' he said. 'Coelia Concordia, Chief Vestal, AD 394. She was the last one, and that was the year the cult was abandoned. Odd that they used Anno Domini, though. Year of Our Lord. The Empire had been Christian for almost a century by that date, but you'd have thought the Vestals would have resisted Christianity to the end. It's what sidelined them, along with the other pagan cults of Rome.'

Costas was silent, and Jack peered at him. 'You still with me?'

'Jack, this is no statue.'

'What do you mean?' Jack struggled to his feet, then slipped on the floor and fell into the statue, holding it close. He winced, and drew back, leaning for a moment while he flexed the knee that had hit the floor, staring at the decayed shape inches from his face. He suddenly froze. It was not limestone at all. It was calcite accretion, a weird, shapeless stalagmite that rose more than a metre from the floor, encasing a stone seat. He looked again at what had startled him. It was a sculpted stone serpent, green, writhing up the back of the chair, staring out at him through a diaphanous mask of accretion.

'Not that, Jack. Over here. Inside.'

Jack moved a step to the left and followed Costas' beam. Then he saw it, trapped inside the calcium, lolling off to one side.

A human skull.

He gasped, stepped back, then stared again. There was more. A sternum, ribs, shoulder blades. Costas was right. The statue was no statue at all. It was a skeleton, a human skeleton. Small, almost childlike, but with the jaw of someone old, very old, the teeth all missing. Then Jack saw something else. She wore a necklace, a neck torque, solid gold, an extraordinary sight in the heart of Rome, some ancient booty perhaps from the Celtic world. And above the skull encased in the accretion were sparkling fragments of gold leaf and jewels from an elaborate hairdo, the coiffure of a wealthy Roman woman, a matron.

Then Jack realized. *She had come here to die*. Coelia Concordia, the last of the Vestals. But a Vestal wreathed in serpents. Not just a Vestal. *A Sibyl*.

Jack's mind was in a tumult. So the cult of the Sibyl had not come to an end with the eruption of Vesuvius after all. She had come back here, back to her cave under Rome, to another entrance to Hades. And the oracle had survived, lived on for more than three centuries after Claudius met his end, after the old world of the Cumaean Sibyl had been consumed by fire. This Sibyl had seen out Rome, seen Rome rise and fall to the end, seen out the pagan world and ushered in a new order, one whose beginnings she had watched all those years before, among the outcasts near her cave beside the Fields of Fire.

'Jack, take a look at her hand.'

Jack peered down, barely able to breathe. He looked again. So that was what had happened to the Sibyls. They had become what they had foreseen. They had fulfilled their own prophecy. She was holding a crude metal forging, two iron spikes joined at right angles. *A cross of nails*.

Suddenly there was a flash of light, a momentary surge. For a second Jack thought he might be hallucinating. Then he was dragged violently sideways, to the edge of the chamber, down to the floor. A hand slammed the side of his helmet and his light went off. He was in total darkness. The hold relaxed, and Costas came over the intercom, his voice tense. 'Sorry about that, Jack. But there's someone else down here.'

13

For a few moments they remained on the floor of the chamber, in utter darkness. Their intercom was virtually inaudible with the external speaker deactivated, though they instinctively talked in low voices. 'Jack, I thought you said nothing else would be living in here.' Costas moved to the edge of the chamber, and peered along the line of the *dromos* tunnel towards the cave at the other end. Jack crawled up behind him. Their headlamps were still switched off, but they had activated the night-vision goggles inside their e-suit helmets. There was just enough natural light for the sensors to work, not enough to be discernible to the naked eye but enough for Jack to make out Costas' form in front of him, speckly and green, an eerie apparition that seemed to be constantly forming and re-forming with every movement. It made sense that there would be light coming from cracks and fissures leading outside, where the archeologists' probe had reached into the cave somewhere ahead of them.

'You're sure it was a torch?'

'Positive. I was looking in the opposite direction, while you were communing with our dead lady. One look at that thing was enough for me. Then I saw the beam. It flashed out from somewhere on the left side of the cave.'

'That's where the other tunnel, the one from the House of the Vestals, should enter,' Jack whispered. 'But God knows how they got in.'

'If we could do it, someone else could.'

'Massimo's map showed entrances into the Cloaca in the Forum of Nerva and under the Colosseum,' Jack said. 'His guys were turned back by a flooded culvert, didn't have the right equipment. Someone with the right gear could have found a way, but not one of his people. He'd have told us.'

'Is this a coincidence?'

Jack paused, then stared into the darkness. 'There's something that's been on my mind since yesterday. It wasn't going to stop us coming to where we are now, and I was waiting to speak to her more, on the phone. You remember Elizabeth at Herculaneum, the superintendency official? My old friend?'

'What's she got to do with this?'

'She caught up with me for a few moments yesterday in Herculaneum before we left the villa.'

'Maria and I noticed.'

'She was taking a big risk, with the guards around. Maurice had already warned us about how somebody seemed to be sitting on the superintendency people, keeping them from talking. She wanted to tell me something. About what we're up against. An organization as deeply rooted in the history of Rome as you can imagine, that goes right back to the time of St Paul. An organization that knew the villa concealed a threat to their very existence, something they had hoped lost for ever in the eruption of AD 79. Elizabeth was whispering, and I didn't have time to question her. She said they will do anything in their power to keep this threat at bay.'

'You think we're being followed?'

'If it's who I fear it is, they'll have tentacles everywhere. And if they know we're in here, they must assume we're on to something. And if they somehow have an idea what it is we're after, it's a prize they'd die for.'

'And kill for.'

Jack drew up behind Costas, and peered over his helmet. All he could make out was speckly green, with darker smudges at the end. 'The only thing we can do is brazen it out. My guess is, it's likely to be only one guy. The entrances from the forum and the Colosseum are pretty public. More than one might be too much of a risk, to get in unseen.'

'Maybe the authorities turned a blind eye.'

'Rome isn't Naples,' Jack said. 'But you may be right. At the moment, whoever's in that cave is going to be kicking themselves for having the torch on as they came out of the tunnel. I should imagine it was a pretty hairy ride, unless they had the kind of equipment we've got. And the longer we keep our lights off, the more likely they'll assume we've rumbled them.'

'You're saying we should carry on as if we've seen nothing.'

'Our intruder might think we've gone down a side passage, a dead end, come back up again. Let's just switch on our lights, go forward. We're going to have to have lights on anyway, to climb up that cavern to find the place beneath the shrine. They're not going to have a go at us until we've found what we're after.'

'Okay. Lights on, sweeping them up from behind as if we've just come up from somewhere. I'm not armed, Jack.'

'I've got the rock hammer in my right hand,' Jack murmured. 'If I hadn't forced our security chief Ben to go on vacation, he'd have insisted that I carry the Beretta. There's even a pocket for it in the e-suit. Lesson learned. Next time.'

'Next time?'

They switched on their headlamps, then stood out in the passageway and began to make their way forward, passing the edge of the pool they had come up through. They knew they were being watched, but had no idea where from. After about ten metres they reached the end of the tunnel and the edge of the cave. They swept their beams around, and could see it was a huge natural cavern, extending at least twenty metres upwards. To the right was an ancient rock-cut stairway, winding up the natural contours of the cave, the tufa steps so heavily eroded they were sloping. About halfway up the cavern was a series of massive fractures and displacements in the rock, and they could see a continuation of the stairs far above that, near the ceiling, above a jagged precipice. Directly below that point on the floor of the cavern they could see an opening identical to the channel they had come through earlier, with rivulets just visible flowing into it. 'That's the other channel,' Jack murmured, scanning the folds of rock around the entrance. 'Can you see anything?'

'Not yet.'

'But thank God for Massimo and his rope. He was right. Looks as if we're going rock-climbing.'

'You are. I'm clambering round the base of the cavern, exploring for lost treasure, right? I might switch off my light, for better light contrast, you know, to see those secret chambers. Sometimes you might not see me.'

'Be careful. This guy's bound to be armed.'

'He won't shoot until he thinks we've found whatever it is we're looking for.'

'That's the theory.'

'Then don't find it.'

'I'll tell you when to move on him,' Jack said. 'Loudly.'

Jack shifted the coil of rope off his shoulder in readiness and began to climb the steps. Costas was quickly lost to view among the folds of rock, and his beam disappeared. Jack hated the vulnerability, knowing that eyes were following his every move. Costas was no assassin, and was not the most inconspicuous of physiques. Jack stopped and looked up, ostentatiously. If they played their cards right, there was a chance. But some kind of showdown was inevitable. He steeled himself and carried on, focusing only on the challenge of the climb ahead. After thirty steps he reached the end, the point where the earthquake had pushed out a huge section of rock, creating a sheer face at least ten metres high. He inspected the rock, carefully judging the holds. It could be done. He clipped the rope to his harness, then unfastened the rebreather from his back, setting it down on the step behind him, unclipping the hoses from his helmet and lifting the visor. For the first time since the fetid blast from the drain an hour before he tasted the air. It was damp and warm, and he could hear water dripping all round him. The rainstorm Massimo had predicted must have started. He pulled himself on to the rock face. The tufa seemed friable, but he knew it was strong, volcanic stone that gave a good grip. He eased himself up, splayed on the rock, using his long limbs to find holds. About five metres up, he hammered in the first piton, the sound ringing through the cavern. He hammered another one in three metres higher. Another two metres and he was above the main precipice, with a ledge in front of him and then the stairs above, continuing into the rock face. To the right, he glimpsed a wide fissure that had walls covered with mosaic decoration, with embedded shells. It must be the fissure the archaeologists had found beneath the House of Augustus. He now knew with absolute certainty that the steps led up under the lost Palatine Shrine of Vesta, to the secret chamber they were seeking, only a few metres ahead.

He turned, hammered in a final piton just above the cliff

edge, then clipped the rope to his harness and under his back, abseiling down the first few metres. He stopped and listened. The rivulet down the tunnel leading towards the forum had greatly intensified, and was now a torrent. The rainwater must have pushed the water reservoir from the spring over its threshold, and the tunnel was doing the job Claudius had designed it for. Jack paused, took a deep breath. This was it. He yelled out, as loudly as he could.

'Costas, I've found it. I'm coming down.'

He bounced down another couple of metres, halfway down the cliff, the hammer in his left hand. Suddenly a grip like a vice held his left ankle, and he began spinning wildly. He looked down. A figure in a black wetsuit was staring up at him, wearing a close-fitting diving mask, legs wrapped around the rope just above the step. One hand held Jack's ankle and the rope, the other held a silenced pistol, aimed at Jack's head. 'Give it to me,' the man said coldly, in a thick Italian accent. Jack looked down, saying nothing. A bullet cracked past his face, followed by the thump of the silencer. It was a warning shot. Jack caught sight of something out of the corner of his eye, a shape. He swung, and aimed the hammer at the man's head, a killer blow. But the arm holding his ankle was closer, and he brought the hammer down hard against the man's wrist. There was an explosive sound as the bones snapped, and the pistol spun off into the cavern. Simultaneously Costas launched himself at the man's legs, bringing him down with a huge crash. The man tried to get up, tripped, tumbled down and hit the channel below with a sickening crack, and then was gone, swept away down the tunnel in the torrent. Jack dropped down to help Costas, who had also removed his respirator and visor. 'You okay?'

'Fine,' Costas panted. 'Only wish you'd put that hammer in the little bastard's forehead.'

'I don't think he'll be troubling us any more,' Jack said.

Costas wiped some blood off his mouth and looked down. 'Well and truly flushed out.' He looked back up the cliff face. 'Right. Hook me up. That's done it for me. The sooner we get what we've come for and get out of here, the better.'

Twenty minutes later they were in a narrow space above the final flight of rock-cut stairs. Jack squeezed himself as far up the crack as he could go, his arms raised above him into a hollowed-out chamber. He could feel nothing. He wriggled further, but it was no use. His head was jammed sideways against the top of the crack, and all he could see was the side of the jagged fissure inches from his face. He felt blindly with his hands, but there was only empty space. He arched his back, pushing hard, and felt himself move fractionally forward, an inch or two. Suddenly his fingers met resistance. Wet rock, smoothed down, different from the irregular rock of the fissure. He parted his hands and felt around. It was a circular chamber, about two feet wide, sunk into the rock. He felt down as far as he could reach, and touched the base of the chamber. He traced his fingers slowly around the edge. Nothing.

It was empty.

Jack slumped slightly, and peered down at Costas' face, just visible below his feet. 'I can feel the chamber.' His voice sounded peculiar, resonating in the chamber but then deadened in the fissure. 'It's a cylindrical hole bored into the rock. I can feel all round the base. There's nothing inside.'

'Try the middle.' Costas' voice sounded distant, muffled. 'Maybe there's another smaller chamber sunk below it.'

Jack shifted as far as he could to the right. He slowly drew his left hand across the bottom of the chamber. It was wet, slimy, with small ridges and furrows, as if it had been left roughly finished. He reached the other side. Suddenly he pulled his hand back again. There was a regularity to the furrows. He felt around, his eyes shut, tracing the marks, trying to read what he was feeling. There was no doubt about it. 'You're right,' he said excitedly. 'I can feel the outline of another circle, an inner circle on the floor of the chamber. I think it's a lid, a stone lid. I can feel markings on it.'

'Is there a handle?' Costas said.

'Nothing. It's flat across the top. I've no idea how we're going to open this.'

'And those markings?'

'I can count twenty so far,' Jack said. 'Wait.' He flinched in pain as he jammed his elbow against the crack, trying to feel every part of the lid surface. He worked his hand round. 'No, twenty-three. They're in a circle, around the edge of the lid. They're letters, raised letters carved on little blocks, set slightly into the stone surface. It's curious. I can actually press them down slightly.'

'Can you read them?'

Jack traced his fingers around the letters. He suddenly realized what they were. 'It's the Latin alphabet, the alphabet of the later Roman Republic and the early empire. Twenty-three letters. Alpha to zeta.'

'Jack, I think what you've got there is a combination lock, Roman style.'

'Huh?'

'We studied these things at MIT. Ancient technology. If there isn't a handle, the lid must have some kind of spring opener, set underneath to push it up. My guess is a bronze spring, set around the edge of the inner chamber. The letters must be a combination lock, probably attached to stone or metal pivots that secure the lid into the rock. The combination might be adjustable, allowing the person using it to reset it each time with a new code. Press the right combination, and bingo, the lid springs up.'

'Twenty-three letters,' Jack murmured. 'And no way of knowing how many we need to press. I don't even want to begin to calculate the number of possibilities.'

'Let's start with the obvious,' Costas said. 'It was Pliny the Elder who put the scroll here, right? What was his full name?'

Jack thought for a moment. 'Caius Plinius Secundus.'

'Okay. Punch in the initials.'

Jack pictured the Latin alphabet in his mind's eye, and traced his finger around the circle until he came to each letter. C, P, S. He pressed them in the correct order, and they depressed very slightly, but no more. He tried again, then in a different order. Still nothing.

'No good,' he said, his teeth gritted.

'Then your guess is as good as mine,' Costas said. 'You may as well try random combinations. We shouldn't be here for more than a week. We really need to get going, Jack. Our friend might not be the only one. We don't know.'

'Wait.' Jack's mind was racing. 'You might have the right idea. Let's think about this. Pliny gets the document from Claudius. He promises to hide it away. Pliny keeps his promises, and never puts anything off. He's got too much else to do, managing the naval base, writing his books. He takes his fast galley up to Rome that night, 23 August AD 79, right up the Tiber, comes straight here to the Admiral's safety deposit box, returns that same night to Misenum on the Bay of Naples, just in time for the eruption. Whose name is fresh in his mind?'

'You mean Jesus? The Nazarene?'

'Not enough there for a code, and it might be too obvious. No. I mean Claudius himself. His name before he became emperor. Tiberius Claudius Drusus Nero Germanicus.' Jack shut his eyes again, moved his hand over the letters and pressed them in. *T, C, D, N, G.* Nothing. He repeated it. Again nothing. He exhaled forcibly. 'No good.'

'Maybe you've missed a letter. Emperor?'

'*Caesar Augustus.*' Jack found the letters, then punched them. Still nothing. He slumped again, then suddenly drew his breath in sharply. 'No. Not *Caesar Augustus*. Claudius was no longer emperor. He would have been at pains to tell Pliny that. Not an emperor. He'd become something else. Something that would have amused them both.'

'Claudius the god,' Costas murmured.

'*Divus.*' Jack reached back around and found the letter D. He pressed it as hard as he could. Something gave way, and the letter depressed at least an inch. Suddenly the lid sprang up, and Jack quickly withdrew his hand to prevent it being trapped. 'Bingo,' he said excitedly. He put his hand back where the lid had been. He could feel the coil of a heavy bronze spring, now holding the lid a foot or more above the opening it had covered. He reached inside and felt a cylindrical shape, loose in the hole. His heart began to pound. He pulled it out, easing it between the metal coils of the spring. The cylinder was heavy for its size, made of stone, about ten inches long and six inches wide. 'I've got it,' he said, pulling the cylinder out of the chamber and into the fissure, then holding it under his headlamp. 'It's Egyptian, a hand-turned Egyptian stone vessel. We've hit paydirt, Costas. It's identical in manufacture to those larger jars in Claudius' library, the reused canopic jars, the ones holding the papyrus scrolls. The lid's still sealed in resin. Looks like Pliny didn't tamper with it. We might be in luck.' He passed the cylinder down to Costas, who reached up from the tunnel below. Jack eased himself back down the fissure, and the two of them squatted over the cylinder in the darkness, their beams illuminating the mottled marble surface as Costas turned the object over in his hands.

'What do we do now?' he said.

'We open it.'

'So this could be it.'

Jack nodded silently, and looked at Costas. They had been here before, the knife-edge moment just before a new revelation, but each time the excitement seemed more intense.

'Not exactly controlled laboratory conditions,' Costas said.

'My call.' Jack took the cylinder, grasped the lid with one hand and the body of the jar with the other, and twisted. It gave way easily, the ancient resin around the sealing cracking off and falling on the tunnel floor. He prised the lid off and set it down, then peered inside. 'No papyrus,' he said, his voice flat. 'But something else, wedged in.' He reached inside with his other hand, and withdrew a flat stone object about six inches long and four inches wide, the size of a small cosmetic mirror. It was made up of two leaves joined together, with a hinge on one side and a metal latch on the other. Jack turned it over in his hands and then put his thumb against the latch. 'It's a writing tablet,' he said excitedly. 'A diptych, two leaves that open up like a book. The inside surface should be covered with wax.'

'Any chance that could have survived?' Costas said.

'This could be another Agamemnon moment,' Jack said. 'It could still be there, but exposure to oxygen could degrade it immediately. I'm going for it. We can't risk waiting.'

'I'm with you.' Costas pulled out a waterproof notebook and pencil, and knelt beside Jack, poised to write.

Jack pressed the latch and felt the stone leaves move. 'Here goes,' he whispered. He opened up the tablet. The interior surfaces were hard, glassy. They could see it was wax, smooth and perfectly preserved, but getting darker by the second. It had writing on it. 'Quick,' Jack said. He passed the tablet to Costas, and grabbed the notebook, feverishly writing down everything he saw. 'Done,' he said after less than a minute. The wax was still there, but the scratchings on the surface had virtually disappeared, gone like a phantasm.

Costas closed the tablet and immediately folded it in a sheet of bubblewrap and a waterproof bag, then slipped it into his chest pocket. He peered at Jack, who was staring at the notebook. 'Well?'

'It's Latin.' Jack paused, marshalling his thoughts. 'Whoever wrote this, it wasn't a Nazarene from Galilee. That could only have been Aramaic, Greek perhaps.'

'So this is not Claudius' precious document?'

'It could have been written by Claudius, or it could have been Narcissus,' Jack murmured, shifting his body in the cramped space. 'Impossible to tell from scratchings on a wax tablet whether it was the same handwriting as that sheet by Narcissus in Claudius' study. Especially when it disappears before your very eyes.' He gazed at Costas. 'No, this is not the document we're after. But it's not the end of the trail either.' He ripped off the page of the notebook and transcribed his scribbled words neatly on to a fresh sheet, then held it in his beam so they could both see:

Dies irae, dies illa
Solvet saeclum in favilla
Teste David cum Sibylla

Inter monte duorum
Qua respiciatam Andraste
Uri vinciri verberari
Ferroque necari

'Poetry?' Costas said. 'Virgil? He wrote about the Sibyl, didn't he?'

'You wily old devil,' Jack murmured.

'Who?'

'I think Claudius was keeping his word, but he was also playing a game, and I think the Sibyl was playing games with him too.'

'Go on.'

'Well, the first verse is easy enough. It's the first stanza of the Dies Irae, the Day of Wrath, the hymn that used to be central to the Roman Catholic requiem mass. It's an incredible find, because the earliest version of these lines before this dates from the thirteenth century. Most people think it was a medieval creation, especially with those rhyming words which you never see in ancient Latin verse, in Virgil for example.' Jack scribbled down an English text beside the Latin. 'Here's how it's usually translated, keeping the metre and the rhyme:

' "Day of wrath and terror looming!

Heaven and earth to ash consuming,

David's word and Sibyl's truth foredooming!" '

Costas whistled. 'Sounds like a premonition of the eruption of Vesuvius.'

Jack nodded. 'I think what we've got here is a Sibylline prophecy, given to Claudius at Cumae. She must have spoken these first lines to others, who remembered them, and preserved them secretly until they resurfaced in the medieval Catholic liturgy.'

'Who's David?' Costas asked.

'That's the fascinating thing about discovering that this verse is so old, from the early Christian period. David in the Dies Irae is usually thought of as a reference to Jesus, who was believed to be a descendant of King David of the Jews. If that's true, then this may confirm that the Sibyl knew of Jesus, that the association of the Sibyl with early Christianity is based on fact.'

'And the second verse?'

'That's our clue. It has all the hallmarks of a Sibylline utterance, a riddle written on the leaves in front of the cave at Cumae. Here's how I translate it:

'"Between two hills,

Where Andraste lies,

To be burned by fire, to be bound in chains,

To be beaten, to die by the sword."'

'Meaning?' Costas said.

'The second part's easy. Extraordinary, but easy. It's the *sacramentum gladiatorum*, the gladiators' oath. *Uri, vinciri, verberari, ferroque necari*. I swear to be burned by fire, to be bound in chains, to be beaten, to die by the sword.'

'Okay,' Costas said quietly. 'You can't spring anything new on me. Gladiators. I'm cool with that. And the first part?'

'Andraste was a British goddess, from before the Romans. We know about her from the Roman historian Dio Cassius, who says that Andraste was invoked by Boudica before a battle. You know about Boudica?'

'Boudica? Sure. The redhead queen.'

'She led the revolt against the Roman occupation in AD 60. The biggest bloodbath in British history.' Jack looked at the word again, then suddenly had a moment of utter clarity, as if he were just waking up. 'Of course,' he said, his voice hoarse. 'That's what the Sibyl means.' He quickly scanned the final lines again. 'The gladiators' oath. *Ad gladium*, by the sword. We're being directed to a gladiators' arena, an amphitheatre.'

'The Colosseum? Here in Rome?'

'There were many others.' Jack looked at the verse again. *A place built between two hills, a place where a British goddess lies*. He suddenly peered at Costas, grinning broadly.

'I know that look.' Costas said.

'And I know exactly where we're going,' Jack said triumphantly. 'Come on. You might not want to hear this until we reach sunlight.'

Costas narrowed his eyes and looked at him suspiciously. 'Roger that.' He heaved himself up, and they both crouched around and made their way down the steps to the cliff face, abseiling down one by one and kitting up again with their rebreathers at the bottom. They both kept an eye on the tunnel exit where their assailant had disappeared, but the flow of water had increased further and there was clearly no chance of a repeat entrance from that direction. They continued heavily down the remainder of the steps to the cavern floor and the water's edge, where they checked their breathing equipment before closing down their helmets. Costas studiously avoided looking down the passageway to the macabre seated figure in the sacred cave, but Jack was transfixed by it for a moment, suddenly aware of the momentous discovery they had made. The pool of water leading back towards the Cloaca Maxima seemed less forbidding now, a way out of the underworld rather than a portal into the unknown. Costas put both hands up, ready to shut his visor, then peered at Jack. 'We're getting to know old Claudius pretty well now, aren't we?'

'He's become a friend,' Jack said. 'We seem to be following his life's works, his achievements. He seems to be standing over my shoulder. Back there I really felt he was with us, egging us on.'

'So he didn't trust Pliny after all.'

'I think he trusted him as a friend, but he knew that curiosity might get the better of him. If Pliny had survived Vesuvius, I've little doubt he would have come back here one day and opened that container. So Claudius gave him a riddle. A Sibylline prophecy. What neither of them knew was that Vesuvius would cut the whole story short. That wax tablet's been sitting there unread since the day Pliny deposited it almost two thousand years ago.'

'For us to discover.'

'I think that's what Claudius wanted. Not for Pliny to take up the trail, not another Roman, but someone far in the future, someone who could follow the clues and find his treasure at a time when it could be safely revealed.'

'What he didn't foresee was that the threat would remain,' Costas murmured. 'So where do we go now?'

Jack said nothing, but looked at Costas apologetically.

'I knew it,' Costas said with resignation. 'I just knew it. Another hole in the ground.'

'We need to find a long-lost goddess.'

14

Twenty-four hours later, Jack led Costas past the great bulk of St Paul's Cathedral in London, into the maze of streets and alleys that made up the heart of the old city. They had spent the previous night on board *Seaquest II* in the Mediterranean, and had flown into London City airport early that morning. Jack's first task had been a meeting with Ben Kershaw, the IMU security chief. After their experience in Rome, what had begun as a secretive archaeological quest had taken on a deadly new dimension. As long as they were still searching, as long as it was clear to those who were following them that Rome had provided only another clue, not the object of their search, Jack felt they were reasonably safe. The fate of the man who had aimed a pistol at his head under the

Palatine Hill was unknown, though the chances of surviving a body surf through the Cloaca Maxima without breathing gear were slim. It seemed almost inconceivable that they should have been followed to London, but Jack was taking no chances. They would keep the lowest possible profile, and Ben and two others would be lurking in the background, watching, waiting, ready to pounce should there be any repeat of their encounter in the ancient cavern under Rome.

'Welcome to sunny London.' Costas grimaced, then stood back too late as a line of black cabs rumbled past, sluicing water up over his ankles. He and Jack both wore blue Goretex jackets with the hoods up, and Costas was fumbling inexpertly with an umbrella. What had begun as a heavily overcast day had now settled into constant drizzle, interspersed with occasional heavy downpours. Costas sniffed noisily, then sneezed. 'So this was where Claudius brought his precious secret. Seems an awful long way from Judaea.'

'You'd be surprised,' Jack said, raising his voice above the traffic. 'The early Christians in Roman Britain thought they had a direct link to the Holy Land, undistorted by Rome. It caused them no end of trouble when the Roman Church tried to assert itself here.'

'So we're on the site of Roman London now.'

'Just entered it. The City of London today, the financial district, is the old medieval city, and that was built on the ruins of the Roman city of Londinium. You can still see the line of the Roman walls in the street layout.'

'This place must have seemed a backwater to the Romans,'

Costas said, splashing across the street behind Jack. 'Who'd have wanted to come here?'

'Look around you now, at the faces,' Jack said, as they navigated through a crowd of people hurrying on the pavement. 'London was just as cosmopolitan in the Roman period. It was founded for commerce, a magnet for traders from all corners of the empire.' He veered left over the road and dodged through traffic which had almost crawled to a standstill, then led Costas up the alleyway opposite. 'It's true that the Celtic background gave Britain a particular stamp, something that made it seem very distant to some Romans, pretty frightening. But this place was no backwater for Roman entrepreneurs, for freedmen and retired soldiers on the make. It offered chances of a fortune and social status they never would have found in Rome.'

'You mean guys like Narcissus, Claudius' freedman?' Costas said.

'Precisely. He may never have lived here, but those British lead ingots with his name stamp we found on St Paul's shipwreck show he was a pretty shrewd investor in the new province.'

'So it was Claudius who invaded this place.' Costas blinked up at the drizzle that was beginning to envelop them, and then pulled the hood of his jacket forward. 'Left Italy for this.'

Jack wiped the sheen of water from his face, and then bounded across another street. They were in Lawrence Lane, heading towards the medieval Guildhall. 'Claudius was on a mission,' he said. 'It was a matter of family pride, living up to his ancestors, taking up where they had left off. Almost a hundred years before, his great-great-uncle Julius Caesar had landed in Britain with his legions at the tail end of the conquest of Gaul. It was more a show of strength than an invasion, a bit of ancient gunboat diplomacy, to keep the Britons on their side of the Channel.'

Costas peered out gloomily from under his hood. 'You mean Julius Caesar took one look at this place, thought better of it and left.'

Jack grinned. 'He had other things on his mind. But he paved the way for traders. Even before Claudius invaded, there was a settlement of Romans at the tribal capital Camulodunum, about fifty miles north-east of here near modern Colchester. They imported cargoes of wine in pottery amphoras, exactly the same type we discovered in the shipwreck of St Paul and saw in Herculaneum. They discovered that the British loved alcohol.'

'Glad to see that hasn't changed.' Costas' muffled voice came from several paces behind, and Jack turned to see his friend's hooded figure standing in front of a pub. Costas pulled down his hood and pointed suggestively. Jack shook his head and beckoned him. 'We're almost there. Time for that later.'

'That's what you always say,' Costas grumbled, then splashed up behind Jack. They walked on for a few paces in silence, then Costas caught Jack's arm and pulled him to a halt. 'One thing been's nagging at me since Rome, Jack.'

'Fire away.'

'It's Elizabeth, your encounter with her at Herculaneum. You said she warned you, told you to be on your guard.'

'It was only a few snatched words.'

'I'm wondering about our assailant in the cave under Rome. Whoever he was, whoever they are, how could they have known we were there?'

'I assume we were being followed. I only really put it together afterwards, but it wouldn't have been difficult to trace us from Herculaneum to *Seaquest II*, then to Rome. A few tapped phone calls, even some hijacked satellite surveillance. We kept our movements low-key but it still wouldn't have been difficult for the right people to know we were trucking IMU diving equipment into the centre of Rome, and going into the Cloaca Maxima.'

'You're suggesting some pretty sophisticated surveillance.'

'That could be what we're dealing with. No holds barred.'

'They seemed to know specifically what we were after. That guy in the cave. The last thing he said. "Give it to me."'

'Are you suggesting Elizabeth could have been part of this?'

'I'm not suggesting anything.'

Jack looked troubled. 'She did say something else. I thought it was personal, about us, but maybe I was wrong.'

'Go on.'

'She said she knew.'

'Knew what?'

'That was it. Just that she knew. It was the last thing she said to me.'

'Do you think she knew what we'd found in Herculaneum?

Do you think she'd been up the tunnel into the villa herself, before we arrived?'

'Maurice was certain that nobody else had been through the crack in the wall before us, and he knows better than anyone the signs of modern interference, tomb-robbers. But Elizabeth could have gone up the tunnel in secret the night before we arrived, seen Narcissus and the carbonized scrolls, looked through the crack into the chamber. She could have known there were scrolls.'

'Why not tell you?'

'There was fear in her eyes. Real fear. And she's one tough lady, brought up in the back streets of Naples. I've left repeated phone messages for her at the superintendency, but no reply. I think she told me everything she could in those few moments. I think she was taking a big risk.'

'You think she's on our side?'

'I don't know what to think, Costas. I haven't known what to think about Elizabeth for a long time. But I do believe she's not pulling the strings. There something very powerful behind all this, powerful enough to put the gag on her. And that frightens me too.'

Costas grunted, peered up at the drizzle again, then nodded slowly. 'Okay. I guess we don't have any choice. We carry on. But I still feel like bait.'

'Ben and the other guy are just behind us.'

Costas nodded, and then walked on. 'Okay. Back to Roman London. A lot of foreigners here, so a lot of foreign ideas too.'

'Exactly.' They came to the edge of Gresham Street, and

Jack pointed to the building opposite. 'That's what we've come for.' Costas gazed at the darkened masonry façade, clearly much older than the towering concrete and glass structures of Lawrence Lane they had just passed through. The façade was broken by five tall windows with a circular window at each end, and the east side in front of them had columns and a pediment embedded in it in a neoclassical style. 'English baroque,' Jack continued. 'Not quite as grand as St Paul's, but same period, same architect. One of the City churches rebuilt by Sir Christopher Wren following the Great Fire of London in 1666.'

'St Lawrence Jewry.' Costas peered at a soggy tourist map he had pulled from his pocket.

'The name says it all.' Jack waited for a taxi to roar past. 'This was the Jewish quarter of London until the Jews were expelled in the thirteenth century. St Lawrence Jewry is Church of England, Anglican, but just up the road there are Catholic churches, Nonconformist chapels, synagogues, mosques, you name it. That's my point. It would have been similar in Roman London. Today most people worship one God, but in some ways it's not that far from the polytheism that Romans such as Claudius would have known, with lots of different temples and forms of ritual.'

'Wasn't there a cult of the emperor too?'

Jack nodded and stepped back against a wall for a moment, out of the spray from the road. 'The Romans built a temple to Claudius at Colchester, and maybe one here in London too. Privately, I don't think Claudius would have bought into it, if he really did survive to see himself being worshipped. It would have smacked too much of his deranged nephew Caligula, and of Claudius' successor Nero. But here in the provinces, the imperial cult was a practical matter, a way of getting the natives to pay dues to Rome, as much as it was about idolizing the individual emperor himself.'

'Didn't the Romans try to stamp out rival religions?'

'Not usually. That's the beauty of polytheism, politically speaking. If you already have more than one god, then it's easy enough to absorb a few more, less hassle than trying to eradicate them. And absorbing foreign gods stamps the authority of your own gods over them. That's what happened in Roman Britain. The Celtic war god was absorbed into the cult of Mars, the Roman war god, who had earlier absorbed the Greek war god Ares. The Celtic goddess Andraste from our inscription was linked with Diana and Artemis. Even Christianity came to adapt pagan rites of worship, including temples and priests. Almost everything you see about that church over there would have been unfamiliar to the first Christians, even the idea of an organized religion with acts of worship. To some of them, it might have been anathema.'

'Maybe even to their Messiah himself.'

'Provocative thought, Costas.'

'Remember, I was brought up Greek Orthodox. I can say these things. In Jerusalem, in the Church of the Holy Sepulchre, the Greeks think they're the closest to Christ, custodians of the Tomb. But then so do all the other denominations there, Armenian, Roman Catholic, you name it, all crowded up against it, competing. It's a bit ridiculous, really. Not seeing the wood for the trees.'

Jack led Costas briskly over the road, past the church and into Guildhall Yard. A few metres behind them was the west wall of the church, and in front of them, set into the paving slabs of the courtyard, was a wide arc of dark stones, like part of a huge sundial extending under the surrounding buildings. Jack's cell phone chirped and he spoke quickly into it, then began to walk towards the entrance to the Guildhall Art Gallery on the west side of the courtyard, following the alignment of the arc. 'Jeremy's there already,' he said. 'And remember this arc on the courtyard. It clarifies what we're about to see.'

Ten minutes later they stood at almost exactly the same spot as on the courtyard but eight metres below ground. They were in a wide subterranean space, backlit around the edges, with brick and masonry ruins in front of them. They had taken off their coats, and Costas was reading a descriptive plaque. 'The Roman amphitheatre,' he murmured. 'Fantastic. I had no idea.'

'Nor did anyone else, until a few years ago,' Jack said. 'Much of the city above Roman London was destroyed by German bombing during the Second World War, and clearance and redevelopment has allowed a lot of archaeological excavation to take place since then. But the chance for a big dig in Guildhall Yard didn't come up till the late 1980s. This was their most astonishing find.'

'That elliptical arc in the pavement, above us,' Costas murmured. 'Now I've got you.'

'That arc marks the outline of the arena, the central pit of the amphitheatre,' Jack said.

'What date are we looking at?'

'You remember the Boudican revolt? That took place in AD 60, about the same time as St Paul's shipwreck. Roman London had been founded about fifteen years before that, soon after Claudius' invasion in 43. Boudica destroyed the first Roman settlement, but it soon recovered and there were big building projects underway within a few years. The amphitheatre was wooden, but the wall you see here around the arena was made of brick and stone, probably begun some time in the seventies.'

'In time for Claudius' second visit, incognito as an old man.'

'That's my working hypothesis, that he came here some time shortly before AD 79, on a secret mission.' Jack pulled out his translation of the extraordinary riddle they had discovered on the wax tablet in Rome. '*Between two hills*,' he said in a low voice. 'That's what London looked like, with the Walbrook stream running down the middle. And then the gladiator's oath. *To be burned by fire, to be bound in chains, to be beaten, to die by the sword.* This has to be the spot.'

'Where Andraste lies,' Costas murmured. 'A temple? A shrine?'

'Some kind of holy place, the home of a goddess.'

'But where exactly?'

'There's one spot here that hasn't been excavated, between the amphitheatre and the Church of St Lawrence Jewry,' Jack said. 'Just behind the wall over there.' At that moment he heard footsteps coming up behind them and he swivelled round in alarm, then relaxed. 'Here's someone who might be able to tell us more.'

15

A tall, rangy young man with glasses and a shock of blond hair came loping up to Jack and Costas, smiling and waving his hand in greeting. With his dripping Barbour jacket and pale corduroys, Jeremy Haverstock looked the quintessential English country squire, but his accent was American. 'Hi, guys. Just got off the train from Oxford. Lucky your call got me at the Institute yesterday, Jack. I was on my way out for a week in Hereford studying the lost cathedral library. Maria gave me complete responsibility for it, you know. It's a big break for me, and I was a little worried about cancelling. I couldn't get her on her cell phone.'

'She's back in Naples by now,' Jack said. 'She and

Hiebermeyer are tying themselves up in red tape. Don't worry, I'll put in a word.'

'I had time for a couple of hours in Balliol College library in Oxford yesterday evening,' Jeremy said. 'Turns out Balliol owned the Church of St Lawrence Jewry from the thirteenth to the nineteenth centuries, and they still have the archive. I looked up what you wanted. I think I found enough for you to go on, but I need to get back there after we visit the church. There's one really intriguing lead I want to follow.'

'Great to see you again, by the way, Jeremy,' Costas said. 'Hadn't expected it so soon.'

'The whole thing still seems like a dream, our expedition,' Jeremy said. 'The hunt for the lost Jewish treasure, Harald Hardrada and the Vikings, the underground caves in the Yucatán. I thought I might try to write it down, but nobody would believe it.'

'Just make it fiction,' Costas said. 'And leave our names out of it. At the moment, we're trying to remain anonymous. We've had a slightly unpleasant encounter in Rome. Underground.'

'So Jack tells me,' Jeremy said quietly. 'You guys seem to make a habit of it. I thought I recognized someone in the art gallery above, from *Seaquest II*.'

'Good,' Jack murmured. 'They're here.'

'We've got half an hour until we can get into the crypt.'

'Crypt?' Costas said.

'Fear not,' Jeremy said. 'It's empty. The first one is, anyway.'

Costas gave him a dubious look, then sat down on a chair

and leaned back, stretching out his legs. 'Okay. So we've got a little time. Some questions. Put me in the picture. Tell me about this place before the Romans. In the lead-up to Claudius,' he said.

Jack looked at him keenly. 'Prehistoric London was a weird place. Not a settlement, as far as we can tell, but a place where something was going on. Best guess is some kind of sacred site. Trouble is, we don't know much about religion in the Iron Age, because they didn't build temples or make representations of their gods that have survived. Almost all we have to go on are the Roman historians, most of them biased, all second-hand.'

'Druids,' Jeremy said, sitting down on the edge of the amphitheatre wall and leaning forward. 'Druids, and human sacrifice.'

Jack nodded. 'When the Roman general Suetonius Paulinus heard of Boudica's revolt, he was attacking the remote island of Mona, modern Anglesey off north Wales. It was the last bastion of the British who'd refused to come under Rome's yoke, and the sacred stronghold of the druids.'

'Guys in white robes,' Costas murmured.

'That's the Victorian image of the druid, a kind of Gandalf figure, Merlin, gathering mistletoe and travelling unharmed between warring kingdoms. The idea of priestly mediators is probably accurate, but the rest is pure fantasy.'

'Tacitus paints a pretty appalling picture,' Jeremy said.

Jack nodded, extracted a book from his khaki bag and flipped it open. 'Tacitus' father-in-law Agricola had been governor of Britain, so he knew what he was talking about. The Romans at Mona were confronted by a dense mass of enemy along the shoreline. Among them were the druids, who he says were "raising their hands to heaven and screaming dreadful curses". After the Romans were victorious, they destroyed the sacred groves of the druids, places where they "drench their altars in the blood of prisoners and consult their gods by means of human entrails".'

'Sounds like a few modern priests I've known,' Costas said wryly. 'Power through terror.'

'There are plenty of historical parallels, as you say.'

'The Church in the Middle Ages, for one,' Jeremy murmured. 'Submission, obedience, confession, vengeance, retribution.'

'All things the earliest Christians would have abhorred,' Jack said.

'And it wasn't just male druids on Anglesey,' Jeremy said.

Jack opened the book again. 'The thing that really terrified the Romans, that awed them to the point of paralysis, was the women.'

'This gets even better,' Costas murmured.

'Hordes of fanatical women, "black-robed women with dishevelled hair like Furies, brandishing torches".' Jack put down the book. 'It was the Romans' worst nightmare. The image of the Amazon, the warrior queen, really kept the Roman male awake at night, and it wasn't lust. Tacitus may have exaggerated this aspect of Britain to play on Roman fantasies about the barbarian world, a world beyond control, a world with no apparent method or rationale. But all the evidence suggests it was true, that the Romans in Britain really had walked into their own vision of hell, a world of Amazon queens and screaming banshees.'

'Boudica,' Costas said. 'Was she some kind of druid?'

'We know of one other British queen, Cartimandua of the Brigantes,' Jack replied. 'And queen usually meant high priestess. There was nothing unusual in that. The Roman emperor was Pontifex Maximus, the Egyptian pharaohs were priest-kings, the queens and kings of England are Defenders of the Faith.'

'A redhead arch-druid warrior queen,' Costas said weakly. 'God help her enemies.'

'And how does London fit into all this?' Jeremy said.

'That's where we really get our teeth into the archaeology.' Jack took a plan from his bag and rolled it out on the floor, and Jeremy knelt down and held the corners. 'Or rather, the lack of it. This shows the London area during the Iron Age. As you can see, there's no clear indication of habitation on the site of Londinium, where we are now. A few finds of pottery, some of the silver coins the tribes began producing in the decades before the Roman conquest. Not much else.'

'What's this?' Costas pointed to an object marked in the river Thames west of the Roman town. 'Armour?'

'The Battersea Shield. One of the finest pieces of metalwork ever found from antiquity, rivalling the best the Romans produced. You can see it in the British Museum. It probably dates to the century before the Romans arrived, and it may suggest what actually went on at this place.'

'Go on.'

Jack rested on his haunches. 'Almost all the other major towns of Roman Britain were built on the site of Iron Age tribal capitals, often right next to the prehistoric earthworks. Camulodunum, where they built the temple to Claudius, was a colony for Roman veterans right on top of the Iron Age tribal capital of the Trinovantes. Verulamium was built next to the old capital of the Catuvellauni. It was an ingenious system, designed to stamp Roman authority on the heart of the tribal world, yet also to maintain the power base of the old tribal leaders who became the new magistrates. It was rule by devolution, maintaining the pretence of native authority, just as the British did in India.'

'But London was the exception,' Jeremy said.

Jack nodded. 'After starting as a river port, London became the provincial capital when it was rebuilt following the Boudican revolt. But something was going on here before the Romans arrived, something really fascinating. The Battersea Shield was almost certainly a ritual deposition, a valued object deliberately thrown into the river as a votive offering. There are other finds like this from the Thames and its tributaries. Swords, shields, spears. It's a tradition that goes back at least to the Bronze Age, and lasted well into the medieval period.'

'Excalibur and the Lady of the Lake,' Jeremy murmured.

'Offerings seem to have been made on tribal boundaries,' Jack continued, nodding. 'Maybe the weapons were to arm the god of your tribe, a way of asserting territorial claims, a bit like the medieval ritual of beating the bounds of parishes on Rogation Day. And London was the biggest boundary site of them all, with at least five tribal areas converging on the river Thames. The distant island of Anglesey may have represented the edge of the British Iron Age world, but London may have been its ritual apex.'

'Yet no Iron Age settlements have been found here, according to this plan,' Costas said.

'Remember Tacitus' account, the sacred groves on Anglesey? London was densely wooded at the time of the Roman invasion, right up to the water's edge. Within the forest, along the edge of the river and its tributaries, were clearings, groves, places now submerged under the streets of London.'

Costas peered hard at the map. 'How about this. In AD 60, when Boudica rose in revolt, the one place the Britons really can't stomach having a new Roman settlement is London, built on their sacred site. They save their worst retribution for it.'

Jack nodded enthusiastically. 'After the rebels had ravaged Camulodunum and driven the Roman survivors into the Temple of Claudius there, Tacitus tells us that the Celtic warriors heard an augury. At the mouth of the Thames a phantom settlement had been seen, in ruins. The sea was a blood-red colour, and shapes like human corpses were seen in the ebb tide. For Boudica, it was a sign of where to go next.'

'What happened when Boudica hit London?'

'There were no survivors. Tacitus says that the Roman general Suetonius and his army reached London from Anglesey before Boudica arrived, but Suetonius decided his force was too weak to defend the place. There were lamentations and appeals, and the inhabitants were allowed to leave with him. Those who stayed, the elderly, the women, children, were all slaughtered by the Britons.'

'Cassius Dio tells more.' Jeremy picked up another book Jack had taken out of his bag. 'As I recall, he's our only other source on Boudica, writing over a hundred years after the revolt but perhaps based on lost first-hand accounts.' He found a page. 'Here's what the Britons did to their captives: "The worst and most bestial atrocity committed by their captors was the following. They hung up naked the noblest and most eminent women, cut off their breasts and sewed them into their mouths, so that they seemed to be eating them; afterwards they impaled the women on sharp skewers run through the length of their bodies. All this they did to the accompaniment of sacrifices, feasts and wanton behaviour. This they did in their holy places, especially in the Grove of Andraste, their name for the goddess of Victory."'

'Sounds like a scene from *Apocalypse Now*,' Costas murmured.

'That may not be far off,' Jack said quietly. 'The name Boudica also meant Victory, and it could be that her sacred grove was some pool up the river, her own holy of holies.'

'Her own private hell, you mean,' Costas said.

'Geoffrey of Monmouth thought there were mass

beheadings,' Jeremy said quietly. 'He wrote in the twelfth century, when human skulls started to be found along the Walbrook, just yards from here. They've been found ever since, when the river's been dug into. Skulls, hundreds of them, washed down from somewhere and embedded in the river gravel, right under the heart of the city of London where the Walbrook flows into the Thames. Geoffrey of Monmouth was the first to link the skulls with the Boudican revolt.'

'I don't get it.' Costas had picked up Jack's copy of Tacitus, and was flicking through the pages, stopping and reading. 'Here we go again. Sacrifices, orgies of slaughter. Whole towns razed, everyone murdered. Men, women, children. Correct me if I'm wrong, but these hardly seem acts of charity. I don't get why Claudius would have brought his precious document with the word of Christ to this place, to the care of some pagan goddess.'

'We don't know what was going on,' Jack murmured. 'The British rebels who knew of Jesus, perhaps even Boudica, may have seen him as a fellow rebel against Roman rule. They may have been sympathetic to early Christians for that reason alone. If Tacitus and Dio Cassius are right about the violation of Boudica's daughters by the Romans, she would have had ample cause for retribution, for vengeance wreaked in the ways of the barbarian, ways which she must have known would cast most fear into the hearts of Romans.'

'She must also have known it was suicidal, that she was on a one-way ticket,' Costas murmured. 'Maybe it unhinged her. Remember *Apocalypse Now*, Colonel Kurtz. A noble cause, unsound methods. Maybe Boudica got swallowed up in her own heart of darkness.'

'Speaking of which, it's time.' Jeremy lurched to his feet. 'The rector's opened the crypt specially for us during the lunchtime concert in the church. Come on.'

A few minutes later they stood just inside the portico of the Guildhall Art Gallery, looking out over the yard with the elliptical line of the Roman amphitheatre arena marked across it. To their right was the medieval façade of the Guildhall itself, and to the left the solid, functional shape of St Lawrence Jewry, reconstructed after the Second World War to resemble as closely as possible the original design built by Sir Christopher Wren after the Great Fire of London in 1666.

'This place seems pristine now, but it's seen three circles of hell,' Jack said quietly, peering out into the drizzle. 'Boudica's revolt in AD 60, the massacre, possibly human sacrifice. Then the Great Fire of 1666. Of the buildings here, only the Guildhall wasn't completely destroyed, because its old oaks wouldn't burn. An eyewitness said it looked like a bright shining coal, as if it had been a Palace of Gold or a great building of burnished brass. Then, almost three centuries later, the inferno visited again. This time from above.'

'The twenty-ninth of December 1940,' Jeremy said. 'The Blitz.'

'One night of many,' Jack replied. 'But that night the Luftwaffe targeted the square mile, the City of London. My grandmother was here, a despatch rider at the Air Ministry. She said the sound of dropping incendiaries was ominously gentle, like a rain shower, but the high-explosive bombs had been fitted with tubes so they screamed rather than whistled. Hundreds were killed and maimed, men, women, children. That famous picture of St Paul's Cathedral, wreathed in flames but miraculously intact, comes from that night. St Lawrence Jewry wasn't so lucky. It went up like a Roman candle, the flames leaping above the city. One of the men standing next to my grandmother on the roof of the Air Ministry watching the churches burn was Air Vice Marshal Arthur Harris, "Bomber" Harris. He said he saw total war that night. He was the architect of the British bomber offensive against Germany.'

'Another circle of hell,' Jeremy murmured.

'My grandmother heard a terrible scream that night, like a banshee,' Jack said quietly. 'It haunted her for the rest of her life.'

'Must have been a lot of horror,' Costas said.

'The scream came from the church,' Jack continued. 'The organ was on fire and the hot air rushing through the pipes made it shriek, as if the church was in a death agony.'

'Shit.'

'You couldn't put that in a horror movie, could you? Nobody would believe you.'

'I think I'm getting the jitters about this place, Jack.'

'It's all still there, under our feet,' Jack said. 'The Boudican destruction layer, charred earth and smashed pottery, human bone. Then masses of rubble from the old medieval church destroyed in 1666, cleared and buried to make way for Sir Christopher Wren's new structures. And then another layer of destruction debris from the Blitz, with reconstruction work still going on.'

'Any unexploded ordnance?' Costas said hopefully. 'That'd make me happy. You owe me one. That stuff you wouldn't let me touch on the sea bed off Sicily.'

Jack gave Costas a look, and then walked briskly over Guildhall Yard. 'Remember where we are, the lie of the amphitheatre,' he said as he stepped over the curved line in the pavement. He pointed to the western wall of St Lawrence Jewry, about eight metres away. 'And remember the proximity of the church.' They reached the church entrance and went inside. The lunchtime concert was about to begin, and Jeremy led them quickly through the nave packed with seated people to a small wooden door off the west aisle. He opened it, ducked inside and beckoned. Costas followed him, then Jack. As Jack shut the door the music began. The concert was a selection of Bach's reconstructed violin concertos, and Jack recognized the Concerto in D Minor for solo violin, strings and basso profundo. The music was bold, confident, joyous, the strident Baroque beat giving order to confusion, structure to chaos. Jack lingered, and for a moment he thought of slipping back and sitting anonymously in the audience. He had always loved the reconstructed concertos, the result of a kind of musical archaeology that seemed to mirror his own processes of discovery, small fragments of certainty put together by scholarship, by guesswork and intuition, suddenly fusing into an explosion of clarity, of euphoria. At the moment, he felt he needed the reassurance, uncertain whether the pieces they had found would meld, whether the trail they were following would lead to a conclusion that was greater than the sum of the parts.

'Come on, Jack,' Costas said from below. Jack followed him down the steps, into an undercroft beneath the level of the nave. The music was still there, but now just a background vibration. He saw an open door, and followed them down into another chamber, smaller and darker. It was old, much older than the masonry structure of Wren's church, and looked as if it had been recently cleaned. A bare bulb hung from the brick vault. Once they were all inside, Jeremy closed and bolted the door at the bottom of the steps, then ran his hand along the masonry wall. 'It's a medieval burial chamber, a private crypt. It was found during the recent excavation work. This is as near as anyone's got to the southern edge of the amphitheatre arena.'

'This must be it,' Jack said. 'Jeremy?'

'I agree. Absolutely.'

Costas eyed them. 'Okay, Jack. I want a damn good explanation for what we're doing here.'

Jack nodded, then squatted back against the wall, his khaki bag hanging from his left side. He was excited, and took a deep breath to steady himself. 'Okay. When we worked out that riddle in Rome, when the location clicked, I immediately thought of Sir Christopher Wren and this church. When I was a boy I used to come here a lot, visit the old bomb sites and help with the excavations. My grandmother was a volunteer, drawn back to the place where she had watched helplessly decades before, trying to atone by helping with the reconstruction work. She took me along for my first excavation, and somehow her description of the inferno in 1940 brought the Boudican revolt to life for me, brought the true horror home, the colour of fire and blood and the terrible noises of human suffering. I've been fascinated by the Boudican revolt ever since, by all the attempts to find Boudica's last place of refuge and her tomb. It became my grandmother's passion too, and when she was dying it was the last thing we spoke about. I made her a promise I thought I'd never be able to fulfil. Later, as a student, having seen myself what the bombing and clearance had revealed of the Roman city, I became fascinated by the other great inferno, by what Wren might have come across in the prehistoric and Roman layers exposed after the Great Fire of 1666. That was before archaeology had begun as a discipline, when most artifacts were never even recognized, let alone recorded.'

'With a few exceptions,' Jeremy murmured.

Jack nodded. 'Wren himself had an antiquarian interest, and mentioned finding Roman artefacts under St Paul's. That's what really fired me up. Then I discovered that the Church of St Lawrence Jewry had been owned by Balliol College, Oxford. One of my uncles was a Fellow of the College, and he arranged for me to visit the archive, to see whether there was any record of finds made here after 1666. That visit was years ago, when I was being drawn away by diving and shipwrecks, and I didn't take detailed notes. That's what I asked Jeremy to check out.'

'And Jeremy came up trumps,' Costas said.

'Jack remembered it was just a scrap of loose paper in an old book, part of the master mason's diary, but I found it,' Jeremy replied, pulling a notepad out of his coat pocket. 'It's fantastic. It was when they were clearing the rubble and burned timbers after the fire, trying to find holes underground to bury the stuff away: disused wells, cesspits, old vaults. One of the workmen broke into a crypt which must be this chamber. The mason described going through into another crypt, then seeing a line of large pottery pipes with handles, upright in a row against the earth wall on one side. He thought they might be drainage pipes, possibly the lining of a well, so they left them intact. They stuffed as much debris as they could into a space off to one side and then bricked it up. They then came back out, and bricked up the entrance from the first crypt also.' Jeremy gestured towards the crumbling wall on the far side of the chamber, opposite the side with the entrance door. 'Over there. That must be it. The brickwork looks hasty, and it's definitely post-medieval. It looks like it hasn't been disturbed since.'

Costas looked perplexed. 'Okay. Drainage pipes. So where does that get us?'

Jack took out a photograph from his bag, and handed it to Costas. 'Where it gets us,' he said excitedly, 'is back to the time of Boudica.'

'Ah,' Costas murmured. 'Got you. Not drainage pipes. Roman amphoras.'

'More than just amphoras,' Jack said excitedly. 'Much more. Intact amphoras by themselves would be a fantastic find, but it's the context that counts. Think of where we are.'

'The Roman amphitheatre?' Costas said. 'A bar, an ancient tavern like the one we saw at Herculaneum?'

'Good guess,' Jack said. 'But that picture's from a place called Sheepen. It shows the amphoras exactly as archaeologists found them. Intact wine amphoras, five of them in a row, along with drinking cups and other goods. They were in a grave.'

'A Roman grave?' Costas said.

Jack shook his head. 'Not Roman. Remember what I said about the Celtic taste for wine? Imported wine had prestige value, a sign of wealth and status. No, the Sheepen amphoras were in the grave of a Celtic nobleman, a warrior.' Jack suddenly felt exuberant. 'All those years ago, when I was a boy, I knew I was on to something really big when I came to the Guildhall site. I just had a hunch. I thought it was the amphitheatre, when they found it years later. But now this, something else, maybe even more extraordinary. I wish my grandmother were here now. Wherever else this trail leads us, this could be another dream of mine realised.'

Costas looked at the photo, then at the bricked-up wall in front of them. He started to speak, but suddenly stopped, transfixed. He looked at the photo again, then at Jack. 'Holy cow,' he said weakly.

Jack looked at him, and nodded. 'Yes.'

'That goddess. Andraste,' Costas whispered.

Jack nodded, wordlessly.

'What do we do now?' Jeremy said.

Jack looked at his watch. 'If everything goes according to schedule, the van with the equipment should be outside in an hour. By then the concert upstairs will be over and we'll be able to get all the gear in discreetly, if the church people agree.'

'I've just got one more guy to talk to, but we'll be good to go,' Jeremy said, eyeing Costas, who gave a thumbs-up.

'We're not taking any chances,' Jack said. 'Full kit. We might be going below the water table, and who knows what else is down there. I'm not even going to tackle that wall until we're ready. Meanwhile, I might just go up and listen to the music.'

'No you don't,' Costas said. 'I still need to get a few things straight. A few big things. Like how Christianity fits into all this warrior queen stuff.'

'Okay,' Jeremy said, pushing up his spectacles and peering at Costas. 'If it's early Christianity in Britain, it's one of my areas of interest. Fire away.'

'Before meeting you this morning we went to the British Library,' Costas said. 'Jack needed to check some source material on this church, and while he was busy I visited the display of ancient manuscripts. Incredible stuff. I saw one of the Bibles brought by St Augustine to Britain, in AD 597. That's almost two hundred years after the Romans left Britain. That's where I'm confused. I thought Augustine was the one who brought Christianity to Britain. I thought, hold on, how can there be Christians in Roman Britain?'

Jeremy leaned forward from where he was sitting against the wall. 'That's a common misconception. And it's what the Anglo-Saxon Church historians would have liked you to believe, even the big names like Bede.'

'I don't get it.'

'The Church of England, the *Ecclesia Anglicana*, was really the Church of the Anglo-Saxons. It traced its origins to the mission of Augustine, who supposedly brought Christianity to the pagan population of Britain well after the Romans had left. It was a political tool, intimately bound up with Anglo-Saxon kingship and with the power of Rome. But even the Anglo-Saxon historians knew there had been Christianity in Britain before that, when the Romans had ruled.'

'The *Ecclesia Britannorum*,' Jack murmured. 'The Church of the Britons. The Celtic Church.'

'To get a handle on it, you have to go to Gildas,' Jeremy said. 'A British monk who lived in the early sixth century, about a hundred years after the Romans left, a couple of generations before Augustine arrived. Gildas is just about the only Briton we know about who may have been alive at the time of King Arthur, probably a British warlord fighting the Anglo-Saxon invaders at that time.'

'Sounds like the original Friar Tuck,' Costas murmured.

'His book's called *De Excidio Britonum, The Ruin of Britain*. It was written in Latin, but I've got a translation.' Jack delved into his bag, and brought out a scuffed blue and grey book with a chi-rho symbol on the front. 'It's a rant about how the kings who ruled Britain after the Romans had failed in their Christian duty. I've got it because Gildas mentions Boudica. It was a present from my grandmother when I was a boy.'

'Gildas called Boudica a deceitful lioness,' Jeremy said, grinning.

'That's all he says, but it suggests that the memory of her rebellion lingered on, even in a churchman who knew virtually nothing of Roman history, and little of Christian history for that matter.'

'But he gives us the first ever account of the founding of the British Church, the Celtic Church in the time of the Romans,' Jeremy said.

Jack nodded, and turned the page. 'Here it is.' He read it aloud: ' "Meanwhile, to an island numb with chill ice and far removed, as in a remote nook of the world, from the visible sun, Christ made a present of his rays, that is, his precepts, Christ the true sun, which shows its dazzling brilliance to the entire earth, not from the temporal firmament merely, but from the highest citadel of heaven, that goes beyond all time. This happened first, as we know, in the last years of the emperor Tiberius, at a time when Christ's religion was being propagated without hindrance; for, against the wishes of the Senate, the emperor threatened the death penalty for informers against soldiers of God." '

'At least he got the weather right,' Costas grumbled. 'So what's he on about? The emperor Tiberius?'

'The Roman emperor at the time of the crucifixion,' Jeremy said.

Jack closed the book. 'Tiberius was Claudius' uncle, ruled Rome from AD 14 to 37. Gildas seems to think that Tiberius was himself a Christian, at odds with a pagan Senate. It's all pretty garbled and probably an anachronism, referring to the problems the Christian emperors had with the pagan Senate in the fourth century AD, after Constantine the Great had made Christianity the state religion. There's no other indication anywhere that Tiberius was a Christian. But what we've found in the last few days, in Herculaneum, in Rome, has set me thinking.'

'About others in Rome who knew of Jesus of Nazareth,' Jeremy murmured.

'The British Church, the Celtic Church of the Roman period, has left no written records,' Jack replied. 'If there ever were any, they would almost certainly have been destroyed by the Anglo-Saxons. But was Gildas recounting a distant truth, a folk memory perhaps, a secret passed on by word of mouth among followers of the British Church for more than five centuries? Was he telling us that there had indeed been a Christian emperor very early on, or an emperor well disposed towards Christians? Not Tiberius, but another emperor who had been alive at the time of Christ?'

'Claudius!' Costas exclaimed.

'It's just possible.' Jack was animated, and gesticulated as he spoke. 'By the time of Gildas, centuries later, the true identity of the emperor could have been confused. Claudius would have been remembered as the invader of Britain, as the deified emperor worshipped in the temple at Colchester. A pretty unlikely Christian. But Gildas would have known of Tiberius from the Gospels, as the emperor who had presided over the death of Jesus. To Gildas, it might have seemed the ultimate triumph of Christianity to suggest that Tiberius himself was a convert. A pretty extravagant fiction, but Gildas lived at a time when many fanciful additions were being made to the story of events surrounding the life of Christ.'

'And he's talking about Britain,' Costas said.

'Gildas was implying that Christianity came to Britain very early on, in the first century AD,' Jeremy said. 'He's even implying that the emperor himself brought it, in person. That's what's really fascinating. It's only through being here ourselves, on the trail of an emperor, that those lines of Gildas suddenly take on a new significance, a real authority. His *De Excidio Britonum* was exclusively a book on Britain, not some wider history.'

'What's the other evidence for early Christianity here?' Costas said. 'From archaeology, I mean?'

'Just like in the Mediterranean region,' Jack replied. 'Incredibly elusive until the second century, and it's not until the fourth century that you start to see churches, burials, overt symbols of Christianity, after it becomes the state religion. But early Christianity was a religion of the word, not of idols and temples. It was secretive, and often persecuted. If it wasn't for the Gospels and a few Roman sources, we'd know nothing at all about Christianity in the first century AD. Remember our shipwreck off Sicily? That scratched chi-rho symbol was the only overt evidence we saw there of Christianity, yet we're talking about the ship of St Paul, one of the key episodes in early Christian history.'

'And remember who we're looking at in early Roman Britain,' Jeremy added pensively. 'There were the immigrants, traders and soldiers who may well have brought the idea of Christianity with them, and may have come to worship Christ as others did Mithras or Isis. But the majority of the population were natives, Romanized to some degree but retaining much of their Celtic way of life and customs. Their religion has left almost no archaeological trace. These were not people who were inclined to build temples and altars or to make statues of their gods. Archaeology was never going to tell us much.'

'Okay.' Costas narrowed his eyes. 'But if there was Christianity in early Roman Britain, why would the Anglo-Saxon Church want to deny it? I mean, wouldn't it have been something to celebrate, that their religion had been in place hundreds of years before?'

'But it wasn't their religion,' Jeremy said quietly.

'Huh?'

'The time of Gildas, the time of King Arthur, wasn't just a formative period in the political genesis of Britain,' Jeremy said. 'It was also a time when a conflict within the Christian communities of Britain first began to play out in a big way. Everyone knows about King Henry the Eighth, his break with the Roman Church in the sixteenth century. But the roots of the English Reformation under Henry go way back to this period, to the time when the British Church stood up against

Rome and proclaimed their direct connection to the Holy Land, to Jesus the man.'

'The Pelagian heresy,' Jack murmured.

Jeremy nodded. 'A lot of the Church schisms are obscure, but this one was straightforward, a really profound one. It went right to the heart of Christian belief. It also went right to the heart of the Church as an institution. It frightened a lot of those in power in Rome. It still does.'

'Pelagian?' Costas said.

'Pelagius was another monk in Britain, earlier than Gildas, possibly Irish by birth, born about AD 360, when the Romans were still in control of Britain. By Pelagius' time the Roman Empire had been officially Christian for several decades, since the conversion of Constantine the Great, and efforts were being made to establish the Roman Church in Britain. Pelagius himself went to study in Rome, but was very disturbed by what he saw there. He came into direct conflict with one of the powerhouses of the Roman Church.'

'St Augustine of Hippo,' Jack said.

'Author of the *Confessions* and the *City of God*. The earlier Augustine, not the one who brought the Roman Church to Britain, the one whose bible you saw in the British Library, Costas. Augustine of Hippo came to believe in the concept of predestination, that Christians were utterly dependent on divine grace, on the favour of God. In his view, the kingdom of heaven could only be sought through the Church, not by free volition. It was a theological doctrine, but one with huge practical benefits for the Roman Church, for the newly Christian state.'

'Domination, control,' Jack murmured.

'It made believers subservient to the Church, as the conduit of divine grace. It made the state stronger, more able to control the masses. Church and state were fused together as an unassailable powerhouse, and the stage was set for the medieval European world.'

'But Pelagius was having none of that,' Jack said.

'Pelagius probably thought of himself as a member of the original Christian community which existed in Britain before the official Roman Church arrived, the community who traced themselves back to the earliest followers of Jesus in the first century AD,' Jeremy said. 'What we've just been talking about, the *Ecclesia Britannorum*, the Celtic Church, many of them probably Romanized Britons of Celtic ancestry. Pelagius is virtually the only evidence we have for their beliefs. It seems possible that they took the concept of heaven on earth at face value, the idea that heaven could be found around them, in their earthly lives. To them, the message of Jesus may have been about finding and extolling beauty in nature, about love and compassion for its own sake. It would have been a morally empowering concept, completely at odds with what Pelagius saw in Rome. When Pelagius was there he stood up against Augustine of Hippo, denied the doctrine of predestination and original sin, defended innate human goodness and free will. It was a hopeless battle, but he was a beacon for resistance and his name resounded through the centuries, in hidden places and secret meetings when any hint of it could have meant arrest, torture, even worse.'

'What happened to him?' Costas said.

'Pelagianism was condemned as heretical by the Synod of Carthage in AD 418,' Jack said. 'Pelagius himself was excommunicated and banished from Rome. It's not clear whether he ever got back to Britain. Some believe he went to Judaea, to Jerusalem, to the site of Christ's tomb, and was murdered there.'

'There were uncompromising forces already within the Roman Church, ready to stop at nothing to carry out what they saw as divine justice,' Jeremy said. 'But they couldn't control what went on in Britain. After the Roman withdrawal in AD 410, after the Roman towns of Britain had crumbled and decayed, the Church which had been brought by Constantine's bishops seems to have virtually died out. That's what Gildas was lamenting. He himself was probably one of the last monks in Britain of the Roman Church of the fourth century, though a pretty confused one. With the edifice of the state removed, the Roman church no longer held sway over a people who were not attracted by Augustinian doctrine. Then the Anglo-Saxons invaded. They were pagan. That's where we come to the second Augustine, St Augustine of Canterbury. He was sent by Pope Gregory in AD 597 with forty monks to convert King Aethelbert of Kent, and after that the Roman Church was here to stay.'

'But Celtic Christianity somehow survived,' Costas said.

'It survived the first Augustine, and it survived the second,'

Jeremy said. 'There was something in its philosophy that spoke to the Celtic ancestry of the Britons, something they also believed was true to the original teachings of Jesus. Something that told a universal truth, about freedom and individual aspiration. Something which had been taught to them by the first followers of Jesus to reach these shores, perhaps even by the emperor dimly remembered by Gildas. A wisdom they had kept and cherished, a sacred memory.'

'People having control and responsibility for their own actions, their own destiny,' Jack said.

'That's the nub of Pelagianism,' Jeremy agreed. 'When Pelagius came to Rome, he saw moral laxity, decadence, and he blamed it on the idea of divine grace. If everything is predestined and the whim of God, why bother with good deeds, or with trying to make the world a better place? Pelagianism was all about the individual, about free will, about moral strength. In his view, Jesus' example was primarily one of instruction. Jesus showed how to avoid sin and live a holy life, and Christians can choose to follow him. And what's really fascinating is how these ideas may also represent a continuity from Celtic paganism, which seems to have championed a person's ability to triumph as an individual, even over the supernatural.'

'What I don't get is how this early Celtic Christianity survived the Dark Age after the Romans,' Costas said. 'I mean, you've got the Anglo-Saxons invading, then the Vikings, then the Normans. This Celtic ancestry stuff must have been pretty fringe by then.'

'It's something to do with the kind of people who chose to come to Britain,' Jeremy responded. 'Not just those famous invasions, but later migrations too, the Sephardic Jews expelled from Spain, the Huguenot Protestant refugees from France and Holland. Some common thread, character traits needed to succeed here. Independence, wilfulness, stubbornness, endurance in the face of authority, strength through hardship. Everything about this place where we are now, the history. The Blitz spirit. All of it makes those ideas espoused by Pelagius seem particularly British.'

'I think it's something to do with the weather, myself,' Costas grumbled. 'You've got to have something extra to survive this place.' He paused. 'So you think this church, St Lawrence Jewry, has all this history in it?'

'There's no proof there was a church here before the eleventh century, when the Normans arrived,' Jack said. 'But nobody knows where the churches of late Roman London were located. Before then, Christian meetings were secretive, and even after Christianity became the official religion in the fourth century AD, congregational worship never really took hold in Roman Britain. But I believe St Lawrence Jewry is a very likely spot. Right next to the amphitheatre, a place that would have been associated with the martyrdom of Christians. And churches were often built on sites of pagan ritual. There may have been more going on here, something very old, sacred long before Roman London. And this place may have concealed an extraordinary secret.'

'The heart of darkness,' Costas murmured, looking at the

bricked-up wall at the end of the chamber.

Jack followed his gaze, excitement coursing through him. He glanced at his watch. The music had finished upstairs in the nave, and there was a knock on the door. He got up, took a deep breath and slung his bag over his shoulder. 'I think we might be just about to find out.'

16

An hour later, Jack and Costas crouched again inside the small chamber of the crypt, this time behind the glare of two portable tungsten lights. An IMU De Havilland Dash-8 aircraft had freighted all the equipment they needed from the Cornwall campus to London City airport, including a fresh pair of e-suits to replace those they had left with Massimo in Rome. Jeremy had obtained immediate permission from the church authorities for an exploratory reconnaissance beyond the bricked-up wall in the side of the chamber. In a huddled conversation with a cleric in the crypt they had agreed on the need for absolute secrecy, and their equipment had been brought in from a borrowed television van in the guise of a film crew. Above them, the lunchtime concert had ended and they could hear Gregorian chant wafting down from choristers practising in the nave, a sound Jack found strangely reassuring as they contemplated another dark passage into the unknown.

'Okay. It's done. There's definitely a space behind there, but I can't see much without getting in.' Jeremy had been creating a hole in the wall, pulling out the bricks and stacking them to either side. The wall turned out to have been poorly constructed with mortar which had not properly set, allowing him to remove the bricks with ease.

'Good,' Jack said. 'Your job now is to hold the fort.' Jeremy nodded, walked over to check the bolt on the door into the crypt and then sat back against the wall, watching them kit up.

'We could be going below the water table.' Costas was staring at an image on a laptop computer as he checked the neck seal on his suit. 'We're about three metres below the present level of the Guildhall Yard, about two metres above the Roman layers. Below that, there's a tributary of the Walbrook stream somewhere just in front of us. With all this rain it's likely to be pretty wet.'

'We're going to need the suits anyway,' Jack said. 'Could be pretty toxic down there.'

Costas groaned. 'Gas leaks?'

Jack gestured around the burial chamber. 'Two thousand years of human occupation, Costas. I'm not going to spell it out for you.'

'Don't.' Costas leaned over and flipped down Jack's visor,

then adjusted the regulator on the side of his helmet to verify the oxygen flow. He quickly did the same to his own helmet. Suddenly they were sealed off from the outside world, only able to hear each other through their intercom. 'The oxygen rebreathers should give us four, maybe four and a half hours,' he said.

'We could be back here in ten minutes,' Jack said. 'It could be a dead end.'

'If only I had our remote-sensing equipment from *Seaquest II*, then we could snake in a camera and see what's behind that wall.'

'Nothing beats the human eye,' Jack said. 'Come on.' He nodded back at Jeremy, who had taken a laptop out of his bag and spread out his notebooks. Jack crouched down on all fours and made his way through the hole in the brickwork, his headlamp illuminating the darkness in front of him. Once he was through, Costas came alongside. They were perched on a stone landing, and in front of them a dozen steps led down to another entranceway, a low arched doorway about four feet high. Jack squatted on his haunches and began to sidle down the steps, playing the torch in his hand across the stone steps in front of him.

'Let's hope the ceiling doesn't give way,' Costas muttered.

Jack glanced up. 'It's corbelled stone, about as strong as you could hope for. The masonry looks identical to the old part of the burial crypt we've just come through. Fourteenth century, maybe earlier. I can see reused Roman tile and ragstone, probably taken from the ruins of the amphitheatre.'

He carried on down the steps, reached the bottom and stood up, his back stooped awkwardly over. In front of him the arched stone entrance was blocked by the partly rotted remains of a wooden door, with a grilled window about ten inches wide directly in front of him. Jack shone his headlamp through as Costas came alongside.

'Looks like a prison cell,' Costas said.

'It's a crypt,' Jack murmured. 'Another burial crypt. Exactly as Sir Christopher Wren's mason described in his diary. And it looks undisturbed.'

'What do you mean, undisturbed? I thought Wren's guys got in here.'

'I mean it looks full. No parking space.'

'Oh no.'

Jack pushed cautiously at the door, and it gave way slightly. 'It's still solid,' he said. 'Damp conditions, ideal for organic survival. We could find some pretty amazing preservation down here.'

'Oh good,' Costas said weakly.

Jack pushed again with both hands, and the door came completely ajar. They peered into the space ahead of them. It was a single vaulted chamber, similar in dimensions to the burial crypt they had just come through but about three times as large. Ranged along either side were stone cavities, some of them crudely bricked over, others open and brimming with old wooden coffins, some intact and lidded, others crumbled and decayed. Dark shapeless forms were just visible within. Jack took a few steps forward, while

Costas remained glued to the spot, staring straight ahead. 'This is my worst nightmare, Jack.'

'Come on,' Jack said. 'It's all part of life's rich tapestry.'

Costas edged forward, paused, then resolutely stepped over and peered closely at one of the erupted coffins, clearly having decided that scientific inspection was the best therapy. 'Interesting,' he murmured, clearing his throat. 'There's a pottery pipe emerging from the top of this coffin, blackened at one end. I never realized people made libations in Christian burials.'

'Nice try, but wrong,' Jack said. 'You brought it up, so I'm telling you. Those pipes were for letting off steam.'

'What?'

'You see them in Victorian catacombs,' Jack said. 'The trouble with a lead-lined coffin is that it can explode, especially if the body's sealed in it too soon after death. It's the first stage of decomposition, you know. Off-gassing.'

'Off-gassing.' Costas swayed slightly, but remained fixated on the coffin.

'The pipes were lit to burn it off,' Jack said. 'That's where the blackening comes from.'

Costas swayed backwards, then slipped on the floor, catching himself just in time on the edge of an open niche on the opposite wall. He pulled himself upright again, then lifted his foot from a sticky pool that extended under one of the niches near the entrance. 'We must be closer to the water level than I thought,' he murmured. 'There's too much here for it just to be condensation.'

313

'I've got more bad news for you, I'm afraid.'

Costas stared at the pool, then at the dark stain running down the stonework towards it from the burial niche above. 'Oh no,' he whispered.

'Saponification,' Jack said cheerfully. 'There's a wonderful account by Sir Thomas Browne, a kind of seventeenth-century Pliny. He loved digging up old graves. Hiebermeyer and I did a course on mummification with the Home Office forensics people, and I can remember it word for word. "We met with a fat concretion, when the nitre of the Earth, and the soft and lixivious liqueur of the body, had coagulated large lumps of fat, like the consistency of the hardest candle soap; whereof part remaineth with us."'

'Body liqueur,' Costas whispered, frantically wiping his foot on a fallen brick. 'Get me out of here, Jack.'

'Mortuary wax,' Jack replied. 'The slow hydrolysis of fats into adipocere. Especially likely in alkaline conditions, where the bodies are sealed off from bacteria, and where it's damp. Like I said, we're going to find amazing preservational conditions here.'

'It couldn't get any worse than this.'

'Don't count on it.' Jack squatted down to peer at the inscribed stone blocks he could now see in front of each intact niche, built into the centre of the brick facings. He moved along, from one to the next. 'Fascinating,' he murmured. 'Normally, crypts in London churches were used for a few decades, maybe a century or so, stuffed full and then sealed up. But this one's very strange. The formula on each of these inscriptions is virtually identical, but they range over a huge time span. Each of them has a chi-rho symbol, followed by a Latin name. Look, here. Maria de Kirkpatrick. And there, Bronwyn ap Llewellyn. They're mostly Latin renditions of British names. And they've got dates, in Roman numerals. The one nearest to you, on the lower shelf by the door, is the latest, from 1664, just a few years before the Great Fire of 1666 destroyed the medieval church.'

'That figures.' Costas was still staring into the middle distance, clearly trying to focus on something other than the physical horror around him. He cleared his throat. 'The diary. It said the crypt was sealed up by Wren's men, in the 1680s. It makes sense there shouldn't be any more burials after that.'

Jack reached the far end of the chamber, having carefully circumvented the sticky slick on the floor. He squatted down again, and shifted a few fallen bricks with his hands. 'And the earliest of these inscriptions is incredibly early,' he murmured. 'The oldest ones at this end have crumbled, but there are two here with Anglo-Saxon names. Aelfrida and Aethelreda. I can't read the name on this one, but I can read the date. AD 535. My God,' he said hoarsely. 'That's the Dark Age, the time of King Arthur, of Gildas. That's even before Augustine brought Roman Christianity back to Britain, yet here's a burial with a Christian symbol.'

'The names are all women,' Costas said quietly.

'This chamber is a lot older than the medieval church,' Jack continued, peering around. 'It looks as if it was kept in repair during the medieval period, up to the time of the Great Fire, but the lower courses of brick and stone look Roman.' He knelt down, and swept his hand under the furthest niche. 'No doubt about it. We're inside a catacomb built in the Roman period. The only one ever found in Britain.'

'Check out the inscription above the doorway.'

Jack peered up, and saw a single register of letters carved into the masonry, covered in blackened accretion. Costas slowly read out the words: 'Uri vinciri veberari ferroque necari.'

'Good God,' Jack exclaimed, standing up and staring, his mind in a whirl. 'It's the gladiator's oath. The *sacramentum gladiatorium*.'

'The Sibylline prophecy,' Costas said, his voice hushed. 'The wax tablet we found under Rome. It's the same wording, isn't it?'

'Identical. *To die in fire, to be bound, to be beaten, to die by the sword*. Good old Claudius,' Jack murmured. 'I think we're exactly where he wanted us to be.'

'And where the Sibyl wanted him to be.'

'This must originally have been the gladiators' mortuary, the death chamber, where the mutilated corpses from the arena next to us were laid out before being taken away and burned,' Jack murmured. 'And then it was used as a Christian burial crypt, for over a thousand years. A burial crypt for women, for women who were somehow bound together, over all that time.'

'Maybe they were a secret society, a guild,' Costas said. 'Maybe they wanted to be buried close to whatever lies beyond that wall.'

'According to the diary, this is where the Roman amphoras were found by Wren's men,' Jack said. 'And this must be the wall, where we are now.'

Costas placed both hands on the brick face in front of them, and cautiously pushed. He flinched as several of the bricks shifted. 'It's not mortared,' he said. 'It looks like they just stacked up the bricks.'

'That makes sense,' Jack said. 'The diary says they decided to seal up the entire crypt back in the first chamber, where we've left Jeremy, so they must have abandoned sealing up this deeper chamber part-way through. We'll have to take it down from the top, brick by brick.'

Costas experimentally pushed a little further, and one of the bricks that had shifted fell out behind. Suddenly the whole edifice collapsed inwards, and they both leapt backwards as the air filled with red dust. Costas narrowly avoided the sticky pool on the floor.

'I was going to say, we don't have time for finesse,' Jack said, wiping the front of his visor.

'Check it out,' Costas said, picking himself up and moving forward.

Jack aimed his hand torch to where Costas was gesturing. Where the brick wall had been was now a gaping hole, but just inside to the left was a row of what looked like sections of old ceramic drainpipe, arranged in a row pointing upwards. Jack edged forward over the pile of fallen bricks and beckoned excitedly. 'Recognize those?'

'Amphoras. Roman amphoras. Just what we're looking for.'

'Right. And they're exactly the same type of wine amphora we found on St Paul's shipwreck, the ones made in Campania near Pompeii and Herculaneum. Remember the date of the wreck?'

'AD 58, give or take a bit.'

'Right. These were the typical wine amphoras of that period. What was the date of Boudica's rebellion? AD 60, 61. If wine amphoras were being left as an offering here, these are exactly the type you'd expect to find at that date.'

Costas squeezed in beside Jack and peered into the darkness beyond. 'Not sure where we go from here. Seems to be some kind of shaft.'

Jack looked intently around. To his left was a precarious mass of rubble, much of it old brick but including charred and blackened timbers, all jumbled and compressed into a tight mass. It protruded into a timber-lined shaft about two metres wide and three metres deep, with water at the bottom. 'What we've got here is destruction debris from the Great Fire of 1666, probably dumped during Wren's rebuilding of the church. If any of his men went beyond this crypt, that's the way they must have gone. We'll never get through all that without a major excavation. It's out of the question. Our only hope now is going down this shaft.'

'What is it?'

'Looks like a well. There were fresh springs in the gravels beside the Thames. London water was remarkably healthy until it was swamped by sewage. Wells were often timber lined like this.' Jack leaned in and peered at the wood.

'Fascinating. Reused ship's timbers. These are overlapping, clinker-built, Viking. Remember our Viking longship in the iceberg off Greenland?'

'I never thought I'd say this, but I'd much rather be there now.'

'I'm going in.' Jack swung his legs over the edge of the hole, pivoting on his arms until he was facing backwards. He grasped Costas' arm as he hung over the edge, his feet dangling a metre or so over the black pool below. 'Let's hope it's not a bottomless pit.' He let go and fell with a huge splash, coming to rest on his knees in mud, his upper body out of the water. 'You next.' He reached his foot experimentally around. 'I think it's a safe landing.'

Costas grunted, then lowered himself gingerly over the edge, his visor pressed up against the damp wood of the well lining. He shifted slightly to avoid falling on Jack. He had moved in front of a small section of wood in the well lining that had partly rotted away, and he suddenly froze.

'What is it?' Jack said.

Costas' voice sounded distant, hoarse. 'About this well, Jack. It wasn't dug through gravel.'

'What?'

'It was dug through bones, Jack,' Costas said, his voice sounding beyond emotion. 'Human bones, thousands of them, packed in around us. It's all I can see.'

'It could be a plague pit,' Jack said thoughtfully. 'But more probably an ossuary, bones cleared from a crypt or a grave-yard. Still, a good thing we've got the e-suits on, just in case.'

Costas let go of the edge of the wall and dropped with an enormous splash, disappearing completely under the water down a hole beside Jack before rebounding in a tumult of mud. The water settled, and he raised his hands, looking at the dark glutinous streaks on his gloves. 'Good old-fashioned dirt,' he muttered. 'I think I've had enough of human remains.'

'What you said set me thinking,' Jack said. 'About a well, dug through an old ossuary. Pretty unlikely. I think I may have got it wrong. I think what we've actually got here is a cesspit.'

Costas wiped his visor, streaking it with brown, and stared speechless at Jack.

'Actually, cesspits were quite hygienic,' Jack said. 'Each dwelling usually had one. It was only when they flooded that raw sewage was a problem, and then after people started using sewers that weren't up to the job.'

'Is that supposed to be reassuring?' Costas sounded close to tears. 'Come diving with Jack Howard. No latrine too deep.' He tried to struggle upwards, and suddenly disappeared out of sight, then bobbed up again. 'I thought so,' he said. 'There's water flowing below us. This shaft has broken through into an underground stream.'

'The tributary of the Walbrook stream, where they found the skulls,' Jack said. 'Maybe we've got a chance after all. If we can get into it and find another opening upwards, we might be able to get beyond that rubble obstruction to the edge of the Roman amphitheatre.'

'Or we might join the city of the dead down here. Permanently.'

'Always a possibility.'

'Okay.' Costas pulled out his waterproof GPS computer unit, and called up a 3D topographical outline he had programmed into it while they were waiting for the equipment to arrive in the church. 'The flow of the stream is easterly, towards the Walbrook, which then flows south into the Thames. The outer edge of the amphitheatre is only five metres to the north of us. If we somehow get beyond that point, then we may as well turn back. We'll be into the area that was dug up in the recent excavations.'

'I'll be right behind you,' Jack said.

'See you on the other side.' Costas dropped below the water out of view. For a few moments there was a commotion as his feet broke the surface, then it settled down and the pool became a glistening sheen of darkness. Jack squatted in the water up to his chest, and listened to Costas' breathing through the intercom. He thought for a moment of his own secret fear, the claustrophobia he fought so hard to control, and realized that his mind sensed a lifeline to this place, an exit route through the ancient crypt and the burial chamber to the church above. What lay beyond this pool was that crucial extra step beyond the escape route that could unnerve him, and he took a few deep breaths as he stared at the limpid surface. He felt vibrations, a slight tremor through his body, and watched the surface of the water shimmer. He guessed it was an underground train, passing through a tunnel somewhere far below. The sensation drew him back to the reality of the twenty-first century, and in his mind's eye all of the tumultuous events of the past, the dark rituals of prehistory, the blood of the Roman amphitheatre, the Great Fire of 1666, the 1940 Blitz, all seemed to speed past him like a fast-motion film, leaving their imprint blasted into the cloying sediment around him.

He shut his eyes, then opened them again. He pressed the digital readout display inside his visor, scanning the figures that showed the remaining oxygen in his rebreather, the carbon dioxide toxicity levels. It was a reality check, and it never failed him. He heaved himself up, and realized he had nearly become stuck fast in more than a metre of mud at the bottom of the pool. After extracting himself he floated face down on the surface with his visor underwater, staring into swirling darkness with the dim patch of light from Costas' headlamp directly below him. Jack arched down, bleeding air from his buoyancy compensator, and sank into blackness. About two metres down he could sense the flow of the underground stream, and he saw a tumult of clearer water where the silt was being swept away. The visibility was still only a matter of inches, but it was better than the black soup at the surface of the pit.

'There's an obstruction.' Costas' voice came over the intercom. 'I'm nearly around it.'

Jack could sense Costas' feet directly in front of him, churning the water as he heaved himself round a bend in the tunnel. Jack stayed back to avoid being kicked, and then as the turbulence subsided he let himself slowly fall forward, his hands splayed out to feel for any obstacle. After about two metres he felt something smooth, metallic, and then his shoulders came to rest on Costas' legs. He felt a wriggling, then no movement at all, then a dull metallic thumping, then everything was still except the sound of their breathing.

'It's a Series 17 fuse. Good.'

'What is?' Jack exclaimed. 'What's good?'

'This is.' There was a clanging noise, then a curse.

'What? I can't see anything.'

'This bomb.'

Jack's heart sank. 'What bomb?'

'German SC250, general-purpose bomb. Carried by the Stuka, Junkers 88, Heinkel 111. They dropped thousands of them over here during the Blitz. Should be pretty routine.'

'What do you mean, routine?

'I mean, they weren't delayed-action fuses, so they're pretty routine.'

Jack had another sinking feeling. He thought of the tremor again, the vibration of the train. Suddenly this place seemed less solid, less stable, ready for history to have another go. 'Don't tell me what you're about to do.'

'Its okay, I've done it already. Done as much as I can.' Costas' legs shifted forward, and Jack dropped another metre in the water. 'The forward fuse pocket was right in front of my nose, and I happened to have just the right socket in my e-suit equipment pouch. The after-pocket's the problem. I can feel it, but it's all rusted over. It's not my style, but we might just have to leave it.'

'Yes, we might,' Jack said quietly. 'How dangerous is it?'

'The usual fill for an SC250 bomb was only 280 pounds of Amatol and TNT, sixty-forty mix.'

'Only?' Jack said incredulously.

'Well, enough for us to be toast, of course, but the financial hub of the world would probably remain intact.'

'I think there's probably been enough human sacrifice at this spot,' Jack said. 'How stable is it?'

'The problem's that corroded rear pocket fuse,' Costas murmured. 'It's been happily dormant for almost seventy years, but with our arrival, who knows.'

'You mean after you tampered with it, who knows.' The silt had settled slightly, and Jack could see the bomb casing about three inches from his face. It was corroded, deeply pitted, with no visible markings, and looked about as menacing as Jack could imagine. He was making the usual mental calculations, and this time the odds were not looking good. He sensed Costas shift forward and upward, beyond the bomb. 'I think it might be time to leave now.'

'Oh no.'

'What do you mean, no? This thing's still live. We need to get out.'

'No. I don't mean that. I mean this, in front of me.' Costas was almost whimpering. 'It's another nightmare. It's just getting worse.'

'Okay. I'm coming.' Jack eased himself deeper, with the corroded bomb casing just in front of his face, until he saw where it curved down to the nose cone and suspension lug. He turned over on his back and put his hand on the lug to keep his body from jolting against the casing, which seemed to be suspended perilously in mid-water. He slowly pulled himself up until he felt the casing between his legs, and then below his e-suit boots. At the point where he imagined the base plate and tail fins should be, he suddenly broke surface, his face inches from a slimy mud wall. He had been fine in the silt, underwater, with his face pressed close to the bomb casing, but now he suddenly felt unnerved, as if those extra few inches of visibility were just enough to give him a sense of how confined the space was. He knew he had to fight hard now, concentrate entirely on what they were doing. He rolled over slowly, careful not to budge the bomb casing, until he was beside Costas and facing in the same direction. He could feel the compacted gravel of the ancient stream bed below his feet, showing they had come under the archaeological layers. He angled his headlamp upwards, and gasped with astonishment. They were inside some kind of structure, a chamber, with unworked tree trunks lining the roof about two metres above them. He saw massive beams of blackened oak, with bracing timbers around the walls. He looked down, following Costas' gaze.

Then he saw it.

He could hardly breathe. He shut his eyes, forced himself to inhale hard, and looked again.

It was a skull, a human skull, blackened with age, lying face up with the jaw still in position, slightly ajar. He could see the vertebrae of the neck, the shoulder blades, all cushioned in a red fibrous material. He looked again. The fibrous material seemed to be coming out of the skull. Then he realized what it was. Human hair. *Red hair.*

He panned his beam down again, to something he had seen lying on the neck bones. He put his hands on a wet timber beside the water's edge, tested it, and heaved himself up slightly. He was only inches away now, and gasped in disbelief. It was gold, lustrous, a solid gold neck ring. Just like one they had seen on another body, deep under Rome. A *torque.* Then Jack realized. This was no medieval crypt burial.

'Looks like we might have found our goddess,' Costas whispered.

'Andraste,' Jack said, scarcely believing what he was saying.

'Not exactly immortal,' Costas murmured.

'Everything looks right,' Jack said. 'That neck torque is Celtic, the amphoras at the entrance are the right date. Some kind of high priestess, buried about the time of the Boudican revolt.'

'Maybe the revolt signalled the end of the old order,' Costas murmured. 'The last of the ancient priestesses, wiped out in the conflagration. Like the eruption of Vesuvius, the disappearance of the Sibyls.'

Jack looked at the skull again. He leaned over, and peered more closely, right over the empty eye sockets. The black accretion covering the skull was not black at all. It was blue, dark blue. He gasped as he realized. '*Isatis tintoria,*' he murmured. 'Well I'll be damned.'

'Huh?'

'Woad. Blue woad. She was painted with blue woad. Must have looked terrifying in life.'

'Couldn't be worse than in death,' Costas croaked.

Jack stared again. It was something Costas had said. *The last of the ancient priestesses, wiped out in the conflagration.* Had they found something people had been seeking for hundreds of years, in the heart of the City of London, in a tiny wedge of undisturbed ground in one of the most dug-up, excavated and bombed-out places in the world? He turned to Costas, who seemed numb, rooted to the spot, splayed out on the edge of the pool of sludgy water, staring through his visor at the skull.

'Another Agamemnon moment?' Jack said.

'That thing's no ghost. It's real,' Costas whispered. 'After the body liqueur and everything. I'll never sleep again.'

'Come on,' Jack said. 'Remember we've got a rusty bomb on slow broil for company.' He crawled over the soggy timber clear of the hole, and Costas heaved himself out. They both slowly stood up, dripping profusely, with their helmets and breathing gear still on, mud slicked over their e-suits like brown paint. Jack flicked his headlamp to wide beam, and took out a halogen torch. They stared in awe at the scene revealed in front of them.

It was a breathtaking sight. Jack instantly saw images that were familiar to him, artefact types, the layout of the grave goods, but nothing this intact had ever been found in Britain before. It looked like one of the tombs he had visited of ancient Scythian nobility on the Russian steppes, girt in massive timbers and miraculously preserved in the permafrost, yet this was the heart of London. Somehow the waterlogged atmosphere and the thick clay that surrounded the tomb had kept the timbers from rotting and the tomb from imploding.

And it had not just preserved the skeleton. Jack could see that the red-haired woman had been laid on a bier, a square wooden platform about three metres across, a metre or so short of the edges of the chamber. There were strange shapes, curved shapes, on either side of the skeleton. Jack drew his breath in as he realized what they were. 'It's a chariot burial,' he exclaimed. 'Those are the two wheels, tilted up towards the body. You can see the spokes on each wheel, the iron rim and the hubcaps.'

'Take a look at this.' Costas was peering closely at the base of the bier, at the legs of the skeleton, and then between the wheels. 'There are cut marks on the bones, slash marks, a couple of healed fractures. Looks like she's been through the wars. This was some lady. And she's lying in some kind of canoe, a wooden dugout.'

Jack shifted over, slipping on the mud. 'Fantastic,' he exclaimed, as he came alongside. 'There are boat burials from the Anglo-Saxon period onwards, Viking ship burials, but I've never seen one like this from the late Iron Age.'

'Maybe this was what they used to get her to this place on her final journey, to her sanctuary up the river. To the heart of darkness.'

Jack stood up as far as he could, and stared for the first time properly at the torso of the skeleton. It was one of the most incredible things he had ever seen, like a computer-generated image of a perfect Iron Age burial. He edged up the side of the bier, then slipped and fell heavily on one knee beside the chariot wheel.

'Watch out,' Costas exclaimed from behind. 'The hub of the wheel's got a metal spike sticking out of it.'

Jack looked at the corroded iron protrusion that had just missed skewering him, and felt his chest tighten as he realized how close he had been. He closed his eyes, forcing himself to concentrate. He looked again. It was a vicious spike, one of three that stuck out from the hub about half a metre, twisted like aircraft propeller blades. This was no ordinary chariot. Jack heaved himself up and moved alongside Costas, who had gone round him and was crouching over the torso of the skeleton. 'I think this lady was preparing to do battle with the gods, in the afterlife,' Costas murmured. 'And I think she was going to win.' They stared in awe at the accoutrements laid over the skeleton. There were leaf-shaped iron spear-points, their shafts snapped where the spears had been broken over the grave. Strewn everywhere were numerous pine cones, charred where they had been burned for incense. Parallel to the body on the left side, from the neck to the hip, was a great iron sword, unsheathed, with a decorated bronze scabbard lying alongside. The incised pattern on the scabbard matched the shape of the inlaid wire decoration on the bronze handle of the sword, gold lines that swirled up towards a great green jewel embedded in the pommel. On the other side of the skeleton was a wooden staff, like a wizard's wand. But the most extraordinary treasure was lying across the torso of the skeleton, covering the ribcage and pelvis. It was a great bronze shield, in a figure-of-eight shape, its central boss surrounded by swirling curvilinear forms in enamel and raised repoussée decoration.

'Amazing,' Jack said, his voice hoarse. 'It's virtually identical to the Battersea Shield, found in the river Thames in the nineteenth century.'

'It's made of thin sheet bronze,' Costas said, peering closely at the edge. 'Not very practical in battle.'

'It was probably ceremonial,' Jack said. 'But that sword looks pretty real. And so do those scythes on the chariot wheels.'

Jack looked again, and suddenly it sprang out at him, imagery that had not registered at first but now seemed to knit together all the artefacts in front of him. There were horses, horses everywhere, swirling through the curvilinear patterns on the shield, racing along the sword scabbard, carved into the timbers of the bier. His mind was racing, daring to believe the unbelievable. *Horses, the symbol of the tribe of the Iceni, the tribe of a great warrior queen.* He saw a scatter of coins below the shield, and reached down to pick one up. On one side was a horse, highly abstract with a flowing mane, and mysterious symbols above. On the other side was a head, just recognizable as human, with long wild hair. An image from a people who left no portraits, who hardly ever depicted the human form in their art, yet here he was standing in front of her, one who had been revered as a goddess, whose true likeness none of her followers had dared capture. Jack carefully replaced the coin, then looked around again, appraising, cataloguing, allowing himself to see the unexpected. 'The dovetail joints in the timbers show this tomb was made after the Romans arrived, by carpenters who knew Roman techniques,' he murmured. 'But there are no Roman artefacts here. She wouldn't have allowed it. Those amphoras must have been outside the tomb, offerings made after her burial.'

'She? Her? You're talking about this woman, Andraste?'

Jack paused, then spoke quietly, his voice tense with excitement. 'Nobody has ever been able to find the location of her last battle. The Roman historian Tacitus tells us that forty thousand Britons died, that she survived but went off and poisoned herself. Dio Cassius tells us her surviving followers gave her a lavish burial, somewhere in secret. For centuries scholars have wondered whether her tomb lies under London. It would have been the perfect place, the city laid waste and uninhabited, returned to the state it was in before the Romans arrived. Site of the sacred grove of the goddess Andraste.'

'You still haven't answered my question, Jack.'

'It all fits perfectly,' Jack murmured. 'She would have been a teenager when Claudius arrived in Britain as emperor in AD 43, in the wake of his victorious army. She would have been brought before him when her tribe submitted to the Romans, a princess offering her fealty, probably a dose of defiance too.'

'You're talking about the warrior queen Boudica.'

'A queen who was herself a high priestess, a goddess, and

had some connection with the Sibyls,' Jack murmured. 'Something that made the Sibyl order Claudius to come here in secret as an old man, to seek her tomb.'

'Jack, you're wrong about there being no Roman artefacts here. Looks like our lady had a gladiator fixation.' Costas had moved back to the foot of the bier, and now gestured down. Jack slithered over and confronted another astonishing sight. It was a row of helmets, five elaborate helmets arranged in a row just below the level of the bier, facing the skeleton.

'Unbelievable,' he said. 'But these aren't gladiators' helmets. They're Roman legionary helmets, fairly high ranking by the look of it. Centurions, maybe cohort commanders. And they've seen some pretty brutal action.' He reached over and carefully tipped back the nearest one, which had a deep dent across the top. It was heavier than he had expected, and it stuck to the timber. He pushed harder, and it gave way. He let it drop, and flinched in shock.

They were still in there.

Costas saw it too, and moaned. 'Beam me up, Scotty.'

Jack looked closely along the row of helmets. They were all the same. Each one held a human skull, leering, several of them grotesquely smashed and splintered. The skulls were white, bleached, from heads that had been exposed and left to rot before they were placed inside the tomb. 'Battle trophies,' Jack murmured. 'Collected from the field, or more likely the heads of executed prisoners, the highest-ranking Romans they captured.' His mind was racing again. The warrior queen's last battle. He remembered the accounts of Tacitus, Dio Cassius. *Living trophies of war, brought with her for sacrifice at the most sacred place, consigned with her in eternal submission.*

Then Jack saw them. Huge, shapeless forms emerging from the far side of the tomb, forms that seemed to struggle and rear out of the earth like the sculpted horses from the Athenian Parthenon, only these were real, the blackened skin and manes still stretched over the skulls, teeth bared and grimacing, caught for ever in the throes of death as they had their throats cut beside the body of their queen. It was a terrifying sight, even more so than the line of Roman skulls, and Jack began to feel unnerved again, aware that he and Costas did not belong in this place.

'Time to go,' Costas said, looking apprehensively at the bier. 'I'm remembering that shrieking again. Your grandmother's nightmare. Maybe there really is a banshee down here.'

Jack tore himself away from the image. 'We haven't found what we're looking for. There has to be something more here.' He slithered back towards the bier, and peered down at the skeleton and the array of weapons and armour. Costas took out his compass and aimed it down the bier. 'It's aligned exactly north–south,' he said. 'It points directly toward the arena of the amphitheatre.'

'The amphitheatre was built later,' Jack murmured. 'If this is who I think it is, she was buried at least a decade before work on the amphitheatre was started.'

'Maybe the Romans deliberately built the amphitheatre on a site they knew was sacred, this grove to Andraste,' Costas murmured. 'A way of stamping their authority on the natives after the revolt.'

'And the perfect place to conceal a secret cult, right under the noses of your enemy,' Jack said.

'Have you seen the chariot axle?' Costas said. 'It's lying under her shoulders. With the chariot pole aligned north–south under her body, it makes a cross.'

Jack grunted, only half listening. 'In Iron Age chariot burials, the axle was usually placed below the feet.' Suddenly he gasped, and reached out to the shield. 'It was staring us right in the face. He placed it right over the shield boss.'

'Who did?'

'Someone who was here before us.' Jack began to reach for the object, a metal cylinder. Then he paused, and drew his hand back.

'You must be the only archaeologist who has trouble taking artefacts from burials, Jack.'

'I couldn't violate her grave.'

'I'm with you there. I wouldn't want to raise this lady from the dead. In this place, it's not as if we have anywhere to run.' Costas paused. 'But if you're right, this cylinder wasn't part of the original grave goods. I'm willing to take the risk.' He reached over and picked up the cylinder, then passed it to Jack. 'There. Spell's broken.'

Jack took the cylinder and held it carefully, rotating it slowly in his hands, staring at it. A chain dangled off a rivet on one side. The cylinder was made of sheet bronze, hammered at the join to form the tube, and one end had been crimped over a disc of bronze to form the base. On the bottom was a roundel of red enamel, and swirling around the cylinder were incised curvilinear decorations. Jack saw that the decoration was in the shape of a wolf, an abstract beast that wrapped itself round the cylinder until the snout was nearly touching the tail. 'It's British metalwork, no doubt about it. There's a bronze cylinder just like this from a warrior grave in Yorkshire. And the wolf is another symbol of the Iceni, Boudica's tribe, along with the horse.'

'What about the lid?' Costas said.

'There's a lot of corrosion, bronze disease,' Jack replied, peering closely at the other end of the cylinder. 'But it's not crimped over like the base. There's some kind of resinous material around the join, pretty cracked up.' He pushed a finger cautiously against the crust of built-up corrosion on the top, then flinched as it broke off. 'Thank God our conservators didn't see me do that.' He angled the cylinder so they could both see the surface. Around the edge were the remains of red enamel, from a roundel similar to the one on the base. But here the enamel seemed to have been crudely scraped back to the bronze, which had an incised decoration. The incision was angular, crude, unlike the flowing lines of the wolf on the side of the cylinder, more like scratched graffiti. Jack stared at it. He suddenly froze.

It was a name.

'Bingo,' Costas said.

The letters were large, shaky, the name curving round the

top, the other word below, like an inscription on a coin:

CLAVDIVS DEDIT

' "Claudius gave this",' Jack said, suddenly ecstatic. 'Claudius did come here, where we are now, and he placed this in Boudica's tomb.' He held the cylinder with sudden reverence, looking at the name and then at the fractured join at the lid, hardly daring to think what might be inside.

'How come Claudius has a British bronze cylinder?' Costas asked.

'Maybe he got it when he first came to Britain, during the conquest,' Jack said. 'Maybe Boudica herself gave it to him, and afterwards he used it to hide away his treasured manuscript, what we're looking for. It might have been less obvious than one of those Egyptian stone jars from his library in Herculaneum.'

'But the bronze cylinder would have fitted inside one of the smaller stone jars, like the one we found in Rome,' Costas murmured. 'Maybe there's one of those lying around here too.'

'If this bronze cylinder was inside a stone jar, then it's been disturbed and opened by someone since Claudius came down here.'

'Are we going to open it?'

Jack took a deep breath. 'These aren't exactly controlled laboratory conditions.'

'I've heard that before.'

Jack looked back at the slurry of water where they had come into the tomb, slopping back and forth and distinctly brown in their torchlight. 'I'm worried the seal on the lip of the cylinder might have decayed. If we take it back underwater, we might destroy what's inside for ever. And I don't want to risk going back to get a waterproof container. This whole place might be atomized.'

'At any moment,' Costas said, looking at the tail fin of the bomb rising above the water. 'Right, let's do it.'

Jack nodded, and put his hand over the lid. He shut his eyes, and silently mouthed a few words. Everything they had been striving for suddenly seemed to rest on this moment. He opened his eyes, and twisted the lid. It came away easily. *Too easily*. He tipped the cylinder towards his beam, and stared inside.

It was empty.

17

Early the next morning, Jack sat in the nave of St Paul's Cathedral in London, beneath the great dome facing the high altar to the east. The cathedral had opened to the public only a few minutes before and was still almost empty, but Jack had chosen a row of seats well in from the central aisle of the nave where they would be less likely to be overheard. He glanced at his watch. He had arranged to meet Costas at nine o'clock, five minutes from now, and Jeremy would join them as soon as he could after arriving back from Oxford.

Jack and Costas had spent the night in IMU's flat overlooking the river Thames, a place where Jack often stayed between projects when he needed to carry out research in one of London's libraries or museums. After the exhilaration of the ancient tomb and then the empty cylinder they had been too tired to talk, and too numb to feel disappointed. Jack leaned back, stretched, and closed his eyes. He still felt drained from their extraordinary exploration the day before, and his morning coffee was only just kicking in. He felt strangely discomfited, unsure whether their quest had gone as far as it could, whether he should look back on what they had discovered, begin to relish the extraordinary finds of the past few days for what they were and not see them as clues to something even bigger. He opened his eyes, and peered up at the magnificent dome far above him, so similar to the dome of St Peter's in the Vatican, to the dome of the Pantheon in Rome built over fifteen hundred years earlier. Yet here Jack felt he was looking not at replication or continuity but at the unique brilliance of one man, the architect Sir Christopher Wren. The interior dome was set below the ovoid dome of the exterior, a way of elevating the cathedral externally yet ensuring that the view of the dome from inside was pleasing to the eye. Jack narrowed his vision. As so often in the best works of human creation, the view was not quite what it seemed.

'Morning, Jack.' Costas came sliding along the seats from the central aisle, and Jack eyed him with some concern. He was wearing one of Jack's fisherman's guernseys from the IMU flat, slightly too small for him around the middle but about two sizes too long, the sleeves pushed up to reveal his muscular forearms. He looked a little pale and red around the nose, and his eyes were watery. 'Don't ask,' he said, slumping down on the seat beside Jack and looking miserable, sniffing and digging in his pocket for a tissue. 'Every decongestant I could find. I'm beginning to float. I don't know how you can breathe when the air's so damp. And cold.' He sneezed, sniffed noisily and groaned.

'I gather the all-clear's been given in the City,' Jack said.

'They're removing the barriers now. The disposal team dug straight down through the Guildhall pavement, craned out the bomb and choppered it away in the middle of the night for a controlled explosion. It was quite a commotion. I made sure they dug in from the east, so I don't think there was any damage to the tomb.'

'I've just been speaking to my friends at the London archaeological service,' Jack said, pointing to his cell phone. 'They've got a real challenge on their hands. They need to make some kind of protective bubble over the site to maintain the atmospheric conditions in the tomb, to keep it from decaying. They've got the best conservation people on standby. It's probably going to take months to excavate, but it should be amazing when it's revealed. I've suggested they leave the tomb *in situ*, make a museum on the spot. It could be completely underground, entered from the amphitheatre.'

'They don't want to be disturbing her.' Costas sniffed. 'No way.'

'Did they let you in on the act?' Jack enquired. 'The disposal team?'

'The CO of the Dive Unit turned out to be an old buddy of mine, a Royal Engineers officer from the Defence Diving

School. We met when I did the Mine and Explosive Ordnance Disposal course at Devonport two years ago. I told him the second fuse on the bomb was too corroded to drill into, that they'd have to fill it with chemicals to neutralize it. But he couldn't let me in to help. Health and safety regulations, you know.' Costas sniffed again. 'That's the trouble with this country. Over regulated.'

'You'd rather we were based in Italy, let's say?'

Costas' eyes lit up. 'Speaking of which, when are we getting back to the shipwreck of St Paul? A couple of weeks in the Mediterranean would suit me just fine. Might even kill this cold.'

'*Seaquest II*'s still on station, and the Embraer jet's on standby,' Jack replied. 'I've just been on the phone to Maurice about timing the press release on the Herculaneum library. Unless Jeremy's got something new for us, I don't see where we go from here with the Claudius connection. It's already a fabulous addition to history, with the extraordinary finds we've made in Rome, and here in London. But the whereabouts of the manuscript might just have to remain one of the great unsolved mysteries of all time.' Jack heaved a sigh, then peered up at the dome again. 'Not my style, but a dead end's a dead end.'

Costas gestured at the laptop on Jack's knees. 'I see you've been scrolling through Maria's images of the Herculaneum library.' He pointed a soggy tissue at the page of thumbnail images. Jack nodded, then peered back at him with an expectant expression. 'I know that look,' Costas said.

'I was just going through the pictures for the press release, then I suddenly remembered something,' Jack said. 'That page of papyrus I found in Herculaneum, lying on the table under the blank sheets. *Historia Britannorum. Narcissus Fecit.*' Jack clicked on a thumbnail, and a page of ancient writing appeared on the screen. 'Thank God Maria took plenty of pictures.'

Costas blew his nose. 'I knew you'd found something.'

'I'd put that page from my mind because I'd guessed it was probably part of a treatise on military strategy, the kind of thing Claudius the armchair general would have relished, to show he really knew his stuff and was worthy of his father and brother. Maybe something on the lead-up to the invasion of Britain, on his planning sessions with his legionary commanders, all painstakingly recorded. But then I put myself back into Herculaneum, into that room. I began to think about the last things Claudius would have had on his mind, what he would have been writing. In the weeks leading up to the eruption of Vesuvius, we know Pliny the Elder was visiting him in the villa. Pliny was a military historian too, an experienced veteran himself, but he'd been there, done that, and what really fired him up in his final years was his *Natural History*, collecting any facts and trivia he could stick in it.'

'Like that page on Judaea, you mean, his additional notes, that we found on the shelf in the room,' Costas said.

'Precisely. And what really would have excited Pliny about Claudius was the Britannia connection. Not the military campaign, the invasion, but anything Claudius could tell him about the natural history, the geography, the people, anything unusual, garish. Pliny would have badgered him about it. I can see him sitting with Claudius in that room, constantly questioning, steering him away from the triumph, the strategy, mining him for any trivia he might have learned about Britain, with wily old Narcissus at the table patiently transcribing everything Claudius said. After all, we know Claudius had seen the place with his own eyes, had visited Britain not just once, for his triumph, but twice, when he came in secret to the tomb as an old man, not long before the eruption. Britain was his great achievement, and he would have loved telling Pliny all about it, playing the old general reminiscing on his conquest for the glory of Rome and his family honour.'

'Go on.' Costas sneezed violently.

'I've now read the entire text preserved on that page from the table, Claudius' *History of Britain*. It's clearly part of a preamble, an introductory chapter, setting the stage.' Jack pointed at the fine handwriting on the screen. 'The Latin's easy, clearly written. We have to thank Narcissus for that. It's about religion and rituals, just the kind of thing Pliny would have loved.'

'And just what we need.' Costas sniffed. 'All that discussion yesterday about the Iron Age, about Boudica, Andraste. There are still some pretty big black holes.'

Jack nodded. 'The first part really staggered me. It's the end of the description of a great stone circle Claudius had visited. "I have seen these things with my own eyes," he says.'

'A stone circle? Stonehenge?'

'He tells us that the stones were set up by the British people in honour of a race of giants who came from the east, escaping a great flood,' Jack said. 'The stones represent each of the priest-kings and priest-queens, who afterwards ruled the island.'

'The Black Sea exodus!' Costas exclaimed. 'The priests of Atlantis. That shows Claudius wasn't being fed a pack of lies.'

'"These giants brought with them a Mother Goddess, who afterwards was worshipped in Britain,"' Jack translated. '"The descendants of these priest-kings and priest-queens were the Druids."' He reverted to the original Latin: '"*Praesidium posthac inpositum victis excisique luci saevis superstitionibus sacri: nam cruore captivo adolere aras et hominum fibris consulere deos fas habebant.*"' He paused, then translated. '"Who consider it their sacred duty to cover their altars with the blood of their victims. I myself have watched them at the stone circle, the place they call *druidaeque circum*, the circle of the Druids."'

'In our last few expeditions, we've had Toltecs, Carthaginians and now ancient Britons,' Costas grumbled. 'Human sacrifice everywhere.'

'The early antiquarians of Sir Christopher Wren's day actually thought Stonehenge had been a druid circle, and they were right after all,' Jack said. 'It's amazing. But this is the clincher. Listen to this. "They choose the high priestess from among the noble families of the Britons. I myself have met the chosen one, the girl they call Andraste, who also calls herself Boudica, princess of the tribe of the Iceni, who was brought before me as a slave but who the Sibyl ordered me to set free.

For the Sibyl of Cumae says that the high priestess of these Druids is the thirteenth of the Sibyls, and the oracle for all the tribes of Britannia."'

'Stop right there,' Costas said.

'End of page. That's it.'

'You're saying Boudica, the warrior queen, she was the high priestess? That Boudica was a kind of arch-druid?'

'I'm not saying it, Claudius is.'

'And this druidess was one of the Sibyls?'

'That's what he says. And Claudius should know. We know he was a visitor to the Sibyl's cave at Cumae.'

'That's because the Sibyl was his drug-dealer.'

'There's something extraordinary going on here, something people have guessed at but never been able to prove,' Jack murmured, putting the computer on the seat beside him and staring up towards the altar. 'Let's backtrack for a moment. Begin at the beginning. Claudius gets a document from a Galilean, a Nazarene.'

'We know who we're talking about, Jack.'

'Do we? There were plenty of would-be messiahs floating round the Sea of Galilee at that time. John the Baptist, for a start. Let's not leap to conclusions.'

'Come on, Jack. You're playing devil's advocate.'

'Let's keep the devil out of this. We've got enough to contend with as it is.' Jack paused. 'Then, as an old man, Claudius makes a secret trip to Britain, to London. He has the manuscript with him, inside a metal container given to him during a previous visit to Britain, perhaps by a princess of the

Iceni.' Jack patted a bulge in his bag. Costas looked at the bulge, then at Jack.

'That's called looting,' he said solemnly. 'It's becoming a habit.'

'Just a precaution. In case that bomb cooked off. We had to have some evidence we'd really seen the tomb.'

'No need to explain it to me, Jack.'

'And like all good treasure-hiders, Claudius leaves a clue,' Jack continued. 'Or rather a series of clues. Some of them are by way of his friend Pliny.'

'I think Claudius was having fun with us,' Costas said, sniffing.

'He's addicted to riddles, to reading the leaves, has done it all his life, all those visits to the Sibyl. She has him wrapped round her shrivelled fingers, of course. Claudius becomes like a crossword freak, a cryptologist. And leaving clues seems to be part of the treasure-hiding psychology,' Jack continued. 'If you have to hide something, you hide it ingeniously, but you have to feel that somewhere along the line someone else might find it. If you leave clues, you're in control of that process of discovery too. A way of assuring your own immortality.'

'So he comes back to Britain and finds her tomb, and here we are too,' Costas said. 'Always hide things in the most unlikely places.' He sneezed. 'The word of the Messiah clutched in the dead hands of a pagan priestess.'

'That's one thread in our story,' Jack said. 'Claudius, his motivations, what drove him. But there's another thread that's been fascinating me. It's about women.'

'Katya, Maria, Elizabeth? Careful, Jack. That's one thing you don't seem to be able to control.'

'I mean women in the past. The distant past.'

'The mother goddess?' Costas said.

'If the priesthood that Claudius writes about did survive from Neolithic times, then there's every reason for thinking that the cult of the mother goddess did as well,' Jack said. 'She's there in the Graeco-Roman pantheon, *Magna Mater*, the Great Mother, Vesta, whose temple we found in Rome, and among the Celtic gods too. But I'm not just thinking about female goddesses. I'm thinking about the earthly practitioners of religion, the priests, the oracles.'

'The Sibyls?'

'Something's beginning to fall into place,' Jack murmured. 'It's been staring at us for centuries, the Sibylline prophecy in Virgil, the Dies Irae. And now we've found the extra ingredient that suddenly makes it all plausible, that tips the balance into reality.'

'Go on.'

'It's about early Christianity.' Jack suddenly felt a surge of excitement as he realized where his thoughts were leading him. 'About women in early Christianity.'

'Huh?'

'What does that mean to you? First thought?'

'The Virgin Mary?'

'The cult of the Virgin probably incorporated pagan beliefs in a mother goddess,' Jack said. 'But I'm thinking about the early believers, the first followers of Jesus, who they were.' He reached into his bag, and pulled out a red hardback book. 'Remember I told you how elusive the written evidence is for early Christianity, how virtually nothing survives apart from the Gospels? Well, one of the rare exceptions is Pliny. Not our old friend Pliny the Elder, but his nephew, Pliny the Younger.'

'The one who wrote about the eruption of Vesuvius,' Costas said slowly. 'And the Vestal Virgins.'

Jack nodded. 'The account of Vesuvius was in a letter to the historian Tacitus, written about twenty-five years after the event. Well, here's the younger Pliny again, in a letter written shortly before he died in AD 113. By that time he was Roman governor of Pontus and Bithynia, the area of Turkey beside the Black Sea, and he's writing to the emperor Trajan about the activities of Christians in his province. Pliny wasn't exactly a fan of Christianity, but then he was echoing the official line. What had started out at the time of Claudius as an obscure cult, yet another mystery religion from the east, fifty years on had become a real concern to the emperors. Unlike the other big eastern cults, Mithraism or Isis worship, the Christians had become political. That was what really put Christianity at centre stage. Far-sighted Romans could see the Church becoming a focus for dissent, especially as Christianity attracted slaves, the great underclass in Roman society. The Romans were always frightened of another slave uprising, ever since Spartacus. They were also thrown off balance by the fanaticism of the Christians, the willingness to die for their beliefs. You just didn't see that in any of the other cults. And there was something else that really terrified them.'

'These Romans you're talking about,' Costas said, sneezing. 'They're all men. We were talking about women.'

Jack nodded, and opened the book. 'Listen to this. A letter from Pliny the Younger to the emperor Trajan. Pliny's seeking advice on how to prosecute Christians, as he's never done it before. He calls it a degenerate cult, carried to extravagant lengths. He tells Trajan he has unrepentant Christians executed, though he generously spares those who make offerings of wine and incense to the statue of the emperor, the living god. But then listen to this. In order to extract the truth about their political activities, he orders the torture of "*duabus ancillis, quae ministrae dicebantur*". Both the words *ancillis* and *ministrae* mean female attendants, but *ministra* is often equated with the Greek word *diakonos*.'

'Deaconesses,' Costas mused. 'Priestesses?'

'That's what really terrified the Romans,' Jack said. 'It's what terrified them about the British, too, about Boudica. She fascinated them, excited them, but also terrified them. Women could be the true power behind the scenes in Rome, women like the emperor Augustus' wife Livia, or Claudius' scheming wives, but it was a male-dominated system. The *cursus honorum*, the rite of passage through military and public offices followed by upper-class Romans like Pliny the Younger and his uncle, would never have admitted a woman. Just like the image of the wild barbarian warrior queen, the idea of this new cult having priestesses on a par with men would have been horrifying, worse still if they were slaves.'

'But I thought the Christian Church was male dominated.'

'That's the really fascinating thing about Pliny the Younger's letter. That one word, *deaconesses*. It implies the Church didn't start out male dominated. Somewhere along the line, perhaps soon after the time of Pliny the Younger, the more politically minded leaders among the Christians must have realized they'd never defeat Rome head-on, that they stood a good chance of being extinguished completely. Instead, you confront the system from within. You make converts of Roman men who can see how the Church fits with their own personal ambitions, with their political careers. Ultimately you catch the emperor himself, as happened two hundred years after Pliny with Constantine the Great. The power of the Roman Church, its political power, was all about men. But in the earliest period of Christianity, before the Church developed as a political force, the word of Jesus was carried equally by men and women.'

'Talk me through the Sibyl again, Jack. The link to early Christianity.'

'Okay.' Jack closed the book, looked up again at the dome, then narrowed his eyes. 'Speculation, and a few facts.'

'Fire away.' Costas sneezed violently.

'By the end of the first century BC, at the beginning of the Roman Empire, the power of the Sibyls was on the wane,' Jack said. 'To the Sibyl at Cumae, the Romans who had come to occupy the old Greek settlements of the Bay of Naples, places like Pompeii, Herculaneum, Neapolis, were a double-sided coin. On the one hand, they kept her in business.

Romans came to the Phlegraean Fields seeking cures and prophecies, or as tourists, gawping at the fire and spectacle at the entrance to the underworld. On the other hand, to many Romans the music of the Sibyl had become ersatz, a contrivance, a Greek embellishment like those statues in the Villa of the Papyri or those phoney philosophers kept for after-dinner entertainment. And, as we now suspect, the Sibyl began to depend more and more for her livelihood on dishing out narcotics than selling divine prophecies that people took at all seriously.'

'But surely the poet Virgil believed in her,' Costas said. 'The Sybilline prophecy in his poem, about the coming Golden Age.'

'It's hard to know whether he took her seriously, or just fancied embellishing his poetry with a Sybilline utterance,' Jack said. 'But the Sibyl may have seen a man whose word would outlast him, a man destined for supreme achievement, just as she saw Claudius a generation later. She may have given Virgil words she wanted to see survive, immortalized in his writing. The Sibyls were shrewd operators. Like most successful mystics, she would always have tried to keep one step ahead of her clients, profess to know more about them than could seem plausible. The Sibyls probably had an extensive network of spies and informants, keeping them abreast of everything going on. Remember the cave of the Vestal Virgins we found under the Palatine, right under the heart of Rome. And remember Claudius' extraordinary statement about the priestesses in Britain, chosen from the families of tribal chieftains, of kings. Maybe the Sibyls at Cumae were also chosen from the wealthiest families of Rome, like the Vestals, even from the imperial family. Maybe the cave under the Palatine was where they were nurtured. And the schooling of a Sibyl was probably all about how to tease private information out of people, without them realizing it.'

'Easy if your client's all drugged up,' Costas said.

'That may be how Claudius revealed his secret to her,' Jack murmured.

'And the Christianity connection?'

'That's where speculation takes over,' Jack said intently. 'But try this. By the time Virgil visits Cumae, by the time of the first emperor, Augustus, the Sibyls already know their days are numbered. Rome has come to rule the world, and the Sibyls see the pantheon of Roman gods solidifying around them like the temples and palaces of the great city itself, built to last a thousand years. But the Sibyls also look east, beyond Greece, and they see new forces which could engulf the Roman world, forces kept at bay while Rome fought within itself and then strove to conquer the ancient lands once ruled by Alexander the Great. The Sibyls foresee the eastern cult of the divine ruler coming to Rome, the emperor becoming a living god. And they see something else. They see it in the slaves and outcasts who hide in the Phlegraean Fields near the cave of the Cumaean Sibyl. They see it in the easterners who flock to the Bay of Naples after the Augustan peace, just as Pliny the Elder must have seen it in his sailors at Misenum. New religious ideas from the east, new prophets, a Messiah. A world where the Sibyls will no longer be able to hold sway, where people need no longer be enslaved to oracles and priests in order to know the word of God.'

'Virgil's coming Golden Age,' Costas murmured.

'By the time of Virgil, the Sibyl at Cumae must have guessed it would come to pass. By the time of Claudius, she knew it. Christianity had arrived.'

'And she heard the rumblings underground,' Costas said. 'Literally.'

'There was a huge earthquake in the Bay of Naples in AD 62,' Jack said. 'You can see the damaged buildings at Pompeii today, still under repair seventeen years later when Vesuvius erupted. And dangling in her cave in the Phlegraean Fields, the Sibyl must have had her ear to the ground in more ways than one, guessed that something catastrophic was imminent. We're talking empirical observations here, not mysticism. Everything was hotting up. The sulphurous smell was getting worse. And maybe the memory of past volcanic catastrophe was part of the ancient lore passed down to the Sibyls, the eruption of Thera in the Aegean in the Bronze Age, earlier eruptions at the dawn of civilization. And perhaps she truly did believe in some divine power behind it all, behind her utterances. She saw signs, auguries, that her age was ended. With the eruption of Vesuvius, her god Apollo would be gone, extinguished for ever.'

'Time for a fast exit left,' Costas murmured.

'Time for the final ingredient, the biggest twist,' Jack said.

'Several decades earlier, in the time of Claudius the emperor, the Sibyl would have seen her prophecy to Virgil come true. The birth of a boy, the imminent Golden Age. She would have seen Christians appearing in the Phlegraean Fields. She would have heard of Jesus, and of Mary Magdalene. She would have known that the Christians included both men and women. She would have seen that there were no priests.'

'We're talking women here again, aren't we, Jack? That's what you're driving at. Girl power.'

'Girl power.' Jack grinned. 'Not goddesses, but real flesh-and-blood women. That's what the Sibyl saw. In Rome, the power of women was on the wane. The Vestal Virgins were virtually imprisoned within the palace walls, almost a despotic male fantasy of female submission. The imperial cult, the cult of the emperor, was male dominated, with an exclusively male priesthood. To the Sibyls, their own vocation was perhaps not really about Apollo or any earlier gods they might have served. It was about matriarchy, about continuation of the female line that extended far back to the Stone Age, to the time when women ruled the family and the clan. In Christianity, the Sibyl may have seen hope for the future, for the continuation of the matriarchy.'

'Why the focus on Britain?' Costas asked.

'Because it's often at the periphery that the biggest changes take place,' Jack said. 'In Rome itself, civilization had become corrupt, decayed. Christianity had come from the periphery, from the eastern boundary of the empire, and it was at the other periphery, far to the north-west, that some saw greatest hope for its success. Britain would have seemed like the New World did to the religious dissenters of seventeenth-century Europe, a place where they could pursue their beliefs without persecution. The Britons themselves, the natives, were fiercely independent, truculent, with a mysterious religion that would never be fully captured and manipulated by the Romans, where the Roman gods would never truly hold sway. The tribes of Britain had been ruled by great warrior queens, by Boudica and those before her. And as we now know from Claudius, their own priesthood, the druids, was ruled by a high priestess. If the druids were dominated by women, then it was women who knit together the warrior tribes of the Celtic world, just as women had done for thousands of years before that, back through prehistory.'

'And how much would Boudica have known about Christianity?'

'Claudius himself may even have talked to her about it, when she was brought before him as a teenager on his first visit to Britain, after the Roman invasion. Something about her, about what he saw and felt in Britain, may even have influenced him to tell her his best story, of his visit to Judaea as a young man. Then remember the reference in Gildas, the monk writing after the Roman period. The memory of a Roman emperor himself secretly bringing Christianity to Britain may have become part of the folklore of the first Christians in Britain. And Claudius may have known about the connection of the Sibyl with the druids, as he was already under the sway of the Sibyl at Cumae. The Sibyl herself may have influenced his decision to invade in the first place, perhaps a way of knitting Britain more closely within her world. She may have given him a message in the leaves.'

'Amazing what people will do for their drug-dealers,' Costas murmured.

'In the years that followed Claudius' visit, Boudica would have learned more about Christianity,' Jack continued. 'Like the children of most vanquished princes, she would have been brought up in the Roman way, learning Latin and perhaps even travelling to Rome, maybe even to the Bay of Naples and the cave at Cumae. Back home in London, she would have heard of sailors and soldiers bringing ideas from the east, Mithraism, Isis worship, Christianity. Then, as she was inducted into the priesthood, preparing for her role as high priestess, as the British Sibyl, she would have become part of the secret network of knowledge that tied together all the Sibyls across the Roman world, the thirteen. And she may have seen the same thing that the Sibyl at Cumae saw in Christianity, something that drew her even closer to its followers after she rebelled against the Romans. A religion on a collision course with Rome, with the Rome which had abused her and raped her daughters, a religion of defiance. And the ideas she heard, the quest for a heaven on earth, may have come easily to the Britons, people whose beliefs were attuned to the natural world and not fossilized in temples and priests. She may not have shown any outward signs of it, but she may have decided that those ideas could work for her, and for the survival of the matriarchy.'

'You're talking about Christianity before the Roman Church,' Costas murmured. 'What you and Jeremy were telling me about in the amphitheatre. The Celtic Church, the Church of the Britons. The Pelagian heresy.'

'I believe that's the reason why the Sibyl at Cumae made Claudius bring his precious document here,' Jack said. 'To provide a secret gift for the early Christians in Britain, something which might strengthen them against what she saw happening before her eyes in the Phlegraean Fields, in the years after St Paul's arrival there.'

'You mean the beginnings of what would become the Roman state religion,' Costas said, blowing his nose.

'There was something in Claudius' document from Judaea, something we can only guess at, that gave the Sibyl hope. Something Claudius must have said when he was in a stupor before her cave. Something that made her realize that what he had was extraordinarily precious, and needed to be secreted away in a place where it might survive, and further her cause. And something she knew some of those around Claudius would do anything to get their hands on, to destroy.'

'She saw the first priests among the Christians. Male priests. And it frightened her. She saw Christianity going the same way as all the other cults in Rome.'

'You've got it.'

'So she threatens to withdraw Claudius' drugs unless he does her bidding.'

Jack grinned. 'She knew exactly why he kept coming back for more, what it was that dulled his pain. Claudius himself might not have been so sure. All he knew was that if he did her bidding, every time he stood in that smoky cavern he felt good again. Probably she offered him something tangible, something else that drew him back to that place at the entrance to the underworld. Maybe like Aeneas in Virgil's story she offered to take him down below, to see his father and brother again. That's what he would have yearned for most. Like any good fortune-teller, she knew her client's psychology.'

'And she knew he loved a good riddle.'

Jack nodded. 'She gives him a prophecy. A message in the leaves. Claudius laps it up, relishes the challenge. It was the one we found in Rome, the Dies Irae. A prophecy of doom, but also of hope. Claudius knows who Andraste was, and knows where to find her tomb. The Sibyl knows that he knows. He writes it down, seals it in that stone cylinder, the one he gave Pliny to take to Rome. All Claudius had to do was fulfil the prophecy, take the manuscript and put it with Andraste, and he would get what he had begged the Sibyl for, his visit to the underworld.'

'Big time,' Costas murmured.

'When it came down to it, in those last moments of hell in front of the crack of doom in the Phlegraean Fields, it may have felt right. Claudius may have shut his eyes, and in his mind seen only those statues we found in his room in the villa in Herculaneum, those images of his father and brother which must have been seared into his mind.'

'Jack, I think you've found another soulmate,' Costas said.

'Move over Harald Hardrada, King of the Vikings, here comes Claudius, Emperor of Rome.'

'I feel like I did on that little island north of Newfoundland, on our search for the Jewish menorah,' Jack said, closing the book. 'Harald had taken us on an extraordinary adventure in search of his treasure, farther than we could ever have dared imagine. I feel the same way now, but I feel Claudius has left us, has taken us as far as he can. I owe it to him to find the clues, to go where he wanted me to go. But I just can't see a way ahead.'

'Speaking of soulmates, here's one of mine,' Costas said, sniffing and gesturing blearily at the figure making his way along the row of seats towards them. 'And maybe he's got what you need.'

18

The woman stumbled as they dragged her out of the car and pushed her over the irregular rocky surface. She was blindfolded, but she knew where they were. The smell had hit her as soon as they had opened the car door, the acrid waft of sulphur that made the tip of her tongue burn. She could sense the yawning space ahead, the warm updraught from the furnace in the pit of the earth. She knew the score. They would either do it here, or take her down below. She had been here many times before, as a girl, when they had tried to toughen her up. She had seen the terror, the pleading, the incontinence, and sometimes the serene composure, the acceptance of the old ways as they always had been, the futility of resistance.

A hand steered her to the left, and pushed her on, down a rocky path. So it would be below. They were taking no chances. The hand pulled her to a halt, and roughly undid her blindfold. She blinked hard, and stared into darkness. She sensed the bulk of Vesuvius over the bay behind her, but knew that if she turned for one last look she would be slapped down, and the blindfold put back on. She knew they had only removed it to make it easier for them to get her down the rocky path to the floor of the crater, but she hoped they would keep it off to the end. It was her only fear, that she should experience that moment in darkness, unable to distinguish between blindness and death.

She kept her eyes ahead, only looking down when she stumbled, her hands duct taped behind her. They reached the bottom. One set of footsteps remained behind, guarding. It was the usual drill. Once, long ago, that had been her job, when they had tried to suck her deeper into the family, before they had found another way for her to serve them. She remembered the interview, the shadowy man from Rome, the man she never saw and never spoke to again. Afterwards, there had been occasional phone calls, instructions, threats she knew to be real, the order that she take the job in Naples. Nothing for years, and then the earthquake, and the nightmare returned, the calls in the night, hissing demands, threats to her daughter, her world of scholarship and archaeology crashing down. She thought of earlier times when she had seemed free of it. She thought of Jack, of the lost years since they had forced her to leave him, of seeing him again two days ago and their fleeting words in the villa. There was something else she had wanted to tell him, but now only her daughter would know, three years from now when she came of age and would read the truth. It was all too late now. Then the other pair of footsteps resonated in the crater, pushing her forward. The hand halted her again, and the blindfold was yanked tight over her eyes. 'No,' she said fiercely in Italian. 'Not this. Do you remember how much it frightened me when we were children? When I looked after you. My little brother.'

There was no response. The hands paused, then relented. The blindfold caught on the superintendency ID card still dangling around her neck, and it was pulled violently off. Her neck felt as if it had been whipped. She kept her eyes resolutely ahead, but caught sight of the fresh plaster cast on his wrist. 'What happened to you, *mia caro*?' she said. There was no reply, and she was pushed ahead, this time violently, the hand against the bun of her hair. She stumbled forward. Fifty paces. Another twenty paces. A hand grasped her hair again, and a foot kicked behind her right knee. She collapsed on to the floor of the crater, her knees hitting the lava with a crack. The pain was shocking. She kept her composure, remained upright. Her legs were kicked apart. Something cold was pushed against the nape of her neck, sending a tingle down her spine. 'Wait,' she said, her voice strong, unwavering. 'Release my hands. I must make my peace with God. *In nomine patris et filii et spiritus sancti.*'

For a few moments nothing happened. The muzzle was still

pressed against her neck. She wondered if that was it, if it had already happened, if this was death, if death meant being frozen in the moment of passing. Then the muzzle was removed, she heard a sloshing metal can clatter on the ground, smelled the petrol, and felt the hands fumbling at her wrists. Her heart was beginning to beat faster now, pounding, and her knees felt weak. She closed her eyes, took a deep breath, savouring it, even the sickly smell of this place. She would not let herself down. She would not let her family down. *The family*. She knew she should be thinking of something else, of those she truly loved, of her daughter, but she could not. She opened her eyes, and looked in front of her. The crack was there, pitch black, solidified lava around the edges. She knew what would happen next. The bark of the silenced Beretta, the jet of blood and brains, strangely self-contained, like water from a hose, pulsing out with the final heartbeats. The body pushed into the crack, the fuel can emptied over it, the tossed cigarette. She wished the crack itself would take her, come alive as it had when the volcano had throbbed like a living heart under this place, the seething core of the underworld. She wanted to be embraced by it. She wanted it to burn.

There was a tearing sound as the tape on her wrists came free, a jolt of pain as it was ripped off. She let her left hand fall, shook it, feeling the circulation return. She slowly raised her right hand in front of her breasts, made the sign of the cross, and touched her forehead. Her hand was firm, unshaking. She was pleased. She let it drop. Her eyes were wide open, staring into the crack. She moved her hands together, felt the delicate ring Jack's grandmother had given her, an ancient treasure of his seafaring ancestors. She felt the muzzle press against the nape of her neck. She bowed her head slightly. The angle would be better. Quicker. She heard a cell phone chirp, and then a voice behind her, a voice that brought back the warmth of childhood, a voice that she had loved hearing in the mornings when she had stroked his forehead, seeing him waken.

'Eminence? *Va bene.* Your will be done.'

The click of the pistol cocking.

Then nothing.

Costas sneezed, as he made space for Jeremy, who had arrived in St Paul's Cathedral five minutes before but had spotted a church official and gone straight off to talk to him. Jeremy came down the aisle carrying a dripping umbrella and briefcase and wearing a red Goretex jacket. Costas and Jack had only just returned to their seats below the dome a few moments before, having made a quick dash to a pharmacy outside on the Strand. Costas was noisily snorting a decongestant and peering at the label on a bottle. He popped a small handful of pills, took a swig of water and leaned back to let Jeremy by, making space on the chair between him and Jack. Jeremy took off his coat, sat down, sniffed the air, removed his glasses to wipe away the rainwater, then sniffed again. He leaned towards Costas, then recoiled slightly. 'Something smells bad around here.'

'Good morning to you too,' Costas said nasally.

'It's kind of sickly,' Jeremy said. 'Really pretty disgusting.'

'Ah,' Jack said. 'Body liqueur. Must have been when we took off the e-suits. Somehow it always stays with you.'

'Ah,' Jeremy replied forcibly. 'I forgot where you've been. Dead bodies. That's why I stick to libraries.'

'Don't say that word. Stick,' Costas said, looking miserable.

'Come on. This way,' Jeremy said, gathering his things and getting up, pointedly keeping his distance from Costas. 'I've arranged a private room.'

'How do you know all these people?' Costas said.

'I'm a medieval manuscripts expert, remember?' Jeremy replied. 'A lot of the best documents are still held by the Church. It's a small world.' Jack quickly packed his laptop, then followed Jeremy down the nave towards a side chapel. Jeremy nodded at a cassocked man who was waiting discreetly nearby with a ring of heavy keys, and who came over and unlocked the grated steel door for them. Jack slipped in first, followed by the other two. They were in the Chapel of All Souls, dominated by an effigy of Lord Kitchener and also containing a pietà sculpture of the Virgin Mary holding the body of Christ. Jeremy led them behind the effigy out of earshot from the aisle outside and squatted down with his back to the statue. He took out a notebook from his bag and looked up at Jack, his face flushed with excitement. 'Okay. You told me on the phone about your finds, about the tomb. Pretty incredible. Now it's my turn.'

'Fire away.'

'I was in Oxford most of yesterday following that lead I told you about. The archivist at Balliol College is a friend of mine. We searched through all the unpublished papers related to the Church of St Lawrence Jewry, and found an accounts ledger from the 1670s' reconstruction of the church by Sir Christopher Wren. Nobody had ever thought much of the ledger, as it seemed mostly to replicate Wren's accounts books that have already been published. But something caught my eye, and we looked at it in more detail. It was an addendum, from 1685. An old burial chamber under the church had been cleared out, and Wren's team returned to seal it up and check the foundations. They found a locked crypt beyond the chamber. They managed to break open the door, and one of them went in.'

Jack whistled. 'Bingo. That's our crypt. Do you know who it was?'

'All of the master craftsmen were present in the burial chamber. It was five years after the church had been completed, and the 1685 visit was a tour of inspection to see how everything was standing up. Edward Pierce, mason and sculptor. Thomas Newman, bricklayer. John Longland, carpenter. Thomas Mead, plasterer. Christopher Wren himself was there, taking a breather from his work here at St Paul's. And there was one other man, a new name to me. Johannes Deverette.'

'French?' Jack said.

'Flemish. My friend the librarian had come across the name before, and we found enough to build up a sketch. He was a

Huguenot refugee, a Calvinist Protestant who had fled the Low Countries for England earlier that year. Sixteen eighty-five was the year the French king revoked the Edict of Nantes, which had given Protestants protection.'

'Nothing unusual in a Huguenot in the London building trade at that time,' Jack murmured. 'Some of Wren's best-known woodworkers were Huguenots, the famous carver Grinling Gibbons for example. You can see his work all round us here in St Paul's.'

'What was unusual was Deverette's occupation. I went over the road to the Bodleian Library and did a name search, came up with more biographical notes. He described himself as a *Musick Meister*, a master of music. Wren apparently employed him on a recommendation from Grinling Gibbons, to soothe Wren's young son Billy, who was mentally handicapped. Deverette sang Gregorian chant.'

'Gregorian music.' Costas sneezed. 'Isn't that the traditional music of the Roman Catholic liturgy?'

'It's a really fascinating ingredient of this whole story,' Jeremy said. 'Like the Anglicans, the Huguenots rejected the rule of the Roman Church, but there were many who clung to the old traditions for purely aesthetic reasons. I discovered that Deverette came from a long line of Gregorian musicians who claimed descent from the time of St Gregory himself, the Pope who formalized the plainsong repertory in the sixth century. I was stunned to discover that Sir Christopher Wren also shared that aesthetic. But then I thought of his architecture. Just look at this place.' Jeremy gestured up at the cathedral interior. 'It's hardly an austere Protestant meeting house, is it? It's a match for the grandeur of St Peter's in the Vatican.' He pulled out a scrap of notepaper. 'This quote is almost all we know about Wren's religious views, but it's extraordinarily revealing. As a young man he was much taken by the country house of a friend. He said it was a place where "the piety and devotion of another age, put to flight by the impiety and crime of ours, have found sanctuary, in which the virtues are all not merely observed but cherished". Nobody has ever seriously thought of Wren as a secret Catholic, but he certainly regretted the killjoy aspects of the Protestant Reformation.'

'Doesn't plainchant originate much earlier than all that, in Jewish ritual?' Jack said.

'Unaccompanied singing almost certainly goes back before the foundation of the Roman Church, to the time of the apostles,' Jeremy said. 'It was probably responsorial chanting, verses sung by a soloist alternating with responds by a choir. It may have been one of the very earliest congregational rituals, sung in secret places where the first followers of Jesus came together. Singing is even mentioned in the Gospels.' He looked at his notebook. 'Matthew, 26:30. "And when they had sung a hymn, they went out unto the Mount of Olives."'

'So this guy Deverette was here in London during Wren's rebuilding of St Paul's Cathedral?' Costas asked.

'He was here from 1685, when he arrived in England. Wren's men had finished the new structure of the Church of St Lawrence Jewry a few years earlier, but the ledger we found in the college library shows that 1685 was the year they broke through into the undercroft, the old crypt. That's where it gets really fascinating. It turns out Deverette had another passion. He was a keen antiquarian, a collector of Roman and Christian relics. Wren was also interested in all the old stuff his men found during his building work in London. He gave Deverette another job, to rescue interesting artefacts. A kind of archaeological watching brief.'

'He's our man,' Jack said excitedly. 'We know somebody got into the tomb and found that cylinder. It must be him.'

'Did he keep any records?' Costas said, coughing.

'I checked everywhere. I went back through all the published Wren papers, everything on the churches, all his personal papers. Nothing. Then I had a brainstorm. I went to the National Archives at Kew, got there just in time yesterday afternoon. I did a search of the records of the Prerogative Court of Canterbury.'

'You found his will,' Jack exclaimed.

Jeremy nodded, his face flushed. 'Many of the ecclesiastical wills are now online, but his was in a newly discovered batch that had been filed wrongly and has only just been catalogued. My librarian friend told me about it. I was incredibly lucky.'

'Let's have it,' Jack said.

Jeremy took out a scanned image from his sheaf of papers. It showed a yellowed page, with about twenty lines of neat handwriting. Below the handwriting was a red seal and a signature, with more signatures and a scrawled probate note at the bottom. Jeremy began to read: '"In the Name of God, Amen. I, Johannes Deverette, Musick Meister to Sir Christopher Wren, Knight, Surveyor General of her Majesty's Works, doe make and ordain this my last Will and Testment as followeth. I desire that my body may be decently buried without pomp at the discretion of said Sir Christopher Wren, herein after named sole Executor and Trustee."'

'My God,' Jack murmured. 'Wren was his executor. He must have known about any antiquities Deverette possessed, anything he'd found in London and been allowed to keep by Wren, anything he'd chosen to pass on at his death.'

Jeremy nodded. 'Deverette died only a few months after making the will, when his son and heir was still a minor, so Wren would have safeguarded any bequeathed possessions. But wait for it. There's the usual inscrutable verbiage about chattel and estates, but the final sentences are the crunch.' He read aloud: '"All of my books, musick and musickal instruments, I give and bequeath unto my sone John Everett. To my said sone too I bequeath all of my antient rarities, my Cabinett of Curositys and Relicks from the divers excavations in Londone of said Sir Christopher Wren, including the Godspelle taken by me from the hand of the Antient priestess. This last mentioned to be kept in Security, in the most sacred Trust, and bequeathed by my said sone to his own sone and heire, and thereafter to his sone and heire, in perpetuity, in the Name of Christ, Jesu Domine. Signed and Sealed by the above named Johannes Deverette as and for his last Will and Testament in the presence of us who have subscribed our names as written in his presence, this sixth of Auguste 1711. Chris. Wren. Grinling Gibbons. Witnesses.'"

'Godspelle,' Costas said. 'What on earth's that?'

Jack's heart was pounding. His voice was hoarse. 'Jeremy said it a few moments ago. It's Old English, meaning "good word". And meaning Gospel.' Jack paused, and swallowed hard. 'It means that Deverette found the scroll in that cylinder, and must have read it.'

Costas attempted a whistle. 'Game on again.'

'It's the only reason I can see why he would have called it that,' Jeremy said.

'It's the first indication we've had of what Claudius' document might have contained,' Jack said, peering at Jeremy. 'I hardly dare ask. Did you get any further?'

'It was easy enough tracing Deverette's descendants,' Jeremy replied. 'The Huguenots kept pretty good family records. Deverette himself anglicized the name, had his son named Everett. The musical tradition seems to have carried on, but they came to make their living as builders and architects. For generations they were worthies of the Carpenters' Company, one of the most prominent London guilds. They settled in Lawrence Lane, overlooking the church, only yards from the crypt where Deverette had made his discovery.'

'Guardians of the tomb,' Costas murmured.

'This is beginning to fit together,' Jack said quietly. 'The secret crypt, the burials of those women we found, the succession of names from Roman times to the Great Fire of

1666. I think they were a secret sect who knew about the tomb, knew about the treasure it held, were the original guardians. But then the Great Fire broke the succession, burned the church and buried the entrance to their crypt and the tomb.'

'Maybe it was like the eruption of Vesuvius for the Sibyl at Cumae,' Costas said. 'Fire and ash foredooming, all that. The end of their time.'

'And then by sheer chance the tomb was found again, the sacred gospel was removed, and the cycle of guardianship was renewed,' Jack murmured.

'The strong Huguenot family tradition counts in our favour again,' Jeremy said. 'There's no reference to relics in any of the later wills, but the power of that original bequest in Deverette's will would have held sway through the generations. And there's something else, a real clincher. In the mid-nineteenth century, Deverette's great-grandson John Everett was associated with a secretive Victorian society called the New Pelagians, who claimed to follow the teaching of the rebel British monk Pelagius. They believed they were the true inheritors of the earliest Christian tradition in Britain.'

'Claudius?' Jack murmured. 'Can we really trace all this back to him?'

'To one he met in Judaea,' Costas murmured.

Jeremy carried on. 'The Everetts continued to be prominent in the City of London in the nineteenth century, always living and working close to St Lawrence Jewry and the Guildhall. John Everett the Pelagian was a Councillor of the

Corporation of London, and a freedman of the City. His son Samuel was master of the Carpenters' Company. But then something odd happens. Samuel's eldest son, Lawrence Everett, was an architect like his father. But almost immediately after his father died in 1912, he closed his business in Lawrence Lane, left his family and disappeared. You can read too much into it, but it's as if Lawrence Everett was the last of the guardians and broke the succession, taking the treasure away to a new sanctuary before hell was unleashed again during the London Blitz.'

'Any idea where he went?' Jack said.

'Immigration records, passenger manifests. A lot of stuff to research. I've got one promising lead, though.'

'You always do,' Jack said. 'You're becoming indispensable, you know.'

'I might be able to make some headway back at the National Archives in Kew. It might take me another day.'

'Let's get on with it then.'

Five minutes later they stood under the entrance to St Paul's Cathedral, looking out through the sweeping curtains of rain and seeking a break in the deluge. Jack felt as if he were on an island, and the solidity of the cathedral with the veiled miasma outside seemed to mirror his state of mind. The astonishing revelations of the last hours had taken the quest forward by leaps and bounds, made it seem as real as the structure above them, yet their goal still seemed like an unseen beacon somewhere out beyond the rain, down some dark alley they might never find. Jack had a sudden, surreal flashback to the lost library in Herculaneum, the image seeming to concertina into a succession of chambers, the doors open as far as he could see but the goal out of sight in the distance. He knew their only hope now lay with Jeremy, that some revelation in the archives would push them towards that last door, to the place Claudius had wanted them to find.

'Don't tell me we're going on the Tube, Jack,' Costas croaked. 'You know I'm never going underground again.'

'As it happens, I've always wanted to see the Great Conduit,' Jack replied, winking at Jeremy. 'An underground channel built in the thirteenth century to bring fresh water from the Tyburn stream, about three kilometres west of here. The stone cisterns sound impressive, but Roman aqueduct engineers a thousand years earlier would have been appalled. It leaked, and the gravity flow was all wrong. A great example of the march of progress, marching backwards. Well worth a visit.'

'No,' Costas said flatly. 'No way. You go. And I'm only doing taxis from now on.'

Jack grinned, then saw a respite in the drizzle and stepped out from the cathedral entrance. At that moment a young man in a City suit disengaged himself from a group of people also sheltering under the entrance and walked in front of Jack, blocking his way. 'Dr Howard?' he said intently. Jack stepped back in alarm. The man handed him a slip of paper. 'Tomorrow, eleven a.m. Your lives may depend on it.' He moved off and quickly trotted down the steps, disappearing into the throng of morning commuters making their way into the City.

Jack quickly stepped back under the doorway and read the note, then passed it to Jeremy. 'Did you recognize him?' Jack asked.

'I'm not sure.' Jeremy anxiously scanned the other people on the steps. 'It's not good news if you've been tracked here, Jack.'

'I know.'

Jeremy glanced at the piece of paper, read the typed words and pursed his lips. 'Right in the heart of things.' He passed it back to Jack. 'You going?'

'I don't think we have any choice.'

'I'd go with you, but I have to stay and find out what I can about Everett.'

'I agree,' Jack said quietly.

'Take Costas with you. You might need a bodyguard.'

Jack looked at the form slumped miserably against the stone column beside them, dripping and sneezing. He walked over, took Costas by the shoulder and steered him towards the steps. The rain had begun again in earnest, and Costas looked as if he were about to dissolve. 'Come on,' Jack said, looking up for a moment and letting the rainwater stream over his face. 'I think we might just be able to do something about that sniffle of yours.'

19

At five minutes to eleven the next morning Jack led Costas across the Piazza San Pietro in the Vatican, heading towards the Ufficio Scavi, the office of the archaeological excavations, on the south side of the basilica. They had flown in that morning from England on the IMU Embraer, arriving at Leonardo da Vinci airport away from public scrutiny, and Jack felt sure they were not being followed. The vast scale of the piazza and the surrounding colonnade seemed to dwarf the milling crowd of tourists and pilgrims, and they passed through as inconspicuously as they could. As they came closer to the Ufficio, Jack began to scan the faces around them, looking for some sign, some recognition. He had no idea what to expect. Then out of nowhere a young man was walking beside him, dressed casually in jeans and an open-necked shirt and wearing sunglasses. 'Dr Howard?' the man said. Jack looked at him, and nodded. 'Please follow me.' Jack glanced at Costas, and they followed the man as he strode ahead. After passing the Ufficio, he approached the Swiss Guard at the entrance to the Arco delle Campane, and flashed his identity card. 'These are my two guests,' he said in Italian. 'A private tour.' The guard nodded, and lifted up his automatic rifle to let them pass. They crossed a small piazza, then entered the south annex of the Grottoes beneath the Basilica. At the third room, the young man motioned for them to wait, and then walked over to a locked door. 'We will not be disturbed,' he said in English. 'The Ufficio has closed this part of the Grottoes for more excavation work. Wait here.' He produced a set of keys and opened the door, slipping through and leaving Jack and Costas alone, suddenly hemmed in by silence and the old walls.

'Any idea what's going on?' Costas said quietly, his voice bunged up by his cold. 'Any idea where we are?'

'First question, your guess is as good as mine. Second, these walls are virtually all that's left of the early basilica, the one built here by the emperor Constantine the Great after he'd converted to Christianity in the early fourth century. Before that, this was the site of a Roman circus, a racetrack. And where our guide has disappeared is the entrance to the necropolis, a street of rock-cut mausolea of the first century AD, discovered when archaeological excavations began here in the 1940s. Their big find was the tomb of St Peter, ahead of us under the high altar.'

The door swung open and the young man reappeared. He handed Jack and Costas each an unlit candle, and flicked a lighter over the wicks. 'Where you see the candle on the floor, go right, but extinguish it and take it with you,' he said quietly. 'There are twelve steps down, then you'll see another candle through another door. Pass through that door, and then close it behind you. I'll wait for you here. Go.'

Costas looked pained. 'We're going underground again, Jack.'

'It's just your kind of thing. A city of the dead.'

'Great.'

Jack paused, looked at the young man for a moment, decided not to speak, then nodded and walked towards the door, Costas following. They went through, and immediately the door was shut behind them. It was pitch dark except for the candles they were carrying and a faint glow somewhere ahead. It had been hot and dry outside, but the air was cool and damp as they descended, becoming musty. Jack led, carefully feeling his way down the steps until he reached a rough stone floor. They could see that the glow ahead of them was a candle on the floor. After reaching it Jack did as instructed, snuffing it out with his fingers and picking it up, then turning right and going down another flight of steps into a rock-cut chamber, evidently an ancient mausoleum long since cleared of its contents. At the bottom to the left was a stone door opened inwards in the rock, and through it they could see another distant pool of candlelight, just as before.

They passed through, and Jack pushed the door back until it was shut, seamlessly fitting into the rock as if it were a secret entranceway.

'Incredible,' he murmured, looking around in the flickering candlelight, making out the niches and decorations on the walls. 'It's a catacomb. The mausolea we've just come through were originally above ground in the Roman period, a street of tombs. But this deeper part must always have been subterranean, cut into the living rock. The Vatican has never revealed this before.'

'Makes you wonder what else they haven't revealed,' Costas murmured.

Jack stepped forward, sensing images on either side of him, inscriptions, paintings. He stopped at one, and held the candle forward. 'Amazing,' he whispered. 'It's intact. The catacombs are intact, the burials are still here.'

'Just what I wanted to know,' Costas moaned.

'They're sealed up, plastered over. Look, this inscription's legible. *In Pace*.' Jack faltered. 'It's early Christian, very early. It dates well before the time of Constantine the Great. A secret burial place, used when the Christians in Rome were outlawed, persecuted. This is a fantastic find. I can't see why they haven't made it public.'

'Maybe something to do with this.' Costas was ahead now, not far from the candle on the floor, and Jack cautiously followed. 'It's a raised area, covered with pottery tiles,' Costas said. He made his way along the left side of the passageway and squatted down beside the candle.

'It's a tomb,' Jack said quietly. 'You sometimes get them in the floor of catacombs, as well as along the sides. Sometimes the floor tombs were the more important ones.'

'Jack, I might be hallucinating. That déjà vu thing you were on about under the Palatine Hill. Maybe a delayed nitrogen effect.'

'What is it?'

'That tile. Below the candle. There's an inscription scratched on it. Either I'm seeing things, or it's identical to a word we've come across before.'

Jack edged up behind Costas. There were decorative scratchings around the edge of the tile, like a wreath of vine tendrils. In the centre he saw what had sent a tremor through Costas. It was a name, unmistakable, a name they had seen scratched on pottery like this before, on an ancient shipwreck hundreds of miles away, lost for almost two millennia beneath the Mediterranean Sea. The name of a man, written in Latin.

PAVLVS.

Could it be? Jack looked around, saw the widening of the passage, the other tombs crowding in on this spot but not built over it, as if their occupants had wanted to be close to it, in reverence. He saw Christian symbols everywhere, a dove on the wall beside him, a fish, the Christian formula in inscriptions again and again, *in pace*. And then as Costas moved his candle over the tile he saw it faintly scratched beside the name, the chi-rho symbol. *The sign of Christ.*

'The tomb of St Paul,' he whispered incredulously, laying

his hand on a tile. 'St Peter and St Paul, interred in the same place, *ad catacumbus*, just as tradition says.'

'It is so.'

Jack drew back, startled. The voice came from a shadowy niche opposite them, in the wall beyond the head of the tomb. He could just make out a black cassock over legs, but not the upper body. The voice was authoritative, with an edge to it, the English slightly accented, possibly east European. 'Do not attempt to approach me. Please extinguish your candles. Sit on the stone bench behind you.' Jack paused for a second, then nodded at Costas, and they did as instructed. The only source of light now was the candle on the tomb, and everything else was reduced to flickering shadow and darkness. The other figure shifted slightly, and they could just make out a hooded head, hands placed on knees. 'I have summoned you here today in the greatest secrecy. I wanted you to see what you have just seen.'

'Who are you?' Costas said.

'You will not be told my name, nor who I am,' the man repeated. 'Do not ask again.'

'This truly is the tomb of St Paul?' Jack said.

'It is so,' the man repeated.

'What about the church of San Paulo fuori le Mura?' Jack said. 'Isn't he supposed to have been buried there, in a vineyard?'

'He was indeed taken there after his death, but was brought back here secretly to be reunited with Peter, at the place of their martyrdom.'

'It is true, then,' Jack murmured.

'They were martyred together by the emperor Nero, in the circus built at this spot by Caligula. Peter was crucified upside down, and Paul was beheaded. The Romans made martyrs of the two greatest fathers of the early Church, and in doing so the pagan emperors helped to bring the Holy See into being at this place. *In nomine patris et filii et spiritus sancti, amen.*'

'You have brought us here to show us this?' Jack said.

There was a pause, and the man shifted again. The candle on the tomb wavered, lengthening the shadow so that for a few moments he was obscured completely, then the flame burned upright again. 'You will by now know that the Roman emperor Claudius faked his own poisoning, and survived in secret for many years beyond the end of his reign in AD 54.'

Jack peered into the shadows, unsure how much to reveal. 'How do you know this?'

'By telling you what I am about to tell, I test my bond with the sanctity of the Church. But it will be so.' The man paused, and then reached into the shadows beside him and lifted an ancient leatherbound volume on to his lap. Jack could now see his hands, strong, long-fingered hands that had seen physical toil, but he could still not see his face. 'In AD 58, St Paul came to Italy from the east, surviving the famous shipwreck on the way. It was as it is told in the Acts of the Apostles, except that the shipwreck was off Sicily, not Malta.'

Costas glanced questioningly at Jack, who flashed an exultant look back at him. Neither of them spoke.

'St Paul came first to the Bay of Naples, to Misenum, and

met with the Christian brethren he found there, as recounted in Acts,' the man continued quietly, almost whispering. 'After the crucifixion, it was the single most important event in the early history of Christianity. Paul was the first to take the word of Jesus beyond the Holy Land, the first true missionary. When he left Misenum for Rome, those whom he first instructed called themselves a *concilium*, the *concilium ecclesiasticum Sancta Paula*.'

'The council of the church of St Paul,' Jack translated.

'They were three in number, and they remain three today.'

'Today?' Jack said, astonished. 'This *concilium* still exists?'

'For generations, for almost three centuries, the *concilium* was a secret organization, a pillar of strength for the early Church when it was fighting for its very survival, when Christianity was still an underground religion. At first they met in the Phlegraean Fields, and then they took over the Sibyl's cave at Cumae, after the last of the Sibyls had disappeared. Later, as Christianity took hold, the *concilium* moved to Rome, to these catacombs where we sit now, to the place where the martyred body of St Paul was buried in secret by his followers after his beheading, near the hallowed tomb of St Peter.'

'And this *concilium* has been meeting here ever since?' Costas said.

'By the time of the conversion of the Roman Empire under Constantine the Great, the leaders of the *concilium* saw its purpose over and disbanded it, sealing up the catacomb of St Paul. Its location was lost, and was only rediscovered during the necropolis excavation following the Second World War. Only since then has this chamber again become the meeting place.'

'The *concilium* was re-created in modern times?' Jack said.

'It was called forth again by Constantine the Great, near the end of his reign. He reconstituted the *concilium* in its original number, three, and in the greatest secrecy. He had invested much in converting the state to Christianity. As a statesman, as a soldier, he saw the need to defend the Church, to create a council of war which would send out soldiers to fight in the name of Christ, who would show no mercy in the face of the devil, who would follow no rules of engagement. Over the centuries, the *concilium* fought off the most pernicious of heresies, the ones the Inquisition of the Holy See were unable to defeat. In Britain they fought the Pelagians, sending Pelagius himself to the fires of hell. They fought the Protestants after the Reformation, a secret war of terror and murder that nearly destroyed Europe. After the New World was discovered, the *concilium* ordered the destruction of the Maya and the Aztec and the Inca, fearing a prophecy of the ancient Sibyl that foretold a coming darkness from the west.'

'And these were men of God,' Costas murmured.

'They were believers in the sanctity and power of the Church, in the Roman Church as the only route to salvation and the kingdom of heaven,' the man said. 'Constantine the Great was an astute statesman. He knew that the survival of the Church depended on unswerving loyalty, on the faith of his holy warriors in the Church as the only route to God. In his revived *concilium*, he created his perfect enforcers.'

'Can you prove all this?' Costas said.

The man lifted the book slightly into the candlelight. 'The records of the *Consilium Ecclesiasticum Sancta Paula*. One day the world will know. History will be rewritten.'

'What does this have to do with Claudius?' Jack said.

The man leaned forward slightly, and the candlelight flickered off the shadowy outline of his face. 'It is the greatest threat the *concilium* has ever faced, and their greatest fear. It is the reason why I have brought you here. You and your team are in the gravest danger, far more so than you may realize.'

'We realize what it's like to look down the business end of a Beretta 93,' Costas said. 'Inside a cavern under the Palatine Hill.'

'He had instructions not to shoot,' the man said quietly.

'Then maybe the *concilium* should employ more obedient henchmen,' Costas said.

'How did you know?' Jack said. 'How did the *concilium* know we'd be diving under Rome?' The man was silent, and Jack persisted. 'Was there someone listening in the tunnel at Herculaneum? Was it the inspector, Dr Elizabeth d'Agostino?'

'We know she spoke to you outside the Villa.'

'How do you know?' Jack felt a sudden chill run through him. What if it was more than fear that had prevented her from returning his calls? 'Where is she now?'

'There are spies everywhere.'

'Even on board *Seaquest II*?' Costas said.

'You need to do everything you can to find what you are

looking for and to reveal it to the world before they get to you,' the man said intently. 'Once they know where it is, they will do everything in their power to destroy you. I have done all that I can, but I cannot restrain them any more.'

'Dr d'Agostino?' Jack persisted.

'As I said, I have done all that I can.'

'Why should you want to help us?' Costas said.

The man paused. 'Let me tell you about Claudius.' He opened the book at the beginning. They could just see the ancient writing in the dim candlelight, extensively annotated in the margins and clearly in several different hands, reminiscent of the page from Pliny's *Natural History* they had found at Herculaneum, but more ragged and stained, as if it had been pored over many times. 'This page recounts the founding of the original *concilium*, in the first century AD,' the man said, shutting the book again and putting his hands over it. 'One of the first three members was a man named Narcissus, a freedman of the emperor Claudius.'

'Good God,' Jack murmured.

'The eunuch? We've met him,' Costas said. 'Lying across the doorway into Claudius' study. Looked as if he was heading in, reaching for something. He got a little singed.'

'Ah.' The man was quiet for a moment. 'You found Narcissus. For almost two thousand years we have wondered.'

'I think I can guess now what he was doing there,' Jack murmured.

'You will know then that Narcissus was Claudius' long-serving *praepositus ab epistulis*, his scribe,' the man said. 'When Claudius decided to disappear from Rome in AD 54, he also engineered Narcissus' fake poisoning so that he could accompany his master to his hideaway in Herculaneum, and help him with his books. But after AD 58, there was another reason for Narcissus to stay on. He always accompanied Claudius on his nocturnal visits to the cave of the Sibyl, where Claudius sought a cure for his palsy. Narcissus came to know the Christians who hid in the Phlegraean Fields, and he himself converted after meeting St Paul there. Narcissus already knew that Claudius had been to Judaea as a young man, that he had met the Messiah and had returned with a precious document. Paul himself had never met Jesus, and was astonished to hear from Narcissus that something written in the hand of Christ might survive. He instructed Narcissus to find and bring the document to him in Rome, where Paul was going next. History overtook Paul, of course, and he was martyred, and Narcissus never found it. Claudius had been too cunning even for him. But the clamour for the document grew among the Christian brethren in the Phlegraean Fields, and word spread that Claudius was an anointed one, that he had touched Christ. The other two members of the *concilium* saw the threat this posed, a threat against their authority, and they implored Narcissus to find the document, to destroy it. They believed it to be false, a heresy, a fable dreamed up by Claudius, a man who they only ever saw delusional, after his visits to the Sibyl. Finally, Narcissus left Claudius one night at the cave of the Sibyl and made his way back to Herculaneum, intending to burn the study and all the books. That was the night of 24 August AD 79.'

'When everything except that room went up in flames,' Costas murmured.

'The *concilium* had no way of knowing whether or not Narcissus had succeeded. But with the utter disappearance of Herculaneum in the eruption, the threat was thought extinguished for ever,' the man continued. 'Over the generations, the document, the false gospel, was remembered as heretical, as the first of many forgeries intended to bring down the Church, and its destruction as the first of many battles won by the *concilium*. Then, in the seventeenth century, more than a thousand years after the fall of Rome, the Bourbon King Charles of Naples began digging at the site of Herculaneum, and an ominous truth was revealed. Herculaneum had not been destroyed in the eruption. It was miraculously preserved. Even worse, one of the first sites to be discovered and explored was the villa of Calpurnius Piso, the Villa of the Papyri, which the *concilium* knew had been Claudius' hideaway. Then, even worse still, books started to be found, ancient scrolls, mostly carbonized but some legible. The *concilium* had to act. For more than two centuries now they have done everything in their power to hamper exploration at Herculaneum, at the Villa of the Papyri. The *concilium* has huge wealth and resources at its disposal, more than enough to excavate Herculaneum in its entirety, or to prevent excavation for ever. Or so they thought. Just as in AD 79, natural catastrophe intervened again. The earthquake last month revealed that tunnel which had been sealed up in the eighteenth century, one the *concilium* knew might lead to more scrolls, even to Claudius' secret room. With all the world's media present, there was no way an investigation could be prevented. The work of the devil might yet see light. That was when your team was called to the scene.'

'Phew.' Costas sat down against the tomb, then suddenly realized what he had done and sprang up, brushing the plaster from his legs. 'That explains a few things.'

'But it doesn't explain who you are, and why you are telling us this,' Jack said. 'Are you a member of the *concilium*?'

There was a silence, and then the man spoke again, more quietly than before. 'For many years I was a Jesuit missionary. Once, in a canoe on the lake at Péten in the Yucatán, I had an epiphany, a revelatory experience. When you are on water, in a small boat, the motion seems at once to focus and to free the mind, until you think about nothing except what you are experiencing, the sensations of the moment.' The man paused, and Jack nodded, but felt uneasy. 'I began to think about Jesus on the Sea of Galilee. I began to think that the sea was his kingdom of heaven, that his message to the others was that the kingdom could be found, just as he had found it. That the kingdom of heaven is all around us, on earth.'

'And that turned you from the *concilium*?' Jack asked.

'Love thy neighbour, because it is easier than hating him. Turn the other cheek, because it is easier than resisting. Free your mind from such preoccupations, and focus your energy on finding the kingdom of heaven. That was Jesus' message.

The *concilium* had a holy cause, but it did not heed this call. The search for heresy, for blasphemy, became all-consuming, and the goal was lost. Their methods became unsound. And now there is one among the three who has turned a dark corner, has been unable to resist the temptation. The devil has reached out and drawn him into his fold. It has happened to others in the past.'

'Who is he? And how do you know about us?'

'You have come to the attention of the *concilium* before. The one of whom I speak was also a member of the Norse brotherhood who guarded the secret of the lost Jewish treasure of the Temple, the *félag*.'

'And who murdered Father Patrick O'Connor,' Jack said grimly. 'My friend, and a devout man of God. Butchered in the name of the *concilium*, it seems.'

'The instruments used by the *concilium* have often been blunt. But now they have enlisted forces of darkness that seem far beyond the reach of God.' The man paused, sinking back further into the shadows, his voice little more than a whisper. 'Father O'Connor was a friend of mine too. He was the other young initiate who found this place years ago with me, the tomb of St Paul. He delved too deep into a past that the *concilium* did not wish to see opened. He knew about the book that I now hold in my hands. He believed that we must face the truth. And so, now, do I.'

'You have put yourself at grave risk,' Jack murmured.

'I have done all that I can to protect you. You must swear to keep secret all that I have said until I reveal myself. I must continue to work from within. And you must understand. Were the true words of the Messiah to be found, the *concilium* would rejoice. Were the words to prove false, as they believe them to be, then the dogs of war would be unleashed to devour those who would convey them, who would peddle such a blasphemy. You must be careful. Do not try to find me again. Go now.'

Half an hour later, Jack and Costas sat high on the rooftop balcony beside the dome of St Peter's, swigging water and soaking up the afternoon sun, gazing out over Bernini's great piazza far below. Beyond the sweeping semicircular colonnades that surrounded the piazza, they could just make out Castel St Angelo, the mausoleum of the Roman emperors beside the river Tiber, and further south they could see the heart of the ancient city, the Capitol and the Palatine Hill. Costas leaned back on his elbows, his face tilted to the sun and his eyes shut behind his designer sunglasses. 'On balance, I prefer being high up to being underground,' he murmured. 'I think I really have had enough of damp subterranean places.' He peered over at Jack. 'You trust this guy?'

'Well, a good deal of what he said we'd already guessed at, and the rest fits into place. But I'm not sure.'

'I don't weasel up to anyone who sends a thug to point a gun at me, turncoat or not. I have to tell you, Jack. I don't trust the guy. I think it's all an elaborate game of charades. Tell us enough that's verifiable and plausible, take us into his confidence, get us to reveal what we know.'

'He didn't answer my question about Elizabeth. I'm worried.'

'Maybe Hiebermeyer and Maria can find out.'

'Maybe.' Jack breathed in deeply, and looked out over the city again. 'Anyway, the crunch time will be if we actually find something.'

'Or if we get no further,' Costas said. 'Either way could be bad news. I can't imagine the *concilium* wanting us to tell the world what we know. If that guy was playing a game with us, then as soon as he started revealing all that history he was also issuing our execution warrant. It was his risk telling us, but if what he says is even half true then he could silence us with a click of his fingers.'

'You're assuming the worst about this guy.'

'I'm being devil's advocate, but we have to be wary, Jack. And it's not just us I'm thinking about. The hit list gets bigger with each person we bring on board. Hiebermeyer and Maria have to be up there at the top. There's your friend Elizabeth. And Jeremy's been seen with us, by that guy who slipped you the message in London. God knows what was overheard when we talked in the cathedral. We should have been more careful.'

'My Reuters friend is only a call away. We'll send out a press release with the images from Herculaneum at the first threat.'

'There's not enough hard evidence for this *concilium*, Jack. As it stands, it could all be a figment of our imagination. It would be yet another conspiracy theory, big news one day, forgotten the next. And any investigative reporter's got to think twice about taking on this lot.'

'We'll just have to hope our man really is what he says he is,' Jack murmured. 'And that Jeremy comes up with something in London.'

Costas grunted, and lay back. Jack was still reeling in astonishment at what they had heard. They had another hour to kill before the taxi to the airport, and he got on his cell phone to update Hiebermeyer and their old mentor Professor Dillen with the latest developments, skirting around what they had just been told until he could be convinced it was all true. Many pieces of the puzzle seemed to have fallen together, but the enormity of what they might be up against was only beginning to register. He focused on the view below, anything to take his mind off it, knowing there was nothing they could do at the moment, no leads they could follow until Jeremy had exhausted all possible lines of enquiry in England. He glanced at Costas. 'A few days ago you asked about the size of St Paul's ship,' he said, pocketing his cell phone. 'Take a look at the centre of the piazza.'

Costas heaved himself up, and peered over the parapet. 'You mean the obelisk?'

'Brought here by the emperor Caligula from Egypt, to decorate the central spine of the circus, the place where Peter and Paul were executed,' Jack said. 'Twenty-five metres tall, weighing at least two hundred tons. Looking at stone like that is the best way to gauge the size of the biggest Roman ships, including grain ships like the one carrying St Paul. The obelisk-carrier was eventually sunk by Claudius in his new harbour at Ostia, filled with hydraulic concrete to make a mole. It's still there today. Pliny the Elder tells us all about it in his *Natural History*.'

'Good old Pliny,' Costas murmured, then slumped back in the sun. Jack peered round at the other people who had come up to the roof of the dome, his eyes alert for anything suspicious, his vigilance heightened after their warning in the catacombs far below. *He might have been telling the truth.* Jack had no reason to believe they had been followed, and they were probably safer here than anywhere else in the city. He relaxed slightly, and looked back over the parapet. He had an eagle's-eye view of the piazza, whose grandeur equalled the greatest monuments of pagan Rome. He watched the people crossing far below. It was as if he were viewing a computer-generated image from a Hollywood epic, of Rome the way people thought of it, not the way it was, as if on closer inspection the people below would be revealed not as flesh and blood but as stick figures, mere embellishments to the architecture, ethereal and meaningless. Jack reached for his wallet and took out a paper sleeve containing the bronze coin of Claudius they had found in Herculaneum, then slid it out and held it up so that it blocked his view of the piazza between the colonnades of the roof.

'My find! You took it. Good man. Nobody would ever have seen it again if we'd left it.' Costas was peering at Jack, and at the coin.

'Borrowed it.'

'Yeah. Right.'

'I'm thinking about Claudius again,' Jack said. 'That history is shaped by individuals, unique personalities, not by processes. Those are real people down there in the piazza, individuals with their own volition, their own free will, and they aren't subordinate to this whole thing.' He gestured back at the dome of St Peter's, and at the huge colonnades surrounding the square. 'Somewhere down there is someone who could create more grandeur than all this, or destroy it. It's individual decisions, whims, that make history. And people have fun. Look where Claudius has taken us.'

'Fun isn't exactly the word that springs to mind, Jack.' Costas rolled over. 'Let me see. Dead rats, sewage, body liqueur, a fossilized Vestal Virgin, a terrifying banshee redhead queen.'

'But you got an unexploded bomb.'

'Didn't even get to defuse it.'

Jack's phone chirped, and he quickly sleeved the coin. He took out the phone, listened intently for a few minutes, spoke briefly and then pocketed it. He had a broad smile on his face.

'Well?' Costas said. 'You've got that look again.'

'That was Jeremy. He had a hunch, and did a search of the international death registries available on the web. All the obvious places Everett could have disappeared to in 1912: Australia, Canada, the States. You're going to love this one. The IMU Embraer's being fuelled up as we speak.'

'Try me.'

'When was the last time you were in southern California?'

20

Jack was struggling towards consciousness, and became aware of the vibration of the aircraft where he had been leaning against the window. Images had been cycling through his mind, flashbacks to their extraordinary discoveries of the past few days. The chi-rho symbol in the ancient shipwreck, the scratched name of St Paul. The shadowy head of Anubis, leering out of the tunnel like a demon, beckoning him into the lost chamber in Herculaneum. More dark places, the cave of the Sibyl, the underground labyrinth in Rome, the blue woaded skull under London, staring sightlessly up at him from her tomb. Images at once vivid yet opaque, disjointed yet somehow bound together, images that flashed up in his mind over and over again as if he were caught in a continuous loop. He felt like Aeneas in the underworld, yet without the Sibyl to guide him back, only some malign force that pulled him down as he struggled to find the light, trapping him in a dark maze of his own devising. He felt disturbed, discomfited, and it was a relief to open his eyes and see the reassuring figure of Costas slumped over in the seat opposite. He realized that the overbearing feeling in his head had been the increased air pressure as the aircraft descended, and he blew on his nose to equalize. The whine of the Embraer's twin jets swept the images from his mind, and reality took over. He leaned forward and stared out of the window.

'Bad dream?' Jeremy slipped into the aisle seat beside him, and closed the dog-eared notebook he had been studying.

Jack grunted. 'It's as if the ingredients are there, but nothing's cooking. This trip's make or break. If we don't get anywhere today, I'm out of options.' He took a deep breath, calmed himself, then glanced curiously at Jeremy's book. 'Cryptography?'

'One of my childhood passions. I collated all the German codes broken by the Allies during the First World War. I was just getting myself back up to speed. It was looking at some of those early Christian acrostics that did it. I've realized you can't have too many skills in this game.'

'It would appear,' Jack said, scratching his stubble, 'that you have the makings of an archaeologist. Maria was right. Maybe I should just give up now and hand it all over to you.'

'Maybe in about twenty years,' Jeremy replied thoughtfully,

then grinned at Jack. 'That should give me time for a stint in special forces, to learn everything about diving, weapons and helicopters, to overcome all fear, and, most importantly, to work out how to handle your esteemed colleague opposite.'

Costas moaned and snorted in his sleep, and Jack laughed. 'No one handles him. He's the boss around here.'

'Trouble is, in twenty years' time, all the world's mysteries will have been solved.'

Jack shook his head. 'The past is like the New World was to the first colonists. You think you've found it all, then you turn a corner and another El Dorado's shimmering on the horizon. And look where we are today. Some of the greatest mysteries may always be there, half solved, constantly drawing you on.'

'Sometimes that's the best way,' Jeremy murmured. 'You remember the Viking sagas? The loose ends aren't always tied up, virtue isn't always rewarded. We don't always want a conventional ending.'

'And you won't always get one, with me,' Jack grinned. 'Something else I've learned, the treasure you find is rarely what you think you've been looking for.'

'There it is.' The aircraft banked sharply to port, and Jeremy pointed to the coastline some ten thousand feet below. 'I asked the pilot to take us into Los Angeles from the north, to give us a view of Malibu. It's pretty spectacular.'

'Beaches,' Costas murmured. 'Good surfing?' He had been asleep for the entire trip from JFK in New York, and before that for most of the transatlantic haul from England. He looked as if he had just come out of hibernation, and leaned his forehead against the windowpane as he peered blearily down.

'Not bad,' Jeremy replied. 'Not that I'd know, of course. When I was here, I was working on my dissertation.'

'Right.' Costas still sounded blocked up, but the worst of his cold seemed to have passed. 'I'm looking forward to finding out what we're doing here, Jeremy, but I'm not complaining.'

'I told Jack the whole story while you were dead to the world. I found Everett in the California State Death Registers. Same date and place of birth, no doubt about the identity. He lived just north of here, in Santa Paula, arrived here after leaving England in 1912. On a hunch I called a friend in the Getty Villa. Turns out he can tell us more, a whole lot more. For a start, Everett was a devout Roman Catholic, a convert.'

'Huh?' Costas rubbed his eyes. 'I thought this was all about the British Church, the Pelagian heresy.'

'That's what I hope this visit will sort out for us.'

'So we're not going surfing.'

'The trail's hotted up again, Costas,' Jack said intently. 'Jeremy's made a real breakthrough.'

'You can see it now,' Jeremy said. 'The Getty Villa. In the cleft in the hills down there, overlooking the sea.'

Jack peered at the cluster of buildings visible just in from the Coastal Highway. Suddenly it was if he was back at Herculaneum, staring at the plan of the Villa of the Papyri made by Karl Weber more than two centuries before. He could see the great peristyle courtyard, extending towards the sea, with the main mass of the villa structure nestled behind at the back of the valley.

'The only big difference is the alignment,' Jeremy said. 'The villa at Herculaneum lies parallel to the seashore, with the courtyard and the main buildings abutting the seafront. Otherwise the Getty Villa's faithful to Weber's plan. It's a fantastic creation, the kind of thing that's only possible with American philanthropy, with unfettered vision and unlimited wealth. It's also one of the finest museums of antiquities anywhere in the world, and the place where I've done some of my best writing. Whatever else awaits us down there, you're in for a treat.'

Three hours later they stood beside a shimmering rectangular pool in the main courtyard of the Getty Villa. They had entered unobtrusively by a small door at the west end, and now they stood stock-still like the statues that adorned the garden, soaking in the sunshine and the brilliance of the scene. It was as if they had entered a movie set for a Roman epic, yet with an intimacy and attention to detail rarely seen in the sweeping panoramas of history. The pool was almost a hundred yards long, extending from the front portico of the villa to the seaward side where they had walked up from the Coastal Highway. At either end were copies of ancient bronzes found in the Villa of the Papyri at Herculaneum, a drunken Silenus and a sleeping faun, and opposite them was a seated Hermes so lifelike he seemed ready to slip into the pool at any moment. Between the pool and the colonnaded portico that surrounded the courtyard were trees and beds of plants that made the marble seem like natural extrusions of the bedrock, surrounded and cushioned by vegetation. The entire garden was an orderly version of the world outside, cocooned and protected by human ingenuity. The pool reflected the columns and trees, creating an illusionistic scene like the wall paintings they could just make out on the interior of the portico, as if they were being drawn beyond the garden to other, fanciful creations of the human mind, not to the disordered and uncontrollable reality beyond. Jack remembered the wall painting of Vesuvius he had shown Costas as they flew towards the volcano, an image that summed up all the Arcadian dreams of ancient Rome, a flimsy sheen over a reality that had blasted its way through on that fateful day almost two thousand years before.

'Everything's authentic,' Jeremy said. 'The plan's based on Weber's original record of the villa he saw in the tunnels in the eighteenth century, and the statues are exact copies of the originals they found then. Even the vegetation's authentic, pomegranate trees, laurels, fan palms brought all the way from the Mediterranean.'

Jack closed his eyes, then opened them again. The California hills had the same stark, sun-scorched beauty he loved in the Mediterranean, and the smell of herbs and the sea transported him back. The villa was not an interpretation of the past but a perfect resemblance of it, full of light and shadow, alive with people, gesturing and breathing. Few other historical reconstructions had done this for him, and here it felt right. As he looked at the villa, rich with colour and precision, in his mind's eye he saw the excavated buildings of Herculaneum, flickering in the background like a photographic negative. He found himself remembering the times he had witnessed death, the moment of transition when the body suddenly becomes a husk, when colour turns to grey. Herculaneum was too close after that moment for comfort, more troubling to behold than sites that had decayed and become whitewashed by time, like old skeletons. It was the blasted corpse of a city, still reeking and oozing, like a burns victim after a terrible accident. Yet here in the Getty Villa it was as if someone had injected a burst of adrenaline into the still-warm corpse and miraculously revived it, as if the ancient site was again pulsating and sparkling with a dazzling clarity.

'Only in California,' Costas said, shaking his head. 'I guess with Hollywood only a few miles down the coast, this is what you'd expect.'

'When the villa opened in 1974, the reaction was amazing,' Jeremy said. 'A lot of the critics panned it. The Romans can get a pretty bad press over here. It's all Pontius Pilate, debauched emperors, throwing Christians to the lions. This place was a stunning revelation. The colour, the brilliance, the taste. Some scholars even refused to believe it was an authentic recreation.'

'This place is all about putting art back in its original context, and that can be a shock to modern sensibility,' Jack said. 'The European aristocrats who plundered Greece and Rome thought they were doing it, arranging statues on pedestals in their neoclassical country houses, but their idea of the classical context was based on the bleached ruins of Greece rather than the Technicolor reality of Pompeii and Herculaneum. Here, you get the real deal, with objects like these bronzes as components of a larger whole, with the villa as a work of art in itself. Classical scholars for too long venerated these things as works of art in the modern sense, in their own right. What the critics didn't like was that the villa makes these venerated sculptures seem frivolous, and the whole setting more whimsical and fun than they'd bargained for. But that's what it was really like.'

'And that's what I like about it.' Costas squatted down with a coin in the crook of his finger and eyed the length of the pool. 'If the Romans could have fun, so can we.' Jack shot him a warning glance as a man appeared through the entrance portico and made his way briskly towards them. He was of medium height with a close-cut beard, and wore chinos and a shirt and tie with his sleeves rolled up. He raised a hand in greeting to Jeremy, who gestured towards Jack and Costas.

'Allow me to introduce Dr Ieuan Morgan,' Jeremy said. 'An old friend, my mentor when I was here. He's on secondment from Brigham Young University. Permanently, by the look of it.'

Costas and Jack shook hands with him. 'Thanks for seeing us at such short notice,' Jack said warmly. 'Are you anything to do with the BYU Herculaneum papyrus project?'

'That's why I came here originally,' Morgan said, a hint of Welsh in his accent. 'I'm a Philodemus specialist, and the infra-red spectrometry on the scrolls from the eighteenth-century excavations was inundating me with new stuff. I needed breathing space, somewhere to put it all in perspective.'

'And where better than the Villa of the Papyri itself.' Jack gestured around. 'I'm envious.'

'Any time you want a sabbatical here, just give the word,' Morgan said. 'Your reputation precedes you.'

Jack smiled back. 'Much appreciated.' He winked at Jeremy. 'Maybe in about twenty years' time.'

Morgan looked intently at Jack. 'I understand from Jeremy that you're on a tight schedule. Follow me.'

He led them along one side of the peristyle, then on to the west porch of the villa and through the open bronze doors that served as the main entrance to the museum. They went up a flight of marble stairs to the upper storey, and came to a second, inner courtyard, another fragrant and colourful place, resonating with the flash and sparkle of fountains. Below the tiled roof, tiers of columns dropped down to surround a garden proportioned in the Roman way, with bronze statues of five maidens in the centre appearing to draw water from a pool. Again Jack felt the extraordinary immediacy of the past. Whatever else came of the day, this Roman villa on the coast of California had been an unexpected revelation, another vivid lens on the ancient world.

Jack narrowed his eyes, and spoke from memory. '"Lovely gardens and cool colonnades and lily ponds would surround it, spreading out as far as the raptured eye could reach." Those are words that Robert Graves in *Claudius the God* has Herod Agrippa, King of the Jews, saying to his Queen Cypros. I've always remembered that description, since I first read Graves as a boy. Herod has always been thought of as anti-Christian, the man who ordered the execution of St James, but to me those words could have been an ancient Christian image of heaven.'

'You're talking about Herod Agrippa, friend of Claudius?' Costas said.

'That's the one.'

Costas scanned the courtyard. 'So if this villa is an accurate replica of the place where Claudius ended his days, he didn't give up on life's pleasures completely,' he said.

'He had all this to look out on, sure, but I doubt whether he would have cared less,' Jack replied. 'As long as he had his books and his statues of his beloved father and brother, he'd probably have been content to eke out his days in a sulphurous cave somewhere up on Mount Vesuvius.'

'Claudius?' Morgan said, clearly mystified. 'Which Claudius?'

'The Roman emperor Claudius,' Costas said.

'Jeremy didn't mention any emperors.' Morgan paused, then eyed Jack quizzically. 'I think you've got some explaining to do.'

'We have,' Jack smiled. 'Lead on.'

Morgan led them a few paces further to a room at the back of the portico. He opened the door, ushered them in and gestured at the marble table in the centre. 'I had the café send up some things. Hungry?'

'You bet.' Costas launched himself at a plate of croissants, and Morgan poured coffee. After a few moments he gestured at three seats on one side of the table, and walked around to the other side with his coffee and sat down.

'Okay.' Jack sat in the middle chair, and leaned forward. 'You know why we're here.'

'Jeremy filled me in. Or at least I thought he did.' Morgan swivelled in his chair to face Jack, took a sip of his coffee and then set his cup down. 'When Jeremy had his fellowship here we worked quite closely together, and when he called me yesterday he discovered I had an interest in Lawrence Everett. I'd always kept quiet about it, a private obsession of mine, but of course I told him when he asked. It's an incredible coincidence, but a man like that can't go completely underground as he might have wished. And I thought there couldn't possibly be anyone else on his trail, but there was another enquiry this morning.'

Jack suddenly looked alarmed. 'Who?'

'No idea. Anonymous hotmail address.'

'Did you reply?'

'After my conversation with Jeremy yesterday, I felt it prudent to claim ignorance. But I sensed that this was someone who wouldn't go away. Somehow they knew there was a connection here, with the Getty Villa. I checked the online ticket reservations for the museum, and someone with the same e-mail address booked a ticket for tomorrow.'

'Could be a coincidence, as you say,' Jeremy murmured. 'I can't see how they'd have known.'

'Known what, exactly? Who are you talking about?' Morgan said.

Jeremy was quiet for a moment, glanced at Jack and then looked back across the table. 'You were right. I haven't told you everything. But what I did tell you was true, that we think Everett had something extraordinary to hide, an early Christian manuscript. That's the key thing. Let's hear what you've got to say, then we'll fill you in.'

Morgan looked perplexed. 'I've got no reason to be secretive. My scholarship, the collections here are open to all. It's the founding ethos of the museum.'

'Unfortunately this has gone way beyond scholarship,' Jack said. 'There's far more at stake here. Let's hear you out, then we'll bring you up to speed before we leave this room.'

Morgan pulled a document box towards him on the table. 'Fair enough. I can start by giving you a potted biography.'

'Fire away.'

'The reason I know about Everett is that he tried to correspond with J. Paul Getty, the founder of the museum. The nuns who looked after Everett during his final illness found the Getty headed notepaper among his belongings, and some architectural drawings. They thought the museum might be interested. I stumbled across the box of papers when I was researching the early history of the Getty villa, and thought they might have some bearing on the Getty interest in antiquities.' He opened up the box and carefully lifted out a handful of yellowed pages covered in words and figures in a precise, minute hand. He spread them out on the table in front of him, including one page with a ruled-out plan of an apsidal structure. 'Everett was fascinated by mathematical problems, by the game of chess, crosswords. There's lots of that kind of stuff here, most of it way beyond me. But before he came to America he'd been an architect, and there's an unfinished manuscript I've been annotating for publication. He was interested in early Church architecture, in the earliest archaeological evidence for Christian places of worship.'

'Fascinating,' Jack murmured. 'But why try to contact Getty?'

'The two men had a surprising amount in common,' Morgan replied. 'Getty had studied at Oxford, Everett at Cambridge. Getty was a passionate Anglophile, and he might have been pleased to discover a kindred spirit in California. And both men had rejected their professional careers, Getty to be a millionaire philanthropist, Everett to be a Catholic ascetic. There may seem a world of difference between those two, but Everett's correspondence shows that he'd liberated himself in much the same way. And there was a more particular reason.'

'Go on.'

'It was well known that Getty had been to Pompeii and Herculaneum before the First World War, had visited the site of the Villa of the Papyri, been fascinated by it. Hence the villa we're in today. Then in the late 1930s Everett heard of an extraordinary new discovery at Herculaneum, and wanted Getty's opinion. Everett was really intrigued by it, to the point of obsession.'

'You mean the House of the Bicentenary?' Jack said.

'You guessed it.'

Jack turned to Costas. 'I pointed it out to you on our quick tour of Herculaneum, when we arrived at the site last week.'

'Another black hole, I'm afraid,' Costas said ruefully. 'I think I was still asleep.'

'Bicentenary refers to the two hundredth anniversary of the discovery of Herculaneum, in 1738,' Morgan said. 'The 1930s excavation was one of the few to have taken place on any scale since the eighteenth century. Mussolini was behind it, part of his own obsession with all things Roman, though there seems to have been Church resistance to his more grandiose excavation schemes and the Herculaneum project was almost stillborn.'

'Why does that not surprise me?' Costas murmured.

'They discovered a room which they called the Christian Chapel,' Morgan continued. 'They called it that because they found an inset cross shape in plaster above a wooden cabinet, which they thought looked like a prayer stand. In a house nearby they found the name David scratched on a wall. Hebraic names are not unusual in Pompeii and Herculaneum, but they're usually Latinized. Jesus was thought to be a descendant of King David of the Jews, and some think the name David was a secret way the early Christians referred to him, before they started to use the Greek word for messiah, *Christos*.' Morgan paused, and looked pensive. 'These were very controversial finds, and plenty of scholars still don't accept the interpretation, but it may be the earliest archaeological evidence anywhere for a place of Christian worship.'

'Only a few hundred yards from the Villa of the Papyri,' Jack murmured. 'I wonder if Everett had any inkling, if he had any idea how close he was to the source of what he possessed.'

'What are you talking about?' Morgan asked.

'First, let's have the rest of your story,' Jack said. 'Do you have anything more on him?'

Morgan nodded, and slid a sheet of paper from the box across the table. 'We don't know whether Getty himself ever responded to Everett, or even knew about him. The headed notepaper we found was just an acknowledgement note from a secretary. But I like to think that Everett's interest helped to fuel Getty's continuing fascination with Herculaneum, in the years leading up to the creation of this villa. After that brief correspondence, Everett slid back into obscurity. This is the only image we have of him, an old photocopy of a picture taken by his daughter. She managed to discover his whereabouts and visit him in 1955, the year before he died. I traced her to a care home in Canada, where she'd emigrated from England, and got hold of this.'

Jack peered at the grainy black-and-white image, the details almost washed out. In the centre was an elderly man, well dressed, hunched over on sticks but standing with as much dignity as he could muster, his face virtually indiscernible. Behind him was a single-storey shack made of corrugated metal, festooned with ivy and surrounded by lush vegetation.

'This was taken outside the nunnery, in front of the shack where he lived for more than thirty years,' Morgan continued. 'The nuns looked after him, cared for him when he became too ill to fend for himself. In return he tended their gardens, did odd jobs. He'd been a choral scholar in his youth, and sang Gregorian music for them. He took in tramps, down-and-outs, fed and clothed them, put them up in his shack, the full Christian charity thing.'

'Sounds a little messianic to me,' Costas murmured.

'I doubt whether he had any delusions about that,' Morgan said. 'But California in his day was the world of Steinbeck, of *Cannery Row* and *Tortilla Flat*, a whole subculture on the margins of society. And these were the ones he felt most at home with, outcasts, drifters, people who had forsaken their own background and upbringing, men and women like himself.' He paused, and then spoke quietly. 'What do you know about the Pelagians?'

'We know there was an Everett family connection. His grandfather was a member of the New Pelagians, the Victorian secret society.'

'Good. That saves a lot of explaining,' Morgan replied, relaxing visibly. 'In one of his letters he reveals his Pelagian beliefs, something he clearly wanted to talk about, and it explains a lot about where we're going this afternoon. It's as if he was living a double life, a devout ascetic Catholic on the one hand, and privately about the most radical heretic you can imagine.'

'When was that letter written?' Jack said.

'About the end of the Second World War. He was already pretty ill by then, rambling a little, and there was no more correspondence.'

'That explains it,' Jack murmured. 'I don't think he would have risked revealing himself before then.' He took a deep breath. 'Okay. What do you know about his origins?'

'It's an amazing story. Born in the centre of the city of London, in Lawrence Lane, where his family had lived for generations. They were Huguenots, and his father was a prominent architect. Went to Corpus Christi College, Cambridge, where he was a wrangler, achieving first-class Honours in Mathematics, and also studied languages. One of his tutors was the philosopher Bertrand Russell. He was offered a fellowship but turned it down, having promised his father that he'd go into partnership with him. Ten prosperous years as an architect, unexceptional, got married, had three kids, then his father died and he suddenly gave it all up, family, job, and disappeared to America.'

'Any explanation given?' Costas asked.

'He'd converted to Roman Catholicism. His wife's father was vehemently anti-Catholic. The father gave him an ultimatum, then bought him off. Seemingly as simple as that. The children's education was paid for by their grandfather on the condition that they had no contact ever again with their father. A sad story, but not unique, given the antipathy that existed between Protestant and Catholic in England, even as late as the Victorian period.'

'But we know the true reason he left,' Jeremy murmured. 'His father's death, the will, his sudden overwhelming responsibility for the family heirloom. The question is why he came here, and what he did with it.'

'Why convert to Catholicism?' Costas said. 'Was that part of the plan? Hide in the least likely place?'

Morgan paused. 'It could have been. But it could have been heartfelt. He'd been Anglo-Catholic, and others like him had taken the step. Remember, the followers of Pelagius, those who traced their Christianity back to the earliest British tradition before Constantine the Great, were not necessarily great fans of the Church created by King Henry VIII either. What had discomfited them about the Roman Church, the ascendancy of the Vatican and the Pope, had an uneasy conterpart in the English monarch as head of the Church of England, divinely appointed. It seemed one step from the emperor as god, the grotesque apotheosis that had ruined ancient Rome. Whether pope or king many had a problem with the Church as a political tool.'

'Yet for some like Everett, the Roman tradition of worship came to have more attraction,' Jack said.

Morgan nodded. 'The letters show that he still saw himself as a follower of Pelagius, and some of his theological views would have seemed heretical to Catholic purists. But the Roman liturgy, the rituals, above all the music, seemed to offer him great spiritual comfort.'

'What Jeremy said in London yesterday about Sir Christopher Wren, missing the beauty of the old rituals,' Costas murmured. 'Speaking as a Greek Orthodox, I can understand that.'

'That was what mattered to Everett. But his fundamental faith remained unchanged.'

'And the thought police were a long way from a remote valley in Califor12,' Jack murmured.

'I believe that was part of the plan. He came here to safeguard what he had with him, to a country where religious freedom had provided a haven for all Christian denominations. He still needed to be careful, to pick the time and place to reveal what he had, to find some way of passing on the secret.'

'So he arrived here in 1912,' Costas said.

Morgan nodded. 'He sailed to New York, gained American citizenship, then worked his way west. After what Jeremy told me, I now believe that what he did took huge strength, a decision to preserve an extraordinary treasure not for his own benefit but for humanity, for the future. Once he'd been assured of his children's upbringing, he made the greatest sacrifice a father can ever make, and walked away assuming he would never see them again.'

'I only hope it was worth it,' Costas said.

'That's what we're here to find out,' Jack replied, turning to Morgan. 'Do you know anything more about his life, anything that might give us clues?'

Morgan paused. 'August 1914. Europe is torn apart. Britain mobilizes. The First World War begins.'

'He goes to fight?' Costas said.

Morgan nodded. 'In the folly and horror of the First World War, people often forget that many at the time believed it was a just war, a war against impending evil. Everett felt morally compelled to join. Winston Churchill wrote about men like him.' Morgan leaned back so he could read the inscription below a framed portrait on the wall, showing a young man in uniform. '"Coming of his own free will, with no national call or obligation, a stranger from across the ocean, to fight and die in our ranks, he had it in his power to pay tribute to our cause of exceptional value. He conceived that not merely national causes but international causes of the highest importance were involved, and must now be decided by arms."' Morgan paused. 'That's a friend of Churchill's, Lieutenant Harvey Butters, Royal Field Artillery, an American killed on the Somme in 1916. J. Paul Getty was a great admirer of these men, Americans who volunteered to fight German imperialism even before the United States joined the war.'

'So Everett returns to Europe,' Costas said.

'He went north to Canada and enlisted in the British Army. By early 1916 he was an officer in the Royal Dublin Fusiliers, on the Western Front. In June that year he was gassed and wounded in a terrible battle at Hulluch, near Loos. During his recuperation his mathematical skills were discovered, and he was transferred to British Military Intelligence, the original MI1. He worked in the War Office in London, and then was seconded to Naval Intelligence at the Admiralty down the road, in a top-secret complex known as Room 40. He was a codebreaker.'

'No kidding.' Jeremy leaned forward, excited. 'Cryptography.'

'They were desperate for people like him,' Morgan continued. 'And he was recruited by intelligence just in time. What happened next may well have won the war.'

'Go on,' Jack said.

'Ever heard of the Zimmerman telegram?'

'Yes!' Jeremy exclaimed. 'Of course! It's what brought America into the First World War.'

'A coded telegram dispatched in January 1917 by Arthur Zimmerman, German foreign secretary, to the German ambassador in Mexico,' Morgan continued. 'It revealed the German intention to begin unrestricted submarine warfare against American shipping, and to help Mexico reconquer the southern States. The plan seems ludicrous now, but it was deadly serious then. The British intercepted and decrypted the telegram, then passed it on to the US ambassador to Britain. Sentiment in the United States was already pretty anti-German because of earlier U-boat sinkings that had killed Americans. A month after the telegram was deciphered, President Woodrow Wilson asked Congress to declare war on Germany.'

'Let me guess,' Costas said. 'The decipherment was done in the British Admiralty Room 40.'

'Correct. The Room 40 codebreakers had a book for an earlier version of the cipher that had been captured from a German agent in the Middle East, but the decryption of the telegram by the London team was still a work of genius.'

'And Everett was involved.'

'His name was never released. After the war, the British went to extraordinary lengths to keep the activities of their codebreakers secret, and only ever released enough to tell the essential story. Some of the Room 40 codebreakers of the First

World War went on to work at Bletchley Park in the Second World War, and their names will never be known.'

Costas whistled. 'So Everett really did have a place in history. Bringing America into the First World War.'

'If you think that's a place in history, wait for what I've got to say next.'

'Go on,' Jack said.

'A lot of the stuff is still classified. But I do know he worked alongside the two men whose names were released and celebrated after the war, the Reverend William Montgomery and Nigel de Grey. Of those two, Montgomery is the one who concerns us most. He was a Presbyterian minister, a civilian recruited by British Military Intelligence. He was a noted authority on St Augustine, and a translator of theological works from German. He was best known for his translation of Albert Schweitzer's *The Quest of the Historical Jesus.*'

Jack suddenly felt the hairs prick up on the back of his neck. 'Say that again.'

'Albert Schweitzer, *The Quest of the Historical Jesus.*'

The historical Jesus. Jack felt himself tense up with excitement. He thought for a moment, his mind racing, then spoke quietly. 'So we've got two men, both brilliant codebreakers, Everett and Montgomery, both passionate about the life of Christ. One a Catholic convert, the other a Presbyterian minister. Everett is guardian of an extraordinary ancient document, something he's hidden away. Maybe the horror of that war, his near-death experience on the front, perhaps a soldier's conviction that he will not survive, gives him an overwhelming need to share the secret, to ensure that the torch is kept alight.'

'He tells Montgomery,' Costas said.

'They devise a code,' Jeremy murmured.

'Pure speculation, but if it happened, it probably happened here,' Morgan said.

Jack looked startled. 'You mean here? In California?'

'In Santa Paula. Where Everett spent the rest of his life. A small nunnery in the hills, where Everett had found what he was looking for when he arrived in America before the war. Peace, seclusion, a community whose fold he could enter effortlessly, where he could follow his faith and seek the time and place to pass on his secret.'

'Just like the emperor Claudius, two thousand years before,' Jeremy murmured. 'And just like Claudius, the tide of history seems to have overtaken his plans, the First World War erupting like a latter-day Vesuvius.'

'Could Everett and Montgomery have been here together during the war?' Costas said.

'May 1917,' Morgan replied. 'Publication of the Zimmerman telegram had just brought America into the war. The two men were invited to the United States to help set up the fledgling US codebreaking unit. It was all top secret. I can't prove it, but there was enough time for a fleeting visit to California.'

'Does the nunnery still exist?' Jack said.

Morgan looked at Jack, nodded, then pushed back his chair,

got up and walked over to the window, his voice tight with emotion. 'All my professional life I've lived and breathed this place. I was here when the museum was inaugurated. There's a spirit here that's infused my work. An ancient Roman villa in the California hills. But it also haunts me. This room, where we are now, is unknown, pure guesswork. The Getty Villa's based on Weber's eighteenth-century plan of the Villa of the Papyri as he saw it in the tunnels, yet this section of the villa is pure conjecture, a part never excavated. With your discoveries in the villa at Herculaneum it's as if the past is catching up, and we risk losing all the solidity and assurance we've created. I want this room to be a library, a scholar's room, but it may never even have existed.' He took a deep breath, walked back over to the desk, picked up a bunch of keys, then sat down again resolutely. 'I'll take you to the nunnery now. But before we go, you owe me the rest of your story. I want to hear about what lay at the end of that tunnel. I want to hear about Claudius.'

21

hree hours later, Jack stood on a wooded ridge above a
small valley outside Santa Paula, in the Californian hills
some twenty miles north-east of the Getty Villa. It was a
brilliant afternoon, the sky a deep azure blue and a refreshing
breeze wafting up the valley from the Pacific coast to the west,
rustling the leaves. He was among a grove of mature black
walnut trees, interspersed with the occasional cottonwood
and stunted oak. The trees had been deliberately planted, not
in regimented rows but artfully arranged along a series of
terraces dropping down the slope, giving each tree the space
to grow and conforming with the natural features of the
landscape. The walnut bark was deeply furrowed, and the
trunks forked close to the ground to give the impression of

two trees grown together, diverging to create bowery hollows and passageways that temped Jack ever deeper into the grove. It seemed a magical, secretive place, cut off from the world outside, yet revelling in all the light and colour that California had to offer.

Morgan came down the path from where they had left his Jeep, followed by Costas and Jeremy. 'Everett's shack was where you're standing, and his grave is somewhere nearby,' Morgan said. 'They're both lost now, but in a way he's everywhere here. He planted all these trees, did all the landscaping. But wait until you see what's round the corner.' He carried on down the path as it veered left along the line of the terrace, descending through a rustling corridor of walnut leaves. Jack lingered for a moment, then quickly caught up with Costas and Jeremy. They passed over a bubbling stream and suddenly were at the entrance to a building, a long, low-set structure that extended along the terrace on one side, and dropped down into the valley on the other. The walls had been built on a base of irregularly cut stone, and above that were made up of long, thin bricks. A course of darker bricks had been laid in the centre, creating a horizontal line that relieved the appearance of the façade. The roof was sloping and covered with large, flat tiles secured by overlapping semicircular ones, in the Mediterranean fashion. Jack stood back and appraised the structure, racking his brain. It all looked oddly familiar.

'Welcome to the convent of St Mary Magdalene,' Morgan said.

'You been here often?' Costas asked.

'I've only been allowed access within the last year. It's still pretty much a revelation for me. Originally this place was a Jesuit retreat, a typical Spanish mission affair, all adobe mud and whitewashed plaster. Then it was completely rebuilt in the early twentieth century. What you see here is one of the unknown architectural gems of California.' He glanced at Jack. 'You've probably guessed it.'

'I can see Getty wasn't the only one re-creating ancient Roman villas,' Jack murmured.

'When Everett first came here in 1912, the old mission building was crumbling, almost uninhabitable,' Morgan said. 'Apart from the war years, building this was his main occupation for the next three decades. He built the whole thing virtually single-handedly, until his health packed in.'

'So he didn't give up his vocation as an architect after all,' Costas said.

'Far from it,' Morgan responded. 'Out here he was really able to indulge his passion, to do something he might never have been able to get away with in Edwardian England. In the 1890s, when he was a student of architecture, people were beginning to realize just how beautiful the country villas of Roman Britain were, places that were first being properly excavated at that time.'

'It took a moment, but then I recognized it,' Jack said. 'One of my favourite Roman sites, Chedworth villa in Gloucestershire. Even the setting's similar, a bit damper there maybe.'

'You've got it,' Morgan said. 'And the setting was crucial to him. The great houses of Roman Italy were enclosed places, inward-looking, cut off from the natural world. Think the Getty Villa, the Villa of the Papyri. There's a magnificent view to be had outside, but the peristyle courtyard excludes it, encloses you in its own order. And instead of windows on the outside world, you've got those wall paintings showing fanciful scenes of gardens and landscapes, deliberately unreal, mythical. The whole place represents control over nature.'

'Or lack of control,' Jack said.

'Or denial,' Costas said. 'More comforting to paint Vesuvius on your villa wall as some kind of Dionysian reverie than to look out of the window and see a reality you could never hope to control.'

'In Roman Britain, something different was going on,' Morgan continued. 'The Britons, the Celtic tribespeople, worshipped in forest glades, and seem to have had no temples. They were attuned to nature, saw themselves as part of it. Nature wasn't something to control. So when the Celtic elite wanted villas in the Roman fashion, they built them as part of the landscape, not excluded from it. That's what Everett wanted to do here. Instead of a peristyle courtyard, there's a single long corridored structure extending along the head of the valley to the south, the nuns' dormitory, just like the west range at Chedworth. It fits beautifully into the contours and the colours of the landscape, becomes part of it. That was Everett's vision.'

'He must have relished the challenge,' Jack said. 'Getty

could call on architects and builders from all over the world for his villa, whereas Everett had only himself. And yet Everett finished this place decades before the Getty Villa was opened.'

'And the Getty Villa was a public spectacle, a benefaction to the world, whereas this place is about as secret as you can get,' Morgan added. 'The constitution of the nunnery forbids outsiders from going beyond the entrance vestibule, or from having any direct contact with the nuns. It's a huge privilege for us to be allowed this far.'

'Can we look inside the vestibule?' Jack said.

'That's why I brought you here.'

Morgan led them on to a patio of irregular flagstones towards a simple, unassuming doorway, surrounded by upright slabs and capped by a lintel in the local yellow-brown sandstone Jack had seen on the terrace. The door was made from chiselled planks of hardwood that looked like walnut, and was slightly ajar, pivoting inwards. Morgan pushed it further in, then stood back and pointed at the floor. 'First, look at the threshold.'

They stared down. In front of them was a black-and-white floor mosaic, made of irregular, crudely cut cubes, tesserae, polished smooth. It was about three feet across and filled the entranceway, half in and half out. The black cubes formed a pattern of letters. Jack had seen a threshold like this before, a black-and-white mosaic in a doorway at Pompeii bearing the Latin words *CAVE CANEM*, BEWARE OF THE DOG. But this one was different. The letters had been arranged in a square, and the message had no obvious meaning. Each line constituted a word:

ROTAS
OPERA
TENET
AREPO
SATOR

Jack stared for a moment, and then it clicked. 'It's Latin. "Arepo, the sower, holds the wheels carefully."'

'Some kind of code?' Costas said.

'Not exactly,' Jeremy murmured. He quickly took out a notebook and pencil from his pocket and scribbled down some words, then ripped out the sheet and handed it to Costas. 'It's a word square, a puzzle. Rearrange the letters and this is what you get.' Costas held up the paper so Jack and Morgan could see it too:

Costas whistled. 'Clever.'

'But not Everett's idea,' Jack said. 'It's ancient Roman, found scratched on an amphora sherd in Britain.'

'That sounds familiar,' Costas said. 'Ever since the graffiti of St Paul from our shipwreck off Sicily, I'm beginning to look at humble old pots in a whole new light.' He took a step forward and peered into the vestibule. 'And speaking of which, that looks familiar too. I think I see a chi-rho symbol.'

'Two of them, in fact,' Morgan said. 'One on the floor, one on the wall.'

They filed inside. The room was simple, austere, in keeping with the exterior of the villa, the plastered walls painted matt red in the Roman fashion. There were no windows, but instead a series of apertures just below the ceiling artfully designed to let shafts of light fall on the middle of the floor and on the wall opposite the entranceway, on the centrepieces of the two decorations in the room. The floor decoration was another mosaic, but this time polychrome. It covered almost the entire width of the room, perhaps eight feet across. The tesserae were each about half an inch square and the palette was limited, no more than half a dozen colours. The mosaic was executed in a bold, linear style with stark images and little subtlety of shading. A series of concentric circles advanced inwards, abstract patterns of tendrils, meanders and scrolls divided by bands of white. In the centre was the image that Costas had seen, a chi-rho monogram inside a medallion about two feet across, surmounted by the head and torso of a human figure. The chi-rho symbol appeared behind the head, as if it were a halo.

'Extraordinary,' Jack murmured. 'Hinton St Mary, in Dorset. It's almost identical to the famous mosaic.'

'Another British villa?' Costas asked.

Jack nodded absently, then squatted down, absorbed in the detail. 'The Hinton St Mary mosaic wasn't excavated until the 1960s, but the medallion design was probably replicated by the Roman mosaicist and Everett must have known of it from somewhere else. He's even used the same materials,' he murmured. 'Brick for red, limestone for white, sandstone for yellow, shale for grey. He had access to plenty of other colours around here, quartzes, greens and blues, the colours you see in the Getty Villa mosaics, but he stuck to a British palette.'

'I take it that's Christ?' Costas said.

'Good question,' Morgan replied.

Jack got up. 'I didn't think there was any dispute,' he said. 'Pretty standard fourth-century representation. Clean shaven, square faced, long hair, wearing something like a Roman toga. It was pure fantasy, of course. Nobody knew what he looked like. This could as easily have been an image of the first Christian emperor, Constantine the Great, or one of his successors. In fact, the emperors might not have discouraged the confusion of their images with Christ.'

'That's the problem,' Morgan said.

'What do you mean?'

'Well, some of the early Christians in Britain seem to have distanced themselves from the Roman Church, to have seen themselves as part of another tradition that drew strength from their own pagan ancestry. You have to ask yourself whether the owner of that villa at Hinton St Mary would have wanted an image of Christ so similar to the image of the emperor on the coins in his purse. And the educated British elite of the late Roman period would have known what people from Judaea looked like. The idea that Jesus should have been clean shaven, almost cherubic, is preposterous. He was a fisherman and carpenter from the sun-scorched Sea of Galilee. But look again. The long hair, those almond eyes, that cloak that might be a toga, might be a gown. Forget about the identification. What does that image say to you?'

'It's a woman!' Costas exclaimed.

Morgan nodded. 'For the earliest British Christians, then for later followers of Pelagius like Everett, Jesus' companion Mary was a powerful part of the story. Not for the Pelagians were the androgynous images you see in some late Roman art, of Christ seemingly embodying both man and woman. They saw the iconography of Christ in the Roman tradition reduced to a mere decorative motif, as imperial propaganda. For the Pelagians, it was Jesus the man, and Mary the woman. And remember where we are. It's an appropriate image for a convent of St Mary Magdalene.'

'Fascinating,' Jack murmured.

'And you'll recognize the painting.'

Jack looked up from the mosaic to the wall. He saw another chi-rho symbol, painted in black on a light blue background, with the Greek letters alpha and omega on either side. The symbol and the letters were surrounded by a dark blue wreath, and Jack could make out other, smaller Greek letters among vine tendrils swirling decoratively around the flowers and leaves of the wreath. Below the symbol was a small cross with ornate finials in the Armenian tradition, and below that the Latin words *Domine Iumius*.

'"Lord, we come",' Jack translated. 'Apart from that inscription and the Armenian cross, it's a version of another famous mosaic, from Lullingstone in Kent,' he said. 'Everett really had a thing for Romano-British villas, didn't he?'

Morgan nodded. 'It's not just these images we're meant to be looking at, it's the setting. Everett wanted us to see art like this in its original context, just as Getty did. And whereas Getty was inspired by Herculaneum, Everett was fuelled by the archaeological discoveries of the nineteenth century in England, a rediscovery of the Romano-British and early

DOMINE IUMIUS

Christianity which had excited him as a young man. He realized that early Christian worship in Britain had taken place in private houses, in villas, probably much as it had done in Herculaneum. Everett called this room the *scholarium*, the learning place. Not a church, not a chapel, but a learning place. A place where people could gather and read the Gospels. A place which had no pulpit, no special place for preachers or priests.'

'A place where he might have envisaged one day revealing his great secret,' Costas said.

Jeremy had been pensive, but now spoke quietly. 'It shows the absurdity of those centuries of conflict between the different denominations, Rome and the Pelagians, Catholic and Protestant. Here, in this Catholic convent in the California hills, he found a place where he could express his convictions with total freedom, create a place where he could get closer to Jesus and his teachings than anywhere before.'

Jack looked around, nodding slowly. Over the years he had learned to accept his own instincts about art, to trust his own sensibility and not force himself to find beauty out of obligation. This place felt familiar to him, somehow touched his own past. The relationship with nature, the choice of colours, the use of light and shade, reflected a particular adjustment to the world that seemed to gel with Jack's own, with the landscapes of his ancestry. But there was more to it than that. Moving from the great monuments of Christianity, from St Peter's in Rome and St Paul's in London, to the intimacy of this place, Jack had begun to sense that he was looking at two different versions of truth, of beauty. He looked again at the face in the mosaic, and thought of Jesus the man, Mary the woman. So much Christian tradition had been wrapped up in high art, creating images that were awesome, remote, unattainable. Yet there was another beauty, one crudely fashioned, perhaps, but with a power wrought through intimacy with men and women themselves, not a creation of idealized forms. Being here today had helped Jack to crystallize these feelings, and to navigate a mystery that was becoming more complex and fascinating the more they delved into it.

Jack snapped out of his reverie, took a deep breath, and looked hard at the mosaic and the painting. 'Come on,' he murmured.

'What is it?' Costas said.

'It's got to be here somewhere,' Jack said. 'If Everett left any kind of clue, it's got to be embedded in these images.'

Jeremy walked up to the wall, and peered at the painted wreath that surrounded the chi-rho symbol. 'Is this an exact copy?' he asked.

'He did make some changes,' Morgan said. 'Those pinnate leaves are walnut and the flowers are orchids, which he loved. He added the Greek letters too. I checked them all after I first came here, tried to match them with every known Christian acrostic, but came up with nothing. I've had to conclude they were purely decorative.'

'That doesn't sound like Everett,' Jeremy said.

'No, it doesn't, but I've tried everything.'

Jeremy stood back, and looked all round the room. 'What's the chronology of this place?' he said. 'I mean, do we know when he did these decorations?'

'I was able to speak to the Mother Superior, through an intermediary,' Morgan said. 'She'd been a young nun here when Everett was dying, and had nursed him in his shack during his final months. Apparently he'd finished building this part of the convent before the First World War, within two years of arriving in America. He seems to have worked with extraordinary fervour, as if he needed to justify the decision he'd made to leave his family and sacrifice his career.'

'And the decoration?'

'He finished the mosaics then too, including the word square at the entrance. But the wall painting he did when he returned from the war. When the Mother Superior was young, some of the older nuns remembered it. Everett had returned a changed man, withdrawn and troubled. Physically he was weakened, his lungs permanently damaged. He virtually locked himself in this room, for months on end. They had no notion of what he'd gone through. How could they? Southern California was a long way away from the hell of a gas attack. But you can see it in that painting. His version of the chi-rho is stark, jagged, pitch black, as if it's been blasted by fire. It's like those black-and-white photographs of towns on the western front, Ypres, Passchendaele, Loos, where he was wounded, utter desolation with only a few shattered fragments standing, like a bleak image of the hill of Golgotha, the empty crosses of the crucifixion blackened and warped by fire.'

Jeremy walked up to the wall painting, and traced his finger over the wreath. 'I count twenty-five letters altogether, all Greek,' he murmured. 'No obvious order, no rationale. They don't seem to read anything, forward or backward.'

'I told you I'd tried that route,' Morgan said. 'Didn't get anywhere. The only legible inscription is those words *Domine Iumius* at the bottom, below the Armenian cross. That doesn't get us anywhere either.'

'He was a brilliant mathematician,' Jeremy murmured. 'He loved puzzles, word games. You can see it in that word square at the door. Then he goes to war, comes back and does this painting, adding these letters to his copy of the Roman original. Why? What had happened to him?' Jeremy stared at the wall, pressing on it with one hand and tapping his fingers, then suddenly turned and looked at Morgan. 'Remind me,

1917. You said he came back here. You mean to the convent, where we are now?'

Morgan nodded. 'After America had entered the war, after he'd been involved in decrypting the Zimmerman telegram. He and William Montgomery came here to California, to this place.'

'Cryptographers,' Costas said, his eyes narrowing. 'Codebreakers.'

'That's it. I've got it.' Jeremy bounded over to the bag he had left by the door, and pulled out a battered notebook. 'Remember this, Jack? It's what I was reading on the plane. I had a hunch it might come in useful.' He flipped it open, thumbed through it and stopped at a page. 'When I was at school, I transcribed the entire Zimmerman code,' he said excitedly. 'That's what happened to Everett during the war. He'd been shell-shocked, wounded, but he'd also become a codebreaker. That's the key. He returns here during the war, and wants to leave a clue, just as Claudius did two thousand years before. He's immersed in codes, and he's got the Zimmerman code running though his head. He lets Montgomery in on his secret. It's the only reason I can imagine he brought Montgomery to this place, in the middle of the war when they must have had precious little time. Maybe they devised a code in this very room. Maybe the ancient document, the gospel, was somewhere here, concealed by Everett in this room while he was building it before the war, and maybe they planned a permanent hiding place for it when they were here together.' He paused, and peered at Morgan. 'You're right. These letters don't fit any ancient acrostic. But I don't think they're purely decorative. I think they're a First World War code.'

'Keep talking,' Jack said.

'The Zimmerman code was numerical, right?' Jeremy flipped to another page. 'The telegram looked like any other except instead of letters there were numbers, arranged in clusters like words. The problem was assigning values to the numbers, equating them to a letter or a syllable or a word. The breakthrough was the secret codebook acquired from a German agent in the Middle East.'

'I think I'm with you,' Costas murmured. 'What about giving the Greek letters on the painting a numerical equivalent?'

'That's exactly what I thought.' Jeremy rummaged for the pencil in his pocket, opened a fresh page and began copying down the Greek letters in sequence as they appeared on the painting, clockwise from the top where the two arms of the painted wreath nearly joined. He then jotted down the Greek alphabet from alpha to omega with the numbers one to twenty-four alongside, and transferred those numerical values to the sequence of letters from the painting, beginning with the first letter from the painting, delta, and the number 4. 'Okay. I've got it.' They crowded round, and he held the notebook up in a shaft of light. They could see the Greek letters with their numerical value below:

Δ P Z T Ξ Φ Ψ H Ω Θ H M Δ Θ I Π Ω A Ξ N Λ O Π B T
4 17 6 19 14 21 23 6 24 8 6 12 4 8 9 16 24 1 14 13 11 15 16 2 19

'Okay. It's pure guesswork, but if I'm right there will be clusters in those numbers identical to clusters in the German codebook, and then we're in business.' Jeremy bounded back to his bag, pulled out a palm-sized computer and activated it, squatting down on one knee. 'When I first became interested in the Zimmerman code, I decided to see how modern computer technology could have aided the decryption,' he said.

'I'm liking you more and more, you know, Jeremy,' Costas murmured.

'I'm sure Everett would have loved the technology,' Jeremy continued. 'But he would have seen that with some decoding, no amount of computer wizardry can replace the human brain. Decrypting the Zimmerman code depended on understanding the Germans who created it, their perception of the world, their vocabulary. You had to know the words they would have used and been familiar with.'

He tapped a command and a page of numerical sequences came up, with words and syllables alongside. 'As it turned out, the key to the German code was quite simple,' he said. 'Each cluster of numbers is a word or a phrase or a letter. You use the codebook like an index. The problem was, the Germans who created the code hadn't anticipated some of the words that were going to be needed for this particular message, so a few words had to be made up from smaller parts. Here, you can see the word Arizona, made up from four different clusters of numbers, for the syllables AR, IZ, ON and the letter A. That's the part of the Zimmerman telegram where the Germans were going to help the Mexicans reconquer the southern states. The intelligence people back in Germany had never imagined they'd need the word Arizona, evidently. This was probably where Everett came in. He may have been more familiar than any of the other British codebreakers in Room 40 with America, having lived there for several years before the war. He may have been the one who suggested that they should be looking out for geographical names, unique place names that might not be in the codebook.' Jeremy paused, tapped the keyboard again and sat back. 'Okay. I'm going to run these numbers. This might take a minute or two.'

'Everett was having fun, wasn't he?' Costas said.

'What do you mean?'

'Well, all this business was deadly serious for him, of course, hiding the ancient gospel and leaving this trail, but he was also having fun.'

'He loved puzzles,' Jeremy replied. 'A codebreaker.'

'A bit like Claudius.'

'A treasure hunt can be like a game of chess,' Jack murmured. 'With someone who thinks they're always one move ahead of you, and leaves openings to make the game last longer, and then you trounce them.'

'I thought you were an archaeologist, not a treasure-hunter, Jack,' Costas said, with a twinkle in his eye. 'I'm getting seriously worried about you.'

'Bingo!' Jeremy said excitedly. 'It worked!' Six words had appeared on the screen.

'Well I'll be damned,' Jack murmured.

'It's in German, of course.'

'Ah.'

'How's your German?' Jeremy asked, scribbling down the words on his notepad.

'Rusty.' Jack paused, scanning the words. 'Grabeskirche. I think that's church, though there might be a more specific meaning. But I know a man who can help.' He dug his cell phone out of his pocket, flipped it open and pressed the number for the IMU secure line. 'Sandy, this is Jack. Please find Maurice Hiebermeyer and have him call me asap. Thanks.' He held the phone expectantly, and a moment later it chirped. 'Maurice? Good to hear you.' Jeremy ripped a sheet of paper from his pad and gave it to Jack, who took it with the pencil and walked outside. A few minutes later he returned, still holding the phone open. 'I read the words to him, and he's going to mull it over for a moment then call me back.'

'How is our friend?' Costas asked.

'He's in a pizzeria in Naples,' Jack replied. 'Seems to have had a change of heart about the place. Says as long as you actually want to string along the bureaucracy, it's a piece of cake. All you have to do is show up at the superintendency in the morning and throw another spanner in the works, then you can go away and relax for the rest of the day. He's on his second circuit of the pizzerias. Says even if we were allowed back into the passageway in Herculaneum again, he wouldn't fit.'

'Cue his latest discovery in the Egyptian desert, the one he's been trying to tell you about,' Costas said. 'No tight passageways, more room to maneouvre. Would we care to join him? Finally?'

'Nope. Didn't even mention it. His mouth was full.'

'What did he say, seriously?'

'He's really taken the initiative. The authorities had already used him as a media figure when they got him in to excavate the tunnel, the famous Egyptologist, showing they'd got the best person in to do the job. He's fluent in Italian, and they probably hadn't reckoned that he'd become an overnight star on Italian TV. He's used it to our advantage. The superintendency wanted him to front a big press event on the Anubis statue, and he insisted it take place in the villa site, outside the tunnel entrance. That way, he and Maria were able to keep an eye on things. He's made a huge play in the media about the dangers of the site, the need to seal it up until the funding's there for a complete excavation of the villa, once and for all. He insisted that the superintendency concrete up the entrance to the tunnel while he watched. They were only too happy to oblige, of course, but at least it means we know that what lies at the end is still intact.'

'Amazing guy,' Costas murmured, then eyed Jack closely. 'Was he able to find out anything about Elizabeth?'

Jack shook his head. 'Nothing.' The phone chirped, and he rushed outside again. He returned a moment later, pocketing the phone, looking at the notebook. 'Here it is.' He cleared his throat, and read slowly: '"The word of Jesus is in the grave chapel."'

There was silence for a moment, and they all looked at the painting on the wall.

'The word of Jesus,' Costas said. 'Surely that means the gospel, what we're after.'

'It might,' Jack murmured.

'And the grave chapel. That must be this room. He's telling us the gospel is somewhere in this room?'

'Or he's simply telling us that this room is a burial chapel.'

'Not much of a clue.'

'It doesn't add up.' Jack looked around the austere interior, then back to the painting. 'He could have hidden it here. But somehow it's too obvious. He would have known that anyone standing here, anyone who'd reached the point of decrypting those Greek letters, would have known something of his life, his background. There's something more, something we haven't recognized. There's a big piece missing.'

'Nineteen seventeen,' Jeremy murmured. 'That's the key year.'

'I can't see what else we can tease out of it,' Jack said.

'Did Everett remain here, after Montgomery left?' Costas asked.

Morgan looked up, distracted. 'Huh?'

'In 1917. When Everett and Montgomery came here. The war was still on, and Everett was still a British intelligence

441

officer. Did he remain in the States, working with the Americans?'

'Ah. I forgot to say.' Morgan cleared his throat. 'I was in London and had a few days in the National Archives at Kew. To my astonishment I found a file of his personal correspondence, mainly related to his wound, doctors' reports, medical board evaluations, stuff that couldn't be classified as top secret because it was routine officers' papers, unrelated to his intelligence activities. What they'd forgotten was that medical reports specify where a soldier's being posted next, on the basis of the fitness recommendation. It turns out Everett already knew his next posting, assigned to him just before the trip to America. The British Army realized they needed decryption experts at the front, ideally officers with field experience. And somewhere along the line, the War Office discovered that Everett was not just a mathematician but had also studied Arabic at university. That made him a real prize. After returning from America in 1917 he became a cipher officer with British Middle Eastern forces, on the other big British front of the First World War, fighting the Ottoman Empire. He accompanied General Allenby in the liberation of Jerusalem.'

Jack suddenly went still. He let his pencil drop, and looked up at Morgan. 'Say that again.'

'Everett was in Jerusalem in late 1917. We only have that faded picture of him as an old man to go on, but I believe you can actually make him out in the famous photograph of Allenby and his staff dismounted, walking through the Jaffa

Gate on the eleventh of December of 1917. I believe he's one of the officers behind T. E. Lawrence, Lawrence of Arabia. We know they walked on through the Old City to the Church of the Holy Sepulchre, where they prayed in the square. Everett stayed on in Jerusalem as an intelligence officer with the British occupying forces for the remainder of the war. They had plenty of time on their hands after the Turkish defeat, and that explains how he drafted an architectural treatise on the Holy Sepulchre, the manuscript of his I told you about that I've been working up for publication. After his demobilization from the army in 1919 he returned to America and spent the rest of his life here in this nunnery. His lungs had been so badly damaged in the gas attack in 1916 that he was unable to travel again, and he eventually became an invalid.'

Jack had his back to them still, and was staring at the painting. 'Well I'll be damned,' he whispered.

'That usually means something,' Costas said.

'I know where Everett buried his treasure.' Jack stood up quickly, and turned round with a broad smile on his face. 'That message in the letters. *The word of Jesus is in the grave chapel.* Not *grave chapel*. Maurice has given us a literal translation. There was no reason why he should have done otherwise. But my German isn't that rusty. I knew that word was familiar. It's from the last time I was in Jerusalem. It's the German for *Holy Sepulchre*.'

There was a collective gasp. Jack felt a huge burst of adrenaline course through him, as all the loose ends suddenly seemed to coil together and point in one direction. He quickly took his cell phone out again, and pressed the number for the IMU direct line. 'Sandy? How soon can you get us to Tel Aviv?'

Morgan gestured, pointing towards himself. Jack eyed him, nodding. 'Four of us. Yes. His name is Morgan.' He listened for a moment, replied quickly and snapped shut the phone. 'We may as well head for the airport now. We'll pick up what you need on the way.' Morgan nodded, and Jack stepped towards the painting with the chi-rho symbol, putting his hand on it. He turned round and looked at the others, his khaki bag slung over his shoulder. 'From now on, we're back in the firing line. We already know someone else has been on the trail of Everett, and may even have tracked us here. As soon as we leave on that flight, things really hot up. They'll know we're on to something. We're all in this now. There's no backing out. Anyone got any questions?'

'Let's do it,' Costas said.

22

'Jack? Jack Howard?'

A woman detached herself from a huddled group of monks on the rooftop of the Church of the Holy Sepulchre and marched across the sun-drenched courtyard, her white robe flowing around her. Jack shielded his eyes as he took in the scene. The dome of the greatest church in Christendom lay before him, rising above the whitewashed walls and flat rooftops of the Old City of Jerusalem. Up here there seemed to be more room to think, above the narrow alleyways and hemmed-in courtyards below, where every square inch was zealously guarded by one of the many factions who had staked a claim in this holiest of cities. Jack looked over at Costas, and rubbed his eyes. He had found it impossible to sleep on the flight from Los Angeles. They had left Morgan a few minutes earlier at the entrance to the Holy Sepulchre, intent on checking accessibility to the part of the church he wanted them to explore. But Jeremy was not with them. At the last minute Jack had asked him to go to Naples, to join Maria and Hiebermeyer and to do what he could to find out what had happened to Elizabeth. Jack had felt uneasy about sending anyone else back there, but Maria and Hiebermeyer were completely wrapped up in the media circus at the villa site and he felt he could rely on Jeremy to do everything possible until he himself could get there.

The car ride from Tel Aviv had been hot and dusty, but as the Old City of Jerusalem opened out in front of them Jack had felt a surge of exhilaration, a certainty that they had come to the right place, that whatever lay at the end of the trail would be here. With the feeling of certainty had come increased anxiety. Ever since he and Costas had met with the mysterious figure in the catacombs under the Vatican he had felt trapped in an inexorable process, a narrowing funnel, with no knowledge of who might be watching them. If what they had been told was true, for almost two thousand years those who were following them had won all their battles, allowed no failure. And with every new person Jack brought into the fold, there was another name added to a hit list. He looked at the approaching woman, then glanced again at Costas beside him. He suddenly remembered his friend's old adage: If you can calculate the risk, then it is a risk that can be taken. But he hated gambling with other people's lives.

The woman came up to him, smiling. She had strips of colourful embroidery down the front and around the wrists of her robe, and wore a gold necklace and earrings. Her long black hair was tied back, and she had the high cheekbones and handsome features of an Ethiopian, with startlingly green eyes. She extended her hands and Jack embraced her warmly. 'My old school friend,' he said to Costas. 'Helena Selassie.'

'That surname rings a few bells,' Costas said, shaking hands with her and smiling.

'The king was a distant relative,' she said, in perfect English with an American accent. 'Like him, I'm Ethiopian Orthodox. This is our holiest place.'

'Virginia?' Costas murmured, his eyes narrowing. 'Maryland?'

Helena grinned. 'Good guess. And you have a hint of New York? My parents were Ethiopian exiles, and I grew up among the expat community south of Washington DC. I was at high school with Jack in England when my father was stationed in London, then I went back to MIT. Aerospace engineering.'

'Really? I must have just missed you. Same faculty, submarine robotics.'

'We didn't mix with the sub jocks.'

'The Old City of Jerusalem's a far cry from moon rockets and outer space, Helena,' Jack said.

She gave him a wan smile. 'After NASA wound down the space shuttle programme, I figured I'd seek the spiritual route. Get there quicker.'

'You knew you'd be coming out here eventually.'

'It's in the blood,' she said. 'My father did it, my grandfather, his father before that. A fair number of women along the way. There are always at least twenty-eight of us up here on the roof, mostly monks but always a couple of nuns, have been for almost two centuries now. Our presence on the Holy Sepulchre is the hub of our Ethiopian faith, helps keep our sense of identity. I don't just mean the Ethiopian Church, I mean my extended family, Ethiopia itself.'

'Seems a little crowded down in the church below,' Costas said.

'You can say that again. Greek Orthodox, Armenian Apostolic, Roman Catholic, Coptic Orthodox, Syriac Orthodox. We spend more time negotiating when we can use the washroom in this place than we do worshipping. It's like a microcosm of the world here, the good, the bad and the ugly. In the nineteenth century, the Ottoman Turks who ruled Jerusalem imposed something called the Status Quo of the Holy Places, in an attempt to stop the bickering. The idea was that any new construction work, any change in the custodial arrangements in the Holy Sepulchre required government approval. Trouble was, it got turned on its head and used for more in-fighting. We can't even clear fallen wall plaster from our chapels without weeks of negotiations, then formal approval from the other denominations. Everyone's always spying on each other. We're never more than one step from open warfare. A few years ago an Egyptian Coptic monk staking a claim up here moved his chair from the agreed spot a few feet into the shade, and eleven monks had to be hospitalized.'

'But at least you're in pole position on the roof,' Jack said.

'Halfway to heaven.' Helena grinned. 'At least, that's how the monks console themselves in the middle of winter, when it's below freezing and the Coptics have accidentally on purpose cut off the electricity.'

'You live up here?' Costas asked incredulously.

'Have you smelled the toilets?' she said. 'You must be kidding. I have a nice apartment in the Mount of Paradise nunnery, about twenty minutes' walk from here. This is just my day job.'

'Which is what, exactly?'

'Officially, I try to get back all our ancient manuscripts, the ones held here by the other denominations. They're easy to spot, with Ethiopian Ge-ez inscriptions and bound in colourful artwork, the signature of our culture.'

'Get back?' Costas repeated.

She sighed. 'It's a long story.'

'The nub of it.'

'Okay. Ethiopia, the ancient kingdom of Aksum, was one of the first nations ever to adopt Christianity, in the fourth century AD. Not a lot of people realize it, but Africans, black Africans from Ethiopia, are one of the oldest Christian communities associated with the Holy Sepulchre. We were given the keys to the Church by the Roman Emperor Constantine the Great's mother Helena, my namesake. But then for centuries we had a very unholy rivalry with the Egyptian Coptic Church, the monks from Alexandria. Things began to go seriously downhill when we refused to pay taxes to the Ottoman Turks after they took over the Holy Land. Then in 1838 a mysterious illness wiped out most of the Ethiopian monks in the Holy Sepulchre. They said it was the plague, but none of us believe it. After that most of our property was confiscated. The surviving monks were banished to the roof, and we kept our foothold here, bringing mud and water by hand from the Kibron Valley to build these huts you see around us. Then came the worst desecration of all. Many of our precious books were stolen from us and burned. They claimed the manuscripts were infected with the plague.'

'In other words, there was something in them they didn't want revealed,' Costas murmured.

Helena nodded. 'They were afraid of proof that we were here at the site of the Holy Sepulchre a few years before them, that we could use our books to claim ascendancy. The tragedy is, we know some of those lost documents dated way before the foundation of the Church of the Holy Sepulchre in the fourth century. There were manuscripts on goat parchment almost two thousand years old. Some of them may still exist, locked away in the libraries of our rivals. My dream is to find just one of these manuscripts, something dating from the lifetime of Jesus and his followers, those who met him and actually heard his word, and to house it up here in a purpose-built library. Something that speaks to all the pilgrims of any denomination who come here seeking Jesus, not the bickering and rivalry you see below. Having that kind of treasure to show the world would put the Ethiopian community firmly on the map again, as something more than a bunch of oddballs camped out on the roof.'

Jack shaded his eyes and glanced past the dingy grey structures of the monks' cells to the holy cross on top of the dome over Christ's tomb, rising behind the west range of the courtyard in front of him. The seeming purity of the scene, the whitewashed walls set against the sky, seemed to bely the complex history Helena had been describing, yet he knew they were standing on the accretion of centuries like an archaeological site. 'I agree, he murmured. 'This would be the perfect place. I'd love to help you.'

'We don't have much of a stake below, near the tomb, but up here we feel we've got the edge. Right over the spot where Christ rose, as high as you can get.'

'You believe this is the place?' Costas asked.

She paused. 'It's like everything else to do with early Christianity. You have to cut away so much encrustation to reach the truth, and sometimes the truth you were seeking just isn't there to be found.'

'The encrustation of history,' Costas murmured. 'Funny, Jack uses that word too.'

'Same school, I guess,' Helena grinned. 'The Church of the Holy Sepulchre wasn't dedicated until three hundred years after Jesus' death, at a time when the search was on among some Christian clergy for a fantasy past, one that fitted the political needs of the emperor Constantine the Great. The story of his mother Helena finding a fragment of the True Cross in one of the ancient water cisterns below the church is probably just that, encrustation. But there's truth here too. This place where we're standing really was an ancient hill, outside the city walls. There were tombs here at the time of Jesus, and it could have been a site for executions. It all adds up.'

'You're sounding dangerously like an archaeologist, Helena,' Jack said.

'It's what lies under it all that I want to get at, the bare bones of history.'

'They're not always bare, in my experience,' Costas muttered.

'Don't mind him,' Jack said, smiling. 'He's recently traumatized.' He turned back to Helena. 'But I understand what you're getting at.'

'There's something about spending time on this rooftop, Jack,' Helena said. 'It's as if everything below is smothered under the great weight of the past. Up here, with nothing but the sky over us, it's like being above a great bowl of history, radiating upwards to some distant focal point. And looking down, all the absurdities of humanity seem trivial, easily dispensable. You seem to see the shape of things for what they really are, the simple truths. It gives me hope that one day I will find the real Jesus, Jesus the man. That's what makes this place precious to us. I sat beside the Sea of Galilee only a few days ago, just water and shimmering hills and sky, and I seemed to see it all so clearly in front of me.'

Jack glanced at Helena. 'I'd love you to share some of that. But first we need your help. Pretty urgently. It's what I called you about. Is there somewhere we can go?'

At that moment Morgan came up the stairs on to the rooftop courtyard. Like Jack and Costas he was wearing chinos and a loose shirt, but he was carrying a straw hat which he put on as he came out into the sun walking towards them.

'Welcome to the kingdom of heaven,' Costas smiled.

'It's hot enough to be the other place,' Morgan said, then looked at Helena apologetically and held out his hand. 'You must be Sister Selassie.'

'Dr Morgan.'

Helena gestured for them to follow her to a line of doors on the other side of the courtyard. The walls and upper structure of the church that surrounded the courtyard kept the noise of the city at bay, but there was a sudden sharp clatter from somewhere nearby followed by a series of percussive echoes. 'Gunfire,' Jack said. 'Sounds like .223, M16. Israeli Army.'

'They've just called a curfew,' Morgan said. 'Apparently there's been some kind of disturbance at the Wailing Wall, and it's spread up to the Christian Quarter. A couple of tourists have been knifed. We got into the Old City just in time. They've shut all the gates. I'd only just started my recce of the Holy Sepulchre, and then they shut that down too, got everyone out.'

'That's another advantage of being up here on the roof,' Helena said. 'We're above all that. But it's pretty unusual for tourists to be attacked. The extremists here rarely resort to that. Doesn't help any cause.'

'Just what we need,' Jack murmured, suddenly feeling

uneasy. 'Curfew, no tourists, police and army distracted. It leaves us vulnerable. I only hope Ben can get through.' He glanced at Helena. 'Our security chief. He flew out of London early this morning, and is due in from Tel Aviv about now.'

'If anyone can get them to open the gates, it's Ben,' Costas said.

'He's already liaised with the chief of police here,' Jack said. 'They knew each other from Special Forces, some combined UK–Israeli operation even I don't know about. Special Forces is a pretty small world.'

'You guys sure do network,' Helena said.

Jack gave her a wry look. 'Anyone thinks being Indiana Jones is a one-man show, forget it.'

They reached a door, indistinguishable from others along the side of the courtyard. Helena unlocked it, switched on an electric bulb hanging just inside and ushered them in. 'Welcome to my office,' she said. They all squeezed in, Jack and Costas sitting on a bench and Morgan standing. It was little more than a monk's cell, with the bench and devotional images on one side, but on the other side there were shelves brimming with books, architectural drawings pinned to the wall and a narrow desk with a state-of-the art laptop. 'I steal electricity from the Armenians, and hack into wireless internet from the Greek monastery next door.' She grinned, and sat down on a stool behind the desk. 'You see, it's really all a sharing community.'

Morgan peered at one of the drawings, showing simple rectilinear structures surrounded by rocky outcrops and terrain contours. 'The Holy Sepulchre?' he asked. 'Is this the early church?'

'I'm doing an architectural history of the Roman Church,' Helena said. 'I'm most interested in what lies beneath, what can be found out about the site before the Constantinian Church was established in the fourth century. There was a lot more going on here in the early Roman period after the crucifixion than people have ever guessed. It's been my secret after-hours project, but now you know. I reckon if I'm going to be sitting on top of one of the most complicated places in history for the next few years, I may as well do more than keep my monks in order.'

'Then you're going to love what I've got,' Morgan said excitedly, patting his bag. 'Someone else was doing the same thing almost a hundred years ago. His work was left unfinished, and has never before been published. It's mostly a detailed record of the early medieval elevations, but there are some observations on the Roman stuff underneath that will take your breath away.' Morgan lowered his voice. 'He thought that when King Herod Agrippa rebuilt the city walls in the mid first century AD, he also put a shrine on this spot, only a few years after the crucifixion. If you can help me follow his clues, we may have one of the most extraordinary revelations ever in the archaeology of early Christianity.'

Helena seemed rooted to the stool, and had gone pale. 'You're kidding me. Wait till you hear what I've found. Who was this guy?'

Jack took out a sheaf of papers from his faded khaki bag, and laid them on his knees. Costas leaned over from where he was sitting and shut the door. 'That's what we couldn't tell you about on the phone,' Jack said.

For the next forty minutes he quietly ran through everything: the shipwreck, Herculaneum, Rome, the London tomb, the clues they had found the day before in the nunnery in California. At the end he glanced at Helena, who was staring speechless at him, and then he placed a photograph on her desk of Everett's wall painting with the chi-rho symbol and the Greek letters. 'Does this do anything for you?'

Helena looked straight at the bottom of the photograph. She seemed stunned, and remained motionless.

'Well?'

She cleared her throat, and steadied herself on the side of the desk. She blinked hard, then peered closely at the image. 'Well, that's an Armenian cross. The lower shaft is longer than the arms and top, and those are the distinctive double tips.'

Jack nodded. 'Does that help us?'

'Well, if you're looking for something Armenian inside the Holy Sepulchre, you'd be thinking of the Chapel of St Helena, below the church in the ancient quarry. It's one part of the church the Armenian monks are responsible for.' She stopped abruptly, gripped the table and whispered, 'Of course.'

'What is it?'

Helena spoke quietly. 'Okay. Here's my take. My particular interest is what lies under the church. Everything above, between the bedrock and the roof, is encrustation, that word again, Costas. A fascinating record of the history of Christianity, but encrustation on any truth this place may have to offer on the life and death of Jesus of Nazareth, Jesus the man.'

'Go on,' Jack said.

'It's what Dr Morgan said about Herod Agrippa, the idea of a first-century shrine. Ever since first standing in that underground chapel, I've been convinced there's more Roman evidence buried under the church, from the time of Jesus and the Apostles. From everything you've just told me, from what you've managed to piece together about the events of 1917, it turns out we've been following the same leads.'

'Explain.'

'You say this man Everett was here during the First World War? A British intelligence officer? A devout man, who spent much of his time in the Holy Sepulchre? An architect by training?'

Morgan patted his bag. 'He's the one who wrote the architectural treatise I mentioned. I've got a CD copy you can have.'

'I didn't know the name, but I know the man,' Helena murmured. 'I know him intimately. I feel his presence every time I stand in that underground chapel.'

'How?' Jack exclaimed.

'Three years ago, when I first arrived here. The key to the main door of the Church of the Holy Sepulchre is held by two Muslim families, a tradition that goes back to the time of Saladin the Great. One family takes care of the key, the other opens the door. They've been more sympathetic to the Ethiopians on the roof than some of our fellow Christian brethren, and I became close to the old patriarch of one of the families. Before he died he told me an extraordinary story from his youth. It was early 1918, when he was a boy of ten. The Turks had been evicted, and the British were in control of Jerusalem. His grandfather remembered from decades before that British officers often had a great interest in the history and architecture of the place, engineers like Colonel Warren and Colonel Wilson who mapped out Jerusalem in the 1860s. Because of this, the caretakers were better disposed towards the British occupiers than the Turks, who were fellow Muslims but had no interest in the Holy Sepulchre. The old man told me that a British officer who spoke Arabic came with two army surveyors and spent many days in the church, mapping out the underground chapels and exploring the ancient quarry cuttings and water cisterns. Afterwards the officer came back many times by himself, and befriended the boy. The officer was sad, sometimes tearful, said he had children of his own he'd not seen for years and would never see again. He'd been badly wounded and gassed on the Western Front, and had difficulty breathing, coughed up blood a lot.'

'That's our man,' Jack murmured excitedly.

'Apparently on his last visit he spent a whole night in the church. The caretakers knew he was a very pious Christian, and left him alone. When he emerged he was muddied and dripping, shivering, as if he'd been down a sewer. He told them they had a great treasure in their safe keeping, and they must guard it for ever. They knew he had been badly traumatized in the war and thought he was probably delirious, and was referring to the Holy Sepulchre, to the tomb of Christ. He disappeared, and they never saw him again. With his lungs being so weak, they thought his final night's exertions might have killed him.'

'Did the old man talk about anything that Everett and his surveyors might have found?' Jack asked. 'Anything in the Chapel of St Helena? We're looking for some kind of hiding place.'

Helena shook her head. 'Nothing. But the custodians have always known there are many unexplored places under the Holy Sepulchre, ancient chambers that might once have been tombs, cisterns cut into the old burial ground. Entrances that were sealed up in the Roman period, and have never been opened up since.'

'Then we'll just have to trust our instincts,' Jack murmured.

'I've spent many hours down there, days,' Helena said. 'There are so many possibilities. Every stone in every wall could conceal a chamber, a passageway. And they're almost all mortared up or plastered over. I know of at least half a dozen stone blocks in walls that have spaces behind them, where you can see chinks through the mortar. But doing any kind of invasive exploration is out of the question. The Armenians are going to take a dim view of me taking you down there in the first place, let alone unleashing jackhammers.'

Jack reached for the photograph of Everett's wall painting

from the nunnery, and opened his folder. 'If we don't try, someone else will. There are others who know we're here, I'm convinced of it. We need to move now. Can you get the door to the Holy Sepulchre unlocked for us?'

'I can do that.' Helena caught another glimpse of the photograph in Jack's hand, then suddenly reached out and grabbed his arm. 'Wait! What's that? Under the cross?'

'A Latin inscription,' Jack said. 'It's not clear in the picture, but it says *Domine Iumius*.'

Helena was still for a moment, then gasped. 'That's it! Now I know where Everett went.' She got up, her eyes ablaze. 'I need at least two of you with me. Two strong pairs of hands.'

Costas gave a thumbs-up. 'I'm with you.'

'Where?' Jack demanded

'You're the nautical archaeologist, Jack. Ships and boats. What's the most incredible recent discovery in the Holy Sepulchre? Follow me.'

23

Half an hour later, Jack stood near the main entrance to the Church of the Holy Sepulchre, in the enclosed court-yard below the façade built almost a thousand years before when the Crusaders took Jerusalem. He had lingered behind talking quietly with Morgan as they made their way down from the Ethiopian monastery on the rooftop, and just before reaching the courtyard had handed him a compact disc from his khaki bag. He had already arranged with Helena for an escort to take Morgan out of the Old City, to the place where he would pass on the disc to Jack's contact. At the bottom of the steps he and Morgan were met by a man in street clothes carrying an unholstered Glock pistol. The man had looked questioningly at Helena, who pointed to Morgan, and the man ushered him away across the courtyard. Ahead of them two Israeli policemen suddenly rushed by, in full riot gear and carrying M4 carbines at the ready. A burst of gunfire echoed through the streets, followed by screams and exclamations in Arabic. The bodyguard pushed Morgan against the wall on the far side of the courtyard. Morgan looked back, and Jack tapped his watch meaningfully. Morgan nodded, and then the bodyguard pulled him up and they both ran out of sight around the corner.

Jack glanced up at the sky. Everything was now in train. The sun had disappeared behind a bank of grey cloud, and the air had an oppressive quality, humid and heavy. He mouthed a silent prayer for Morgan, and then followed Costas and Helena to the doors of the church. Two men in Arab headdress appeared on either side. Costas stepped back in alarm, but Helena put her hand on him reassuringly. One man passed a ring of ancient keys to the other man, who then proceeded to unlock the doors. They pushed them open, just enough. Helena glanced at the two men, bowing her head slightly, then led Jack and Costas forward. The doors closed behind them. They were inside.

'There's been a power cut in the entire Christian quarter of Old Jerusalem,' Helena said quietly. 'The authorities sometimes flip the switch. Helps to flush out the bad guys.' It was dark inside, and they remained standing for a moment, their eyes getting accustomed to the gloom. Ahead of them natural light was filtering through the windows that surrounded the dome over the rotunda, and all round them the shadows were punctuated by flickering pinpricks of orange. 'Joudeh and Nusseibeh, the two Arab custodians who unlocked the door, came in and lit the candles for us after I told them we'd be coming.'

'Does anyone else know we're here?' Jack asked.

'Only my friend Yereva. She has the key to the next place we're going. She's an Armenian nun.'

'Armenian?' Costas said. 'And you're Ethiopian? I thought you people didn't get along.'

'The men don't get along. If this place had been run by nuns, we might actually have been able to get somewhere.'

She led them forward to the edge of the rotunda. Jack looked up to where the circle of windows let in the dull light of day, and peered above that to the interior of the dome, restored in modern times to the same position as the dome of the first church built by Constantine the Great in the fourth century. He thought of the other great domes he had stood beneath in the last few days, St Paul's in London, St Peter's in Rome, places that suddenly seemed far removed from the reality of the life of Jesus. Even here the momentous significance of the site, the truths embedded in the rock beneath them, seemed obscured by the church itself, by the very structures meant to extol and sanctify the final acts in life of one who millions came here to worship.

'I see what you mean about the encrustations of history,' Costas murmured. He was staring at the gaudy structure in the centre of the rotunda. 'Is that the tomb?'

'That's the Holy Sepulchre itself, the Aedicule,' Helena

replied. 'What you see here was mostly built in the nineteenth century, in place of the structure destroyed in 1009 by the Fatamid caliph al'Hakim when the Muslims ruled Jerusalem. That destruction was the event that precipitated the Crusades, but even before the Crusaders arrived, the Viking Harald Hardrada and his Varangian bodyguard from Constantinople had come here on the orders of the Byzantine emperor, to oversee the rebuilding of the church. But I think you know all about that.'

'I thought we'd left Harald behind in the Yucatán,' Costas murmured. 'Is there anywhere he didn't go?'

'The ancient rock-cut tomb inside the Aedicule was identified by Bishop Makarios in AD 326 as the tomb of Christ,' Helena continued. 'You have to imagine this whole scene in front of us as a rocky hillside, half as high as the rotunda is now. Just behind us was a small rise known as Golgotha, meaning the place of the skull, where most believe Jesus was crucified. The hill in front of us had been a quarry, dating maybe as early as the city of David and Solomon, but by the time of Jesus it was a place of burial and probably riddled with rock-cut tombs.'

'How do we know the bishop got the right tomb?' Costas said.

'We don't,' Helena replied. 'The Gospels only tell us the tomb was hewn out of the living rock, with a stone rolled in front of it. You had to stoop to look in. There was room inside for at least five people, sitting or squatting. The platform for the body was a raised stone burial couch, possibly an *acrosolium*, a shelf below a shallow arch.'

'All of which could describe a typical tomb of the period,' Jack said. 'According to the Gospels, the tomb wasn't custom-built for Jesus, but was donated by Joseph of Arimathea, a wealthy Jew and member of the Jerusalem council. It was apparently a fresh tomb, and there would have been no further burials, no added niches as you see in so many other rock-cut tombs. It was never used as a family tomb.'

'Unless . . .' Helena hesitated, then spoke very quietly, almost in a whisper. 'Unless one other was put there.'

'Who?' Jack exclaimed.

'A companion,' she whispered. 'A female companion.'

'You believe that?'

Helena raised her hands and pressed the tips of her fingers together briefly, then gazed at the Aedicule. 'It's impossible to tell from what's there now. Constantine the Great's engineers hacked away most of the surrounding hill to reveal the tomb, to isolate it. By so doing, they actually destroyed much of the tomb itself, the rock-cut chamber, leaving only the burial shelf intact. It was almost as if Constantine's bishops wanted to remove all possible reason for doubt, any cause for dispute. From then on, the Holy Sepulchre, the identification of the tomb, would be a matter of faith, unassailable. Remember the historical context, the fourth century. When the Church was first becoming formalized, some things that were incon-venient, contradictory, were concealed or destroyed. Other things were created, spirited out of nowhere. Holy relics were discovered. Behind it all lay Constantine the Great and his bishops. Everything had to be set in stone, a version of what went on here in the first century AD that suited the new order, the Church as a political tool. They were editing the past to make a stronger present.'

'And behind Constantine lay a secret body of advisers, guardians of the earliest Church,' Jack said. 'That's one thing we haven't told you yet.'

'I know,' Helena replied quietly.

'You know?'

'As soon as you told me what you were seeking, I knew you would come up against them. The *concilium*.'

Jack looked at her in astonishment, then nodded slowly. 'We had an audience with one of them, in Rome two days ago.'

'At the tomb? The other tomb?'

Jack stared at her again, stunned, then nodded. 'You know about that too?'

'They're tight, Jack. There are never any chinks. You need to be incredibly careful. Whoever you saw, he may have told you some truths, but he may not be who you think he was. The *concilium* has been stalled in the past, but never defeated. They're like a bad dream, endlessly returning. We should know.'

'We?'

'The memory of that other tomb, the tomb of St Paul in the secret catacomb under St Peter's in Rome, was not entirely lost. The truth was passed down by those who were there, and reached the kingdom of Aksum, Ethiopia. Remember, we Ethiopians are one of the earliest Christian communities, derived from the first followers of Jesus. There are others like us, on the periphery of the ancient world. The British Church, in existence since the first century AD, since the word of Jesus first reached the shores of Britain. We share the tradition of an emperor and Christ, the British story that an emperor brought Christianity to their shores, ours that an emperor and a king sought the Messiah in the Holy Land, during the time of the Gospels. And we have always been good at keeping secrets. You know we have the Ark of the Covenant, Jack.'

'We were going there after we graduated, you remember, but Mengistu refused to lift the ban on your family. Have you actually seen it since then?'

'Eyes on the prize, Jack,' Costas murmured. 'We can plan that one by the pool later.'

'If there is a later,' Jack said, peering at Helena. 'The other thing you said. You've never told me that before. An emperor in the Holy Land.' He thought for a moment. 'The British tradition must be the one alluded to by Gildas, in the sixth century. Is there any ancient source for yours?'

'Passed down through my family,' Helena replied. 'A tradition, no more, but a cherished one.'

'So how did you survive the *concilium*?' Costas asked.

Helena paused. 'We were an inconvenience, one of those bits of untidiness that Constantine's advisers wanted swept away. Ever since the fourth century we have been persecuted by the *concilium*, hunted down, just as our brethren in Britain were. Always we maintained our link with our sister churches, our strength. We women, followers of Jesus and of

Mary Magdalene. In Britain they came to link her with the cult of their high priestess, the warrior queen Andraste.'

'We've met her,' Costas said.

'What?'

'The tomb in London,' Jack added. 'Where we found the empty cylinder, left there by Everett's ancestor. I've got a lot more to tell you.'

'Then it all falls into place,' Helena whispered.

'That plague you talked about, the extermination of the Ethiopian monks in 1838?' Jack said. 'The destruction of the libraries? Are you saying the *concilium* was behind all that?'

Helena looked behind her furtively, and whispered again. 'I'm only just beginning to get to the bottom of it, and it terrifies me. Something sinister was behind all of the rivalries in this place, all the absurdities. Something that wanted us destroyed, and wanted this place kept in a state of virtual lockdown. Look at the tomb, the Holy Sepulchre. You can hardly see it for the encrustation. The little chapels of the rival denominations, crowding in on it, suffocating it. It's almost as if they've devoured as much as they can of the tomb, right up to the burial platform, and are locked together in a permanent standoff. It's madness.'

'It'd serve them right if it wasn't the actual tomb, wouldn't it?' Costas said.

'Yet keeping you all there, keeping all the denominations in permanent standoff, might also serve the purpose of the *concilium*,' Jack murmured. 'Maybe there is something else here, something they don't want revealed. Another inconvenience.'

Helena gave Jack a piercing look, and glanced at her watch. 'Come on. My friend Yereva's due to meet us any time now.'

She led them back the way they had come, and then past the entrance. A few moments later they stood at the top of a flight of steps that dropped down into total darkness. Jack had been here before, and knew that the steps led to the Chapel of St Helena, an ancient cave and quarry cutting five metres below the level of the church. It was a mysterious, labyrinthine place, filled with walled-off spaces and ancient water cisterns, dug deep into the rock. Jack stood alone as Helena and Costas went off to find candles. For a moment all he could hear was a sound like a distant exhalation, as if the echoes of two millennia of prayers were caught in this place, resonating through history. He thought of all the pilgrims, those who had survived uncharted roads fraught with peril and uncertainty, standing at last inside their holy of holies. He hoped that nothing would ever sour the sanctity of this place, where so many had found strength in the events of one extraordinary life two thousand years ago.

Helena and Costas returned, each carrying several lit candles, and they began to descend. On the damp walls Jack saw hundreds of small crosses, carved deep into the rock by medieval pilgrims. He knew that every inch of the bedrock around them had been shaped by human hands, but as the three of them went deeper he felt as if they were walking away from human fabrication, towards the truth of what had actually happened on this bare rock almost two thousand years ago. He stopped to listen, but heard nothing. He glanced at his watch and thought of Morgan. Less than two hours to go now. It was a gamble, but he knew he had to take it, that it could be their final line of defence. *The written word*. Now they must do all they could to reach their goal. He was only a few steps from the floor of the chapel, and all he could see ahead were deep shadows and pools of orange cast by the candles. Then they were on the stone floor, walking past columns towards a grated steel door on the far side, beside an altar.

'Through this door is the Chapel of St Vartan,' Helena murmured, placing two candles in holders on the wall. 'The ancient quarry cuttings below us were only excavated in the 1970s, and part of the enclosed space was made into a little Armenian chapel. It's not open to the public. We have to wait for my friend Yereva to bring the key.' She glanced at her watch. 'She'd hoped to be here by now, but she works for her patriarch and often has trouble getting away.'

There was a rustling from the stairway they had just come down and a figure came out of the gloom towards them, wearing a brown robe and the distinctive triangular hood of the Armenians. The hood was swept back to reveal a young woman with olive skin and curly dark hair. She held a candle in one hand, and a large black ring with a single key in the other. She went straight towards the steel door, nodding at Helena. 'These are your friends?' she asked quietly, her English heavily accented.

'The ones I told you about. Jack Howard and Costas Kazantzakis.'

'I had to tell the patriarch I was coming here.' The woman spoke in a low voice.

'You were allowed out in the curfew?' Jack asked.

'We have our own private passageway.'

'Yereva is the unofficial custodian of the chapel,' Helena said. 'But being a lowly nun, she's not even allowed to look after the keys. She has to apply for them every time from the patriarch.'

'Officially, I've just come to light the candles and say a prayer,' Yereva said. 'But I'm going to return immediately, just in case there are any suspicions. If I'm back with the patriarch, then nobody will have cause to come looking for me. You should be undisturbed until the curfew is over, which will be at least a couple of hours.'

'You said nothing else to him?' Helena asked.

'Nothing else. Nothing different from our usual routine.'

'You two have met here before?' Jack asked.

'Helena will tell you,' Yereva said. 'I would love to go in there now with such a famous archaeologist, but I hope we will meet here again when times are easier.' She turned the key in the lock, and swung the door open. 'God be with you.'

'God be with you too, Yereva,' Helena murmured. 'And be careful.'

Jack eyed Helena, and saw for the first time that she looked anxious. Yereva pulled up her hood and left quickly, pattering across the stone floor and up the steps. Helena turned to the doorway. 'Come on. We may not have much time.' She led them into a gloomy passageway, lighting candles on the wall with her own candle as she went. Jack could see the rough-hewn bedrock around them, the pickmarks of ancient quarrying. The surface seemed old, much older than the stone in the Chapel of St Helena, and it was pitted like corroded metal. Below a modern metal railing on one side was a dark space, the bottom invisible. Jack had a flashback to the cavern under the Palatine Hill, to the Phlegraean Fields and the Sibyl's cave, other bottomless places where the underworld seemed visible. He cast the thought aside and followed Helena into a chamber to the right, stooping low through the entranceway. In front of them was a section of ancient wall, three courses high, the blocks thickly mortared together, with retouching that looked recently done. Helena lit more candles, and they could see another wall, different in style, with the rough surface of rock cuttings all round. She knelt down beside the wall and placed her candle in front. The farthest block to the left of the middle course was covered with a hanging blanket, and she lifted it and folded it above. Where the blanket had hung was a frame with a glass window covering the block, and behind that Jack could make out what was on the surface of the rock.

He knew what he was looking at even before she raised the blanket. It was the most extraordinary find made when the quarry was excavated. *The St Vartan chapel ship graffito*. It was a drawing of a ship, an ancient Roman merchantman, with words below. He knelt down, Costas beside him. He could see the lines of the drawing clearly now, crude but bold, the confident strokes of someone who knew what they were depicting, who got the details right even in this place so far from the sea. An experienced seafarer, a pilgrim, one of the first. Jack's eyes strayed down from the drawing to the words below. Then he remembered. Suddenly his heart began to pound. He slowly read them out:

DOMINE IVMIVS

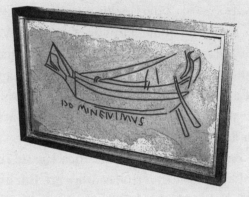

'Of course,' he whispered.

'What is it?' Costas asked.

'It's the same words as the inscription from California, from Everett's painting.' He glanced excitedly at Helena. 'This is what you recognized in the photograph.'

'That's when I knew,' she said. 'It just had to be from here.'

'Everett must have found this chamber, more than half a century before it was opened up and made into a chapel,' Jack exclaimed, keeping his voice low. 'He was here, right here where we are now. These words are the clue in his painting. Somehow, this stone's the key to the whole thing.'

'What's your take on that ship, Jack?' Helena said.

'It's Roman, certainly,' Jack murmured, trying to control his excitement, narrowing his eyes. 'High curving stern, reinforced gunwale, distinctive prow. A sailing ship, not an oared galley. The mast has been stepped down, which was done in harbours. It's got double steering oars, and what looks like an *artemon*, a raking mast at the bow. All of that suggests a large ship. My guess is we're looking at the kind of vessel that would have been seen in the harbour of Caesarea Maritima on the coast of Judaea, one of the grain carriers that stopped off there on the way north from Alexandria in Egypt before heading west for Rome. The kind of ship a Christian pilgrim from Rome might have taken back on its return voyage.'

'Can you date it?'

'I'd have said early Roman rather than late. If I'd seen this anywhere else, I'd have said first century AD. But in this place, the Holy Sepulchre, there's hardly anything that's been dated that early.'

'The inscription was clearly done at the same time as the ship, the same width and style of line,' Helena said. 'But you're the expert.'

'Well, it's Latin, which in this neck of the woods means no earlier than the first century AD, when the Romans arrived in Judaea. Beyond that it's hard to say. The lettering style certainly could be first century.'

'It's usually translated as "Lord we shall go", or "Let us go to the Lord",' Helena said. 'Some scholars have associated it with the first verse of Psalm 122, one of the Songs of Degrees sung by pilgrims approaching Jerusalem. "I was glad when they said unto me, let us go unto the House of the Lord.'"

'That doesn't really help us pin the date down,' Jack murmured. 'The Psalms were originally Hebrew, and were probably chanted by the earliest Christians, here at the tomb and in other places where they gathered in the first years after the crucifixion. So they could date to any time from the first century onwards.'

'I've checked, and these two words *domine iumius* don't actually appear together in the Latin of the Vulgate, the Roman Bible of the early medieval period,' Helena said. 'If they are a translation of Psalm 122, they could be very early, before the Latin translation that appears in the Vulgate was formalized. They could be a translation done by a very early Christian pilgrim, maybe from Rome.'

'Ships come and go, don't they?' Costas said. 'I mean, it doesn't have to be a pilgrim arriving here. It could be someone going, leaving Jerusalem. Your first translation, "Lord we shall go". Maybe it was one of the apostles, practising a bit of Latin before heading out into the big wide world, telling his Lord he was heading off to spread the word.'

Helena remained silent, but her expression was brimming with anticipation. Jack peered at her. 'What aren't you telling us?' he asked.

She reached into her robe, and took out a small plastic coin case. She handed it to Jack. 'Yereva and I found this bronze coin a few days ago. We did a bit of unofficial excavation.

There was some loose plaster under the graffito. The coin was embedded in the base of that stone, in a cavity made for it. It's like those coins I remember you telling me about that the Romans put in the mast steps of ships, to ward off misfortune. A good luck token.'

Jack was peering at the case. 'Unusual to put an apotropaic coin like that in a building,' he murmured. 'Do you mind?' He clicked open the case and took out the coin. He held it up by the rim, and the candlelight reflected off the bronze. He saw an image of a man's head, crude, thick necked, with a single word underneath. 'Good God!' he exclaimed.

'See what I mean?' Helena replied.

'Herod Agrippa,' Jack said, his voice hoarse with excitement.

'Herod Agrippa,' Costas murmured. 'Buddy of Claudius?'

'King of Judaea, AD 41 to 44,' Helena said, nodding.

Jack touched the wall beside the graffito. 'So this masonry could be centuries older than the fourth-century church above us.'

'When that wall was revealed during the 1970s excavations, there was nothing to pin the date down. But it was clearly earlier than the basement wall of the fourth-century Constantinian church, which you can see over there,' Helena said, pointing off to the side wall of the chapel to her left. 'The only ancient record of any building at this site before the fourth century comes from Eusebius' *Life of Constantine*. Eusebius was a contemporary of the emperor Constantine, so he's probably pretty reliable on what went on here in the early fourth century. That was when Bishop Macrobius of Jerusalem identified the rock-cut chamber under the Aedicule as the tomb of Christ, and Constantine's mother Helena had the first church built here. But Eusebius also says that the site had been built on two hundred years before his time, when the emperor Hadrian refounded Jerusalem as Colonia Aelia Capitolina.'

'Hadrian built a temple of Aphrodite, apparently,' Costas said, peering in the candlelight at a battered guidebook Jack had given him.

'That's what Eusebius claims,' Helena replied. 'But we can't be sure. He was part of that revisionist take on early Christian history under Constantine. Eusebius wanted his readers to think Hadrian had deliberately built on the site of the tomb of Christ to destroy it, to revile it. And Aphrodite, Roman Venus, the goddess of love, was regarded as a particular abomination by the Church fathers in his day, so the identification of the building as a temple of Aphrodite could just have been something Eusebius or his informants dreamed up for their Christian readership.'

'Bunch of killjoys,' Costas muttered. 'What was their problem? I thought Jesus was all about love.'

Helena gave a wry shrug. 'Eusebius was probably right about the date of the building, though. There are other sections of wall here that are clearly Hadrianic, judging by construction technique. If there was a structure here before that, all memory of it had clearly gone by Eusebius' day.'

Jack was staring at the wall, his mind in a tumult. 'That

coin,' he exclaimed. 'Herod Agrippa. This begins to make sense.'

'What does?' Costas said.

'It's one of the biggest unanswered questions about the Holy Sepulchre site. I've never understood why nobody has properly addressed it. Maybe it's the resurrection, fear of treading too close to an event so sacrosanct.'

'This is beginning to sound familiar,' Costas murmured. 'Go on.'

'There is one event soon after the crucifixion that gives us an archaeological possibility. King Herod Agrippa had grandiose schemes for Judaea, for his capital Jerusalem. He fancied himself as Emperor of the East, a kind of co-regent with his friend Claudius. It was Agrippa's undoing. Before he died in AD 44, probably poisoned, one scheme he did complete was to increase the size of Jerusalem, building an entirely new wall circuit to the north-west. It encompassed the hill of Golgotha and the ancient quarry site, where we're standing now.'

'Bringing the old burial ground, the necropolis, within the city limits,' Helena said.

Jack nodded. 'When city walls were extended like that, old tombs were often emptied, sometimes even reused as dwellings. In Roman tradition, no burials could exist within the sacred line of the *pomerium*, the city wall. Herod Agrippa had been brought up in Rome, and may have fancied himself enough of a Roman to observe that.'

'What date are we talking about?' Costas said.

'The wall was built about AD 41 to 43, probably just before Claudius became emperor.'

'And Jesus died in AD 30, or a few years after,' Helena said.

'So about a decade after the crucifixion, the tombs here would probably have been cleared out,' Costas murmured. 'Would Herod Agrippa have known about Jesus, about the crucifixion?'

Jack took a deep breath, and reached out to touch the wall. 'Helena's probably one step ahead of me on this, but yes, I do believe Herod Agrippa would have known about Jesus. There was a time earlier in Herod's life when contact between the two men was possible. And from the crucifixion onwards, I have no doubt that this place would have been venerated by Jesus' family and followers, become a place of pilgrimage. When Herod built his walls, he himself in the Roman guise of *pontifex maximus*, chief priest, would have ordered all the tombs within the walls to be emptied. But at the same time, this coin and the wall here suggest that he ordered a masonry structure built above or very close to the tomb. Why? Was he reviling Christ, trying to eradicate the memory?'

'Or trying to protect it,' Helena murmured.

'I don't understand,' Costas said. 'Herod Agrippa?'

'It's not necessarily what you might think,' Jack replied. 'He could have been genuinely sympathetic to the Christians, or there could have been some other factor at play. An augury that led him to believe he had to protect the site, a chance encounter with a Christian that swayed him, some early experience. Or politics. He could have been at loggerheads with the Jewish authorities, and done it to spite them. We may never know. The fact remains, we seem to have a structure built at the likely site of Christ's tomb only a few years after the crucifixion, at a time when this hill was probably already sacred ground to early Christians.'

'Then there's another thing I don't get,' Costas said. 'The tomb of Christ, the Holy Sepulchre, is behind us in the rotunda, at least eighty metres west of here by my reckoning. Let's imagine this wall in front of us was built by Herod Agrippa as some kind of shrine over the tomb. If that's the case, then the ship graffito must be on the inside, painted by someone who was actually within the structure. That just doesn't make sense to me. You'd expect the interior of the tomb to be sealed up, hallowed ground, and any graffito to be on the outside wall. And looking at the lie and wear of the masonry around that graffito, I'd say we're actually more likely on the outside of a structure. Something's not quite right.'

Jack nodded, and squatted back. 'We need some hard archaeology. The ball's in your court now, Helena,' he said, passing her back the coin of Herod Agrippa. 'Have you got anything more, anything at all?'

'Keep hold of the coin,' she murmured. 'There are others here who may suspect I have something, and it's safest with you until this is over.' She pointed to his khaki bag, and Jack replaced the coin in its case and slid it deep into the bag. She turned to face the ancient wall again, then reached out to either side of the glass pane over the graffito, lifting it up and out. She placed the pane carefully on the floor, then knelt down and began to work her fingers into a section of mortar beneath the stone block with the graffito. 'There is something I haven't shown you yet,' she said, flinching as she scraped her hand. 'I want an objective assessment.'

'About the graffito?' Jack said.

Helena winced again, and then gripped two points under the mortar. She pulled, and there was a slight movement. 'Done,' she said. She jiggled a broken section of mortar out, and laid it carefully beside the glass pane. The base of the block was now revealed, with a dark crack beneath where the mortar had been. She knelt down and blew at the lower face of the block, pulling back quickly to avoid a small cloud of dust. 'There it is,' she said, moving back further.

Jack and Costas knelt down where she had been. Jack could see more markings, inscriptions. There was a chi-rho symbol, crudely incised into the rock. Beside it was another inscription, a painted word, clearly by the same hand as the ship graffito and the *Domine Iumius* inscription, the same-shaped letters and stroke of the brush. Costas was closest, and peered down further to get a better angle. He sat back, and looked at Jack. They both stared back at the rock, speechless for a moment.

'Jack, I'm getting that strange sense of déjà vu again.'

Jack felt faint. He suddenly realized where he had seen that style of letter before. The serifs on the V, the square-sided S.

The ancient shipwreck off Sicily.

The shipwreck of St Paul.

'My God,' he whispered. '*Paulus*.' He swallowed hard, and slumped back. St Paul the Apostle. St Paul, whose name they had seen only a week before, a hundred metres beneath the sea, scratched on an amphora in an ancient shipwreck. *Impossible*. Jack closed his eyes for a moment, then stared again. No. Not impossible. It made perfect sense. He sat back, and stared at Helena.

'Are you thinking what I'm thinking?' she said quietly.

'You asked for an objective assessment,' Jack replied. 'And here it is. That graffito was carved by St Paul. That's his ship. *Domine Iumius*. Lord we go. Costas, you were right. The man who drew this was going, not coming. He came here to tell his Lord that he was about to set out on his great mission, to spread the word beyond Judaea. Paul was here, sitting on the hillside at the very spot where we are now, beside the wall built by Herod Agrippa only a few years before.'

'At the place of pilgrimage,' Helena murmured. 'At the tomb of Christ.'

'At the tomb of Christ,' Jack repeated.

Helena pointed at the space under the block. 'Jack, take a look in there. Is hasn't been mortared. You remember I told you I knew of some areas of masonry down here with spaces behind them? Most of the mortar you can see around the block is modern, dating from after the 1970s excavations when the graffito was revealed. But there's another sealing layer beneath that that's also relatively recent, dating within the last hundred years or so.'

'Let me guess,' Jack murmured. 'Nineteen eighteen?'

'I'm convinced of it.'

'You're talking about Everett,' Costas exclaimed. 'You're saying he found this, and removed the block. Can we do it too?'

'That's why I needed both of you here,' Helena said. 'When Yereva and I first found the Paul inscription, we realized there was a space beyond. You can see it through the crack. It could just be a dead space beyond the wall, or another water cistern. There are at least eleven cisterns under the Holy Sepulchre for collecting rainwater, most of them disused and sealed over. Or it could be something else. There was no way we could move this block, and if we'd been caught trying there would have been a couple more crucifixions at this spot.'

'Have you told anyone else about the Paul inscription?' Jack asked.

'You're the first. But we're certain others know, and have kept it secret. The mortar over the inscription was recent, from the 1970s excavation. They found it, then concealed it.'

'I don't understand,' Costas said. 'Surely a discovery like that would give the Armenians huge extra clout, really put them on the map?'

'It's all about keeping the status quo in this place,' Helena murmured. 'Whoever made the decision might have feared jealousy from the other denominations in the Holy Sepulchre. It could have pulled the rug out from all the checks and balances, threatened rights and privileges they'd worked so hard to maintain over the centuries. Better to keep a discovery like this as their own secret, to bolster their own private sense of superiority, to save as ammunition should it be needed in the future.'

'And there could have been other factors at play,' Jack added.

'The *concilium*?' Costas said.

'A fear of bringing dark forces down upon themselves, forces that would do anything to suppress them simply for what they knew, just as so nearly happened to the Ethiopians.'

'Come on,' Helena said, her voice suddenly urgent. 'Let's get going.' She began to prise away more sections of ancient mortar around the block with her fingers. It came away surprisingly easily, in chunks which had clearly been removed before and then sealed back into place. After a few minutes the entire block was clear, leaving a crack around the edge a few centimetres wide, enough to slot in a hand to palm depth. Jack rummaged in his bag and took out a climber's headlamp, flicking it on and pushing it through the crack at the widest point on the right-hand side. 'I see what you mean,' he murmured, his face close to the crack. 'With the block removed we'd be looking at a space about a metre by half a metre wide, just big enough for a crawlway.'

'Do you think you can do it?' Helena said. 'Move it, I mean? Yereva and I couldn't.'

'Only one way to find out.' Jack passed her the headlamp, then motioned to Costas. They each put their hands under a corner of the block. 'We'll have to try to rock it out,' Jack said. 'Gently does it. Towards you first.' They heaved, and the block budged. Costas yelped in pain. 'You okay?' Jack said. Costas drew out one hand, shaking and blowing on it, and grimaced. He slid it back in under the block, which was now a few centimetres out of the wall. 'Again,' he said. They pushed back and forth another half a dozen times, each time pulling it out further. It came surprisingly easily. They shifted position so they were facing each other, both hands under the stone. 'Heave,' Jack said. With one hand under the outer edge of the block they each moved their other hand back fractionally every time the stone came forward, keeping close to the wall. Helena pulled up a pair of short wooden planks she had found beside the railing outside the chapel, positioning them under the stone. 'Okay. This is it,' Jack said. 'Let's try to take it out a good metre. Careful of your back.' They both straightened up as much as they could, looking each other in the eye, and nodded. In one swift movement they heaved the block out from the wall and placed it on the planks. They withdrew their hands, shaking them and exhaling forcefully. 'Right,' Jack panted, looking at the hole where the block had been. 'What have we got?'

Helena was already peering into the space, holding Jack's headlamp as far in as she could reach. 'It goes in about five metres, then there's another wall, rock-cut by the look of it,' she said. 'Then the tunnel seems to veer down, to the right.' She knelt back up, and passed the light to Jack. 'If it's a cistern in there, it could be underwater,' she said. 'We're in the deepest accessible place under the Holy Sepulchre, and it's been raining a lot over the past few days. What now?'

Jack looked at Costas, who looked back at him, his face expressionless.

'Jack, we had a deal,' Costas said. 'No more underground places.'

'You're off the hook this time. Too narrow for you.'

'Are you okay with this?' Costas said, looking hard at Jack. 'I mean, going in alone?'

Jack peered into the space. 'I don't think I'm walking away from this one.'

'No, you're not.'

Jack opened the straps on the lamp and slipped it over his head, then picked up his khaki bag and pushed it as far ahead as he could into the hole.

'His lucky bag,' Costas said to Helena. 'He never goes anywhere without it.'

Helena glanced back nervously at the entrance to the chapel. 'Make it quick,' she said. 'We need to get out of here soon.' She looked at Jack, then touched his arm. '*Domine iumius*,' she murmured. 'Godspeed.'

Moments later Jack was inside the space where the stone block had been, inching his way forward on his stomach, stretched out with his bag ahead of him. The entrance into the wall lay only a few metres back, but already he felt completely isolated, away from the chapel behind him, part of another space he could see ahead in the beam from his headlamp. He remembered Herculaneum, the extraordinary feeling of stepping back in time as they entered the lost library. He felt it here too, part of the same continuum, as if he had edged back further, close to the beginning of the story that had led

Claudius to be in that villa. He felt strangely comforted by the old stone, cocooned by it, his usual anxieties gone. Helena's last words kept running through his head, the two words of Latin, and he found himself murmuring them, a low chant that helped to keep him focused. He pulled himself forward, trying to keep his elbows from scraping on the rock. There was now no light at all visible from the entrance behind his feet. He paused, sweeping his headlamp around the walls. To his right was masonry, clearly a continuation of the first-century wall with the graffito, at right angles to it. To his left and above him was bedrock, scored and cut by quarry marks, so old that they seemed almost part of the natural geology, as if the ancient imprint of man had become just another process of erosion and transformation that had gone into shaping this place.

Ahead of him the tunnel ended abruptly where Helena had spotted the quarry wall, and he could see where it joined a space to the right. He pushed his bag into the corner and angled his body around, squeezing into the opening. It was tight, and the sharp edges of the rock ripped his shirt. He pulled himself through, wincing where the rock caught him. He was in a larger space now, enough to crouch on his hands and knees. To his right, the masonry wall of the entrance tunnel continued at right angles, at least five courses of large stone blocks. His face was only inches from it, and he saw that it was the same stone as the wall outside with the ship graffito, only here the surface was unworn, fresh. He realized that the crawlspace had taken him along the sides of a rectilinear structure built up against the quarry face, and that he was now behind it, inside a cavity that the structure concealed. He turned to the left, towards the quarry face. The rest of the stone was natural, bedrock. Above him were large rectilinear cuttings, where blocks had been chiselled out. Below that he saw a narrow opening into a rock-cut chamber, its ceiling and the upper few feet of the sides visible. Inside he could see that it was filled with water, a black pool that glistened in his headlamp. He crawled over to the edge and peered in. It looked bottomless, like the cistern he had seen beyond the railing on the way into the Chapel of St Vartan.

There was just enough room to maneouvre, and he struggled on to his back, kicking off his boots and stripping off his clothes. He crawled back to the edge of the pool, his headlamp still on, and slipped into the water. It was icy cold, but felt instantly cleansing. For a moment he floated motionless on the surface, face down, eyes shut. Then he looked. Without a mask the image was blurry, and his eyes smarted with the cold. But the water was crystal clear, and he could see the beam from his headlamp dancing off rock, revealing walls and corners. He was floating above a deep cutting, at least four metres deep, rectilinear. He twisted sideways for more air, then put his face under again. As the beam swept down he saw a wide opening in the side of the chamber, cut into the rock in the direction of the quarry face. The opening was arched above and flat below, forming a shelf, wide enough for two to lie side by side. He ducked his head down and stared into the cutting, but was blinded by a dazzling sheen of light that reflected off the polished surface of the shelf. He remained there, staring into the speckly radiance, registering nothing, his mind frozen.

This was no water cistern.

He came up for air, then quickly looked down again. Out of nowhere he had an image of Elizabeth, then of Helena, and for a split second he thought he saw something, a trick of the light perhaps, a reflection of his own form floating over the edge of the shelf. He jerked his head upwards, gasping for air, and his headlamp slipped off, spiralling down out of reach through the water. He blinked hard, then looked down again. The shelf was lost in darkness, and all he could see was the bottom of the pool where the light had fallen, a blurry image of shadows and light. He took another breath, then arched his back and dived, pulling himself down with strong strokes, relishing the freedom of being underwater again, where he belonged.

Then he saw it.

A stone cylinder resting on the bottom, white, just like ones he had seen before, in an ancient library under a volcano, a library once owned by a Roman emperor who had come here to the Holy Land to seek salvation in the words of one who had dwelt beside the Sea of Galilee.

Then he realized.

Everett had found the tomb.

He reached down.

24

Jack crawled back to the entrance of the tunnel where he and Costas had removed the stone block, pushing his bag ahead of him. He dropped it on the floor of the chapel, then stretched his hands down and used them to walk himself out. He had still been dripping wet when he put his clothes back on, but he hardly noticed the cold and damp. All he could think about now was getting out and to safety. He looked around. The candles in the chapel were still lit, but there was nobody to be seen. 'Costas?' he said, his voice echoing back down the tunnel. 'Helena?' There was no reply. He squatted down, putting the strap of his bag over his neck. He shook his hair and wiped his face. Maybe they had gone back to the first chamber, to the Chapel of St Helena. He checked his watch.

Twenty minutes to go. He prayed that Morgan had made it. He clutched his bag. Whatever happened now, the world would know.

He got up and walked cautiously towards the chapel entrance, then out into the passageway. He wiped his face again with the back of his hand, and saw how grimy he was. Ahead of him was the grated door into the Chapel of St Helena, wide open. He could see the candlelight flickering over the central columns of the chapel, and in the gloom at the back the steps that led up to the Church of the Holy Sepulchre. He took a few steps forward, then stopped. Something was wrong. Then he heard a sound, out of place, metallic. *The sound of a gun cocking.* So this was it. He braced himself, his heart pounding. He had no choice now. There was only one way out. He walked slowly into the chapel.

'Dr Howard. We meet again.'

The voice was instantly familiar, with the hint of an east European accent. It was the voice of a man from another underground place two days before, a man Jack had only seen in shadow. He suddenly felt a cold grip in the pit of his stomach. *Helena had been right.* Jack said nothing, but made his way cautiously over the irregular stone floor, keeping his eyes averted from the candles to accustom them to the gloom. The figure stood in front of him, in the shadows again, beside the chapel altar and a statue of a woman holding a cross: St Helena. Jack stood still, his feet apart, glancing from side to side, trying to discern others in the darkness.

'Show them to me,' he snarled.

There was a pause, then a sound of fingers clicking, and someone in a dishevelled monk's robe was pushed forward, tripping and falling heavily on one elbow. It was Yereva, her face bruised and swollen. 'I didn't say anything, Helena,' she blurted out, peering into the darkness behind her. 'They followed me.' Then Jack saw the silencer of a pistol rammed into her neck, and she was yanked back into the shadows.

'You see, we knew where you were all along,' the man said to Jack, his face obscured. 'We have eyes and ears everywhere. Many willing brethren.' Jack saw him click his fingers again. Another figure was pushed out from the shadows, a bearded man wearing an episcopal robe, a bishop, clutching an ornate Armenian cross to his chest. Jack saw the silencer thrust out of the darkness towards the man, who looked imploringly at Jack, twisting sideways. Jack looked back towards the man in the shadows, and snorted. 'One of your willing brethren?' he said.

The bishop spoke rapidly in his own language, beseechingly. The man in the shadows turned on him, his voice low, vicious. He said something in Latin. The bishop stopped talking, stood rooted to the spot, then started shaking, weeping.

'You see?' the man said, turning to Jack. 'Everyone is willing, who serves our cause.'

'Show me them,' Jack snarled again.

The man spoke into the darkness to one side, in Italian. '*Pronto*,' he said. The fingers snapped again. There was a tussle, and a grunted exclamation. Costas was suddenly pushed into the candlelight, tripping and then standing upright, a strip of duct tape over his mouth and his hands tied behind his back. He was breathing stentoriously, sucking in the air through his blocked sinuses, his chest heaving. Jack could see a silencer behind his neck, and the dark outline of a figure behind. A man with his arm in a cast. Jack's mind was working overtime. *Their assailant in Rome.* Costas caught sight of Jack, his eyes wide, desperate.

'Take off the tape,' Jack snarled. 'He can't breathe.'

'He has nothing further to say,' the figure by the altar said. 'And nor do you.'

Jack suddenly knew, with cold certainty. This was no longer a sanctuary. It was an execution chamber. He glanced at his watch. Only ten minutes to go. He needed to string it out. 'I take it that little affray out in the streets was no coincidence,' he said. 'The knifings by the Wailing Wall, the curfew, the power cut.'

'It served our purpose,' the man said. 'And it has always been easy to infiltrate extremist groups, on both sides.'

'When we met before, you said you wanted an end to it.'

'I needed to convince you.'

'You told us the truth about the *concilium*, about Claudius and the last gospel.'

'I needed to convince you. Enough for you to carry on your quest, to bring us to this place. You have served our purpose well. From Narcissus we knew that Pliny had taken what Claudius gave him to Rome, and that Claudius had visited the tomb in London. The rest was your work. The Getty Villa, the nunnery at Santa Paula, here. It was not difficult to follow. Your young American colleague trusts his friends too much. Not that it need concern him now.'

'Jeremy.' Jack felt another cold jab in the pit of his stomach.

'He is alive. For the time being. As are your colleagues in Naples. Safe in the folds of our extended family.' The man nodded towards the shadowy figure behind Costas. 'When the time comes, it will be quick. A bullet in the head, another soul sent to hell. That has always been their way.'

'How did you know I wouldn't tell others? About the *concilium*?'

'Because you needed to keep it secret until you had found what we seek. I told you that others were searching for it, that you were in grave danger. And I was telling the truth. I saw through you, Dr Howard, when you were sitting in front of me in Rome, beside the tomb of St Paul. I took you into my confidence, and you thought you saw something sympathetic, something kindred. But you cannot escape the *concilium*. We will always prevail.'

'You mean *you* can't escape it,' Jack said, playing for time. 'You're wrong. *I* saw through you. You weren't just telling us the truth about the *concilium*, you were telling us what you really felt. You needed to confess, even though you were living a lie. You wanted to break free, but you didn't have the strength.'

'Blasphemy,' the man spat out, his voice quavering. 'I could never break my covenant. That is my strength.'

'Do you really think St Paul would have wanted all this?' Jack said.

'St Paul was our founder,' the man replied.

'Really?' Jack said. 'I thought it was Constantine the Great. You told us yourself. The *concilium* was re-created as his secret council of war.'

'He foresaw the battles we have had to fight, the sacrifices we have had to make. *In nomine patris et filii et spiritus sancti*. Our war is the war of all humanity. The devil is omnipresent.'

'Only in your mind,' Jack said. 'The *concilium* sought out dissent, and created fire. Self-fulfilling, and self-consuming.'

'I think not, Dr Howard,' the man said icily.

'You won't get far with these thugs as henchmen.'

'There are plenty more where he came from.' The man gestured into the shadows behind him. 'Our extended family, as I said.'

'Family? And how does your family treat their relatives? Elizabeth d' Agostino was a friend of mine.'

'Ah, Elizabeth. She was my pupil, I drew her in, but when the time came she lacked the strength to pledge the covenant. It is always honour that has ruled in her family, and we have always found that most convenient. Their honour was to serve us, and she betrayed them. We know she tried to warn you, when you were in Herculaneum. Even then she knew her fate.'

'What have you done to her?'

'The path will be cleansed. We will prevail.'

Jack felt anger well up inside him, but knew he had to keep his cool. 'If I were you, I'd be careful who I trust,' he said, his voice level. 'They're drug-runners now, not servants of the Lord. One day they'll come for you.'

'Blasphemy,' the man hissed again. 'They have been our faithful servants always. Nothing has changed, and nothing will change.'

'Wrong again,' Jack said. 'Others will seek you out, for what you have done. Once the world knows, the weight of your own history will destroy you.'

'Nobody will know. We never leave a trail.' The man gestured into the darkness beside him. 'There are eleven water cisterns dug deep into the rock below this place. You are already inside your own tomb.' He pulled a cell phone out of his pocket and held it up. 'When we are finished here, I will go outside and call Naples. By the end of today, your colleagues will all be gone. None of this will ever have happened.'

Jack glanced at his watch. *Two minutes*. 'The smell of death,' he said. 'You can't hide the smell of death.' He looked at Costas, who was suddenly staring at him, and seemed to have stopped breathing.

'Everything here smells of death,' the man sneered. 'Have you ever been to the Mount of Olives? That sickly-sweet smell is everywhere. And you won't be the first. From Pelagius onwards, others have brought their delusions here, and gone no further. We will not let blasphemy visit the tomb of Christ, our Lord.'

'You believe that? That he was buried here?' Jack said.

'This was the place of the resurrection. We know little of Jesus the man.'

'That's your trouble.'

'Enough of this,' the man said, his voice suddenly shrill. 'You will give us what you have found. It makes no difference whether your companions die now or over your dead body.' He clicked his fingers into the shadows, and Costas and Helena suddenly lurched out, the man with the silenced pistol behind them. 'Give it to me now, and the end will be quick.'

Jack took a deep breath, reached into his bag and felt around, deliberately smearing what he was searching for with the wet grime that was still on his hands from the tunnel. He pulled the object out, walked forward and placed it on the altar, beside the statue of the woman with the cross. He stepped back. Costas and Helena both stared at it, transfixed, but said nothing. It was the bronze cylinder from the tomb in London, the cylinder Claudius had put there. Jack had carried it with him to California and then to Jerusalem, convinced that somewhere along the line it still had a role to play. The man had stepped back into the shadows as Jack approached, but now reached over and snatched the cylinder, holding it at arm's length behind his shoulder, shielding himself from it. 'It is as it should be,' he whispered. 'The will of the *concilium* is done.'

Jack glanced at his watch. *Zero hour*. He pointed at the cylinder. 'You might want to check inside,' he said quietly.

'I will not gaze upon blasphemy,' the man said, his voice contorted. 'It is a falsehood, created by that fool Claudius. A falsehood that has deluded all who have sought it. I will burn it and crush it and throw it into your tomb. You can cherish your treasure in oblivion.' He clicked his fingers, and Costas was pushed towards a dark hole in the floor beside him, the barrel of the pistol in the nape of his neck.

Jack threw himself forward and held his hands up. 'Wait!' he exclaimed. 'There's something else you should see.' He reached towards the flap of his bag. The pistol swung abruptly towards his head. He stopped his hand in mid-air. 'It's just a computer.' Nobody moved, and there was silence. Jack cautiously withdrew a palm-sized laptop from his bag. The gun was still trained on him. He walked slowly back and set the laptop on the altar in front of the statue, flipping the lid open. He had already switched it on when he was fumbling in his bag. The screen showed the IMU logo, with a headline and three paragraphs of text beneath. 'I set up this page an hour ago, when we were on the roof of the Holy Sepulchre. We used Helena's wireless connection to e-mail it to our press agency contact here. Morgan has taken a disc with the full text in person to the agency. I wrote it during our flight from Los Angeles.' He tapped a key to enlarge the text. The banner headline was now splashed across the top of the screen:

THE LAST GOSPEL? LOST TOMB REVEALED

Jack turned to the man in the shadows. 'You see?' he said coldly, his temper barely in control. 'I too have friends. Willing brethren, as you would say. As we speak, this story is being syndicated around the world. I arranged for the press release at nineteen hundred hours, three minutes ago. The whole story. My name, your name. This place. Two thousand years of terrorism and murder. Everything you so helpfully told us about the *concilium*.'

The man said nothing, and then there was a sneering laugh. 'You don't even know my name.'

'Wrong again,' Jack replied. 'That's one thing Elizabeth did manage to say to me, Cardinal Ritter.'

The man twisted in rage and tripped backwards, scrabbling for the wall. At that moment there was a clatter and a blinding light from the stairway at the entrance to the chapel. Everything suddenly happened at once. Costas ducked forward, then swung his left shoulder back at the figure behind him, catching him in the stomach and sending him sprawling. There were shouts in Hebrew, and two uniformed figures advanced out of the light with M4 carbines trained ahead. One of them pulled the gag out of Costas' mouth and slashed his wrist tie. Costas sneezed violently, then lurched over to Jack, breathing hard. 'That came in handy,' he panted, nodding at the bronze cylinder. Helena stumbled over to help Costas.

Jack looked back to the light, and could see Ben standing guard at the entrance to the room, an Israeli police inspector and Morgan alongside. He reached out and held Costas by the shoulders. 'Thank Christ for that,' he said, suddenly exhausted. He gave Costas a tired smile, then gestured at the bronze cylinder. 'And now you know. I haven't become a treasure-hunter after all. I only loot artefacts if there's something bigger at stake.'

'Don't try to tell me you planned this back then,' Costas panted.

'Just a contingency. But sending Morgan to orchestrate the press release and find Ben was a big gamble.'

'A serious bit of time management.'

Jack jerked his head towards the dark opening of the cistern in the floor. 'I just thought something like this might happen.'

'So Elizabeth really told you his name?'

Jack shook his head, and paused. 'We only spoke for a few moments outside the villa in Herculaneum. Maybe she was about to tell me, or thought she'd be able to tell me later. Anyway, Jeremy and I worked through all the possibilities. Our man's mention of the Viking félag was the giveway, when he gave us his spiel under St Peter's. We've been head to head with this guy before. That narrowed it down.'

'I'm really sorry about Elizabeth, Jack.'

'We don't know anything yet for sure. I'm going to get Ben and the police to give this guy a going-over before we leave this place, though I doubt whether he'll spill anything.'

'His henchman might.'

Jack looked at the unconscious figure sprawled on the floor beside them, a policeman standing above him. 'God knows, he was probably related to her.'

Helena stood up, and put her arms around Jack. He could feel her shaking, but she was putting on a brave face. 'That was nicely choreographed. Not the Jack Howard I remember. Planning ahead was never your strong point. You always followed your nose.'

'That reminds me,' Costas said, sneezing again. 'Thanks for the bit about the smell of death. A nice little touch. I nearly threw up into that gag.'

'I thought you needed a little incentive.'

'Never mention that stuff again, Jack. Never.'

'Never,' Jack said solemnly.

Cardinal Ritter had been rooted to the spot beside the altar, a policeman guarding him. Suddenly there was a commotion as the gunman on the floor regained consciousness and grabbed the leg of the policeman guarding him, before being kicked back. The other policeman swung round instinctively, taking his eye off his charge for a second. In that moment of inattention the cardinal lunged forward and grabbed the bronze cylinder, then stumbled with it towards the entrance to the Chapel of St Vartan. 'I have it now,' he said. 'I will destroy it. You will never know what it contains.'

'Wrong again.' Jack reached into his bag, and carefully pulled out another cylinder, a marble one, the cylinder he had taken from the underwater chamber only twenty minutes before, from the place where Everett had hidden it in 1918. 'What you've got there is a bronze cylinder from a tomb in London. A very nice artefact, remarkable really. Probably late Iron Age. And it's empty, by the way.'

The cardinal snarled, and tore the lid off the cylinder, peering inside. He swayed, then seemed frozen to the spot. Jack passed the stone cylinder to Costas, caught his eye, then launched himself forward. In an instant he had the cardinal in a headlock, forcing his right arm behind his back and pushing it up until the man bellowed in pain. Jack was tempted to squeeze the headlock fractionally tighter, to jerk upwards, to hear the crack. But it was too easy, too quick, and there was an off-chance the police interrogation might work. He relented slightly, keeping the man's arm pinned with one hand, and took the bronze cylinder off him, placing it back beside the altar. Then he pushed the cardinal's arm up again until he whimpered in pain. Jack held him like a vice, and pressed himself close behind Ritter's left ear. He could smell the sweat, the fear.

'You see?' Jack whispered, steering the cardinal's head in the direction of the press release on the laptop screen, and then pushing his face close to the precious cylinder in Costas' hands. 'You of all people should know, Eminence. A preacher of the Holy Gospels. The power of the written word.'

25

The next morning they crammed into a four-wheel-drive Toyota, and Helena drove them up the great rift of the Jordan Valley from Jerusalem towards the Sea of Galilee. Costas and Jack were sitting beside Helena, and Morgan, Maria and Jeremy were in the back. Maria and Jeremy had joined them straight from Tel Aviv airport. Jack had called them immediately after coming out of the Holy Sepulchre the day before. He knew that much of his anxiety about their safety could now be dispelled, but it was still a huge relief to have them alongside. Hiebermeyer was another matter entirely. The world's press corps seemed to have converged on him in Naples, and he had refused to budge. Jack knew he would be relishing every moment, but it was also a way of deflecting press attention from their activities in Israel. They still had one final act to play out, a final folding-back of history to the event that had led them on one of the most extraordinary quests of Jack's career.

'Any word?' Costas said to Jack. His voice juddered as Helena slammed the vehicle over a patch of potholes.

'Nothing yet.' Jack had taken Jeremy aside the instant he arrived at their hotel in Jerusalem that morning. The news was not good. Elizabeth had vanished the evening after Jack had spoken to her, walked away from the site at Herculaneum and never returned. Jeremy's enquiries had been met with only shrugs and silence. 'But maybe that's Naples for you,' Jack said. 'And we hadn't spoken for fifteen years, since she left me. So I can hardly expect an instant pick-up.'

'I'll pray for her, Jack,' Helena said, fighting the wheel. 'But she may just have walked away. Sounds like she's done it before.'

'I had a strange vision in the tomb below the Holy Sepulchre, you know,' Jack said. 'I seemed to see her through the water, but it was a kind of odd composite, as if there were someone actually lying on the stone slab.'

'An Agamemnon moment?' Costas said.

'She'd always been on my mind, you know, over all those years,' Jack said. 'It was the way it ended between us. It never really did end, she just left. It all came welling up when I was holding Ritter down in the chapel yesterday. It was what he said, about bringing Elizabeth back into the fold. In that instant everything seemed to be his fault. I nearly broke his neck, you know. I could do it now.'

'At least he's out of the way.'

'For the time being. But he'll be back. He and his hench-man are only being held under the rules of the curfew, for carrying an open weapon and for assaulting a police officer. Kidnap would have been more serious, but the patriarch refused to press charges. That's why Ben's interrogation won't get anywhere. Ritter knows he'll be on a plane back to Rome within days. And all the press exposure, the naming of names, what I wrote in that article, that'll dissipate like leaves in the wind. Organizations like his have weathered this kind of thing before. He'll be quietly absorbed back.'

'With public awareness of the *concilium*, the law might be able to exert a stronger arm,' Maria said.

'Whose law, exactly?' Jeremy asked.

'And it depends how much people believe all this,' Costas said. 'I mean, you said it, Jack, big exposés about Church conspiracies quickly become yesterday's news, unless you can actually pin murder and corruption on them. And we're hardly the first to claim we've found some kind of lost gospel.'

'We haven't seen it yet,' Maria said, nudging Jack.

'Remember what Jack said to Ritter,' Helena said. 'The power of the written word. If we've truly got it, then people will believe.'

'Even if it rocks the foundations of the Church?' Maria asked.

'Freedom for people to choose their own spiritual path, without fear, guilt, persecution, the *concilium*,' Helena said.

That's why I'm here. If we've found something that will help people make that choice, then we'll have done some good.'

'I'll second that,' Morgan said from the back.

'We still have to find out what's in that cylinder,' Costas said. 'If Jack will let us.'

'Have patience,' Jack said.

'We're heading in this direction because of Pliny's note in the *Natural History*, right? The scroll we found in Herculaneum? That Claudius and his friend Herod visited Jesus on the Sea of Galilee?'

'Right.'

'No holes in the ground?'

'Well, I promised Massimo in Rome that you'd be back. There's a huge job opening up the entrance to the Vestals' chamber. Absolutely tons of sludge to clear out.'

'Jack.'

'Okay, no holes in the ground. This time.'

They passed signposts with names redolent of the rich history of the Holy Land: Jericho, Nablus, Nazareth. At the sign for the Sea of Galilee they veered left, past the resorts and thermal springs of modern Tiberias, then to the edge of the lake. They carried on a few miles further beneath the imposing flanks of Mount Arbel until they came to the entrance to Kibbutz Ginosar. The land around them was scorched, desiccated, and the shoreline of the lake had receded some distance over the mudflats to the east. Helena pulled into the kibbutz and they all got out, tired and hungry after the four-hour journey. Jack was wearing khaki shorts with a grey T-shirt and desert boots, and he had his trusty khaki bag slung over his side. Costas had on his usual garish selection of Hawaiian gear and the designer sunglasses Jeremy had given him, now seemingly a permanent fixture. Jeremy, Maria and Morgan were all dressed like Jack. The only one who seemed oblivious to the heat was Helena, who had on the Ethiopian white cassock she had been wearing when they first met her on the roof of the Holy Sepulchre the day before.

'This is the site of ancient Migdal, also called Magdala,' Jack said. 'Home of Mary Magdalene. This shore is where Jesus of Nazareth lived as a young man, where he worked as a carpenter and fisherman and went among the people of Galilee, spreading his word.'

After a quick lunch in the kibbutz canteen, they trooped into the Yigal Allon Museum and stood around its centrepiece exhibit, silently absorbing one of the most remarkable finds ever made in the Holy Land. It was an ancient boat, its timbers blackened with age but beautifully preserved, a little over eight metres long and two metres wide. Costas tipped up his sunglasses and leaned over the metal cradle that held it, inspecting one of the timbers. 'Polyethylene glycol?'

Jack nodded. 'It didn't take long to impregnate the timbers with PEG, as the boat was found in fresh water and there was no salt to leach out. It was the summer of 1986, a drought year like this one, and the level of the Sea of Galilee had dropped. Two local guys searching for ancient coins found these timbers sticking out of the mud, the prow facing towards the lake. It was clearly an ancient boat, and caused an immediate sensation. It was also a flashpoint. The Israeli Ministry of Tourism revelled in the possible Jesus connection, seeing a new magnet for tourism at a time when the intifada was putting people off visiting Israel. But some ultra-Orthodox Jews demonstrated against the excavation, seeing it as a green light for Christian missionary activity in the area. There were even people praying for rain so the site would be inundated and the excavation thwarted.'

'That sounds familiar,' Costas murmured.

'That's one reason I wanted you to see this, before we go out to our final destination,' Jack said. 'All of that nonsense is forgotten now. This boat's one of the star archaeological attractions of Israel, for Christians, for Jews, for all the people of Galilee, whatever their faith. It's their shared heritage.'

'The planks are edge-joined in the ancient fashion, with mortice-and-tenon,' Costas said.

'It's a unique find, the only Sea of Galilee boat to survive from antiquity,' Jack said, pointing out the features. 'It probably had a mast with a single brailed sail, with space for two oarsmen on either side and an oar that served as a quarter-rudder. It had a recurving stem and a pointed bow, with a cutwater. The wood's mainly oak for the frames and cedar for the strakes, cedar of Lebanon.'

'I've just realized why it looks familiar,' Maria murmured. 'Maurice showed me pictures of a boat about this size from the foreshore at Herculaneum, found in 1980 when they discovered all those skeletons huddled in the chambers below the sea wall. The gas and ash from the eruption flipped the boat over and carbonized it, but the interior face of the timbers was well preserved. It was immaculately built, maybe a pleasure boat for one of the rich villa-owners.'

'Maybe old Claudius snuck out on it, for a bit of fishing,' Costas said.

'There's a lot of recycled timber here, scraps cleverly reused,' Jack said. 'The Kinneret Boat may not have the finesse of the Herculaneum boat, but it has a lot of style. Whoever built and maintained it had an intimate feel for the Galilee area, for its resources and how to use them.'

'Any radiocarbon dates?' Costas asked.

'Forty BC, plus or minus eighty years.'

Costas whistled. 'Wide latitude, but pretty good odds. Jesus died around AD 30, right? Close to the end of that spectrum. But boats like this could have lasted for generations on the lake, repaired and refitted. Even a boat made at the beginning of that timeframe could still have been in use during his lifetime.'

'The only artefacts found associated with it were a simple cooking pot and an oil lamp, both probably from the same period.'

'So what about Claudius and Herod Agrippa?' Costas said. 'What date are we looking at for their visit?'

'I believe they came here in AD 23,' Jack said quietly. 'Jesus of Nazareth would have been in his mid twenties, maybe twenty-seven or twenty-eight. Claudius was thirty-two or thirty-three and Herod Agrippa was the same age, both born in 10 BC. A few years later Jesus went into the wilderness and renounced his worldly occupation, and the rest is history. Claudius must have returned to Rome soon after his visit here, and never came again. We know what happened to him. And Herod Agrippa went on to become King of the Jews.'

'How do you get the date?'

'Something I remembered in Jerusalem. Something that had been niggling me ever since we first saw those words in the lab on board *Seaquest II*, on Pliny's page from the *Natural History*. There's no reference anywhere else to Claudius travelling to the east. I'd guessed it must have happened when he was living in obscurity as a scholar in Rome, before he was dragged to the imperial throne in AD 41. It was obviously before Jesus was crucified, about AD 30, in the reign of Tiberius. It was also probably before Jesus was surrounded with disciples who would surely have remembered a visit from Rome, left some record of it in the Gospels.'

Helena cleared her throat. 'We have our tradition, in Ethiopia. That an emperor sought the Messiah.'

'If Herod Agrippa was king of Judaea, he might have visited Galilee then,' Costas said.

Jack shook his head. 'That was much later. It was Claudius who gave him Judaea in AD 41, as a reward for loyalty. Until then Herod Agrippa had lived mainly in Rome. No, I'm thinking of another time, years earlier. Herod Agrippa was grandson of Herod the Great, king of Judaea, but was brought up in Rome in the imperial palace, adopted by Claudius' mother Antonia. He and Claudius became the most unlikely of friends, the hard-living playboy and the crippled scholar.

One of Herod Agrippa's drinking buddies was the emperor Tiberius' son Drusus, who used to get drunk and pick fights with the Praetorian Guard. There was some murky incident one night, and Drusus died. Herod Agrippa was immediately packed off to Judaea. That's what I remembered. It happened in AD 23.'

'Bingo,' Costas said.

'It gets better. Herod Agrippa's uncle, Herod Antipas, was governor of Galilee at the time. He got his wayward nephew a token job as a market overseer, an *agoranomos*. Guess where? In Tiberias, on the shore of the Sea of Galilee a few miles south of here. We passed the site on the way.'

Costas whistled. 'So Herod Agrippa really could have crossed paths with Jesus.'

'Herod Agrippa would probably have got to know everyone worth knowing in Tiberias, pretty quickly,' Jack replied. 'He was a gregarious man, boisterous and charismatic, and would have spoken the local Aramaic as well as Latin and Greek. He would have felt a real affinity with the people here, his own people who he would one day rule. Perhaps he heard tavern talk of some local healer, someone who really did seem a step above the rest. Perhaps he sent word to Rome, to his crippled friend Claudius, who might still have harboured a youthful hope that a cure could be found, maybe somewhere in the east.'

'So we've got Herod Agrippa and Claudius and Jesus of Nazareth here in Galilee at the same time, in AD 23,' Costas said slowly. 'A meeting recorded nowhere else, only in the margin of an ancient scroll we found at the end of a lost tunnel three days ago in Herculaneum.'

'Correct.'

'Jesus was a carpenter,' Costas said thoughtfully, stroking the edge of the timber in front of him. 'That could mean boatbuilder, right?'

Jack nodded. 'In ancient Greek, as well as in the Semitic languages of the time, Aramaic, old Phoenician, the word we translate as "carpenter" could have a whole range of meanings. Architect, worker in wood, even builder in stone or metal. There would have been plenty of work like that around here. Herod Antipas founded Tiberias in AD 20, and there was a palace to build, the city walls. But you're right. The staple woodworking trade would have been boatbuilding. Later in the first century AD the historian Josephus wrote about the Sea of Galilee and said there were 230 boats on the lake, and that probably didn't include the smaller ones. Boats here would have lasted longer than on the Mediterranean, with no saltwater woodworms. But even so there would have been all the usual repair work as well as construction of new vessels. The twenties AD could have been a boom time for this as well, with a lot of scrap wood coming off the building sites at Tiberias. The hull in front of us has some odd-shaped timbers.'

Costas nodded, and put his hand on the edge of the timber in front of him, then looked at Jack. 'A lifetime ago, I think it was last Tuesday, we were diving on the shipwreck of St Paul, off Sicily. You told me then that the archaeology of early

Christianity is incredibly elusive, that hardly anything is known with certainty.' He paused. 'Now tell me this. I am touching a boat made by Jesus?'

Jack put his hands on the boat as well, scanned the ancient timbers and then looked over at Costas. 'In the New Testament, one problem is working out how Jesus regarded himself, whether or not he saw himself as the *Christos*, the Messiah. When he's asked, when people wonder who he is, he sometimes replies with a particular turn of phrase. It's in translation, of course, but I think this gets the gist of it. He says, "It is as you say."'

'What are you saying?'

'It is as you say.'

Costas was silent for a moment, looked at Jack imploringly, then sighed and took his hand off the boat. 'Archaeologists,' he grumbled. 'Can't get a straight answer out of any of them.'

Jack gave a tired smile, then gently patted his khaki bag. 'Come on. There's one final place we need to go.'

Half an hour later they stood on the edge of the mudflats on the western shore of the Sea of Galilee. It was now early evening, and the shadows had begun to steal up behind them and advance across the flats. In the distance the water still sparkled, and Jack remembered the strange pixillation he had sensed in the sky off Sicily the week before, as if his eyes were being drawn to the parts rather than the whole, the view too blinding to comprehend. Now, clutching his bag, he felt the same thrill of anticipation he had felt then, the knowledge that he was on the cusp of another extraordinary revelation, a promise that had brought them to the place where the treasure in Jack's hands had begun its journey almost two thousand years before. He knew with utter conviction that Claudius had stood at this spot, that he too had gazed at the distant shoreline of the Golan Heights, felt the allure of the east. He wondered whether Claudius had sensed the disquiet too, the lurking danger of this age-old faultline between east and west, known the calm of the sea was an illusion like the eye of a storm.

As Jack watched, the sun set lower behind them and the scene became coherent in his mind again, more like a painting by Turner than by Seurat, the sparkles smudging together into pastel hues of blue and orange. He took a deep breath, motioned to the others, and they began to pick their way on to the mudflats, through a tangle of twigs that had been blown up over the shoreline like tumbleweed.

'*Ziziphus spina-crista*, if I'm not mistaken,' Jeremy said. 'Christ-thorn. It has an excellent fruit. You should try it some time.'

'You sound just like Pliny the Elder,' Maria said.

They walked on, Jack in the lead, the rest forming a ragged line over the flats. Jeremy splashed through the puddles and caught up to Jack, out of earshot of the others. 'About Elizabeth, Jack. There's one thing I didn't mention.'

Jack kept on walking, but glanced at Jeremy. 'Go on.'

'Did you know she had a daughter?'

'A daughter?'

'She's at school in New York, and lives with two of Elizabeth's old friends, both university professors. Elizabeth didn't want her brought up in Naples, with her own family. She kept her daughter secret from almost everyone. One of the other superintendency people told me, a man who seems to have been close to Elizabeth. He was very emotional.'

'Does she know? The daughter, I mean?'

'Elizabeth's only been missing for two days, and she kept her daughter completely out of the loop about her life in Naples. But she tried to speak on the phone every few days. She'll soon know something's wrong.'

'Can you put me in touch with this man?' Jack said. 'Can I get the daughter's contact details?'

'I'm there already, Jack,' Jeremy said quietly. He passed over a slip of paper. 'He'll do it, but he said you should be the one.'

'Why would he suggest me?'

'He and Elizabeth had talked about you.'

They walked on in silence. Jack felt as if he were on a treadmill, the ground below his feet moving but the world around him stock-still, as if everything, the play he was in, were suddenly frozen in time, and only the path he could see in front of him had any significance. He began to speak, but caught his breath. When the words came out they sounded as if they came from another person.

'How old is she?'

'She's fifteen, Jack.'

Jack swallowed hard. 'Thanks for telling me,' he said quietly. Jeremy nodded, then stopped to join the others who were coming behind. Jack carried on walking, but his mind was fragmented, seeing images of Elizabeth over and over again, willing an anger that would not come, a rage against all the forces that had made this happen, against the man he had nearly killed the day before and all that he stood for. But instead all he could think about was the last fifteen years, and what he had done.

What he had missed.

After ten minutes skirting the shallow mudpools they came to a raised patch about a hundred yards in front of the shoreline. It was a fishermen's hard, a temporary landing area used during the drought, and was suffused with the odour of fish and old nets. In the centre a large rock lay deeply buried where it had been used as a mooring stone, a frayed old rope emerging from the mud in front and trailing off towards the shore. Jack pulled away some decayed netting and sat down, and the others did the same on two old railway sleepers which had clearly been dragged out for this purpose. Jack laid his bag on his lap, and they all looked out to sea, caught by the utter tranquillity of the scene. They watched as a man and a woman wandered languidly along the shoreline, the sheen of water on the mud making it look as if they were walking on water, like a mirage. Far away they could make out the fishing boats on the lake, the lights on their masts dotting the scene like a carpet of candles.

'This shoreline was where Jesus spent some of his formative years,' Helena said quietly. 'In the Gospels, his sayings abound with metaphors of fishing and the sea. When he spoke of the red evening sky presaging a fine day, he was not being a prophet, but a sailor and a fisherman, someone who knew that dust in the air meant a dry day to follow.'

'And people have come here to the Sea of Galilee seeking him ever since,' Jeremy murmured. 'Early Christians came after the conversion of the Roman Empire under Constantine the Great, the ones who created the Church of the Holy Sepulchre. Then pilgrims of the medieval world, from the British Isles, from the Holy Roman Empire, from Byzantium. Harald Hardrada was here, leading the Viking mercenaries of the Byzantine emperor's bodyguard, bathing in the river Jordan. Then the Crusaders, riding on a tide of blood, thinking they had found the kingdom of heaven, only to see it collapse before their eyes as the Arab armies rolled in from the east.'

'I bet this place hasn't changed much, though,' Costas said, skipping a pebble along a shallow pool, then eyeing Jack. 'Are you going to show us what you've got?' Jack nodded absently, then looked back to where he had been staring at the man and the woman walking off in the distance by the shoreline.

'Did you know Mark Twain was here?' Jeremy asked.

'Come again?' Costas said, turning to him.

'Mark Twain, the writer. In 1867, one of the first American tourists in the Holy Land.'

'I memorized his words,' Helena said. 'I read them last time I was here, and they made a real impression on me. "Night is the time to see Galilee, when the day is done, even the most unimpressible must yield to the dreamy influences of this tranquil starlight. In the lapping of the waves upon the beach, he hears the dip of ghostly oars; in the secret noises of the night he hears spirit voices; in the soft sweep of the breeze, the rush of invisible wings.'"

'There were others like him,' Jack said, clearing his throat and taking a deep breath. He was still reeling from Jeremy's news, and had been unable to suppress the bleakness he felt about Elizabeth's disappearance, a feeling of culpability he knew was irrational. What had happened to her had been set in train the day she was born. He had seen it in her eyes when they were together all those years ago, only he had seen it then as something else. And yet, as he had watched the shoreline, the boats on the horizon, he had suddenly felt the weight lifted from him, a sense of peace he had never known before. Part of him seemed to accept Jeremy's news as if he had known it all along. He wiped his hand over his eyes, then looked at Costas, who had been watching him closely. He clutched the slip of paper from Jeremy tight in his hand. In the face of despair, there was huge yearning, and an overwhelming responsibility. And he still had to hope that Elizabeth was alive after all, that they had stopped Ritter and his henchmen in time.

'There were others who believed the stories in the Bible were not just allegory and fable,' Jack said. 'It was the time when archaeology came of age, when Heinrich Schliemann and Arthur Evans proved the reality of the Trojan Wars and the Greek Bronze Age. Ten years after Mark Twain, Lieutenant Horatio Kitchener, Royal Engineers, cut his teeth in Galilee with the Survey of Palestine, before becoming Britain's greatest war leader. And then T. E. Lawrence came here studying Crusader castles, before returning as Lawrence of Arabia, leading the Arab legion over those hills towards Damascus. Great movements of history sweep past this place, and the biggest fracture line between the eastern and western worlds runs through here along the Jordan valley. But Galilee has so often been an eddy pool of history, a place where the individual can stand out.'

'People who came here with the future ahead of them, on the cusp of greatness,' Maria murmured.

Jack reached into his pocket and pulled out a small snap-lid box. He opened it and took out two coins. He held them up, one in each hand, letting the fading sunlight catch the portraits, the features accentuated by shadow as he slowly moved them from side to side.

'It looks to me as if you've been borrowing again, Jack,' Costas said quietly, still peering intently at his friend. 'It's a slippery slope to becoming a treasure-hunter, you know. I always wondered when you'd cross the line.'

Jack flashed him a smile, but kept silent, staring at the faces on the coins. He had needed to view them one last time, to reach out and touch them before opening up his bag and revealing what they had all come here to see. The coin on the left was a tetradrachm of Herod Agrippa, the one that Helena and Yereva had found in the Church of the Holy Sepulchre. The portrait was worn, but it showed a thick-set, bullish face, the image of a fighter more than a thinker, but with large, sensitive eyes. It was idealized in the eastern tradition, a Hercules or an Alexander more than Herod Agrippa. He wore a laurel diadem, normally only seen on coins of Roman emperors. The man on the other coin was wearing a diadem too, but this time rightly so. It was the sestertius of Claudius they had found in Herculaneum. Jack saw Claudius as he had imagined him sitting at his table in the villa, working with Narcissus and Pliny on his history of Britain, then standing before the tomb under London. He saw the full head of hair, the high forehead, the eyes set back and thoughtful, the pursed mouth. Not Claudius the cripple, not Claudius the fool, but Claudius the emperor at the height of his powers, an emperor who built aqueducts and harbours and brought the Roman world back from the brink of catastrophe, paving the way for the Christian west in centuries to come. Both coins showed men who had reached the pinnacle of their lives, a future they could scarcely have foreseen that day in AD 23 when they came here together as young men, beside the Sea of Galilee. Herod Agrippa, prince of the East. Claudius the god.

'I wonder if they sensed the darkness ahead,' Helena murmured.

'What do you mean?' Costas said.

Jack put away the coins, slipped the box back into his pocket, and then took out a swaddled package from his bag. The others watched him intently. 'Herod Agrippa came from one of the most volatile dynasties of the east, and had grown up in Rome,' he said. 'He knew all about the fickle nature of power. Claudius was intimate with that too, and was also a historian. Even as early as AD 23 he would have seen the seeds of decay in the reign of Tiberius. And the one they met here, the fisherman from Nazareth, may have lived his life in Galilee away from the momentous events of history, but he may have known what lay ahead. When Claudius made his final visit to Britain to hide his treasure, he was doing it to last beyond Rome. And when Everett came to Jerusalem in 1917, he was doing the same. His world was one of terrible darkness, closer to apocalypse than Claudius could ever have imagined. And both men knew how the fickle winds of history might snatch away their prize.'

Jack removed the bubblewrap from the object in his hands and revealed a small stone cylinder. There was a murmur of excitement from the others, and both Helena and Morgan held their hands together as if in prayer. Jack held the cylinder out for Helena. 'Will you break the seal?'

Helena made the sign of the cross and took the cylinder from Jack's hands. Slowly, carefully, she twisted the lid. It came away easily, breaking the blackened resinous material that had sealed the join. She handed it back to Jack, who finished removing the lid. The others crowded round, Maria and Jeremy kneeling in front and Costas and Morgan peering over Jack's shoulder. There was another gasp as they saw what was inside. It was a scroll, brown with age but apparently intact, still wound round a wooden rod.

'The cylinder was airtight,' Jack breathed. 'Thank God for that.' He reached in and held the edge of the scroll between two fingers, gently feeling it. 'It's still supple. There's some kind of preservative on it, a waxy material.'

'Clever old Claudius,' Maria murmured.

'Clever old Pliny, you mean,' Jeremy said. 'I bet that's who Claudius learned it from.'

They were silent, and all Jack could hear was a distant knocking sound, and a faint whisper of breeze from the west. He held his breath. He drew out the scroll, and put the cylinder on his lap. There was no writing to be seen, just the brown surface of the papyrus. He held the scroll up so it was caught in the remaining sunlight that shone over the hills behind them. Carefully, without a word, he unrolled a few centimetres, peering closely at the surface as it was revealed.

'Well I'll be damned,' he murmured.

'Got something?' Costas said.

'Look at the cross-layering, where the strips of papyrus have been laid. You can see it where the light shines through. This is first-grade paper, exactly the same as the papyrus sheet we found on Claudius' desk in Herculaneum. And there it is.' His voice was hushed. 'I can see it.'

'What?'

'Writing. There. Look.' Jack slowly unrolled the papyrus. First one line was revealed, then another. He unravelled the entire scroll, and they could see about twenty lines. Jack's heart was racing. The ink was black, almost jet-black, sealed in by the preservative wax. The writing was continuous, without word breaks or punctuation, in the ancient fashion. 'It's Greek,' he whispered. 'It's written in Greek.'

'There's a cross beside the first word,' Jeremy exclaimed. 'You see that in medieval religious manuscripts too.'

'There's some scrubbed-out writing underneath it, older writing,' Costas said, squinting at the paper from behind Jack. 'Just the first few lines. You can barely make it out, but it looks like a different hand, a different script.'

'Probably some older writing by Claudius,' Jack murmured. 'If so, it'd be in Latin. Maybe something he'd started then erased, notes he'd made on the journey out to Judaea. That'd be fascinating. We don't have anything yet in Claudius' own handwriting.'

'Mass spectrometry,' Costas said. 'That'd sort it out. Hard science.'

Jack was not listening. He had read the first lines of the visible text, the lines that overlaid the scrubbed-out words. He felt light headed, and the scroll seemed to waver in his hands, whether from his own extraordinary emotion or from a waft of breeze he could not tell. He let his hands slowly drop, and held the scroll open over his knees. He turned to Helena. '*Kyriakon*,' he said. 'Am I correct in using the literal translation, House of the Lord?'

Helena nodded. 'It could mean congregation as a whole, Church in the broad sense.'

'And *naos*? The Greek word for temple?'

'Probably used to mean church as a physical entity, as a structure.'

'Are you ready for this?'

'If these are his words, Jack, then I have nothing to fear.'

'No, you do not.' Jack paused, and for an extraordinary moment he felt as if he were looking down from a great height, not at their gathering on the mudflat but at a pinprick of light on a vast sea, on two shadowy forms hunched across from each other in a little boat, barely discernible in the darkness. He closed his eyes, then looked at the scroll and began to translate.

'"Jesus, son of Joseph of Nazareth, these are his words . . ."'

Epilogue

Summer AD 23

The eager young man in the white tunic stopped, and sniffed the breeze. He had never been to the east before, and the sights and smells of the last few days had been strange, startling. But now the breeze that wafted over the hills from the west came from the Mediterranean Sea, bringing with it the familiar smell of salt and herbs and faint decay, a smell which had been purged the day before by a sharp wind from the heights of Gaulantis on the opposite shore. He looked again, shielding his eyes against the glare. The mudflats extended far out to the edge of the lake, a wide shimmering foreshore where the water had evaporated in the long dry summer. The distant surface of the lake was glassy smooth, like a mirror. On the edge he spied a wavering shape, a fishing boat perhaps, with movement around it. He listened, and heard the far-off screech of a gull, then a tinkering sound, a distant knocking like rainwater dripping off a roof. It was becoming hot, suddenly too hot to keep up the pace he had set for himself. He turned towards the mountain they called Arbel, raised his face and yearned for that breeze again, for the cool air from the west to waft over and envelop him.

'Claudius!' It was a girl's voice. 'Slow down! You need water.'

He turned awkwardly, dragging his bad leg behind him, and waited for his companions to catch up. It was only ten days since they had landed at Caesarea on the coast, and five days since they had set off from Jerusalem, up the valley of the river Jordan to the inland sea they called Gennesareth, in the land of Galilee. They had spent the night in the new town of Tiberias, built by Herod's uncle Antipas and named after Claudius' own uncle Tiberius, emperor in Rome now for almost ten years. Claudius had been astonished to find images of Tiberius everywhere in Judaea, in temples and statues and on coins, as if the living emperor were already worshipped as a god. It seemed to Claudius that he could never escape them, his benighted family, but that morning as they had walked away from the bustle of construction in the town he had felt an extraordinary contentment, a sense of liberation in the simplicity of the coastal flats and the shimmering shore of the lake with the hills of Gaulantis beyond.

Afterwards, after this day, they planned to go over those hills to Antioch, to give offerings at the place where his beloved brother Germanicus had been poisoned four years before. Claudius still felt the pain, the stab of anguish in the pit of his stomach. He tried to push it away, and turned to watch as those dearest to him came up the dusty road from the south. His beloved Calpurnia, with her flaming red hair and freckled skin, not yet out of her teens but as sensuous a woman as he had ever beheld. She was wearing the red of her profession, the oldest one, but now only out of habit, not necessity. And beside her Cypros, wife of Herod, veiled and bejewelled as befitted a princess of Arabia, gliding along like a goddess beside her wild-haired companion. And striding behind them was Herod himself, black bearded, his long hair braided like an ancient king of Assyria, his cloak hemmed with real Tyrean purple, his big, booming voice regaling them with songs and bawdy jokes all the way. Herod always seemed larger than life, always the centre of attention, yet he was Claudius' oldest and dearest companion, the only one among all the boys in the palace who had befriended him, who had seen past the stutter and the awkwardness and the withered limb.

Claudius took the skin of water offered to him by Calpurnia, and drained it. Herod pointed towards the distant speckle of movement on the shoreline, and they left the road and began to pick their way across the mudflats. Claudius had seen the tower of Migdal, the next town along the coast in a hollow in the hills, but now it was lost in the haze that rose up and obscured the shoreline like a shimmering veil.

Then the sun broke through and reflected off a myriad shallow pools across the flats. To Claudius the view seemed to fragment, like a shattering pane of glass, the sunlight reflecting blindingly off each pool, and then regain its whole again in the haze. A hint of a rainbow hung in the air, a suspension of colour that never quite materialized, that stayed just beyond reality. Soon all he could see was the movement around the boat ahead of them, and even that seemed to waver and recede as they walked further on. Claudius wondered if it was real after all, or a mere trick of the eye, like one of the phantasms that Herod said he had seen in the desert, a reflection of some distant, unattainable reality.

Herod strode up and pushed him playfully, his voice big, booming, his breath smelling of last night's wine. 'Do you remember the Aramaic I taught you in Rome, when we were boys?'

'My dear Herod. How could I forget? And these past years while you've been playing the rogue, I've been teaching myself Phoenician. I'm planning a history of Carthage, you know. You just can't get by without reading the original sources. I don't trust anything a Roman historian has to say about barbarians.'

'We're not barbarians, Claudius. It's the other way round.' Herod pushed Claudius again, almost toppling him off balance but catching him just in time, with his usual tenderness. 'Anyway, I don't trust Romans, period. With one noble exception, of course.' He shouldered Claudius again, then embraced him to stop him from falling, and they both laughed.

'Does he speak Greek, this man?' Claudius asked.

'Yes.'

'Then let it be Greek, not Aramaic. My dear Calpurnia is a real barbarian, you know. Her grandparents were brought as slaves by my great-uncle Julius from Britannia. A fascinating place. Calpurnia tells me such amazing things. One d-day I will go there. I believe the Phoenicians reached those shores, but I do not believe they left the Britons any knowledge of their language.'

'Very well then, my dear Claudius. For your lovely Calpurnia. Greek it is.'

They came closer to the shoreline. Claudius was walking ahead again, and could now see that the boat was real, not a mirage, and was drawn up a few yards from the edge of the water. It was a good-sized boat, with an incurving stem and a single high mast, a bit like the one Claudius had sailed on the Bay of Naples as a boy and still kept in its shed at Herculaneum. He looked more closely. Under an awning behind the stern sat a woman, heavy with child, working at something on her lap. Beside the hull were loose pieces of wood, fragments of old boats, and a plank with a careful arrangement of tools, a handsaw, a bow drill, chisels, a basket of nails. Claudius realized that this was the origin of the tinkering sound he had heard. Then the carpenter came round from the other side, holding a plane. He was lean, muscular, wearing only a loincloth, his skin a deep bronze, with crudely shorn black hair and a full beard, just as Herod had looked when he came back from a hard season's campaigning. Claudius hobbled up to the boat, keeping his eyes on the man. He could have been one of the gladiators in Rome, or one of the escaped slaves from the marble quarries who Claudius had befriended in the Phlegraean Fields near Naples, where his mother had tried to abandon him but where he had been taken in, befriended by outcasts and others afflicted as he was.

'I am C-Claudius,' he said in Greek, clearing his throat. 'My friend H-Herod has brought me here from Rome, to seek your help. I am ailing.'

The woman smiled up at Claudius, then looked down and carried on with her work, mending the cotton strands of a fishing net. The man gazed at Claudius full in the face. His eyes were intense, luminous, like nothing Claudius had seen before. The man held his gaze in silence for a few moments, then looked down and pushed his plane forward and backward, carrying on working the wood. 'You are not ailing, Claudius.' His voice was deep, sonorous, and the Greek was accented in the same way as Herod's.

Claudius made as if to reply, then stopped. He was dumbfounded, could think of nothing to say. The words when they came were stumbling, inconsequential, instantly regrettable. 'You are from these parts?'

'Mary is from Migdal,' the man said. 'I was born in Nazareth, in lower Galilee, but came here to this lake as a youth. These are my people, and this is my vessel.'

'You are a boatwright? A fisherman?'

'This sea is my vessel, and the people of Galilee are my passengers. And we are all fishermen here. You can join us, if you like.'

Claudius caught the man's gaze again, and found himself nodding, and then looked back and gestured at the others. Herod bounded up, the mud spattering against his bare shins, and embraced the Nazarene in the eastern fashion, murmuring greetings in Aramaic before turning to Claudius. 'When Joshua comes with me to Tiberias for an evening in the taverns we call him Jesus, the Greek version of his name. It trips off the tongue more readily, especially after a few jars of Galilean.' He guffawed, slapped the Nazarene on the back and then knelt down beside Mary, gently putting his hand on her belly. 'All goes well?' he said in Aramaic. She murmured, smiling. He leapt back up, then caught sight of someone on the shoreline towards Migdal, a distant figure waving, then loping on. Claudius followed Herod's gaze, and saw a man with black skin, tall and slender, wearing a white robe, carrying a stringer of fish.

'Aha!' Herod guffawed, slapping the man again. 'You have a Nubian slave!'

'He is Ethiopian, from a place called Aksum,' the man replied. 'He is a free man. And he is a good listener.'

'Everyone listens to you, Joshua. You should be a king!'

The Nazarene smiled, then raised his hand in greeting to Calpurnia and Cypros as they came walking towards him across the mud, barefoot. He passed beside them wordlessly and heaved over a crude stone anchor which had been mooring the boat, then detached a thick hemp rope which had been looped through a hole in the centre of the stone. Herod and Calpurnia and Cypros placed the baskets they had been carrying in the boat, and Mary made as if to lift a pitcher beside her, but the Nazarene quickly took it off her and placed his hand on her belly, smiling. He coiled the anchor rope and tossed it over the sternpost, then braced himself against the stern and heaved, every muscle in his body taut and bulging. As Claudius watched him work, the Nazarene seemed like the bronze statues of Hercules and athletes he had seen in the villa of his friend Piso below Vesuvius. The keel slid along the mudflat until it was half in the waves, and the Nazarene stood back, glistening with sweat, while the others splashed past him and clambered on board. Claudius came last, awkwardly pulling his leg up and over. A few more heaves and the boat was afloat, and the Nazarene quickly leapt up over the gunwale and released the square sail from its yard, while Mary sat by the tiller oar.

Claudius and Herod sat side by side in the middle of the boat, each with an oar, and began to pull in unison as the wind took the sail and pushed the boat beyond the shallows. The hull and the rigging creaked, the water gurgled and crackled under the bow. Claudius relished the exercise, his face flushed and shining. If only he had been allowed into the gymnasium in Rome before the palsy took hold, then he might have led the legions in Germania just like his beloved brother. But now, in this boat, as they slipped further offshore, until the line of the coast was all but lost in the haze, the pain and unhappiness that had begun to cloud his life seemed to slide away, and for the first time he felt whole, no longer battling against himself and others, those who would rather have seen him never return when he was pushed towards the mouth of the underworld as a frightened little boy.

They drifted for hours, blown along by wafts of breeze, talking and dozing in the shade under the sail. The Nazarene cast his net, and caught only a few fish, but enough for him to cook in a pot over a small brazier. 'Oh prince of fishermen,' Herod had joked, 'you tell us your kingdom is like a net that is thrown into the sea and catches fish of every kind. Well, it looks as if you have a pretty small kingdom.' He guffawed, and the Nazarene smiled, and continued to prepare the food. Later, Mary played the lyre, making music that seemed to shimmer and ripple like the surface of the lake, and Calpurnia sang the haunting, mystical songs of her people. They ate the food they had brought with them, bread, olives, walnuts, figs, and a fruit Claudius had never eaten before, produced by the thorn tree, all washed down with pure water from the springs of Tiberias. Afterwards they played dice, and arm-wrestled across a loose plank, and Calpurnia made diadems for them out of the twigs of the thorn tree, solemnly crowning Herod a king and Claudius a god. Herod kept them entertained with a stream of stories and jokes, until his thoughts began to turn to the evening. 'They say you can work miracles, Joshua son of Joseph,' he said. 'But you can't turn water into wine, can you?' He guffawed again, then scooped up a handful of water from the lake and splashed it over the man's head. The Nazarene laughed along with him, and the two men jostled playfully, rocking the boat from side to side. 'Anyway,' Herod said, sitting back. 'We can't stay out here much longer. I'll die of thirst. Anyone for the taverns?'

Dusk was colouring the sky red an hour later when Claudius again pulled the oar, this time sitting alongside the Nazarene. They had landed, and Herod had set out on the road back to Tiberias, eager to seek out the young bloods in the officers' mess for an evening's cavorting. The three women had gone back to Migdal, to Mary's home. But Claudius had wanted to stay on with the Nazarene, to make this day last for ever, to ask more. He had offered to help the Nazarene set his seine net, a few hundred yards offshore from the mudflat where they had first set out.

The Nazarene rowed silently alongside him. Then he stopped, and gazed at the deep red sky where the sun had set, the colour of spilt blood. 'The weather will be fine tomorrow,' he said. 'The net will be safe here overnight. Then, tomorrow, it will be time for the autumn sowing of the fields. The autumn wind will blow up from the west, bringing heavy downpours, coming over the Judaean hills and cleansing the land. The Sea of Galilee will once again be filled, and where we once stood there will be water.'

'Herod says you are a prophet,' Claudius said.

'It does me good to see Herod,' the Nazarene replied. 'I have that same fire within me.'

'Herod says you are a scribe, a priest. He says you are a prince of the house of David.'

'I minister to the *ha'aretz*, the people of this land,' he said. 'But I am no priest.'

'You are a healer.'

'The lame and the blind shall walk the farthest and see the most, because it is they who yearn most to walk, and to see.'

'But who are you?'

'It is as you say.'

Claudius sighed. 'You speak in parables, but where I come from our prophets are oracles of the gods, and they speak in riddles. I go to the Sibyl, you know, in Cumae. Herod thinks she's an old witch, but I still go there. He doesn't understand how much better it makes me feel.' Claudius paused, self-conscious. 'Virgil also went there. He was our greatest poet.' He closed his eyes, declaiming from memory, translating the Latin verse into Greek:

'"Now is come the last age of Cumaean song;
The great line of the centuries begins anew.
Now the Virgin returns, the reign of Saturn returns,
Now a new race descends from heaven on high.
Only do you, pure Lucina, smile on the birth of the child,
Under whom the iron brood shall at last cease
And a Golden Age spring up throughout the world!"'

The Nazarene listened intently, then put his hand on Claudius' shoulder. 'Come on. Help me with my net.'

'Have you ever seen Rome?' Claudius said. 'All the wonders of human creation are there.'

'Those are things that stand in the way of the kingdom of heaven,' the Nazarene replied.

Claudius thought for a moment, then picked up a chisel with one hand, the edge of the net with the other. 'Would you renounce these?'

The Nazarene smiled, then touched Claudius again. 'Let me tell you,' he said, 'about my ministry.'

Half an hour later it was almost dark, and the boat had gently grounded on the foreshore a few miles from where they had set out. The burning torches of Migdal and Tiberias twinkled from the shore, and other faint lights bobbed offshore. The Nazarene took a pair of pottery oil lamps from a box beside the mast step, filled them with olive oil left over from their lunch and deftly lit the wicks with a flint and iron. The lamps spluttered to life, then began to burn strongly, the flames golden and smokeless. He placed them on a little shelf on the mast step and then turned to Claudius.

'Your poet, Virgil,' he said. 'Can I read his books?'

'I'll ask Herod to bring them to you. He's supposed to be at Tiberias for the rest of the year, banished from Rome. Maybe he'll even do a translation for you himself. It might keep him out of trouble for a while.'

Claudius dropped the dice he had been carrying, his habit for years now. Before reaching down he shut his eyes tight, unwilling to see the numbers, the augury. The Nazarene picked them up, placed them in the palm of Claudius' hand, closed his hands around them. For a moment they remained like that, then he let go. Claudius opened his eyes, laughed, then tossed the dice overboard, not looking. 'In return for Virgil, you must do one thing,' he said. 'You must write down what you have just told me. Your *euangelion*, your gospel.'

'But my people do not read. Mine is a ministry of the spoken word. The written word stands in the way of the kingdom of heaven.'

Claudius shook his head. 'If your kingdom of heaven is truly of this earth, then it will be subject to violence, and violent men will maltreat it. In thanks for this day, I will do all I can to ensure that your written word remains safe and secret, ready for the time when the memory of your spoken word has become the word of others, shaped and changed by them into something else.'

There was a silence, then the Nazarene spoke. 'You have paper?'

'Always,' Claudius said, reaching for the slim satchel he kept slung over his back. 'I write down everything, you know. I have one last sheet of first-grade, and some scraps. I had the first-grade made to my special instructions in Rome. It's the best there is. You'll see. Lasts for ever. I used up my gall ink on the voyage here, but I picked up some concoction that passes as ink in Tiberias.'

The Nazarene lifted up the board he had used to chop fish, cleaned it over the side and then dried it on a twist of his loincloth. He placed the board on his knees, then took the sheet of papyrus and the reed pen that Claudius offered him.

Claudius opened a small pot with a wooden lid and held it out, and the Nazarene dipped the pen in the ink. He held the pen in his right hand over the upper left corner of the papyrus, poised for a moment, motionless.

'The Sibyl writes her prophecies on leaves of oak.' Claudius chuckled. 'When you reach out for them, the wind always blows them away. Herod says it's some demonic Greek machine, hidden in the cave.'

The Nazarene looked Claudius full in the face, then began to write, a bold, decisive hand, slow and deliberate, the hand of one who had been taught well but did not write often. He dipped the pen into the ink every few words, and Claudius concentrated on keeping the pot steady. After the Nazarene had started the fourth line, Claudius stared at the script, and then blurted out, spilling the ink on his hand, 'You're writing in Aramaic!'

The Nazarene looked up. 'It is my language.'

'No.' Claudius shook his head emphatically. 'No one in Rome reads Aramaic.'

'I write these words for my people, not for the people of Rome.'

'No.' Claudius shook his head again. 'Your word here, in Galilee, is the spoken word. You said it yourself. Your fishermen do not read, and have no need of this. Your written word must be read and understood far beyond the Sea of Galilee. If you write in riddles, in a tongue few understand, your word will be no clearer than the utterances of the Sibyl. You must write in Greek.'

'Then you must do it for me. I speak Greek, but I do not write it.'

'Very well.' Claudius took the board with the paper and pen, and handed the ink pot over. 'We must start again.' He fumbled in his satchel, thought for a moment, then reached across and took a cut lemon from the fruit bowl. He squeezed the lemon over the writing, then rubbed it vigorously with a cloth from his bag. He held the paper up to catch the last rays of the setting sun, and saw the faded imprint of the Nazarene's writing as he waited for the lemon juice to dry. A breeze wafted over them, making the paper flutter, and Claudius quickly took it down and pressed it against the board on his knees. He dipped the pen in the ink and tested the paper, inscribing a cross mark as he always did at the start of a document, to see whether the ink would spread. It had better not. The paper was his own first-grade. He grunted, then wrote a few words across the top, in the careful hand of a scholar conscious that his writing was usually legible only to himself.

'I am speaking Greek to you now, but I speak my gospel to my people in Aramaic,' the Nazarene said. 'You must help me to find the words in Greek for what I have to say.'

'I am ready.'

An hour later the two men sat motionless opposite each other in the boat, a silhouette that was growing darker in the moonless sky, and would soon be no more. The lamps spluttered between them, then one went out. The Nazarene shifted along the plank he was sitting on towards one side of the boat, then put his hand on the space beside him.

'We must pull the oars together.'

Claudius looked up from the paper, and smiled. 'I should like nothing better.' He looked down one last time, scarcely able to see now, and read the final words the Nazarene had spoken, that Claudius had translated:

The kingdom of heaven is on earth.
Men shall not stand in the way of the word of God.
And the kingdom of heaven shall be the house of the Lord.
There shall be no priests.
And there shall be no temples . . .

Author's Note

According to the ancient sources, the Roman emperor Claudius died in AD 54, probably by poison. He was succeeded by Nero, who ruled until AD 68, and then by Vespasian, who ruled until AD 79, the year that Vesuvius erupted and buried the towns of Herculaneum and Pompeii. The idea that Claudius should have faked his own death, disappeared with his freedman Narcissus and survived in secret for all those years is fictitious, though in keeping with what can be surmised of his character. Claudius had been a famously reluctant emperor, sidelined for years because of a crippling condition, probably a form of palsy, and then dragged from behind a curtain to assume the royal purple in AD 41 when he was already well into middle age. He learned to accommodate himself to the role, and achieved much as emperor – public reforms, practical building projects, the invasion of Britain – but by the end had been worn down by corruption and a succession of scheming wives. He may have looked back wistfully to his earlier life as a scholar, to his histories of Rome, of the Etruscans, of Carthage – all now lost – and yearned for the same again, perhaps with a plan to write a history of Britain; he himself had visited Britain in the aftermath of the invasion, in AD 43. Had he survived, he would have mourned Calpurnia, his mistress probably also poisoned in AD 54, but he could have been driven on by the need to complete his account of his British triumph and maintain the family honour of his revered brother Germanicus and father Drusus – a reverence seen in the commemorative inscription on the coin in this book, a genuine issue of Claudius from the beginning of his reign.

Narcissus was Claudius' freedman secretary, his *ab epistulis*. He reputedly amassed a huge personal fortune as only Imperial freedmen could do, with dealings in Gaul and Britain. He appears to have served his own interests, and sometimes Claudius' wives' interests, more so than he did those of his master, yet there was evidently a transcending bond that kept Narcissus in Claudius' employ after the emperor must have been aware of his nefarious activities. It is not known whether Narcissus was a eunuch, though Claudius had several eunuchs at his court – one was his taster – or whether Narcissus had Christian affiliations, though it is possible. According to the sources, Narcissus' reputation was such that he was forced to commit suicide after Claudius' death, so my fictitious escape route would have been an attractive lifeline.

Pliny the Elder – the most famous encyclopedist from antiquity – was a young army officer on the German frontier when Claudius was emperor, and it is quite likely that the two men met. Before the end of Claudius' reign Pliny had already written a history of the wars against the Germans, the lost *Bella Germaniae*, the result, his nephew claimed, of a vision his uncle had of Claudius' father Drusus (Pliny the Younger, *Letters* iii, 5, 4). As a veteran Pliny would have cherished the memory of Drusus and Germanicus, and his mentions of Claudius in the *Natural History* are respectful, almost familiar, and rarely refer to him by the official designation *Divus*, which Claudius would have scorned. The *Natural History* was dedicated to the Emperor Titus, who had succeeded his father Vespasian on 23 June AD 79, so was completed only a short time before Pliny's own death in the eruption of Vesuvius on 24 August that year. It is entirely consistent with Pliny that he should already have been at work on additions to his great work; Pliny the Younger inherited 160 notebooks from his uncle, 'written in a minute hand on both sides of the page'. He had watched from Misenum as his uncle departed by galley towards Herculaneum on that fateful day of the eruption, and was told of his final hours (*Letters* vi, 16).

Herod Agrippa, grandson of King Herod the Great of Judaea, is the King Herod of *Acts of the Apostles*; his formal name was Marcus Julius Agrippa, and his coins refer to him as Agrippa. He and Claudius were the same age, born in 10 BC, and were brought up in the same household after Herod Agrippa was adopted by Claudius' mother Antonia. Whether or not Claudius visited Judaea and the Sea of Galilee as a young man is unknown, though little is certain about his life at this time, just as little is known of Jesus of Nazareth during his years in Galilee. What is recorded is that Herod Agrippa was appointed *agoranomos* at Tiberias on the Sea of Galilee (Josephus, *Jewish Antiquities* xviii, 147–50). The appointment was on the instigation of his wife Cypros, and occurred after the sudden death in AD 23 of his companion Drusus, the dissolute son of the emperor Tiberius. Years later, as King of the Jews, Herod Agrippa appears in *Acts* as the man who allowed the execution of James, son of Zebedee and brother of John the Apostle, yet his attitude towards Christianity is far from clear. The idea that his new walls around Jerusalem may have included building at the site of the Holy Sepulchre is speculation. As for Claudius, he knew what it was to be an outcast, he may have felt let down by his own gods, and he may have been attracted by the Stoic philosophy later associated with Christianity; he would certainly have known of Christians by the time he was emperor in Rome, but there can be no certainty of his thoughts on the matter.

The archaeology of Herculaneum on the Bay of Naples – buried by the eruption of Vesuvius in AD 79 – has advanced greatly in recent decades, not least with discoveries along the shorefront that have included an ancient boat and the skeletons of many of the town's occupants, huddled together in their last refuge in the cellars by the sea. Nevertheless, our picture still largely derives from the excavations of the eighteenth century, and large areas have seen little exploration since. One exception is the House of the Bicentenary, investigated in 1938; the discovery of a possible household 'chapel' led some to speculate on an early Christian presence. The room was extraordinarily well preserved, showing how the pyroclastic flow from Vesuvius in AD 79 could bypass some places, leaving them miraculously intact.

Much attention has focused on the Villa of the Papyri, a palatial structure which was tunnelled into during the eighteenth century but remains largely unexcavated. A wonderful sense of it can be gained in California at the Getty Villa, based on plans made by Carl Weber when he oversaw the eighteenth-century tunnelling. The finds included bronze statues as well as carbonized papyrus scrolls, many of them by the little-known Greek philosopher Philodemus. Work continues on reading those scrolls, with remarkable advances being made through multispectral imaging, but scholars yearn for more excavation to search for additional Greek scrolls and a possible Latin library which many believe must exist. The excavation in this novel is fictitious, though the finds are plausible and suggest the extraordinary revelations that could await archaeologists in the villa.

Cumae was an important early Greek colony on the Bay of Naples, but was destroyed in the thirteenth century AD and remains a remote and overgrown place. The Sibyl's 'cave' – first identified in 1932 – is a trapezoidal corridor, or *dromos*, hewn out of the rock, some 44 metres long, 2.5 metres wide and 5 metres high. At one end is an *oecus*, an inner sanctum, and on either side are openings, some leading to chambers that may have contained lustral waters. This seems likely to be where the Roman poet Virgil – buried somewhere nearby – had his Trojan hero Aeneas visit the Sibyl on his way to found Rome (*Aeneid* vi, 42–51). The image in the Prologue draws on the account of Virgil, who describes prophecies written on oak leaves, and the Roman poet Ovid, who recounts the story of Apollo condemning the Sibyl to wither away for as many years as she could hold grains of sand (*Metamorphoses* 14). The use of opium is conjectural, but seems consistent with the trance-like state of the oracle, as well as the pliability she may have wished of her supplicants. The Sibyl is said to have sold a book of prophecies to the last king of Rome, Tarquinus Superbus, in the fifth century BC, and these were consulted as late as the fourth century AD. The cult was important in the ideology of the first emperor, Augustus, and it is possible that he and subsequent emperors secretly visited the Sibyl in her cave.

The Temple of Jupiter at Cumae was transformed into a Christian basilica in the fifth–sixth century AD, and the cave of the Sibyl shows evidence for Christian occupation and burials. An association between Sibylline prophecy and early Christianity has long been proposed on the basis of Virgil's fourth *Eclogue*, where he has the Sibyl foretelling a future 'golden age', heralded by the birth of a boy; it is also seen in the medieval *Des Irae*, which has no known ancient source but may derive from this tradition.

The final resting place of St Paul may be Rome, where a fourth-century sarcophagus found in 2006 beneath the Church of St Paulo fuori le Mura has been associated with him. The tradition that he was martyred along with St Peter in the Circus of Caligula and Nero, the site of Piazza San Pietro in the Vatican, led me to imagine that his original tomb may lie under St Peter's Basilica, close to the tomb identified as that of St Peter. The extension in this novel to the ancient necropolis excavated during the 1940s under St Peter's is fictional, but its early Christian burials, symbols and inscriptions are based on actual catacombs I have explored elsewhere in Rome and in North Africa.

The shipwreck off Sicily is based on a wreck of about AD 200 excavated under my direction at Plemmirio, off Capo Murro di Porco south of Siracusa. This was where the British Special Raiding Squadron landed in July 1943, in advance of the disastrous glider assault recounted in this novel; my grandfather Captain Lawrance Wilfrid Gibbins gave me a first-hand account of this action, as he was close inshore that day with his ship *Empire Elaine* of the assault convoy. The seabed around the Roman wreck was strewn with ammunition, thrown into the sea after the Italian garrison surrendered. We had been led to the site by an account of one of Captain Cousteau's divers, who had seen the wreck in 1953 during a *Calypso* expedition. The description of the site is largely factual up to the point where Jack and Costas follow the shotline beyond fifty metres depth. Nevertheless, the deep wreck they discover, with Italian wine amphoras from the first century AD, is itself closely based on other sites I have seen, with the same form of wine amphora found in the taverns of Herculaneum and Pompeii. One of those wrecks, off Port-Vendres in the south of France, is dated to the reign of Claudius by the stamped inscriptions on lead ingots in the cargo. The ingots of Narcissus are fictional, but the inscription is closely based on the actual formulae found on British lead-silver ingots of this period, some of which have also been found at Pompeii.

One of our finds from the wreck was an amphora sherd with the painted graffito *Egttere*, meaning 'to go'. Other finds included a sounding lead with a cross-shaped depression underneath, as described in the novel, and – uniquely from a wreck – a Roman surgeon's instrument kit.

Another Roman wreck, off Italy, has produced the contents of an apothecary's chest – numerous small boxwood phials filled with substances including cinnamon and vanilla. So far, nobody has identified opium from an ancient shipwreck, though its use is well established in the ancient sources. Pliny the Elder devotes a chapter to the poppy and its sleep-inducing extracts, telling us that 'the seed cures leprosy', and describes the overdose taken by the father of one Publius Licinius Caecina, a man of praetorian rank, who 'died of opium poisoning at Bavila, in Spain, where an unbearable illness made his life not worth living' (*Natural History* xx, 198–200).

We searched for an ancient Greek wreck also reported by Cousteau's divers, in deep water beyond the Roman wreck. On our last dive we discovered a scatter of amphoras, several of seventh or sixth century BC date. At this point the sea bed dropped off to abyssal depth, three thousand metres and more, and we could only imagine what treasures lay in the darkness beyond. You can see a picture of me holding one of those amphoras at the moment of discovery on my website.

In 2007 archaeologists announced a stunning discovery in the heart of ancient Rome. Probing beneath the Palatine Hill – home of the emperors, and site of Rome's earliest settlement – revealed a subterranean chamber, some 16 metres below the House of Augustus. The chamber measures seven and a half metres high and six metres wide, and was formed partly from one of the natural fissures that honeycomb the hill. A camera lowered into the grotto revealed lavish mosaics studded with seashells, and in the centre of the floor a marble mosaic of a white eagle, an imperial motif. This may be the long-lost Lupercale, the cave where Rome's founders Romulus and Remus were supposed to have been suckled by the she-wolf, and decorated by Augustus to form the focus of a cult which lasted until Christianity eclipsed the old rituals. Nearby was a circular shrine of Vesta, as described in the novel, part of a cult which survived until the time of the last known Vestal Virgins, Coelia Concordia, in the late fourth century AD.

The 'urban speleologists' of my novel are inspired by true-life heroes of underwater archaeology, a group of divers and explorers who have charted the fetid passageways of the Cloaca Maxima – the 'Great Drain' – beneath the city of Rome. The main line of the Drain runs from the forum to the river Tiber beneath the Arch of Janus, where another branch runs in from under the Palatine Hill. The entrance beneath the Arch is fictional, though the appearance of the circular staircase is inspired by one that leads into the Aqua Virgo, the aqueduct that feeds the Trevi Fountain. The description of being in the Cloaca and inside an aqueduct is based on my experience and on the accounts of 'urban speleologists' who have gone further, revealing many areas under Rome that remain to be explored. The continuation of the tunnel beneath the Palatine is conjectural – the central chamber is based on the appearance of the Cave of the Sibyl at Cumae – though it follows a plausible route between known points of the main drain; the idea that such a project should have been the brainchild of Claudius is consistent with his bent for utilitarian projects, including his aqueduct in Rome, the Aqua Claudia, his huge rock-cut tunnel to drain the Fucine Lake and his construction of the great harbourworks at Ostia, the port of Rome.

Whether or not there was a church on the site of St Lawrence Jewry in London before the Norman period is unknown, but it is a plausible location for one of the lost churches of Roman London. St Lawrence Jewry has endured successive destructions, most recently by German bombing on the night of 29 December 1940, in the same raid that produced the famous image of the dome of St Paul's rising miraculously above the devastation. The bombing was watched from the roof of the Air Ministry by Air Vice Marshal 'Bomber' Harris, who famously remarked that 'they have sown the wind'; thus was born the British bomber offensive against Germany. In the City, air was sucked into the vacuum created as the fires consumed oxygen and hot air rose, creating violent winds which fuelled the fires further and spread burning debris. The account of St Lawrence Jewry shrieking that night is true: a soldier on leave who had been an organmaker recognized the noise of hot air rushing through the pipes. Unexploded German ordnance such as the SC250 bomb still lies under London, and the Royal Navy Fleet Diving Squadron bomb disposal teams are called out frequently to deal with discoveries such as the fictional bomb in this novel.

Almost three centuries earlier the medieval church had been destroyed in another firestorm, 'a most horrid, malicious, bloody flame, not like an ordinary fire', as Samuel Pepys described it in his diary of 2 September 1666. And sixteen hundred years before that, the newly laid-out town of Londinium, created soon after Claudius' conquest, had been laid waste by the forces of Boudica, the warrior queen, who razed the buildings and slaughtered the inhabitants during a terrible rampage in AD 60 or 61. There is no surviving description of the sack of London, but in the estuary of the Thames had been seen a frightful vision: 'the Ocean had appeared blood-red . . . the ebbing tide had left behind what looked to be human corpses' (Tacitus, *Annals* xiv, 32).

The Roman historian Dio Cassius wrote that Boudica's followers exacted their retribution to the accompaniment of sacrifices in their sacred places, particularly 'the grove of Andate' – probably the same as Andraste, who Boudica herself invokes in a speech – who they regarded 'with the most exceptional reverence' (lxii, 7). As for Boudica, after her death following the final battle against the Romans, 'the Britons mourned her deeply and gave her a costly burial'. The location of this burial has been sought ever since, but it is possible that both the tomb and the 'grove of Andate' lie somewhere under modern London. The fictional tomb in this novel incorporates features from actual Iron Age discoveries in England, including the chariot burial, the horse iconography of the Iceni, Boudica's tribe, and the golden neck torque – 'a great mass of the tawniest hair fell to her hips; around her neck was a large golden necklace' (Dio Cassius lxii, 2.4). The decorated bronze cylinder is based on one actually found in a chariot burial in Yorkshire. Some of the artefacts described in the novel can be seen in the British Museum, including a row of Roman wine amphoras from an Iron Age burial at Sheepen and the magnificent Battersea Shield, found on the bed of the river Thames.

Apart from the tomb and the gladiators' chamber, the picture of archaeology in the Guildhall Yard owes much to actual finds. You can go underground and visit the remains of the Roman amphitheatre, discovered in 1988; and beneath the restored Church of St Lawrence Jewry lies a vaulted burial chamber, forgotten since the seventeenth century and discovered by chance in 1998. It contains the only surviving part of the medieval church. As these extraordinary discoveries show, underground London may continue to harbour untold secrets. Much of this can be appreciated in the marvellous displays and publications of the Museum of London, which has overseen many excavations during the regeneration of the City following the bomb damage of the Second World War.

This rich archaeological potential was recognized during the rebuilding following the Great Fire of 1666, when Sir Christopher Wren recorded a Roman road and other remains during his rebuilding of St Paul's Cathedral and the City Churches. Wren did indeed employ the four craftsmen mentioned in the novel, Edward Pierce, mason, Thomas Newman, bricklayer, John Longland, carpenter, and Thomas Mead, plasterer, all of whom worked on the rebuilding of St Lawrence Jewry in 1671–80. Johannes Deverette is fictional, though his Huguenot background is plausible at this period; the wording of his will is based on Sir Christopher Wren's Will, which can be seen at the National Archives website. Wren did have a mentally disabled child, Billy, and the idea that Wren himself may have found Gregorian music appealing springs from his own documented sympathies for another age '. . . in which holy mothers and maids singing divine songs, offering the pure incense of their prayers, reading, meditating and conversing of holy things, spend almost all day in the company of God and his angels' (recorded by his son Christopher in *Parentalia: or, Memoirs of the Family of the Wrens*, 1750, p. 195, and quoted further here in Chapter 18).

The fictional character of Deverette's descendent John Everett draws inspiration from the lives of my great grandfather, Arthur Everett Gibbins (1877–1956), and his brother Norman (1882–1956). They were from a Huguenot family, based in Lawrence Lane, London, overlooking the church of St Lawrence Jewry in the heart of the City; their grandfather Samuel Gibbins had been Master of the Carpenters' Company and a Common Councillor of the City of London, working in the Guildhall. Arthur followed his father John and became an architect, but shortly before the First World War he left his young family and went to America, never to return. He had been Anglo-Catholic, but converted to Roman Catholicism before his departure. He became a US citizen and lived out the remainder of his life in California, where he spent his final years in Santa Paula playing organ, singing Gregorian chant and doing odd jobs for a convent, whose nuns looked after him. He never saw his family again.

For years Arthur had managed a remote estate in the mountains above Santa Paula, and in the first part of his life he and his father had designed and built country villas in southern England. I have a plan of one of those houses, St Mark's Parsonage in Kemp Town, Brighton, from *The Building News* of 1 March 1889 (John George Gibbins, F.R.I.B.A., architect), showing a façade with the alternating courses of bricks and stone so characteristic of Roman construction. As an architecture student Arthur would have known of the Roman villas then being discovered and excavated in Britain. His cousin Henry de Beltgens Gibbins, an economic historian, wrote in his bestselling *Industry in Britain* (1897) about seeing traces of these villas, 'with their Italian inner courts, colonnades and tessellated pavements'. Henry was interested in the relationship of these villas to the landscape, and Arthur may have shared that fascination too. In a fold of the Cotswold hills, not very far from Warwick School where Arthur was educated, is Chedworth – my favourite Romano-British villa – where the layout and vista from the buildings seems perfectly attuned to the landscape, outward-looking by contrast with the enclosed splendour of the great Italian houses such as the Villa of the Papyri at Herculaneum.

Arthur's brother Norman was a 'wrangler' at Cambridge University, achieving first class honours in mathematics, and later became a school headmaster, a published mathematician and a prominent figure in British chess. In 1915 he was commissioned into the Royal Dublin Fusiliers, and was severely wounded near Loos on the Western Front in June of the following year. In April his battalion had been devastated by a German gas attack at Hulluch, one of the worst gas attacks of the war. During his recuperation he worked as a cipher officer in Room 108 of the War Office in London, encoding and decoding telegrams. While he was there, in January 1917, the famous Zimmerman Telegram – revealing German plans to attack America – was decoded in the nearby

Room 40 of the Admiralty Building. One of the codebreakers was the Rev. William Montgomery, translator of Albert Schweitzer's *The Quest of the Historical Jesus* (1910). Montgomery's visit to America in my novel is fictional, though plausible given the great interest by the US in British decryption work at the time. The decoding of the Zimmerman Telegram was one of the greatest intelligence coups in history, the single act that brought the United States into the First World War.

In October 1917, Norman became a cipher officer with British Army HQ in Italy, on the front facing the Austrians, and he remained there until 1919. The other British war in the Mediterranean was against the Ottomans, culminating in General Allenby's victorious entry into Jerusalem in December 1917. My character Everett's activities in Jerusalem are fictional, though there had been a long tradition of British officers devoting themselves to the archaeology of the Holy Land. I myself was fortunate to spend time with the Ethiopian Coptic monks on the roof of the Church of the Holy Sepulchre in the days leading up to the First Gulf War, when Jerusalem was virtually empty of tourists. One day, when the Old City was in lockdown because of violence, I had the extraordinary experience of being in the church alone, and descended past the carved pilgrim crosses to the Chapel of St Helena. The ship graffito described in this novel is preserved in the Chapel of St Vartan, normally closed to visitors. The passage beyond the graffito is fictional, though there are many cisterns and unexplored spaces nearby and much still to be discovered about the site of the Holy Sepulchre in the first century AD.

The quote at the beginning of the book is from *Letters of the Younger Pliny* vi, 16 (trans. Betty Radice, Harvard 1969); the same source is used for quotes in Chapters 6 and 17, the latter from x, 96. In Chapter 9, the quote from the Elder Pliny's *Natural History* is from xi, 79 (trans. John L. Healey, Penguin 1991), and in Chapter 10, from v, 70–4 (trans. H. Rackham, Harvard 1942, with place-names rendered by me in their ancient form); the discussion between Pliny and Claudius in Chapter 4 derives material from the *Natural History* too, including the account of different types of ink. In the Prologue, the line *Facilis descensus Averno* is from Virgil's *Aeneid* (vi: 126), as is the quote in Chapter 5 (vi, 237–42, trans. H.R. Fairclough, Loeb 1916); the other Virgil quotes are from his fourth *Eclogue*, including the passage spoken by Claudius in the Epilogue (trans. H.R. Fairclough, ibid., but rendered in verse by me). The quotes from *Acts of the Apostles*, in Chapters 1, 5 and 25, and from *The Gospel of Matthew*, in Chapter 18, are from the King James Version. The *Dies Irae* is a traditional part of the Requiem Mass; the translation used here, in the Prologue – in the utterance of the Sibyl – and in Chapters 5 and 12, was made by John Adams Dix (1798–1879), American Civil War general, Governor of New York and a remarkable classicist, who preserved the trochaic metre of the medieval Latin.

In Chapter 15, the quotes from Tacitus are from *Annals* xiv,

30 (trans. John Jackson, Harvard 1937), also the source of the line of Latin read by Jack from Claudius' fictional history, in chapter 17; from Dio Cassius his *Roman History*, lxii, 2–13 (trans. Earnest Cary and Herbert Baldwin Foster, Harvard, 1925); and from Gildas his *De Excidio Britonum*, 'The Ruin of Britain', 15 (trans. Michael Winterbottom, Phillimore, 1978). The 'sacramentum gladiatorium' is my translation of the gladiators' oath in Petronius, *Satyricon* 117.

In Chapter 2, the hieroglyphics on the Anubis statue are text from the 'Instruction of Merikare', an Egyptian Middle Kingdom document preserved in several eighteenth Dynasty papyri. In Chapter 7, the inscription of Piso, though fictional, is worded after an actual inscription of Piso found on the Greek island of Samothrace. In Chapter 12, the fictional inscription under the Palatine Hill, including the archaic spelling *Caisar*, is based on the inscription of Claudius on the Porta Maggiore, originally part of his aqueduct – the *aqua Claudia* – where you can still see masonry in the 'rusticated' style typical of Claudius. In Chapter 16, the delightful baroque prose of Sir Thomas Browne in treating the grim business of saponification and 'body liqueur' can be appreciated throughout his *Hydrotaphia, Urn Burial, or a Discourse on the Sepulchral Urns lately found in Norfolk* (1658). In Chapter 20, the words of Winston Churchill are from his obituary of Harvey Augustus Butters in the *Observer*, 10 September 1916. In Chapter 21, the 'Paternoster' is based on an actual word-square found scratched on a second-century Roman amphora sherd from Manchester, once thought to be the earliest evidence for Christianity in Britain. In Chapter 24, the quote from Mark Twain is from his *The Innocents Abroad, or the New Pilgrim's Progress* (San Francisco, 1870), p. 497.

DOMINE IVMIVS is the painted inscription under the St Vartan's Chapel ship graffito in the Church of the Holy Sepulchre; the other inscription found there in the novel is fictional. The illustrations in the text are based on the ship graffito, still *in situ* in Jerusalem, on the Lullingstone Villa Chi-Rho mosaic and the St Mary Hinton 'Christ' painting – both on display in the British Museum – and on the map of Rome by Giovanni Battista Piranesi in *Antichità Romane de'tempo prima Repubblica e dei prima imperatori* (Rome, 1756), Vol. I, Pl. II. The Roman painting of Vesuvius described in Chapter 5 is from the House of the Centenary in Pompeii, and is now in the Naples Archaeological Museum. Other images, including the coins of Claudius and Herod Agrippa and finds from the Plemmirio shipwreck, can be seen on my website www.davidgibbins.com.

Atlantis

David Gibbins

ATLANTIS
The fabled island which disappeared beneath the
waves at the dawn of history

ATLANTIS
One of archaeology's most enduring mysteries

ATLANTIS
Fact or myth? No one has ever known – until now . . .

One day, on a dive in the Mediterranean, marine archaeologist Jack Howard gets lucky. Very lucky. He and
his team uncover what could be the key to the location
of the lost island.

Jack is on the verge of making an astounding breakthrough, but someone else knows about Atlantis's
location. And Jack and those closest to him are
suddenly locked in a life or death game with con-
sequences that could destroy thousands of lives. For
what Jack discovers is beyond his wildest dreams –
but it comes at a terrifying price.

ATLANTIS is an unputdownable read which throws
light on a story still shrouded in mystery. Part thriller,
part history lesson, part adventure story, ATLANTIS
is *The Da Vinci Code* for a new generation: only this
time, it really could all be true . . .

978 0 7553 2422 4

headline

Crusader Gold

David Gibbins

THE HOLIEST OF TREASURES

The gold menorah, symbol of the Jewish faith, stolen by Romans who sacked Jerusalem's Holy Temple.

A HISTORICAL SYMBOL

Carried in triumph through Rome, it came to represent the Empire's ruthless conquests. When the Romans moved to Constantinople, the menorah went with them . . .

THE FINAL CRUSADE

. . . But it had vanished by the time bloodthirsty Crusaders pillaged the city in 1204.

AND TO THIS DAY NO ONE KNOWS WHERE IT IS.

Turkey, present day. In Istanbul's harbour, on a dive for lost Crusade treasure, archaeologist Jack Howard discovers something wholly unexpected. Meanwhile, in an English cathedral library, a long-forgotten medieval map is unearthed. Together they could alter history. Suddenly the clock is ticking for Jack – and the stakes are already too high . . .

What unfolds is a thrilling but lethal quest, stretching from Harald Hardrada, greatest of the Viking conquerors, to the fall of the Nazis and the darkest secrets of the modern Vatican.

An exhilarating blend of history, fact and fiction, CRUSADER GOLD is another unputdownable read from the author of the worldwide bestseller *Atlantis*

'What do you get if you cross Indiana Jones with Dan Brown? Answer: David Gibbins' *Mirror*

978 0 7553 2424 8

headline

Now you can buy any of these other bestselling books from your bookshop or *direct from the publisher*.

FREE P&P AND UK DELIVERY
(Overseas and Ireland £3.50 per book)

Atlantis	David Gibbins	£7.99
Crusader Gold	David Gibbins	£6.99
Wicked	Gregory Maguire	£7.99
Atlantic Shift	Emily Barr	£7.99
Run The Risk	Scott Frost	£6.99
A Passion for Killing	Barbara Nadel	£7.99
Flint's Code	Paul Eddy	£6.99
Vinegar Hill	Manette Ansay	£7.99
Eleven on Top	Janet Evanovich	£7.99
The Roaring of the Labyrinth	Clio Gray	£7.99

TO ORDER SIMPLY CALL THIS NUMBER

01235 400 414

or visit our website: www.headline.co.uk

Prices and availability subject to change without notice.